To Lisa,

A motivational / inspirational quote . . . . the purpose of life is to discover your gift. The meaning of life is to share your gift.

Happy discovering!

Jay ~ July '22

ALL FALL DOWN

A Novel by Jay Fortune

Author's Note

I began writing All Fall Down in January 2016. It started with a simple vision: a young girl seeing her father floating above their garden. I had no idea where the story would go as it began to unfold. Daily life soon got in the way and I put the half-finished story to one side. But the characters haunted me night and day demanding to have their tale told. It was when a friend of mine persuaded me to finish it during Lockdown in 2021 that the narrative took on a pace of its own and I finally managed to get the characters out of my head and onto these pages. Peace at last!

No author is a one-man-band. I owe thanks to Graham Hey for harassing me to finish writing this tale, my publisher Taryn Johnston for believing in my work and bringing it to print, my VIPers who voted for the cover design and my soul-mate Jen Allen for designing said cover and being my constant source of inspiration and strength when the creative juices run low. A final huge thanks to you, the fine human who is reading this; with so many distractions vying for our attention in our lives, your commitment to spending a few hours reading my story makes all the doubt, all the late nights, re-writes and editing worthwhile. Thank you.

Become a VIPer and stay up-to-date with my writing and art. Join my Free VIP private email list today! Sign-up at jayfortune.co.uk

DEDICATION

This one's for Graham
For encouraging and believing.

The Cast
(In Alphabetical Order)

Paula Asketh
Luke Brown
Jamie Carter/Slim
Daniel Chad
Tasha Davies
Cyrus 'Cy' Enfield
Adam Fletcher
Jared Gibson
Jordan Harris
Mike Hegessay
Nicholas 'Nick' Holmes
Nancy Johnson
Keanne
Doug Kinsman
Lihua Kwok/Chinese
Lucy Peters/Business
Angela Pinkney
Paul Ross
Aabid Wakin
Ahmed Wakin
James Whitbourne
Saffron 'Saffi' Williams
Nigel Woods

'We're spinning round on this ball of hate,
There's no parole, there's no great escape,
We're sentenced here until the End of Days,
And then, my brother, there's a price to pay.'
- **Alice Cooper,** *Brutal Planet*

'Stand-up for freedom!'
Dr. J. E. Mordrake, *The Eden Game*

AT THE END
ADAM - THE LAST MAN

Despite his namesake, Adam wasn't a religious man. The irony of what had happened wasn't lost on him either; one moment he'd been in the garden of Eden with Eve--

(*No, not Eve... what was her name? The woman in red? The one who had the white light all around her?* He had felt safe with her. Safe.)

And now he was in Hell, trapped in the dark with the walking dead all around him.

He didn't know how long he'd been here, alone with just his thoughts for company.

And the dreams and nightmares, of course.

The world above had fallen down maybe hours or was it days ago?

Maybe weeks?

He had no idea.

The power was still out.

He was sure it was a trick of the mind, but he felt he could occasionally sense some lost soul wandering among the shadows. They came close, close enough for him to think he could see their outline, before they would pass out of sight again.

Impossible in this darkness. He couldn't see his hand only inches from his face.

He wasn't totally sure he could even move his hands.

I'm unsure if they know I'm here.

Sometimes they even seemed to know his name.

He was vaguely aware of other voices that came and went.

For now, he'd just stay here, a floating consciousness in a world devoid of light.

Maybe soon I'll try to find out where the voices are coming from.

Maybe.

He slept.

BOOK ONE

PART ONE

THE FIRST FLOATERS

CHAPTER 1
MIKE - INSIDE

He tapped the side of his briefcase, a thrill rushing through his thighs. He'd read somewhere that those large muscles held the most muscle memory and gave the greatest feeling of thrill.

Maybe that was why some people tended to rub their thighs when excited. He considered this only briefly before stroking the briefcase one more time.

Patting his dirty little secret - the one inside the case.

A lot of fun awaited him today, just him and his secret. The thrill, the tease of it made his dick semi-hard again.

No, mustn't.

I'm too old. If I cum now, then I can't enjoy myself later.

His daughter knocked on the bedroom door.

'Dad?'

Mike stood, straightening his tie, looking at himself in the full-length mirror.

'Yes, darling?' he said, smiling as she entered the room.

She looked so cute; pig tails, beaming smile. Their morning ritual had begun again.

'Yes, they look ten out of ten today, sweetheart,' he said.

She smiled even more to show them off.

'Well, mum helped a bit. But I did most of the brushing.'

He lifted his briefcase and laid it on the bed, giving it another unconscious tap as he did. He crouched and she ran to him.

'See!'

'And a quick huff puff?' he said.

She blew breath into his face and he pretended to inhale.

'Oh, totally minty.'

'Score?'

'Nine out of ten'

'Nine?!'

'Well, tomorrow you'll have to swill your mouthwash for just a little longer I guess,' he said. She turned and sulked out of the room, shouting to her mother.

'Dad says only nine out of ten, mum!'

'Well, I'm sure you'll do better tomorrow,' replied her mother playing her part in the family game.

Mike Hegessay rose, his knees cracking. As he stood, he rubbed his thighs gently, his thoughts returning to his secret once again.

He smoothed his trousers, took one final glance in the mirror, picked up his case and left the bedroom.

CHAPTER 2

MIKE

'You off darling?'

'Yes Katie. Early meeting.'

Another lie. Well, not entirely.

He did have a meeting. In the office's disabled toilet cubicle; the only one with a lock. Just him, his hand and his secret.

His boner was coming back again.

She came close and he put his briefcase between them both, not wishing her to feel the throb through his trousers.

There were certain things you can't lie about if you're in a relationship.

'Nine out of ten?' she whispered.

He smiled.

'Gives her something to aim for tomorrow,' he replied.

Casey didn't hear them. She was packing her bag for school. Mike wondered what things she kept in there. Had she any secrets? More likely one's on her phone.

'I can't believe you convinced me to give an 8-year-old a smart-phone,' he said in a whisper.

Katie looked at him quizzically.

'That was ages ago,' she said aloud.

'Well, you just don't know what secrets she has on there, what with all the bloody sexting or whatever the kids are doing nowadays.'

Katie regarded him coolly. Uh-oh, what had he said? She was pissed now.

'I'm just saying,' he said gently putting his briefcase down, taking Katie by the hips, pulling her toward him, using his semi-hard-on as further sway to bring her on-side, 'we should perhaps keep up with her on what she does with that phone, that's all.' He kissed her on the lips.

She fell for it, as he knew she would, and purposely tensed his cock into her through his trousers as they hugged.

His wand had worked its magic.

'Mike! Later.'

She blushed, pulling away from him and knocking his briefcase over.

His heart stopped. His case stayed closed.

He willed his heart to beat again. Maybe he wanted to get caught. Isn't that what they say about serial killers? He'd daydream about this exact scenario; the loving father and husband, respected in the local community. In his fantasy, he'd walk about the town, attending meetings, all with his briefcase clasped but unlocked, knowing at any moment it might fall open and reveal the pictures. In the dream it had made his heart rush.

In reality, it was making his heart stop.

Am I dying? he thought.

'Right,' he coughed. 'Gotta go.'

He kissed Katie once more, then bent and kissed his daughter, his heart beating in his ears.

'Bye Dad'.

'See you both tonight.'

That was a lie. But he didn't know it then. He'd see them throughout the morning.

And the whole world would see him too.

CHAPTER 3

MIKE - OUTSIDE

The Toyota gleamed on the drive. Pristine car, tidy house, pretty wife… perfect cover for a paedophile.

Mike stepped from the porch; car key held before him. He felt himself stepping up into the air. As if it would solve the unfathomable situation, he looked at his key fob and tried to press the unlock button. But still he continued to step up, as if riding an invisible escalator.

Insanely, he sought an explanation in his key fob.

'What the fuck?'

He didn't like swearing near his family or house. He worked hard to keep his reputation clean. That thought made him reach and check the locks on his briefcase. If that fell open now…

Yet his right hand couldn't pass in front of his body to reach the case hanging by his left leg. He continued on the invisible treadmill higher into the air.

His head hit a ceiling which, like the invisible escalator, wasn't there. His chin was forced onto his chest, making him stoop.

Despite his university education and liberal upbringing in a middle-class household with a tolerance of most world views and religious beliefs, his next sentence betrayed his background.

'What… the… fucking… hell?'

His back flattened against the glass ceiling, his legs still stepping until they were also flattened. He looked downward and could see his car. Could see the top of the small tree in their front garden. With a slight but difficult turn of his head he could see along the street. Just a little more of a turn and he could see the roof of his own house. And there he stayed, suspended, spread-eagled like a magical Jesus on an invisible floating cross.

But with a briefcase.

Mike's heart thundered powerfully in his chest; boom, boom, BOOM. Maybe this was his last moment.

He prayed to a God that he'd never believed in, a God that he had spent his adult life knowing wasn't there (but acting the lie every Sunday for his wife and daughter's sake at the local Church) praying, begging that his case would remain shut.

Even in his wildest fantasy daydreams he had never imagined floating above his entire street, his entire *community*, with a briefcase load of kiddie porn pictures.

CHAPTER 4

MIKE

The front door was opening.

No, please Christ, no.

A white mittened hand appeared.

Casey's.

'NO!'

She was chatting away to her mum, something about brushing for more than thirty seconds tomorrow, when she glanced up.

She knew I was here, thought Mike.

At first, she stared…. One… Then opened her mouth. Two… Then screamed… Three.

As if she'd learned it from a textbook. 'What to do if you find your dad floating'.

'What Case-'

Katie looked up… one.

A sharp intake of breath… two.

But no scream. No three.

'Mike?'

He gulped. *Ok, how do I lie my way out of this one?*

'Hi honey.'

Now, where the fuck had that come from?

Katie shook her head. Casey stopped screaming. She pointed and laughed. Just the way kids handle things.

That's great, I'm up here for the whole fucking world to see, like a human fucking kite with a case full of-

Shit. He'd forgotten about the pictures.

Shit.

'Mike, I'll call someone,' said Katie, trying to collect her thoughts. 'The Police.' Talking to herself. She asked him something that made the whole episode completely ludicrous.

'Or shall I call the Fire Brigade, Mike? Are you… stuck?'

He clenched his eyes shut. This had to be a fucking dream. A fucking *nightmare!* His mind drifted to his case. To his pictures. He'd looked at them as he'd printed them-

What was I thinking? Printing them?!

- seeing flashes of a child's thigh here-

Thighs, always fucking thighs!

- smooth lump of budding breast there. And boys! Oh, he had boys.

Stop Mike. Be calm. Focus. Don't you dare get a fucking boner up here. Don't you dare.

'Of course, I'm stuck love,' he replied, hearing the worry in his voice and not liking it.

He didn't know if he was worried because he was floating around thirty foot in the air without explanation or means of support or that he might be exposed as a fucking paedo.

He knew the answer.

'Whatever you do, just get help. And quick.'

'Alright, Casey get in quick.' And to her husband; 'Don't move.'

Ludicrous.

Fucking ludicrous.

CHAPTER 5
MIKE

By 9:06am, what was at the start a regular routine of saying goodbye to the family, for Mike Hegessay had become the stuff of nightmares. Of fantasy. Here he was, suspended above his own home, floating on invisible wires, his wife phoning desperately for a rescue team. He was totally vulnerable.

Especially with the pictures in his case.

Casey.

No, never, *ever* would he ever think of her that way. But what would she think of him, should the lock's snap? Vaguely in the back of his mind he recalled a documentary he had seen (or read) about how higher altitudes can affect materials in different ways. But had he really gone to a different altitude? He thought not. After all, he could still breathe relatively comfortably. Although his heart was hammering and that didn't help matters.

By 9:07am, he had had time to think so many thoughts none of which had helped him. He thought how he would be ashamed, probably to the brink of suicide, should his case ever fall open here like this; thought about teenage anxiety dreams, being naked at GSCE exams; thought how he didn't deserve this; thought how he *did* deserve this given his secret; thought how he'd never be able to eat up here, drink up here. He even thought about how he'd shit up here. So many thoughts. He needed an anchor, metaphorically and for real. Something to drag him down, to hold him steady.

Steady.

Mike became aware that he wasn't steady at all. He was drifting. When he'd first floated up, he could see the guttering of his house (and made a mental note to have them cleaned). But now he was already going over the roof of his house, toward his back garden.

He was drifting like a cloud.

What the fuck is happening?

Around 9:09am he began to cry.

CHAPTER 6
PAULA - OUTSIDE

Three doors down, Paula Asketh was heading off for a trip to the garden centre in preparation for the coming Spring. She was a keen gardener and also a keen shoplifter. Nothing heavy. Just the odd bit here and there.

She'd become quite adept.

And an addict.

Her last steal was a blinder; she managed to sneak away a charity collection pot for the Blind when nobody was looking. The irony was not lost on her, chuckling as she made off with her loot. The sheer thrill of it made the little money actually accumulated for her effort paltry in comparison, but the thrill? *That* was priceless.

While walking out to the car, Paula was lifted into the sky alongside Mike.

Suspended.

CHAPTER 7
PAULA

Paula felt sick. In the true sense of the word. Heights had never been her thing. One of her earliest memories was of being held upside-down over the banister by her father as a joke.

Yeah, that worked didn't it.

Made her a freak for most of her life whenever she came anywhere near both men and high places.

But there was another reason she didn't trust men. Most of all her dad.

She was unsure what to do next. She could scream, but the actual height wasn't that bad. About level with the roof of her house. And she wasn't alone. Turning her head, she could see one of her neighbours also up here with her.

Maybe this is Heaven?

A daft thought. Why would she be granted a place in heaven?

Maybe after what he did to me?

She pushed the thought away and realised that if this *were* heaven, if she *were* dead, then she wouldn't have been able to hear people calling up at her.

'I'll call someone… or I can get a ladder. Stay there!'

The words were clear and daft. Stay there. Best instruction ever, yeah, thanks …although that simple statement of fact began to become increasingly more difficult than Paula had first realised. She wasn't stuck to the hard invisible surface but slowly floating, sliding along it. As if blown by a gentle breeze making her feel nauseous.

Sure she was going to puke.

CHAPTER 8

PAULA

'Have you called someone?' shouted Paula, realising the curtain twitchers, (especially the nosey bitch in number eleven who had the cheek to actually open the curtains fully and move the netting to one side to get a really, really good look) were already checking her out, embarrassment having long left her. Anyway, what good would embarrassment do now? She was more a star if anything.

Actually floating like one too, she thought. *But am I burning bright?*

That odd thought caused sudden panic. What if the sun rose higher today? What if she were led up against glass and she was ignited by its magnification?

No, it's only mid-January. And this is the UK. No chance of sunshine!

She remained unconvinced, suddenly wishing to be down. Down now. Surely someone must have called the fire brigade.

Feeling sick. Dizzy.

Panic sinking its claws in.

Don't freak out.

CHAPTER 9
MIKE

Mike spied the woman from a few doors down out of the corner of his eye. He tried to move, being oh-so careful not to jerk the case too much. Every slight movement meant he had to crane his neck to check the locks weren't slipping. A rainstorm of child porn would never do. Amazingly, he caught himself laughing at the thought. The laugh scared him. It was the first sign of losing control. And if he did that, then this would end badly.

With a slight swimming motion, he began to move not only along the glass ceiling by the gentle breeze but also through his own efforts. He realised he could change course. Slightly, like being in a small boat on a lake.

Or being up a creek without a paddle, he thought.

If I can reach her… then…

What?

He hadn't planned that far. It didn't even make sense to try and reach her. That instinctive thought of not being the 'Only-One-In-It' made him feel it was the right thing to do.

Slithering like a fish, like a body in a sleeping bag, Mike edged his way toward the woman.

He need not have worried about being isolated. Before he reached her, more were coming to join him.

CHAPTER 10

AHMED - INSIDE

The mirror was still foggy from the hot water in the basin below.

Cucumber.

That was what he needed. Wipe a mirror with a slice of cucumber and it will de-mist.

He'd never tried it, but apparently it worked. And his mum swore it de-aged you too. He remembered being a child, bursting into the bathroom to find his mum lying in the bath, the door was always left unlocked.

How he hoped today would be just as simple. No locks. No security. Just burst straight in.

He looked down at his handwritten to-do list. Focusing on it kept his mind steady.

He breathed out slowly, feeling if he was afraid. No, he was calm. Controlled.

That was good.

Item One - shit.

That was a funny one, but they had told him it was really important to drink plenty of laxative solution a few hours before, to clear his system out as best he could. Ahmed wondered why. After all, if you're hoping to cause maximum damage then isn't it even more effective to blow shit over everyone? Like anyone would notice anyway.

What if it doesn't go off?

No. Stop.

Focus on the list.

Item Two - shave. Done.

Why bother? If they had his photo, then it would be one where he had his beard. He considered taking a quick selfie now and leaving it on his laptop when he left the flat. Show him without his beard. That'd mess with their heads even more when trying to pin his motive on 'religion'.

Although, it wasn't just his face that required shaving and he'd taken longer than he wished, longer than he thought it would actually take. Some places were just hard to get to. Funny; he'd been with him every step of the way but now his brother had left him to shit and shave alone. It was now he needed his help most.

Item Three - talc.

He took another breath, ensuring he remained cool and collected. Ahmed held his hands before him checking for their steadiness. A slight tremor. Probably from the few drinks he allowed himself the evening before. Opening the cabinet, he was glad to lose contact with his own eyes in the mirror reflecting back at him; judging him.

What if it doesn't go off?

'Stop. Stop. STOP!' Pounding his fist into the wall. His neighbour banged back. What life was this anyway? He gazed up at the single light bulb illuminating the bathroom, taking in the damp and the mould.

Focus.

Removing the talc from the cabinet, Ahmed threw handfuls over himself. He shook himself down.

Checked the list.

Item Four.

Only two more to go after this one.

Another breath.

He went into the lounge where the bomb vest was prepared and waiting.

CHAPTER 11

AHMED - INSIDE
BEFORE

'You know why you've been chosen, Ahmed.'

He'd tried his best to hold back the tears, so confused.

His brother had encouraged him. A friendly arm around his shoulder.

'Come now. It is your path. It is God's will. We go with you.'

Like fuck you do, he thought but didn't say. Wouldn't dare.

Trapped.

What sort of life was this?

Aabid led him to the single sofa in the damp, cold flat.

Once settled, he quickly fixed him a drink.

'OK, so some things are against the rules, but hey-'

You only live once was almost out of his mouth before he could stop himself. That would have been a bad move. No, the sentence worked ending just there. Aabid turned his eyes upward, silently thanking his god for that one.

'Come. Drink with me. For this is your last hour trapped here. Soon you'll be in Paradise!'

Last hour?

Time seemed to be frozen for Ahmed, his world feeling unreal.

Yet he was settled a little by that thought. It would soon be over, this life ended and his new one in Paradise begun. The idea of Paradise had calmed him since he first agreed to do this.

Had he agreed?

It was all a blur now.

'And… I can't speak to mum before I…'

Aabid hugged him close, both squeezed onto the tiny sofa. The hug said it all.

'I'm your family, Ahmed. And as your brother, I go with you.'

Finishing their drinks, Aabid departed, leaving Ahmed on his own.

Scared.

Trapped.

But ready to end this life.

CHAPTER 12

AHMED

As he walked over to the vest, he slipped on the discarded bottle Aabid had brought.

He'd fallen toward the table, somehow managing to cheat gravity and fall away from the vest.

That would have been premature.

And wasted.

With extreme care, checking his breath throughout, Ahmed loaded himself into the vest. He paused periodically, wiping the sweat from his armpits and forehead. It was running down his back but there was little he could do about that.

It took time, but it felt right somehow. With each strap on his body, each buckle clipped in, he became more and more convinced that he was chosen. He was here to do something special.

God's work.

He continued to dress silently and slowly.

His eyes caught sight of the empty bottle now and then as he maneuvered with great care into his clothes.

What was it Aabid had said? Something about rules and how they can be broken?

Could this one?

'Stop Ahmed. Focus.' He felt oddly calm speaking his own name aloud.

'There's been time for doubts, but you have gone this far. A few more steps.'

He looked skyward.

'Please, give me the strength. I will be with you. Be with me.'

He gulped. Collected the To-Do list. Turning it to show the map of the underground. It was a small overland journey and that train should be quiet now the rush-hour had passed. Then off at Liverpool Street Station and onto the Central Line.

Then-

Focus.

Step Five - Get the 9:24 to Liv. St.

He tucked the list in his pocket. Checking his watch, he had six minutes to get to the station. Somewhere overhead he heard a helicopter. They couldn't know about him surely?

'Focus, Ahmed.'

With one final steadying breath he walked to the front door. Despite having the weight of the vest, he felt oddly light. And calm.

Acceptance.

Alone, Ahmed Wakin left his flat with nobody to wish him a happy 17th birthday.

CHAPTER 13

PAULA – OUTSIDE

I need to get across to him, thought Paula, seeing the neighbour with the briefcase sliding away from her. Another guy was near him, a copper by the looks of it. She'd heard a commotion and the approach of their vehicle but then lost sight of them over the trees. She'd heard the conversation quite clearly until the policeman had reached the glass ceiling. Then she could no longer hear anything from the two men. Realising her predicament, Paula began to move toward the policeman. Maybe his plan had been to join them up here in an aid to rescue them. Maybe he had answers too.

If he's local, he might recognise you from CCTV and nick you for shoplifting.

The thought made her pause. She pushed it away, choosing to risk the slim probability of being ID'd or even arrested whilst floating.

Something told her the police had bigger things to worry about at present.

But a charity box for the blind? What kind of sicko does that?

That was one of the locals she had overheard near The Kings Head from where she had made her steal. In retrospect, floating up here, Paula did feel a pang of guilt. Nothing compared to the rush of the steal, but maybe this was justice after all.

If so, if this was God's way, then what crimes had the guy with the briefcase and the copper done? Before this… this…

Happening.

That was the right word. It popped into her mind like a comic strip speech bubble. Pow!

Happening.

That was what this event might be referred to.

Now, above the tree, she had a clear glimpse of the side window of the house a few doors down. A kid stood there filming everything.

Now she may very well be ID'd.

Well, if I go down then I'll take that piece of shit down with me.

Where did that come from?

Paula caught herself beginning to sob. Instead of feeling free, feeling like she was soaring, she began to feel more and more depressed.

Because you're dragging the past up. You always are.

No, mum, I'm not. But if you knew…

Don't you dare say such things! Don't you dare. He would never, never lay his hands on you. You've created this whole paranoia Paula and you won't ruin my life.

That had been the first row where the fully-known-but-left-unspoken had been spoken for the briefest of time.

But no. Just too taboo.

Too horrific. Too unimaginable in her mother's world for it to even be *thought* of, let alone said out loud. For that would make it real. Make it spoken.

Abracadabra.

She'd read that somewhere. Abracadabra, the magician's famous incantation. It meant 'it is created as it is spoken.' Or, had someone told her that?

Her dad used to like magic tricks. And he could keep a secret.

And so could she it seemed. One she had kept for over 41 years.

While all of these past memories went through her mind like a slideshow, moment by moment, Paula hadn't realised her eyes had remained fixed, her neck at an awkward angle pressing against the glass ceiling, staring at the neighbour with the case.

He wasn't old enough to be her dad, yet somehow reminded her of him.

She tried to think of his name. Wasn't he a councilor or something to do with the local authority?

She didn't know how she knew him, not really. Had they even spoken before? She remembered a broken memory, like a distant dream. He and her together, sat in a circle, a group. White walls.

'The church. He must be part of the church group,' she muttered under her breath.

She felt there was something dodgy about him. He was just too nice. And strangers didn't smile like that if they had nothing to hide.

Let it go. This is not the time. Deal with your shit later. Right now, just get down off this thing.

But she knew it had already gone too far. For whatever reason, God had decided to put her and that neighbour up here, and with a copper between them to make the arrest no less (Lord, it was just too perfect to *not* be right), the thoughts of her dad, long buried, now streaming through her conscious mind, like a diver rushing for air, perhaps this was all meant to be.

As she slid, swam and shimmied closer to the two men, Paula felt that feeling of depression, the sense of something righteous about to unfold, the past and present coming together right here, right now, growing stronger, filling her with a mix of dread, anxiety and-

Hope.

Despite everything to the contrary, there was hope.

CHAPTER 14

MIKE

Cold.

Despite all his efforts, Mike had not been able to reach the lady from down the road. Thankfully, the briefcase had remained shut. And it hadn't rained. So there were some things to be grateful for.

A bit of food and drink would have been the icing on the cake. So far, nothing or no-one had got to them yet.

Mike felt tired, like he'd been awake for hours. He wanted to sleep, to wake up in his own bed.

There was the constant movement and noise below.

And the dogs.

They hadn't stopped barking from the first moment he hit the Breaker (he didn't know how he knew, but that was what they had been calling it. Maybe he had heard someone below describe it as that).

Exhaustion physically and mentally was creeping over him. Endless thoughts were going through his mind.

How long can a human last without food? Six weeks, wasn't it? And without water? Was it three weeks or three days? He had kept his breathing as calm as possible, as the Lady Down the Road had freaked out shortly before, having some kind of panic attack. It was horrible to see. Nobody could get to her.

Floaters.

That was the other name being bounded about. Like they were annoying pieces of shit that couldn't be flushed.

Maybe I am, he thought. *If they saw what was in my case, then maybe I am.*

He realised that was the real reason he refused to close his eyes, even for a moment. If his case should float away from him, or fall open while he slept, that would be the end of him.

And his dirty little secret.

CHAPTER 15
PAULA

Paula had hyperventilated and passed out. When she awoke she could no longer recognise the area. Had she drifted while she was unconscious?

I'm a poet and I don't know it.

I'm not.

She began to cry.

I'm a cheating whore. A shoplifter. And I'm sorry for what I've done.

The tears streaked her cheeks.

'I'm so sorry.' Her words broken by her sobs.

Paula's tears didn't fall. They ran upwards onto the Breaker itself.

CHAPTER 16
PAUL & DANIEL

Paul Ross and Daniel Chad were the first of the emergency services to respond to the event. Paul had been in the Police for just over two years and Daniel, 'Chaddy the Daddy' to his mates, under his supervision for the last two weeks. The pair had gotten off to a favourable start, having similar interests in music and, it seemed, each other - although not one of them had actually said it out loud.

The unspoken bond had quickly grown between them, Chaddy often getting aroused when on duty with his superior and wondering what, if anything, to do about it. He'd come from a military family, so going into the police was seen as the less manly of the options the rest of his kin had taken. With his mother's mantelpiece a dedicated shrine to his older siblings wearing their various military uniforms and displaying polished medals, he was pitied as being 'just a copper' - something his dad would remind him of at every family gathering. His mum would always pat his arm gently offering a 'he's only joking love' without uttering a word.

To be 'just a copper and gay' would only make things worse.

As they had approached the first Floater, Paul had been making a joke about Floaters, and how they usually just get flushed, although the stubborn ones need a bit of encouragement from the trusty bog brush. Usual bullshit.

The smile had been wiped from his face as he turned the drive to see a guy hovering without any means of support in the air just above the roof of his house.

'What the…'

He jumped from the car, applying the handbrake in the same motion, bringing it to a sudden bumping halt, mounting the curb and missing the front garden wall by millimeters.

'How did he get up there?' he inquired of nobody as he leapt from the car. The answer was no clearer to him as he began his own ascent toward the floating guy.

CHAPTER 17
PAUL, DANIEL & MIKE

Chaddy was out the car and after his partner almost instantaneously. He saw Paul's legs moving, cycling into the air, as if he were running up an invisible wall. He had a flashback to watching the muscle guys on 'Gladiator', one of his favourite TV shows as a kid, and the final hurdle of the assault course known as the Travelator. His friends and family all cooed after the female warriors, but Chaddy knew in his heart-of-hearts even at that age that he felt something, unsure what, for the male warriors.

And now his latest crush was leaving him in quite an odd way.

He leapt over the front of the car, sliding his butt across the metal and managed to grab hold of Paul's leg at the knee… then the ankle… then the foot itself. The force lifting him was incredible. He clenched his teeth and tried to hold Paul down with all his strength.

It was no use. Paul's shoe came off and fell uselessly to the floor. Paul Ross, the third Floater on the street, hit the Breaker around three feet from Mike.

'I thought you were here to help?' asked Mike, unsure why he felt the need to be jovial.

'How did you get up here?' asked Paul.

Mike looked at the floor, then twisted his head to look along the Breaker at the officer.

'You just done it, so guess we've both got no idea!'

Paul turned his head to see his partner back in the car and radioing for back-up. Back-up for what exactly Paul had no idea. He turned awkwardly, looking across at Mike once more, asked a question that felt oddly correct, as if this floating situation wasn't happening and he was here instead to find out what this floating guy had been up to.

'What's in the case?' he gestured, straining the muscles further in his neck.

Mike instinctively felt the need to reach over and pat the case, ensuring it was tightly locked. But his arms wouldn't budge, pinned as he was to the Breaker.

'This is like being crucified but without the nails,' he retorted in panic, hoping the humour would change the subject. *How can he be interested to know what's in the fucking case when we're marvels of the modern world at this precise fucking moment?*

Fortunately for Mike, the copper's partner below came to the rescue.

'The team's on their way Paul, don't…' He was about to say the bleeding obvious. And he'd called his boss by his first name. First time ever on the job.

On the job.

Floaters.

Chaddy rubbed his eyes, trying to erase away what was happening. Reality didn't behave like this. He'd seen a lot in his first few weeks; stabbings, a glassing, even the death of a baby at the hands of a drunk mother, but this? No, this wasn't reality. In some primal way he could understand all he had witnessed until today. But how do you explain this?

And why wasn't *he* floating?

'Can't be an Act of God,' he muttered.

'What Dan?' said Paul from above.

Dan shook his head, clearing his thoughts. 'Just that… erm, it can't be an Act of God.'

Paul looked around at the ground below, aware he was shifting, sliding along something, above the roof of the house. *Like a human cloud*, he thought.

'Why? Why not? It makes the most sense at the moment!' he called.

Dan took a breath. *Can't be God. Otherwise, I'd be there too. God hates gays, isn't that what the Bible teaches?* But he can't say that. No, never. Saying it aloud would make it real. Confirm his deepest, darkest yearnings.

'Not like this,' he said quietly.

'Dan, I can't hear you. Look, can you get to the back garden… do you have a back garden, Sir?' Still playing the role. Although not a psychologist, it was by staying professional that Paul's grasp on reality was holding firm; *stay in character. Be who you know. Always be at service to the public.* Isn't that what the book says? *Yeah, whilst floating unexplainably, always be at the service of the public.* He felt his public mask slipping. He'd never had time for any of that Freudian shit. Subconscious trauma by not being loved by a father figure? Yeah, right. His dad had fucked him up and he'd been a bit of a wanker himself. Something he'd blamed on his upbringing. The therapy hadn't helped. And he'd gotten into many a fight, usually after drinking, trying to cover what he knew was an obvious feeling inside.

What's happening? Why bring all this up now?

'Dan!' he regained composure. 'Get to the back.'

It appeared his partner was already on his way around, having entered the house.

'Does he have a warrant?' laughed Mike, becoming more certain by the moment he was losing his mind.

Paul didn't laugh. Instead, he tried to latch his thoughts back to anything real.

That briefcase.

He enquired again to its contents.

CHAPTER 18
PAULA

Trying to get closer, Paula could still not hear anything from the copper or briefcase guy. Below her, dogs continued to bark. Had there been that many dogs on the estate? From the noise it seemed every house now owned one.

In a few moments she'd be alongside the copper, close enough to hear them.

Before she could reach them, she passed out.

CHAPTER 19
MIKE

'I asked you what's in the briefcase?'

Fuck this copper.

Mike tried to control his breathing. There was simply no way the police could be onto him. And this situation… whatever it was… clinging to this invisible ceiling. Surely this couldn't be an elaborate trap? No. Floating behind the copper was a woman he recognised from a few doors down. What was her name? Pauline? Paula? One of those.

He hoped he hadn't blushed at the question, trying to remain composed. Given the factors he was experiencing, it was not easy. But if he did look flushed, at least he had an excuse.

'Just work stuff. Was on my way to work when this happened. Why?'

Paul went to speak, but held his tongue. He actually had no idea how to answer. Why had he asked? To try to get control on this situation. Yes, that was it. Keep it real.

Interrupting his thoughts, Mike changed the subject; 'Do you have any idea what's happening here? Is it a terrorist attack?'

Mike thought that was a good one. Blame the foreigners. Wouldn't hurt to move the spotlight off of him. They were both white men after all.

'I'm… I'm not sure,' said Paul, quickly regretting his lack of professionalism. He was supposed to know God damn it! He was the authority here. Although, take away the badge and uniform, they were just the same. Mike, being a few years older, probably had more idea than Paul at this moment in time.

Mike took advantage of the weakness shown. 'You don't know? That's not good enough! Isn't it your job to know?' Quite happy to be a little red in the cheeks now. It would look like anger. That was good.

With great effort, Paul turned his head away. He felt a static feeling across the back of his head. He'd now drifted so much that Chaddy was out of sight.

'Did you feel that?' asked Mike.

Paul turned back, again scraping his head on the Breaker and again that static pulse.

Before he could reply both men passed out.

CHAPTER 20

AHMED

Calm.

It felt good. The vest felt right.

He turned on the footpath, locking his front door, wondering why he was bothering. Unless something went wrong, he'd not be coming back here again.

Ever.

As he removed the key from the door, he felt the familiar lightness of being pulse through his whole body.

I'm getting closer to God.

As if a miracle, that thought became a reality. Ahmed was lifted into the sky shoulders first, hanging by the scruff of the neck, like a cub in its mother's mouth.

Like a martyr in the hand of God.

But this felt wrong. Had they been onto him? Was this some new-found gadget to stop suicide bombers? He looked around; eyes barely visible over the top of his coat hood. He thought it may soon be pulled off over his head. And there he'd be, suspended, the vest on full display, with everyone to look at and throw stones.

A modern rack for the village crackpot.

The vest.

He stretched his hand down and gently felt for the trigger wired to a simple switch in his pocket.

Remote controlled.

Sweating, shaking with despair and fear, Ahmed had the sudden desire to run. But where would he go?

His finger gently touched the tip of the switch.

He could, of course, leave anytime he wanted.

INTERLUDE - DURING THE FIRST HOUR

Tiredness, the need for water, food and the desire to move bowels and bladders were all beginning to take their hold on the first Floaters. Many more bodies were floating up to join them. Yet, not one of the Floaters had noticed something even stranger than their own predicament. Many of the people below and alongside were starting to flicker. Shimmer. Blinking in and out of existence for the merest moment of time.

PART TWO

CHAPTER 1

ANGELA - IN THE AIR

Captained by Angela Pinkney, with her passenger lover, journalist Tasha Davies, the helicopter had been sent up to get the first shots of the floating guy.

Now, with little fuel left, Angela was stumped at just how to get the damn thing down again. They had their photos, had their frank discussions on what the hell was happening and, for the last hour or so, had been silent.

It seemed that getting up through the Breaker was no problem, as if it wasn't there at all. But now, desperate to land, having flown miles across a sea of bodies, she was unable to set the chopper down.

The Breaker wouldn't allow her to pass back through.

And when they had tried to land on it (Angela repeatedly saying how difficult it was to land on something you couldn't see) they had felt an electric shock ripple through the entire chopper.

Angela and Tasha exchanged a frantic look.

If they didn't land soon, then they'd fall out of the sky.

Simple as that.

CHAPTER 2

ANGELA & TASHA

'Baby, are you getting this?' Angela exclaimed.

Tasha barely heard, her finger tapping on the shutter button. The flash was now turned off as it made a bluish glow on the surface of whatever this invisible thing was that the people beneath were sticking to.

'I've never seen anything like it,' continued Angela mainly to herself.

Tasha mumbled something, leaning out to get a better shot. She unfastened her belt. Angela reached over and grabbed her arm. 'No wait! You're my passenger and you're under my command. Understand?'

Tasha stopped snapping long enough to look Angela in the eyes. She saw there was no point arguing.

'Well, cool, but can you get a bit lower? Maybe tilt it so I'm nearer to this thing?'

Angela sighed, considered and flew as low as she dared.

That was when the bottom of the helicopter first touched the Breaker.

The whole thing shook and was suddenly thrown upwards, both passengers barely held in their seats by their buckles. Angela's headphones slid forward over her eyes.

This was not good.

'What the fuck was that?' said Tasha. Her camera had dropped to her chest, landing with an audible thump. Another strap to be grateful for.

Angela consulted all dials. Everything appeared normal.

'I've… no idea.'

'Can you try radioing someone again?'

The previous attempts had been pointless. No response. Just static. They were on their own. Angela was an experienced pilot and she'd be calling the shots. She calmed herself by breathing slowly through her nose. Her yoga training was needed more now than ever.

'No, look, just get your shots baby, we're going back in one minute.' She almost convinced herself they were going to get through this; literally and metaphorically.

It was Tasha's turn to grab Angela's arm.

'Sorry, but hey. We're shooting something miraculous here. Look. I mean… just look!' Tasha extended her arm, taking in the sea of bodies increasing beneath them. As they looked, more people floated up, as if on wires, to join those already there. They filled empty spaces, often being trapped facing up, their features crushed against the Breaker.

Men in suits, women joggers, teenagers. As of yet, neither saw a kid. But more were joining them all the time.

'I really don't like this Tash. I want to help you, but-'

Tasha searched her lovers' eyes for an answer.

'But?'

'I want down now. You've got what you need, yeah?'

Tasha inhaled. Yes, she had what she needed. This would make her name.

Another bolt shot the chopper up into the sky, this time flinging it sideways. It rotated a full 360 degrees. Angela fought hard to get it back under her control.

'Ange, what was that?'

Angela gulped. She had no idea.

'Time to get this baby down before it happens again.'

This time there was no argument.

CHAPTER 3

ANGELA

She'd been flying since her mid-twenties. It was an author who got her into it. And he wasn't even a pilot. She'd read a motivational quote about how one needed 10,000 hours flight time to truly master anything. If you wanted to be a great pianist, spend 10,000 hours playing the piano. But she wanted more than music, she wanted to fly.

Her childhood dream. Flying. Of being free.

From her.

The Wicked Witch.

Her mother had died when Angela was only young. Her dad never told her for years - in fact it wasn't him who had told her in the end. The Wicked Witch had enjoyed scarring with that particular knife. A scar deep across Angela's heart.

Her father had said her mother had run away when Angela was just a baby. Nothing to do with the birth, just that she had problems and had not been able to cope with life.

That part had sort of been true. Her mother had committed suicide after walking out of a hospital shortly after a drug overdose and thrown herself off the cliffs near their house.

Angela had been three months old.

Her dad, wishing to protect his baby from the facts, had concocted the run-away story, and had been telling it to Angela as long as she could remember. He'd met Marianne when Angela was a toddler. It was made clear to her that her 'birth mummy' had ran off, but her 'home mummy' was always here to help them all be happy.

And they had been. Between the hours of 7pm and 8am Monday to Friday. Those times her father would be home and life would be good. But when he was at work, her step-mum would transform from the Loving Mother to the Wicked Witch.

At first it had been simple telling off. Not that Angela had been a bitch baby by any means. You'd hardly have known she was there. Around the age of four, the Wicked Witch had begun to slap. Not too hard, but enough to make the tears come. Angela had told her dad at first when he had come home from work, but that had caused him and the Wicked Witch to shout. Her dad had been upset and she was afraid he'd run off too and go and live with her birth-mummy.

Then she'd be all alone with the Wicked Witch.

Angela had lost herself in fairy stories, having learned to read at an early age. As she devoured the tales of Cinderella, Snow White and Sleeping Beauty, she had projected all her anxieties onto her step-mum. She was the Wicked Witch made real. She wasn't in any fairy story that could be closed forever and put away. No, this Witch was real and in her house.

And she was clever.

Around her father her step-mum was the ideal wife. Loving, caring, cook and cleaner. But when he left, things changed. Angela did her best to be as good as possible. She looked forward to school days and dreaded the holidays. Her friends thought her odd.

'How can you be so sad that it's soon gonna be summer, huh?'

She'd ignore them, shrugging, keeping her thoughts to herself. What should be six weeks of family fun for her could be six weeks of Hell.

Roll-on September.

Her father was still with the Wicked Witch, but Angela had 'faced her fears and done it anyway' (another motivational self-help book she'd read) and had survived her 10,000 hours of flight time with Marianne.

Fright-time seemed more appropriate. But that changed when she was fourteen. It then became fight-time.

As the little girl became an angry teenager, the Wicked Witch had grown ever more fearful of being found out. Of the abuse. Of the slaps, pinches, punches. The kicks, the cuts, the bruises. Of the lunch being put over her head. Of the humiliation of telling her friends that came knocking asking her out to play that she was a 'bad girl' and was cleaning up the house. In reality, the Wicked Witch had decided to empty cans of food, sometimes the waste bin, the food bin - once a sack of doggy doo she'd brought home from the top of a Dog-Bin - all over the house. The latter she had made Angela watch as she had rubbed it into the lounge carpet. The cream carpet.

'What will you father say, when he sees… what… (rubbing, smearing) his… (wiping, smiling) little… (on the curtains, on the sofa) bitch of a princess has done?'

Angela had returned the smile, much to the dissatisfaction of her step-mum.

Marianne didn't like that smile. It revealed not only disobedience, but something scarier. It hid more than it showed. It hid a plan.

And plans could be very tricky. Especially if the plan was to 'catch you out'.

No, can't be. Outdone by a teenager?

But she was. Mentally at least. Angela had cleaned up on that particular occasion, her step-mother for the first time ever not hanging around to inspect and dish out further insults as the girl worked.

Angela had cleaned not for herself but for her father. He had enough to put up with, what with her mum running away, and didn't deserve to come home to this-

She remembered a laugh from behind her.

'Is that what he told you?'

She remembered she'd spoken aloud and wished to God she hadn't…

'That she ran away? Oh, my dear girl.'

No, no, no!

And so, she had found out. It was the last attack. But it was the one that cut the deepest.

Angela was ever grateful for her ability to read and lose herself in books. She'd kept her composure. Had kept her cool.

Until the fire.

No, not now. Focus.

Now, hovering above a sea of people, many seeking out her face (those that faced upwards), seeking some kind of recognition from another person that this situation was being sorted, she was relying heavily on that learned behaviour. That absolute control. If she could beat the Wicked Witch, she could handle this.

She went down in flames. I won't.

Not now.

Stay grounded.

That was her internal voices' advice. She wished it had spoken up before she'd even taken off.

As it was, there didn't seem to be any way down.

CHAPTER 4

TASHA

Bullied at school, a poor home life, lack of role models and involved in petty crime. Tasha didn't have the calm head on her shoulders gifted by the gods to her lover. Tasha was angry. Would flash out and strike. A cobra in clothes. Angela had told her the various pieces of her life jigsaw as they had become closer over the last few years. Although not complete, Tasha had enough of the jigsaw to put together an almost complete picture.

And, like her own upbringing, it wasn't great.

She hoped that their relationship had allowed her lover to add a huge new piece to her life jigsaw; a happy, smiling one, replacing the older miserable ones.

Tasha rarely talked about her past. It was Angela's compassion, patience and understanding that had brought them together. And it was the spark of finding a kindred soul, someone who understood the misery of being isolated, that allowed them to overcome their fears and find a new path.

Together.

Angela had encouraged Tasha to follow her journalist and photographer ambitions, quoting from many of her self-help books. Not much of a reader, Tasha relied on her partner for the quick-fix quote to help her when times were tough.

'Hey baby, if I can fly then you can too! You could take photos from above. Maybe get some traction on that?'

Tasha had smiled. Angela always called her baby. 'Thanks, but I don't think your boss would be happy with me writing about the rich and famous you chaperone around the skies, do you?'

Angela knew it was a no-go when she had said it. But the idea? That was sound. She could write about it.

'You don't have to be physically with me to write about it? I'm sure that Stephen King hasn't really been attacked by monsters or served time in a penitentiary to write his stories!'

Shawshank Redemption.

One of her favourite films. It offered hope.

And so, she had begun her journalism course. It wasn't the most exciting, but it did give her a potential career. It was her Redemption.

It had given her hope.

And the Gods had given her this gift; unfolding below her was the greatest story of the millennium. If not of history itself.

But up here, trapped above the Breaker unable to land, hope was running out.

As was their fuel.

CHAPTER 5
ANGELA

There were bodies floating everywhere, like an oil slick of suits and boots. All at the same level, trapped just beneath whatever this thing was that kept the helicopter trapped above. As she flew, looking for a gap in the sea of bodies, Angela began to feel waves of panic creeping in, threatening her composure.

'If we don't land soon baby…'

There was no need to finish the sentence. A blue pulse, like a shimmer, skated across the Breaker.

'Did you see that?' asked Tasha.

Angela nodded, not speaking out loud, fearing that if she confirmed she had seen it, then it made this ever-increasing series of bizarre events even more real. Tasha hadn't seen the nod, instead taking pictures. This wasn't about notoriety now or getting published; this was coping. Angela's coping mechanism was to concentrate on landing, Tasha's was to photograph. It was their hook on the old reality. The safe one.

Keep your mind busy.

Panic threatened to rise in her, she felt her chest tightening.

Please God, not now. Concentrate on the fuel.

She needn't have worried about something to occupy her thoughts.

Beneath them an explosion happened, sending a rippling wave of fire and white light cascading along the underside of the Breaker.

CHAPTER 6
AHMED

He'd been lifted and placed gently against the ceiling thing. Thank God for small mercies. And now he was drifting. More bodies, floating like balloons, even a couple holding hands, were floating up, joining them.

Ahmed blinked, clearing his eyes as the couple appeared to momentarily flicker in and out of view, like an illusion.

Looked like there was a change of plan after all.

He didn't care. They were still the infidel. He'd still take some of them out.

He was ready. His finger hovered over the trigger.

'Help me, please?'

A fat man.

'My… my wife. She won't cope without me there!' Ahmed turned his neck looking to where the voice was coming from. He didn't know this guy.

'How… how can I help you? I'm here too!'

The fat guy was drifting toward Ahmed, his speed quicker than Ahmed was being dragged.

It's the vest. It's weighing you down. Slowing you down. Lose the vest.

No. Never. He was prepared. He was ready.

Maybe I don't have to die? Maybe this is God's way to punish them all anyway?

Stop.

His thoughts tumbled through his mind. He thought he was sure. Then he felt otherwise. Without realising it, Ahmed began crying.

'Listen kid, I can… I can help you.'

The fat man again. He was reaching out toward Ahmed, his fingers now inches from Ahmed's shoulder.

'Don't… Touch… Me.' Ahmed stuttered between sobs. His tears flowed freely.

I don't want to die.

'It's… my… birthday,' he said.

The fat man sucked in a breath.

'Happy Birthday kid!' he said. 'Not really a way to celebrate this is it, but hey, I guess you'll always remember it!'

Ahmed opened his eyes and looked toward the fat man. The fat man shimmered.

'You're not real,' said Ahmed, confused and scared.

Numb, he pressed the trigger.

CHAPTER 7

PAUL

They were speeding up.

Without a wind in the air, it wasn't apparent just how they were gliding with such speed across this thing. He was aware of a lady who had been gradually trying to get closer to him. He prayed she wasn't about to ask for help. If only he could lose this fucking uniform.

But then he'd be naked. Naked and drifting across the sky. What a sight!

Who'd want to see that? he thought.

He knew.

Chaddy.

Dan would want Paul to be his 'daddy' anytime. The thought made him aroused. He had time to consider how fucked-up humans were. Hovering like this, on display to the world, worried, scared, wondering if he might die and here he was getting a boner thinking of male domination.

That's why God's punishing us.

That wouldn't wash with him. He was an atheist. Although, this was testing his beliefs.

'Mike, listen, is there anything you have on you, that might be able to help us get down? Or contact someone?' Ever the helpful policeman.

Mike's eyes flashed to the briefcase. He felt the urge to reach across and tap it, ensuring it was safely shut. Those clasps. If they go…

'No, don't think so.'

Paul nodded his head slightly, regretting it as it banged on the Breaker.

He glanced beyond Mike and could make out a rather large guy reaching toward someone. Someone dressed entirely in black.

Special ops?

No, too…

What?

Paul didn't know but felt that whoever it was wasn't there to do any good.

Ridiculous but he knew. Deep down he knew.

His heart sped up.

Mike tried to follow his gaze. 'What's wrong?'

Paul didn't answer. The fat guy was almost at the kid now. Paul blinked as the fat guy momentarily vanished and then reappeared.

What the fuck?

He forced his attention back to the kid.

Yeah, he's only young. Maybe late teens? Do I know him?

The pieces of the jigsaw all fell into place with such ferocity that Paul thought he would simply fall from the sky.

'Don't touch him!'

CHAPTER 8

PAUL

It was pure instinct, something no police training manual taught. He'd recognised his face. Even from that distance.

No, not his face. It was the *weight* of him. He was too skinny a kid to have that much mass about him.

Paul had a brief second before the explosion to consider how, if circumstances were different and he wasn't floating around up here, he may have not been so quick to say something. Racism and all that.

But he knew. Somehow, he knew.

Didn't matter anyway. It was too late.

The explosion rippled outwards like a wave, liquid fire incinerating those immediately around the kid, and pushing the others along the Breaker through sheer force.

The Breaker had reacted to the explosion, emitting an electrical pulse across its entire (and still expanding) length. The pulse had caused everyone touching it to pass out.

Into a blessed sleep.

Had he lived, Ahmed would've been disappointed to see the damage inflicted upon his supposed enemy. He took out himself of course (that part of the deal was not negotiable) and one other; a fat man.

INTERLUDE - AFTER

Ahmed's body defied the laws of science and, despite being burned beyond recognition, remained whole.

There he stayed along with the fat man, whose body also remained in the same position it was in at the moment of the blast. They were like pencil drawings on a glass roof. A modern take of Michelangelo's Creation of Adam in charcoal.

Their charred bodies drifted among the sleeping others.

PART THREE

CHAPTER 1
DOUG'S CAR

Always serious on the way, always a laugh on the way back. Well, not always, he guessed. There was that one time when they never closed the deal.

That one time.

From the backseat, Adam interrupted his thoughts; 'So, that's all the paperwork in-hand and Doug, you've got the gift for them in the boot, yes?'

Adam, always the planner with the attention to detail, knew the answer to most of the questions he asked in these situations, but felt the need to hear it out loud. So there'd be no fuck-ups.

'Yes Adam. All's in hand.'

Next to Adam in the back, Nick laughed uneasily; a rarity, their humour was usually kept under wraps until after. The last thing they needed was to laugh their tits off in the middle of doing the deal.

Doug had reached the single-track road that led to the golf club. He took a moment to check himself in the mirror. He looked cool, but felt a growing anticipation. That was good. Meant he was alert.

And with guys like they were meeting, you had to be on your toes. Ready to answer any question.

'I think they'll take it boys, I really do,' he offered.

'Don't jinx us,' replied Nick.

Doug glanced over into the passenger seat and thought of Nicky. That was where she usually sat. Now there was just a bunch of boring papers. But in the glove box…

He smiled again, pleased with how his life had turned out. It hadn't all been plain sailing. But he was getting back on form. 'Back On Top' as he said to himself in moments of privacy.

And with Nicky. She liked to be 'Back On Top'. His mind drifted to the glove box again and the secret package he had there. He'd be celebrating for sure when this deal was wrapped up. It could be their biggest yet.

And he deserved it. Plus, he knew Nicky liked getting surprises. Especially naughty ones. A naughty surprise for a good girl.

He felt himself getting hard.

Nick reached over and tapped him lightly on the shoulder, making him jump.

'Sorry mate. You OK? Adam was asking you about the meeting room?'

Doug took a deep breath. 'Yeah fine, he knows!' answering both questions at once.

Nick sat back and glanced at Adam who was flicking through his many sheets of paperwork as if trying to memorise it all.

Or looking for something he'd forgotten.

Too late now anyway.

They turned onto the golf course. Nick put his elbow on the windowpane. It was a comfy car, loads of room. He allowed his thoughts to drift. Surprisingly, there were few golfers out and about.

'Bit of a miserable day for being on the course at half-nine anyway', he muttered to himself.

Nobody replied. Nick knew they were all getting into their own zone now. Preparing to do the deal.

Loads of hours had gone into it. Late nights, burning the midnight oil. Sacrificing family time, dinners, bed-time stories. But it was all worth it. This deal could make them all a year's salary in half-hour. And more. *Much* more if they played their cards right.

'What. The. Fuck?'

Doug's utterance brought Nick out of his daydream. He leaned forward.

'Nowhere to park as usual?'

Doug didn't reply, simply slowed the car to a crawl and stared out of the windscreen. Nick couldn't see what he was looking at and went to put his window down. Thankfully for him the child controls were activated. Had they not have been, Nicholas Holmes may have been dragged out of the car and into the sky.

CHAPTER 2

DOUG

As a golfer himself, Doug was used to seeing abandoned golf carts, as it was unlikely you'd get anything stolen way out in the sticks as the club was.

Away from the riffraff. A favourite saying of his mum.

But what you didn't expect to see, ever, was a golfer hanging suspended in the air.

Doug brought the car to a slow stop. He sensed Nick trying to get his window open and see what Doug was going on about. Adam was still flicking through papers.

'No, Nick, don't do that!' the words came out far more violently than he had intended.

'Do what? What is it Doug for fuck's sake?!' All their silent 'Getting Into the Zone' work had been shattered instantly. This wasn't good.

Adam glanced up for the first time.

'Something's wrong. Doug, what have you forgot?'

Blaming, always blaming. Everything had to be just-so with him. Doug often made the joke how, if Adam had OCD, he'd have to rearrange the letters to CDO to put them in their proper order.

'Look,' was all Doug could manage. His mouth was completely dry. Water, he needed water. He opened the glove box without thinking, the pink ribbon-wrapped package falling to the footwell. It appeared the other two didn't see it. Doug had a feeling that seeing he had a sexy gift for his girl would not even come into the discussion given what he felt unfolding around them.

He dragged other bits out of the glove box. Nick sat forward again, releasing his seatbelt. An alarm beeped indicating that he'd broken the 'Rules of the Car'.

'Nick you're freaking me out. What have you forgot?'

'Nothing! Nothing! Where is it?' Doug was going through the stuff in the footwell now. 'I always keep a bottle here.'

Adam and Nick exchanged an anxious look.

'Nick, you want a drink? To what? Steady your nerves?' Adam giggled uncharacteristically high-pitched. It sounded like a girl. Adam noticed and coughed trying to bring himself under control. This was all going wrong.

'Oh, for fuck's sake!' Doug slammed the glove box shut. He started the car abruptly and wheel-spinned over the gravel, creating a dust cloud. Nick fell into Adam. He corrected himself and mockingly blew a kiss at Adam. 'Later' he mouthed attempting to grin.

Later. The joking always came later. Not before the deal went down.

Doug slammed the breaks on, Adam and Nick darting forward. Nick head-butted the back of Doug's chair. It was his turn to curse.

'Fucking hell Doug!'

Doug ignored him, pointing out of his side window.

'Now… now can you see?' he was panting.

Nick rubbed his forehead thinking how he'd now look like a flustered twat in front of their clients. This would not do. Not at all.

Adam shifted across, his hand on Nick's lap. Nick thought to joke about 'later' again but was so caught with Adam's open-mouthed expression that, at first, he was unable to turn his head and see what they were gawking at.

Turn Nick. Just turn!

But he couldn't. The tendons in his neck felt like lead. Adam snapped the trance with a simple, unbelievable sentence; 'He's floating!'

CHAPTER 3

DOUG

Like kids looking in through a window of a lap-dancing club, the three businessmen sat open-mouthed in silence, their meeting forgotten.

The window gradually began to fog up.

'Turn on the air con quick!' said Nick.

Doug fumbled, searching for the button. He suddenly felt like he'd never seen this car before. He searched and finally found it, the air conditioning bursting into life. He felt his eyes compelled to the floating golfer. He didn't want to look away, even for a moment in case he missed something. This felt bigger than 9-11.

'Is it a PR stunt do you reckon?' said Adam.

'I dunno, just…' Doug paused.

'What?' said Nick, his voice distant.

'Just, don't get out of the car.'

'Why not?'

Adam jumped in; 'Do you think it's like chemical or something? Terrorists?'

'I don't know,' said Doug, barely a whisper.

While contemplating what to do next, a golfer walking out of the clubhouse was suddenly hoisted into the sky to join the first.

CHAPTER 4

ADAM

Adam unfastened his seatbelt.

'What if the guys we're meeting are…'

Nick finished the sentence for him. 'Up there?'

Questions followed questions, no answers to be had.

'Did you just see what happened? How did he just float up there?'

Silence.

Finally, an answer of sorts from Nick. 'Put the radio on Doug!'

More fumbling, windscreen wipers came on, the de-mister and then, finally, the radio. A music channel. He pressed to the programmed talk-show channel.

'…the A10 is highly congested in Enfield after a lorry has broken down near the…'

Tried another.

More music.

Adam felt an inner calm stealing over him. He took his mobile out and checked the signal. The calm vanished as smoothly as it had come. 'Tits! No 4G!'

Doug realised his hand was shaking. He went back to the talk show, surely someone must be talking about this-

'…all I can say is that this video appears to show an absolute miracle. It was posted by a kid and appears to show a man hovering in the sky outside his house. Now, this has gone viral. In the background we can see other people being apparently lifted somehow into the air. I've no idea what is happening, but more and more Tweets and videos are being posted of similar happenings across the UK. I…' the presenter gulped trying to get the breath to continue in his excitement, '…we've… I'm just hearing that… Oh my God…'

The goosebumps ran over all three men at the same time.

CHAPTER 5

DOUG

'I've got to call Nicky.' Doug was throwing more stuff everywhere. 'Where's my phone, have any of you seen my-'

Adam extended his, then thought better of it. 'No signal, sorry,' he shrugged.

Nick removed his from his jacket pocket. Even worse. No battery.

'It's got to be here… can you guys see if there's a bottle of water under the seats?'

He calmed himself, lifted himself up off the seat, head crunching against roof, and felt in his back trouser pocket. Wallet. Tried the other one. Phone.

Good.

He slipped it from his pocket, praying that it would have a signal. He clicked the screen.

No signal.

Another fuck was shouted.

'Keep your phones out, I'll drive round 'til we get a signal.'

'Can't we just go in the club house and use theirs? This is an emergency, Doug!' said Nick.

Doug turned, looking awkwardly over his shoulder at Nick. 'Just trust me, Nick. Something isn't right here. We need to stay in the car and see if we can get things sorted. First, families, right? Check they're safe. Then we can try to work out what the-'

He slammed the car brakes as one of the receptionists from the private members club had run into the front of the car. Panicking, she ran around to his window and banged on the glass.

'Let her in Doug for Christ's sake!' Nick was trying the lock on his own door. The girl noticed and jumped windows, front to rear. She was pleading through the glass. Her nose started to bleed. Nick stopped trying to open the door, suddenly grateful of the child locks. Her nose dripped onto her white blouse. She was Eastern European. Sandy? Cindy? Had he even seen her before? Usually they wore name badges, something Nick liked as he had ample opportunity to check their tits out under the guise of reading their badge. Something he knew every guy did. And the reason, he assumed, why most women chose to wear their badges right there. They wanted the guys to look. Especially the married ones.

She banged again, slamming a bloody hand against his window. This was getting freaky.

'Drive Doug, just drive,' his voice low, barely audible.

Doug had already begun, spinning off again across the gravel. In the back seats, Nick and Adam turned and stared at the receptionist, her nose bleeding. And then, as if by magic, she raised her arms to her side, and lifted off of the ground into the air.

The similarity to the image to Christ on the cross was burned into their minds. Doug saw the event unfold in his mirror.

The girl's form moved in and out, like a strobe was being flashed before their eyes.

CHAPTER 6
JAMES – THE RADIO STATION BEFORE

James had been broadcasting the breakfast show ever since his lucky break; banging the daughter of a media mogul at an award's ceremony back in the early naughties. He was handsome, charismatic and good company. Plus, he knew he was good at what he did.

Charm.

That was how he'd always got by. 'Liddle Prince Charmin' his mum always used to say, always missing the g, pinching his cheek (a habit that caused embarrassment into his teenage years as she did it wishing him a goodbye as he went out with his mates) in the way only a loving mother can do. Substituting the Ts for Ds only made it sound even more cringing.

It didn't affect him in the way perhaps a less confident, less charming kid would have been. But not James. Calm, confident and full of life, he had no problem pulling any girl he wanted (although in his heart of hearts, he knew it was both sexes that he had the urge to be with but he'd only ever acted on the first of those impulses). They would all expect him to be a good lover and a bit of a playboy. He was convinced he would lose a lot of street cred if he were gay. Although, he also knew from the magazines he read online in secret during spare hours late at night with his iPad tucked under the duvet with him, that many chicks found the gay guy a real turn-on. Apparently because they were not 'turnable'. Only had Eyes for The Guys. How that made his appeal sexier to the ladies he didn't quite understand.

When he was twenty-two, he had been invited to an awards ceremony for a piece he had written in his blog, The Commentari-Crap. His attempt to find a dot com nobody had thought of and the one that was the least pathetic of his choices, allowed him to vlog and blog about all things he felt the world needed to hear his opinion on.

And he'd covered a lot of topics. He had thought of writing under a pseudonym and blogging as a gay guy on matters too. Offering a unique slant. But he never got round to it. Perhaps because he secretly fantasised about such a project, about being Found Out. That was hot. So, the idea stayed as a fantasy.

The Commentari-Crap had won a large following and had been nominated for the highest number of followers in Hertfordshire. He had been invited to the awards ceremony and along he did trot. He was playing around with two girls at that time and hadn't invited either to accompany him. His mother had wanted to go, but he couldn't have that just in case she decided to have one drink too many and share stories of his youth. And worse, maybe grab his cheek at the most inopportune time. Like when he met Gina Barclay in the reception of the event. He'd actually grinned to himself when the conversation had been going so well and she had asked after his parents. He could imagine his mum being right there, gripping, shaking, distorting his oh-so pretty face saying 'My Liddle Prince Charmin'. Gina was hot, *smoking hot* as his mates would say. Slim, fantastic figure and single. Ticked all the boxes. They were sat at different tables during the meal and ceremony, but they could see each other throughout. He would wink, mock boredom at certain points, roll his eyes, always offering his best Prince Charmin grin to whack it home. By the main course she was putty in his hands. By dessert, he knew he'd have her by morning.

Easy.

The icing on the cake was long after they had had sex, her inviting him back, seeing her awesome pad; a converted barn in the countryside. One side had full glass windows which she assured him they could see out of, but nobody could see into. Not that there was anybody too see in. Her father owned the land (he later found out) and the lake they looked out on (also her father's) ensured there wasn't anybody around for at least a mile. Which was a good thing as he had fucked her naked with her arms and breasts up against the glass, on the upper floor where her bedroom overlooked the lake.

When they awoke the next morning, his first smile had been at the sight of Gina's tight tush walking to the bathroom. His second came from seeing his award for 'Best Blogger South-East 2006' on the bedside table. A gleaming gold pole with a flag on it, the meaning of which had escaped him entirely. The morning light gleamed off of the award

(The pole the shaft)

and his mind turned to thoughts of the other impulse he had been harbouring for a long time.

Gina broke his trance, coming back to bed to see if he was able to go again already. At that age he was. His body was with her during their second fuck but his mind wasn't; he fantasised about doing a guy. God knows what she was thinking of; he pushed her head into the pillows, driving into her hard from behind. He didn't care.

After a few more well-planned dates and screws (balanced between his other two girls), Gina had invited him to meet her parents, moreover her dad. She was terrified of him, that much he knew instinctively. He hadn't bothered to delve too deeply into her past, her relationship with her parents (she had the cash to get a therapist without him needing to put up with her trash) and the tone she spoke in when referring to her father was always one of a scared little girl. He smiled, confident that he would be her Prince Charming and take her away on his white horse, away from the evil father forever. Or with her riding his white cock. The day finally came when he met with the Big Bad Man (in his mind, he'd already had a fantasy going about tying the old man up and fucking Gina in front of him. See how Daddy liked that. That was the thing about these wealthy old men; thought they could control the world. Well, James would show him.)

Like most things in life, it didn't turn out anything like he expected. The old man was a real nice guy. Simon Barclay had welcomed James into the family home as if he were himself a long-lost son. The whole experience had shaken James' facade to the very core. He didn't like that feeling. Suffocation. That was the word he had in his mind whenever Gina mentioned going round to see them any time after that first visit. They suffocated you, with food, drink and, God forbid, love.

But when the talk over that first dinner had turned to James' ambitions as 'a young up-coming successful award-winning journalist' (Gina's words not his) James had mentioned about doing more of his videos, as he liked to speak his opinions rather than write them down. He talked about an idea for an online platform where listeners could interact with him live, maybe even making their web-cameras live at the same time, so other viewers could see the debates. See the rows.

That was appealing to James. As he spoke, more and more ideas tumbled out of him. He was surprised at just how many ideas he had, must have been storing them up subconsciously for just such a meeting.

Simon had heartily approved of the idea and mentioned to James that he would consider backing the idea financially (of course he would, as long as he had control. James couldn't have that. Nobody censored his comments. Nobody). Simon had gone on to discuss how the platform could be rolled out offering other presenters the chance to share their opinions on all matters. And they could have a training course and… Before long, James realised he'd have to keep his ideas under wraps going forward. This was getting out of his control and he didn't like that.

That night, in revenge, he'd establish his dominance once again and force Simon's daughter's head into the pillow, fucking her hard from behind. The thought caused a smile to cross James' lips. He then realised Simon had stopped talking, they all had. They were looking at James expectantly. Had he muttered something?

Oh Christ, please don't say I said anything out loud.

No, they were smiling. He grinned further, turning to Gina for help. He needed his charm now more than ever.

'Well, what do you say to Dad's offer?'

That was one thing he liked about Gina. She called him Dad, never Daddy. He always believed posh-totty called their folks Daddy and Mummy. Like they were five or something.

James gulped. He'd clearly not heard an actual offer, instead drifting into a sex premonition with Gina.

'I… I think it's an amazing idea! Thank you.'

Gina had yelped like a little dog (something he would make her do again later, he thought) and her mother had wiped her eyes as if whatever James had just agreed to was *that* emotional.

Christ, I haven't just said I'll marry her, have I?

The colour ran from his face, but the well-honed smile remained.

He could lie so well; he could be a politician.

CHAPTER 7
JAMES

As it had turned out, the offer he had agreed to was much better than marriage. Her father had offered him a chance to grow his experience before doing talk-videos by having a slot on his radio station. He had a controlling share and blah, blah, blah. James had turned off after that bit.

Still smiling, he enjoyed a brandy with Simon while the ladies congratulated each other and talked bullshit about ladies-things he assumed.

It was all too traditional. Here he sat, in Simon's study, surrounded by books and more bottles of spirit than he had ever seen outside of Ibiza. The brandy was good. The offer was good. The pay was very good. It seemed his charm had paid off. He'd landed a good girl, a good opportunity and a good platform to build his name. His *good* name.

And he'd landed into money. Although the feeling of suffocation was still haunting him. He relied on his charm to get him through.

At one-point charm became panic as the topic turned to the future.

Their future.

Gina and his.

James felt the smile, the confidence, the charm dwindling away with each word Simon spoke. Yes, he was a charmer, but this guy? He was a businessman, a deal sealer. Simon had a way to get what he wanted. James was no match for his experience. And he had all the cards up his sleeve, only a few on the table so far, and already he'd got James to a place where he would've liked the shoe to be on the other foot. 'Take my daughter (*clang!* The first chain around him), I've given you a great job (*clang!* Next chain), excellent pay, opportunity - oh and the people I can introduce you to! Well, they can only help you go even further. How would you like that?' (*Clang, clang, clang!*) James quickly realised that in the first few hours of meeting Gina's folks he had become their slave.

He looked at Simon sat behind his desk in the big leather armchair (noticing it was also higher than James' - no doubt another trick to gain the upper hand) and tried to push away the thought which refused to go. *Slave.* Would I like to be this guy's sex slave? Be dominated by an older guy?

No.

No, no and NO!

Push, push it away.

He gritted his teeth. Suffocation. Panic creeping back in. He was losing control.

I'll get control back again in a few hours, pushing her face into the pillow. Pushing it. Hard. Hard.

Simon leaned forward.

'Are you OK James?'

James coughed, clearing his throat. He pinched his skin on the back of his hand hard under the edge of the desk, out of Simon's view. The pain made him jump back into the now.

'Y..yes, sorry, drifted there.'

Smile, smile James.

The winning grin came back and his confidence returned. It was like putting on his favourite mask. He'd win this one. Silly old fuck didn't - wouldn't - have him under any control.

That's right, my liddle Prince Charmin', always missing the final g.

'She never, ever said the G' he muttered and caught himself.

'Sorry?' Simon's eyebrows raised.

'Gina,' James offered, smiling further to restore the upper hand. He stood, reaching for his brandy glass on the edge of the desk. 'I thought it was probably getting late and Gina would need to get to bed soon

(Bite the pillow, bite it bitch!)

as she has to be up early tomorrow, I think she said.'

The older man smiled. Shit, he had a winning smile too. James knew he could be outsmarted here. The old guy could probably smell a bullshitter from a mile away. *You don't make money like this without treading on a few folk on your way up,* he thought. *Unless you're born into it.*

Time to go.

'Listen Simon, thank you again for all of the kind opportunities…' he extended his hand for the final shake, the one that would say Deal Done. And James knew to let the old guy have the upper hand here. He knew how to make them feel they had won. That they had come out on top.

Simon moved from behind the desk, leaving James with his hand stuck out. He avoided the hand completely, pulling James in for a hug.

He was family now.

CHAPTER 8
JAMES - NOW

Today. Hosting the radio breakfast show. Two years and running (although to James it felt more like only a couple of weeks). Ratings up, advertising up, the list of celebrities growing longer by the week. He was becoming a star.

The morning of Thursday 19th January 2017, James was preparing to come off the back of the latest travel update, when the first news began to come in on his many screens; Tweets, emails, posts, pictures.

And the video.

The one that had gone viral.

Someone had filmed their neighbour, a normal looking business guy with a briefcase, hanging suspended in the air just above the trees in the garden of (he assumed) his house. James first saw it briefly just after ten past nine while broadcasting. Must be a hoax, his experienced mind had told him.

But then more came in.

It appeared hundreds of people were floating in the sky. At the radio station, Joanne had begun with the traffic update as normal. 'Problems on the M25 anti-clockwise on the Hertfordshire stretch. I can't see on my cameras what the problem is but people seem to be driving very slowly. The A10 is highly congested in Enfield after a lorry has broken down near Southbury Road. Back in Hertfordshire, I'm just getting news of an event that is causing disruption…'

For the first time in its history, certainly in James' broadcasting career anyway, he cut off the traffic report. In radio News and Traffic are King. They were never cut off. Ever.

Until today. He wasn't going to miss out on this one. This could be his 9-11.

'Sorry Jo.' Charm was out of the window. 'There's something going on. Twitter has gone crazy! Go to my website (that was a sackable offence right there, self-promotion) '… I mean our website and check out this video I've just put up. Nothing is verified yet but all I can say is that this video appears to show an absolute miracle. It appears to show a man hovering in the sky outside his house. Now, this has gone mental online. In the background we can see other people being apparently lifted somehow into the air. I've no idea what is happening, but more and more Tweets and videos are being posted of similar happenings across the UK. I…'

James gulped trying to get his breath to continue in his excitement.

'…we've… I'm just hearing that… Oh my God…'

CHAPTER 9

JAMES

The calm exterior had collapsed at the sight which met him as he glanced at the cameras covering the outside of the busy studio. Based in London, James was used to seeing heavy foot-traffic immediately outside of their doors. The cameras were a security aid, given that some of their topics got a little heated, and provided a glimpse of any would-be attackers when the talk-show host left the building. More applicable to the grave-yard shift guys for sure, but James was always checking them out. You never knew just who you may have offended.

On radio, nobody can see your award-winning smile.

What met his eyes caused all his professional composure to vanish like a girl under the magician's command. The feet of passers-by were simply leaving the pavement. They continued to walk, but upwards, on an imaginary path. Without needing to see further, he knew they were destined to join the others in the sky.

CHAPTER 10
JAMES

By the time his show finished at 10am, James Whitbourne felt exhausted, exhilarated, *excited* and was seeking advice on how he would make it home. He had a wife waiting for him there.

And a pillow she needed to bite.

CHAPTER 11
NIGEL – IN HIS BLACK CAB

Polish not Po(e)lish. That was one of his motto's.

Sure, he'd share it at the greasy spoon with his mates, but not beyond that. Can't say a thing these days without upsetting someone it seemed. Even voting 'Out' in the Referendum had caused rows in his family and, it seemed, he couldn't have any possible reason except 'blaming it on the immigrants'.

He was more educated than that. More liberal.

But yeah, getting rid of a few more of them wouldn't hurt, would it?

His black cab was his pride and joy and he kept that shining. Polished so you could see your face in it. Gleaming, black, slick and… pride. That was it. He had pride in his business.

In his country.

Nigel had been drinking his second coffee of the morning (one for every three fags and, despite what happened to his wife

Maggie, Nigel couldn't find the will power to give the fags up once and for all) when the mobile starting buzzing with the news. Something was amiss in Hertfordshire. Quite how that would affect him in London he had no idea. But it soon became apparent, when his cabbie mates had similar alerts coming through on their phones. It suddenly seemed like they were going to be busy.

'Whassit? Another strike or summink?'

Nigel hadn't looked up from his phone to reply to Derek. For a second, Nigel couldn't recall Derek's name, yet he'd known him for…? Nigel tried to think back. Maybe it was actually less time than he realised. Maybe only a fortnight or so.

'Nah, not a strike Der. Something else.'

That was the first oddity that struck Nigel, right there. No jokes. The guys and him were always bantering. No matter what the disaster, no matter who was involved. Jeez, even when his own wife had died, he made a joke and followed it up himself with 'too soon?' which got another laugh (and several well-meaning pats on the back. They were good guys. Hard exteriors but… what was the saying? Giant teddy-bears underneath).

Yes, Nigel was a giant teddy-bear.

Gruff, chain-smoking widow who had had a loving wife and, until Maggs death, two loving daughters. He was a hard worker. They all were, the whole cabbie clan.

Not like those Uber Fuckers.

Upon seeing this was the beginning of a humanitarian disaster, he thought two things; one, this was going to be a busy day. Busy with a capital B. And two; there was no way those immigrant Uber Fuckers were taking his clientele.

No way.

He'd voted Out.

CHAPTER 12

NIGEL

The morning banter session had been cut short, each giving the other a look that said the same unspoken thing. Get busy and get out there before *they* do.

Nigel had eagerly jumped into his cab, pulled out and then suddenly realised, despite his knowledge (*The* Knowledge, something those Uber fuckwits didn't have to take) and his experience, he was momentarily frozen. Unsure exactly where to go.

The radio was on. James Whitbourne.

'Stir-It-Up Shitbourne,' he muttered, the remnants of ash spitting from his lip. He put the window down, then immediately changed his mind. If what he had read was true, something was dragging folks into the air, and he didn't yet know if it was poisonous.

Go Home, Big Bear.

'Nah, Maggie. Wait. You know things have been hard. This is going to be a good day.'

He often heard his wife speak to him during the many hours he spent alone in his cab. Even when he had passengers, he was alone. They didn't speak. Most didn't even speak his language these days.

Like those Uber Fuckers.

But you don't know what it is. It might not be safe.

'It is, love. Course it is. Look, there's no more police than usual. And traffic's not too-'

That was when the first one took off.

Right in front of him.

At first, he had stopped, used to seeing the London pedestrians dashing out in-front of his cab. But this guy…

One moment he was walking out into the road. The next walking up, into the air.

Nigel stopped mid-sentence and applied the brakes.

Come home, love.

He heard Maggie clearly in his mind but, for the first in a very long time, he failed to reply.

CHAPTER 13

NIGEL

He leant on the dashboard, trying to track the floater with his eyes, until the guy went out of view. Nigel went to get out of the car, but Maggie's counsel stopped him cold.

Don't, love.

His fingers fell from the door handle. *That was a close one. Need to think. What to do?*

He maneuvered the cab, trying to keep one eye on the road and one on the floater. No use, he had gone out of view.

Nigel turned the radio volume higher. Stir-It-Up was still talking. '…and check out this video I've just put up. Nothing is verified yet but all I can say is that this video appears to show an absolute miracle. It appears to show a man hovering in the sky outside his house. Now, this has gone mental online. In the background we can see other people being apparently lifted somehow into the air. I've no idea what is happening, but more and more Tweets and videos are being posted of similar happenings across the UK. I…' Stir-It-Up gulped, Nigel heard him struggling to get his breath back. Even Nigel's heart was hammering.

'…we've… I'm just hearing that… Oh my God…'

CHAPTER 14

NIGEL

The Chinese lady and the business lady brought him out of his trance. They almost put his window through.

'Get off me!' shouted Business.

'My child, no, my child….' said Chinese.

Nigel went to lower the passenger window to stop them banging on the glass and shattering it with their hands. But Maggie stopped him cold.

Drive on. Don't even let the air in. It could be in the air.

'What was that film, love? The one with… oh, whassis name?' Nigel began drumming his fingers on the steering wheel encouraging the cogs of his memory to work faster. 'Oh, you know, the one where the monkey has the disease and they find out it's airborne?'

Bang, hand on glass. Chinese interrupted his thoughts again.

'No, you don't. This is my cab love. Any damage caused you PAY FOR!' he mouthed the last two words slowly. She was holding a baby wrapped in a blue blanket.

This is no way to behave, he thought to himself. His head lulled back and forth considering what to do. Open, close, drive on or stay?

'Ahh! Sod it!' he clicked open the back-door lock.

'Get in!' he shouted.

Both did. There was plenty of room. Business was in first. She tried to close the door on Chinese, but Chinese had fight in her. Slim, almost anorexic in Nigel's opinion, but strong. Chinese literally threw the baby in. A girl. He didn't know how he knew that, wrapped as she was, but he knew. The baby was shrouded in a blue cloth. The colour for a boy. But this was a girl. Nigel just knew.

Throwing the baby in was a desperate but smart move. It secured Chinese's place in the safety of the cab.

Business made no attempt to catch or care for the baby, pulling her feet in as Chinese threw the baby onto the back seat, as if it were the plague itself.

That one move, that tiny selfish act of pulling in her feet, as if she'd been contaminated, made Nigel hate Business from the off.

Ah, you're a teddy bear love, always was, always will be, he heard Maggie say.

'GET IN!' shouted Nigel.

Chinese smiled and, after what seemed like an eternity, stepped into the back of the black cab.

'Close the door!' he said. Stating the bleeding obvious.

Foreigners.

Chinese reached to do so, as a hand clamped onto the door.

CHAPTER 15
NIGEL'S CAB

Chinese screamed.

Nigel fumed. More handprints to wipe off of his wax work. Had these people no idea of the care and love he had for his cab? It was his place of work for Chrissake.

Business yelped.

Chinese showed her strength again, yanking the door with considerable force. The hand stopping it was big. Strong. It belonged to a guy in a woollen cap, track suit and earphones. Nigel could make him out through the passenger window. And there were others coming now. He could see pedestrians pointing, even lip-reading a guy nearby; 'There, that one's free!'

'Mate get in or fuck off!' yelled Nigel. The beauty of being your own boss.

The decision was made for him. Strong Guy's hand kept hold of the door but his body lifted around him until he was doing an impressive one-arm handstand, with only the top of the cab door for balance. And then that too gave way.

A miracle.

The human balloon drifted up, earphones and all.

Chinese reached out and slammed the door shut. 'Go, go, go!' shouted Business, each word coming with a bang on his glass.

'Don't touch my fucking glass! Just had that polished too!' he shouted back.

He could see Business through the Trip Advisor sticker on the glass partition between him and her. He was quite sure that he wasn't going to get a tip from this, let alone five stars. He laughed. It felt good. A release. He had to control it though, or it could become manic. Things were coming apart at the seams.

Despite all this, the noise, language, shouting, screaming and all-round negative energy, the baby had still not uttered a sound.

CHAPTER 16

NIGEL

Nigel knew the streets like the back of the proverbial hand. He had 'The Knowledge'. Those slime turds at Uber were using the same cut throughs though, often blocking his access as they didn't know many of the backstreets were one-way.

'Bloody satnavs, ban them too,' he said to nobody.

Chinese had settled, taking a few moments to get her breath back. The baby still lay on the seat beside her. Business now had her back to him, taking the folding seat up against the glass partition. Her shoulders were heaving, the adrenaline in them all still finding an outlet, looking for a fight that wasn't happening.

Fight or flight.

That simple sentence summed up more than the situation they had just been through.

Whatever was happening right now, outside of his cab, was a case of fight or flight. Literally. If there *was* anything you could do to fight it, of course.

Nobody spoke.

Nigel driving, his cab still having hands reign down upon his proudly polished bodywork as he darted to and fro between other vehicles and pedestrians. Coming around one corner, he slammed on the breaks, a sight before him he would remember vividly until his dying day.

A double-decker bus had mounted the pavement. Its hazard lights were on, as if it had pulled in for passengers to board. And some had. Others were holding on to windows, the rear access poles, fingers scrapping metal work as people were being lifted into the air. Some went silently, a look of bemusement on their faces. Others went up while still holding conversations on the phone. One elderly man went up, his walking stick falling to the floor, clattering off the bus roof as he went (Nigel thought the walking stick vanished as it fell, seeming to disappear and then re-appeared as it hit the ground). The old man took the opportunity to stretch his back, actually bending backwards, on his way up. His face hit something, Nigel couldn't see anything actually blocking the ascent, and the old man simply slid into place; until he was led facing the sky, about thirty feet from the pavement. Nigel's mouth hung open.

'Maggs, love, you ain't going to believe this…' his words trailing off.

I believe you. Go. Just drive. Get out of the city. Now.

He needed no further convincing. He put the car into gear, driving out around the bus, almost hitting a lady pushing a pram. He beeped, something he rarely, if ever, bothered doing. But this was close. The lady turned to him, everything seemed to be in slow motion.

'Get. Out. Of. The. Road!' he mouthed through the windscreen. She was about twenty, long blond hair, pretty. She smiled at him. The gesture creepy on her face. This was simply no time to be polite. There was horror unfolding all around them. Then, glancing back, so slowly, at the baby in the pram, she leaned forward, kissing her fingers and transferring the kiss to the baby. And, just like that, she turned, leaving the pram. Facing Nigel, she stared directly into his eyes and, still smiling, lifted her arms and floated skywards. As she did, she flickered. In and out of existence. On. Off. Like a lightbulb.

Nigel thought it a trick of the sun. He tried to speak, to make sense of what had just happened. His mouth opened and closed; a fish gasping for air.

Business brought him back to his senses.

'Driver, listen, I've no idea what the fuck is going on, but in here we seem to be… safe somehow.' She had turned, shifting to the other folding seat, now behind the front passenger seat. For the first time Nigel could see her clearly. She too was pretty, her features taught, make-up plastered on. A high-flyer in some corporate world.

Probably shagged her way to the top, he thought absentmindedly. He grinned.

She was still speaking.

'Did you hear me? We need to get out of London. Now! Look, I have money.' Her hands played in her lap, then her head went from shoulder to shoulder, looking for a handbag that wasn't there. 'No, no. Fuck, fuck, FUCK!' She pulled her long blonde hair hard with both hands.

'Don't do that, love,' said Nigel.

Chinese, now with the wrapped baby on her lap, reached gingerly across and stroked Business's hands, gently easing them from her hair. Nigel saw scars on Businesses' wrists, make-up unable to cover these completely. They were faded but they were there.

We all have stories, he told himself. *Most of our scars are beneath the skin. Across our hearts.*

Business tried to calm down, but then began clawing at her face, raking her nails (bright red, highly polished) down her cheeks, drawing blood.

Bet that's not the first time, Nigel said to himself.

He didn't have time for this.

Chinese was shushing Business, herself the embodiment of calm composure.

'What's her name?' asked Nigel, hoping to divert Business' attention away from harming herself.

Chinese looked at his eyes reflecting in the rear-view mirror. She forced a smile and went back to hushing Business, trying to stop her raking her face. Business finally did, her hands falling into her lap. The brief moment she had to inflict pain on herself had been effective. Incredible damage had been done in such a short space of time. Her mascara, a moment ago part of her stunning make-up regime, now streaked down her face. Her immaculately straightened hair, now knotted and dishevelled. For the first time Nigel saw she was younger, much younger than she had at first appeared. Whatever mask she hid behind had crumbled. Now she was vulnerable. And scared.

Nigel hated to admit it to himself, but he was too. One big teddy bear.

'The baby,' he gestured with his eyes in the mirror. 'What's her name?'

Chinese looked down at the baby wrapped and soundless in the blue cloth. She glanced back up, the ghost of a smile still trying to become real.

'Chunhua,' she said. 'It means…'

'Spring flowers,' finished Business.

Nigel and Chinese exchanged a surprised glance. Then Business began to sob.

'I've got no money. I've lost my bag.'

Nigel hoped another tantrum wasn't coming. Heck, she was barely older than his eldest daughter.

Big Bear would protect her.

That made him smile again. Whoever these two girls are, he thought to himself, fate has thrown them into my cab. And I'll protect them. And Spring Flowers.

In his mind's eye he pictured Maggie smiling. Big Bear.

'I'll look after them love,' he said under his breath.

Unlike he'd been able to look after her.

CHAPTER 17
NIGEL - BEFORE

Maggie and Nigel met when they were both in senior school. She had been quite plump and, despite his shared fascination with his mates goggling at the latest stolen porn from one of their fathers' secret collections showing slim-bodied beauties, Nigel had always liked his girls with a bit more bosom. A tad more to grab. Being pudgy himself, maybe he had convinced himself of that at a young age. As if a chubby kid like him would ever catch a slim beauty. No chance.

Fat chance.

Maggie had walked into his life by accident. They weren't in the same class. Not even in the same year. He was a year above her and had been sent back out after lunch one day to retrieve his blazer from the school playing fields. He'd always used his blazer as a make-shift goalpost, crumpling it up for the lunchtime kick-about. Not that he ever did much kicking or running about. Usually just hanging around, chatting and having a laugh. He'd gone to History class after lunch and forgotten the blazer. So, Mr. Higgins had sent him back out for it.

He was a good kid, but liked a smoke, so took his time, taking the moment to have a drag as well. The football fields were well out of view of any of the main school buildings, so the chances of someone catching him were slim.

As he'd gone out that day, he'd walked around the corner of the geography block, his mind a million miles away, and smacked right into Maggs.

'Shit, sorry Miss.' He'd actually said that.

Maggs had laughed. 'That's alright. You OK?'

Checking Maggie out, he manned-up pretty quick realising that his first instinct was wrong; it wasn't a teacher and second; that using a curse word was not now going to land him in further trouble.

'Am I OK? Yeah course! Are you OK, that's the question? I mean, I'm not exactly…'

Slim. It almost slipped out.

His hand was probably on his way to his mouth to stop even an utterance of betrayal about his self-image, when he forced it to change course and touched her arm instead. She had blushed. Mr. Hargreaves had broken the magic spell then.

'What are you two doing out of class?' Always shouting. Nigel and his mates had guessed Hargreaves would have a stroke by the time he was forty. They were wrong by eight years. Hargreaves died from a stroke aged forty-eight.

After that first encounter, he and Maggie would exchange cursory glances across the playground from time-to-time. He, being fourteen, was already seeing her most nights in his imagination, his hand working fast, tissues being abused in the process. He finally bottled up the guts to ask her out; would you like to come with me, just as mates like, to have a drink, only soft drink like, at the youth bus. Not a date like, just hang out like.

She said she 'would like'.

The taunts of Cradle-Snatcher from his mates soon stopped after they realised that Nigel and Maggs were an item. They celebrated their second anniversary before even leaving school. And even then, their life routine was implemented and wouldn't change much for another thirty years.

Both stayed local. Alternate Sunday dinners with the other's family. Friday night was Lads Night for him. Saturday night Girls Night for her. Monday through Thursday were their nights. Sunday, family time. It worked well. Then they stopped the Lads and Ladies nights when Maggs gave birth to their first daughter Sally. They were over the moon.

Maggs stopped her temporary work at the local pet store to bring their daughter up. Four years later they gave Sally a sister, Erika. Maggs didn't go back to work after that. Nigel had started the cab business and, with London being on their doorstep, meant he was never out of work. Until Uber of course. But that was a long way down the line for them yet.

The cancer came before that.

CHAPTER 18
NIGEL - BEFORE

After thirty years together, many of their friends from senior school were still their best friends. Seeing their two daughters grow and find lovers of their own, Nigel and Maggie had the sort of relationship that only comes from quality time together and time apart. Nigel always thought that was the secret of their success. They had always allowed time for the other to indulge in their hobby and social circles. They shared the same friends on many occasions and had a happy home (as happy as any home could be given the ups and downs of life). Nigel knew he was blessed. Sure, he liked to see pretty girls, enjoyed flirting when he had the opportunity with a particularly attractive passenger in his cab. Only ever talk, never more than that. He loved his wife too much.

Trust.

An easy word to say but one that was learned over time. It was given by yourself to another. A gift. And it was one you never threw back in the giver's face. Ever.

Nigel truly believed that.

He'd never wandered, never wanted too. He assumed (although with trust you never asked) that Maggs had never played away either. They had spent almost all of their adult lives together every night. Only once, when the kids were young and they needed some extra money, had he decided to work the late shifts at the weekends. But a young group of girls puking in his cab put a stop to that. A fine was issued and they paid, but the stench? He couldn't get it out of the cab for months.

He and Maggs were lucky, they both knew that. Had a chance to buy their own home and had seen the value skyrocket over the years. Had enough for a family holiday each year. And still had valuable time with their parents at Christmas, both sets of grandparents spoiling the kids rotten.

Coming from chubby parents, the kids were plump too. That was fine. *More of them to love*, Maggs always reminded them. They exercised as a family, walking most days to school and back. Sundays was always a family stroll through the park. They had planned bike trips but they never materialised. Life always seemed to get in the way.

But he was grateful of the time they had to spend together. Nigel knew so many of his friends who had been through different partners, had their lives ripped apart through divorce, losing custody of kids, homes and one, Ryan Cadwell, even taking his own life over it. Him and Maggs had always stayed strong.

'You have to work on it.' That was the advice he'd give his mates when they had asked how he and Maggs had stayed together. 'You have to give and take; you have to give trust and you have to take time. Folks give up too easily these days. In this culture of swipe-a-wife, it's too easy to be tempted.' Being chubby, he never had. Maybe knowing instinctively as he did when only a teenager that, unlike him, his chances were slim. So why bother starting a race you could never win?

But no. It was more than that.

He was content. He simply didn't want another.

After thirty years of riding life's rollercoaster together, surviving many of the downs and riding a lot of highs, there came the big final loop-the-loop. And they couldn't survive that one, no matter how strong their love.

Maggie had died two days before her 44th birthday. The cancer came quick and ate her fast. To the last she had joked saying how she'd have a while to live yet, given there was so much of her for the cancer to eat. Nigel had been with her night and day. And his mates… the lads he laughed and joked with day in and day out at the cafes, they stood by him, helping him through every stage.

After only three months from being diagnosed, despite being given a possible time frame of eighteen months to two years, Maggie had slipped away in her own bed, Nigel at her side.

Nigel had held her hand until the last, kissing her lightly on the forehead when he knew she was gone.

That had been just over two years ago.

He was still blessed.

He talked to her every day.

CHAPTER 19
NIGEL - NOW

The two passengers in his cab were about the same age as his daughters. He'd protect them. He tried to protect Maggie always from any kind of suffering, even when they were burgled, putting himself in harm's way blocking any of the attackers from hurting her, if that was their intention. But how can you protect someone from being attacked from within?

'I'll look after them love,' barely a whisper.

I know you will. My big bear!

'I need you both to concentrate. Stay calm. I know how to get us out of here, but it's not going to be easy. The doors are securely locked. Whatever this thing is'… he paused… 'I think we're safe if we stay in and keep the windows shut.' He was talking to them while simultaneously glancing from mirror to road, road to mirror.

Business was still breathing heavy but her sobs had stopped. Her face was running with blood. She'd dug deep.

Definitely not the first time.

'So, let's get some rules sorted. This is *my* cab. That means there's no money needed today OK. It's a special day or whatever, free travel. For you two only!'

Chinese looked worried.

Nigel forced a grin. 'And for Spring Flowers of course! That goes without saying. Kids Go Free Right?' he mouthed the words sounding each loudly to make sure Chinese understood.

She did.

'So, my names Nigel, right? What's yours?'

Chinese looked to Business, who was still looking at her hands in her lap, seemingly lost. The handbag fiasco had caused something to snap. The hook she had used to keep a grip on reality had slipped. So had the mask. Behind the make-up lay the true face of the girl and she was vulnerable.

'I am Lihua,' said Chinese, touching her heart as she spoke.

Nigel, without meaning to, touched his own chest again, repeating his name. 'Nice to meet you, Lihua.' His eyes shifted in the mirror to Business.

'And yours love?'

Nothing, the hands now working hard on each other, fingers entwining, jaw clenching. *She's going to freak out any minute*, he thought. If he were back there, he'd slap her. She needed something to snap her back to the here and now. He unclipped his seat belt, trying to both navigate the human obstacle course that was growing more and more intense in the roads about him and shift position so he could open the partition, grab Business and force her to look at him. He had almost succeeded in accomplishing both, his eyes leaving the road for a moment, when he happened to glance at Lihua. Her face told him something was wrong but he didn't have time to react.

With crushing force, the black cab hit the front of another car coming in the other direction. Had it of been a normal day, the case would have eventually gone to court and Nigel would have had another reason to hate his Uber competitors. The other driver was going the wrong way.

Despite only going 43 miles per hour, it was enough to throw Nigel, all nineteen stone of him, out through the front windscreen and onto the bonnet of the hire car.

CHAPTER 20
LIHUA

Lihua had foreseen the crash, but not wearing a seat belt herself, she and baby were flung into Business. Business' head had smashed back against the partition, opening a new cut, one she would have been proud of had she inflicted it herself. Blood poured down the glass. Lihua had bit through her upper lip with her own bottom teeth. The pain was intense and brought her to the edge of collapse.

Must stay strong.

Business was alive, but unconscious. She flopped forward onto the cab floor, her head taking another whack as it landed.

Lihua didn't know if the lady was dead or not. She tried the door handle.

Don't get out.

That was the warning the driver had said. Lihua sat back down, holding the baby closer to her chest, making shushing sounds again.

Yet, still, the baby made no sound.

CHAPTER 21
NIGEL

Nigel was aware that something had happened. Something bad.

Got to protect them Maggs, he thought.

Get up love. You're OK. A skinny guy would have been broken. Not you, Big Bear.

He struggled up, shattered glass all around him. He put his hand onto the hire car's bonnet, smoke coming from somewhere close by, engulfing him. He straightened his arm, lifting his torso.

'Argghh!' The pain shot up his arm.

You're alive. Now, go!

'Linhow?' Not quite right, but he was close.

He squinted, looking through the smoke, through the hole where his windscreen once was. A face stared back at him. She was trapped in the back, alive, Spring Flowers clutched to her chest.

The automatic locks.

'Got… to... protect…' he rolled off the bonnet, wincing with pain at every turn.

'Business?' he tried.

Nothing.

Lifting his shirt to cover his mouth, he walked around to the cab back door on legs that felt alien to him. If there was something in the air, he didn't want to be joining those in the sky.

Locked. Of course.

He lowered the shirt, coughing. Smoke was getting heavier.

'See the red button? The Red Button!' Was she understanding him? He momentarily thought about re-entering the cab through the windscreen, but that wasn't really an option.

Not for a Big Bear.

A skinny guy could do it, he thought.

A skinny guy would be dead now. D. E. A. D. Dead. Now stop faffing and go, love!

Faffing. One of Maggs pet words. He was a faffer. He knew that.

'Just press the red button. Look, red.' He mocked scratching his own face, then showed the tips of his fingers. 'Blood, yes? Red!' Comprehension came to Lihua's eyes.

'At last!' Nigel exclaimed, hands reaching to the sky in triumph. He immediately dropped them, daring a quick glance up, fearing he'd be snatched up by those unfortunate enough to have already left terra-firma.

Nobody was reaching down for him. But up there, a few feet above him, it was like the Gates of Hell. Bodies piling over each other, sticking to something up there. And they were moaning.

This is it, he thought, *this is the End of Days. They always said it was coming.* The thought wasn't comforting.

'Mate, quick, in here! You're bleeding!'

A voice from behind. Nigel turned, eyes still watering from the smoke.

'Quick before that thing blows!' said the voice. A hand was reaching to him.

Cockfosters. I'm in Cockfosters, right outside the tube station. Whether fate or…

No, he knew better than that. For some reason two women, similar in ages to his daughters, had gotten into his cab. And he'd just driven, not really thinking to where. But Maggs had known. She'd guided him here.

The Underground.

How much safer could you be from being dragged into the air, than underground?

He smiled, thinking that 'they' always said that if an attack did come (if this even *was* an attack) it would be on the underground. Now that very same place could be his haven.

'The lady... and the baby!' said Nigel, his shirt once again lifted over his mouth. The man considered this and Nigel thought he was going to desert him, but quickly darted out.

'Stand back mate, yeah,' he said. He rubbed his elbow and smashed the back glass.

Nigel wondered why he had even bothered to have the cab waxed and polished.

The guy

(Slim, he's a slim one Maggs!)

(Yes, then send him in through the windscreen)

reached into the broken window, pressed the button and opened the door. Business' head lolled out. The slim guy was quick, catching her before she took another knock. Nigel saw blood oozing through a gash on her head.

Had she done that to herself?

No love, the impact. Now go. There's little time.

Above him, the moaning. Behind him, in the station, people calling, threatening to close the shutters if they weren't in and quick.

Slim grabbed Business under the arms and dragged her to the Station. Others were also piling into the station now from the street, eager to be out of the pull of the force.

'No more! Close the doors! There's too many down there already!' said an authoritative voice from within.

No, three more, mate, thought Nigel. *Three more. You can squeeze them in.*

Nigel reached into the back seat, hands outstretched, offering to take the baby. Lihua pulled the baby closer to her bosom. Nigel searched her eyes desperate to get in and get safe.

'Please, Linhow. Please.'

'Too late mate. Too late,' said a voice from behind. The shutters were being lowered.

'Not like this. I'm not going like this.' Nigel's mind conjured up the image from a film he'd seen a long time ago. Human beings trapped behind shutters. Some kind of threat about to wipe them out. Titanic maybe? He couldn't remember.

You always were naff at quizzes, love.

Lihua paused. That pause cost them their safety. Then her eyes grew wide again, her having seen something over Nigel's shoulder.

Not again, he thought. *What now?*

She handed him the baby. He turned, baby in arms and ran to the descending shutters. He slid the baby under, like sending a bowling ball down the lane. He turned back to the cab; arm extended to help Lihua out over the broken glass. His shirt now useless as any form of protection against whatever might be in the air.

INTERLUDE - FATE

A second.

The merest moment. A blink of an eye.

In that moment, that briefest slice of life, everything can change.

As it did that morning for Nigel Woods and Lihua Kwok.

CHAPTER 22
NIGEL

The pause. That was what did it. Time slowed down, or so it seemed, as Nigel's mind ran through so many thoughts all in the space of a second.

If that.

The hesitation to hand over Chunhua, a mother's natural instinct to protect her baby from danger, was all it took for Nigel and Lihua to end up outside the station. But Chunhua…

Nigel had turned to see the shutters being lowered, many standing inside the safety of the station with bowed heads. There was still plenty more room in there. Even Business was in there lying on the floor, having been dragged by Slim. There was enough room for her it seemed, even lying down taking up floor space, so why not him and Lihua?

The shutter was lowering like a slow blinking eye.

(The blink of an eye.)

Nigel knew he couldn't get Lihua under there, not enough time. Couldn't get himself under there.

(Not you love, my Big Bear!)

Don't hesitate love.

'No Maggs,' he whispered. *I just need to check…* Something felt wrong.

Crouching, he looked for the baby. The bundle had stopped against Business.

CHAPTER 23

NIGEL

Lihua placed a hand gently on Nigel's shoulder, encouraging him to stand.

They had to move. Had to get somewhere safe.

Nigel's fingers were wrapped around the brick-patterned shutters, steadying him. He felt sure he was going to lose it. How can Business, the only one who seemed intent on killing herself, be the one inside the station, in safety? How can the baby be separated from her mother? How can he have tried so hard to save them all and failed?

Lihua now patted his shoulder harder, asking him to stand, to move, to get away.

To help.

Protect her, love.

Nigel stood, confused, angry and emotionally wrecked.

Move. Now.

He turned, grabbed Lihua by the arm and dragged her away.

****

Behind them, in the station, a grinning man flickered, shimmered and disappeared.

CHAPTER 24
SLIM/JAMIE

Jamie Carter had run faster than he had in the last few months. Since he was a kid, he had always had ants-in-his-pants. Everyone had told him so. His teachers, parents, friends. *Jamie won't sit still!* written in his earliest school reports. Why they had bothered trying to make him sit still was beyond him. He knew that he was put on this planet to run, jump, swim and be free. A 'sit-there I-say you-repeat' education was not for him. He ran everywhere, including away from home several times as a teenager. Then, when forced to go to school, he ran away from there too.

Always running.

But when he saw the couple from a few doors down leaving their house, parting hands as they left their happy home - him for work by bike, her for work by cab - they parted in more ways than they had planned. She went toward the cab waiting at the curb. He went toward the sky, leaving the bike propped up against the front fence.

And for reasons that escaped him even now - standing safe behind the shutter of the underground station - Jamie had run. He could have simply turned and gone back inside his flat.

Could have.

Instead, he went back to his survival instinct. Something wasn't right. So, he ran.

Nothing was chasing him, but as he ran, he felt as if something was. He imagined hands, claw-like with huge talons, were coming at him fast, reaching out from the sky, reaching to drag him up there too.

Had he taken just a moment to check over his shoulder he would've known that was wrong, nothing of the sort was coming at him.

But it felt good to be chased.

Being chased meant somebody cared. Somebody wanted him.

As he ran, others began to lift off the pavement. He sprinted on, residential estates giving way to commercial. Shoppers appeared out of doorways with their morning purchases. Coffee lovers, newspaper readers, chewing gum buyers, many stepped out and stepped up. Into nothingness. The sky wanted them all.

But it wouldn't have him.

Jamie ran. Long strides, something he felt in his very core, he was made to run. Nobody had taught him; he just knew how to push his body to get the best out of it.

He'd reached the underground, by now seeing so many people flying all round him, he knew that getting down, getting underground, was the key to surviving this. Chaos was erupting as he darted through streets, back alleys, jumping over fallen bins, even hurdling one or two dogs. Some folks stopped and stared at this running man. Others too busy trying to flee their own inner nightmare of the sky monster.

Jamie ran on. Everything around him becoming a blur.

He didn't see the man staring at the sky, a huge grin on his face. Didn't see him flicker. One moment there, solid. The next moment, gone.

CHAPTER 25

JAMIE

The tube station was busier than usual, but only at the entrance.

Once inside the main entrance, the crowds fizzled out. Passers-by were taking video on their phones of those unfortunates being lifted off the pavement before their eyes. Others opting to stay inside the safe confines of the tube station.

Hands to his knees, he bent over, drawing breath. Around him people were shouting, screaming. Chaos.

The air. It tasted funny.

It might be something in the air. A chemical attack?

It didn't matter. He had to draw air. Had to get oxygen into his gasping lungs.

What will be will be, he thought.

Que sera sera.

The tattoo on his forearm had his motto forever there to remind him.

A mighty crash came from just behind him, outside one of the smaller entrances. He saw two cars had hit each other head on. A black cab and-

He couldn't quite make the other car out.

The driver of one of the cars had not been too lucky, having been thrown through the windscreen. Or was that a passenger caught in between?

Jamie winced at the thought. He was up and moving again before he even realised he was doing it.

Always the Good Samaritan.

People were standing, crowded between the doorway and the cars. Eager to get a look, but fearful of the force.

Jamie knew that there would be no emergency services today. This wasn't a normal day. People don't just walk out of their house and float upwards on a normal day.

He pushed through the crowd of onlookers, some still filming. Jamie had the desire to knock their phone out of their hand, stamp on it and scream in their face. What was wrong with these people? The world was falling apart around them and they wanted to capture it on film!

He got to the front. The fat guy had gotten himself off of the bonnet but was bleeding badly. He appeared to have been thrown through the black cab window. The other driver, the one Jamie had first assumed was the better off of the two, didn't look it now he was closer. As Jamie looked away, the driver shimmered.

'Mate, quick, in here! You're bleeding!' he shouted to the guy now at the back door of the black cab. The guy turned, tears in his eyes.

Maybe he's not the driver. Maybe he's a passenger and his wife and kids are in the back?

Jamie tried again, aware of the smoke pouring out of the cab.

'Quick, before that thing blows!' shouted Jamie.

The guy replied, although Jamie was unclear as to precisely what he had said. He was covering his mouth with his shirt. Was there something in the air?

Jamie frowned, trying to back track on what he thought the guy had said. Something about a baby? Jamie darted out of the station.

Come on legs, we're only just warming up.

He'd reached the cab in a few sprightly bounces.

'Stand back mate, yeah,' he said. Jamie recalled a film he'd seen where the hero had smashed a window to save a damsel in distress. The hero had wrapped his arm in a cloth. No, that was wrong. He'd rubbed his arm. As if to make the skin there hard. Jamie rubbed his elbow and with a silent prayer that he didn't cock this up and look a right idiot (there were people filming everything. He could outrun most things, but the internet?) smashed the back door glass.

Smiling at his achievement, he glanced at the guy who looked forlorn.

Maybe he is the driver after all, thought Jamie.

Jamie reached in through the broken window and de-pressed the back-door lock. The door swung open and Jamie, reflexes as quick as ever, caught the head of a blond lady who was about to tumble out onto the floor.

She's dead.

That was his first thought. Blood was congealing from a cut on her forehead.

Must be from the crash.

Above him, more moans and screams caused his flesh to break out into goosebumps. There wasn't much time. Behind him, people were now shouting for the station shutter door to be shut. He had to get this lady inside. She needed help.

God help them all.

Jamie managed to drag the lady across the pavement and into the entrance, when a guy in a yellow vest called for the shutter to be closed.

There was another in the back of the cab. A lady holding something. He hadn't had a clear view when the blond lady had made her appearance, but Jamie knew-

He spotted a man who looked out of place, yet familiar somehow. He was staring with a broad grin right at Jamie. He rocked his arms back and forth like he was cradling-

A baby.

The other passenger in the cab had been holding a baby. Jamie was sure she must have been. The way she had held it so preciously close to her chest like that. Unless…

Jamie realised she was foreign.

No, couldn't be a bomb. Could it?

He felt sure it was a baby.

He turned, pushing back through the onlookers, this time actually forcing his shoulder into a guy filming the situation on his phone.

'Don't film fuck-wit, help!' he said as he barged past. Jamie hoped the guy wouldn't react violently. He was getting tired now, all the sprinting and now the rescuing. Adrenaline was coursing through his veins, but it would soon stop and if he were stuck inside with this guy in the next few moments, he didn't want a fight.

Not safe outside. Not safe inside. What a choice.

Maybe I should've just turned and gone back in the flat.

Too late now.

Que sera sera.

'No, there's others.' His call fell on deaf ears. The shutters were already coming down. He tried to push to the front, but couldn't. His path was now blocked by other guys in high vis jackets.

Through the mesh he could see the cab guy leaning in the back of the car. He turned, dropped out of Jamie's sight and then the guards stepped aside.

A wrapped bundle came sliding along the floor under the closing shutter.

In the road, the grinning man with rocking arms, flickered once, twice and then went out like a light.

CHAPTER 26

JAMIE

Inside the station the crowd at the door soon dispersed. Something had just been thrown under the shutter. Jamie saw people run, trample over each other, shove and push. He saw one girl cross herself, two guys hug and many simply close their eyes. And surprise-surprise, a few were still filming.

The guards in high vis pushed people back, allowing the package to sail through along the floor. It came by Jamie's feet. The body of the blond lady from the cab stopped it. Jamie tensed waiting for the bang.

CHAPTER 27
JAMIE

The guy from the cab was back at the shutters, fingers through the mesh, shaking it violently. He was shouting, something about spring flowers. Jamie looked at him briefly, then stepped toward the blond lady still passed out on the floor. He got closer and saw something pinkish wrapped in the blue package.

Another step and he could see a tiny hand.

He had been right.

It was a baby.

She's why I'm here.

The thought didn't make much sense to him, yet deep down felt right.

She's why we're all here.

CHAPTER 28
JAMES - INSIDE - THE RADIO STATION

He hadn't wished to stop. Everything in his body told him to stay on-air, but the next host was chomping at the bit to get in on the action. Whoever was broadcasting now would be famous overnight. They were the most listened to talk show station in the UK and, with the communications being affected by whatever was happening over their heads, people across the country would be trying to seek a radio station for news.

Someone to give them an answer.

And hope.

He could give them that.

Debbie Strickland was already taking over the air telling people to call, James silently wishing her the best of luck. The phones had failed to ring for him, so what chance did she ha-

A full switchboard.

The problem wasn't that they weren't phoning him, just they weren't being put through. Walking (running) toward the exit, he passed the producers room and saw all of the staff, except the dedicated and terrified looking producer, had gone. In, out, up? James had no idea.

He descended the stairs three at a time, not bothering to wait for the lift.

In the lobby he saw no need to use his security pass at the reception, that too was deserted.

They must have all just run away, he mused. Gone to see family, friends? 'Share the end of days,' he muttered. He stopped, checking himself in the reflection of the inner door glass, a skill he had mastered long ago. He could do it while holding a conversation or doing up a shoelace, totally deceiving those who may think they have his undivided attention. He had even faked waving to someone through the glass once. All to get his look checked out before heading into the wider world to meet his public.

His fans.

And his critics.

Granted, there were a few. But they rarely, if ever, hung around to catch him coming off-air.

A quick glance, the smile was there. Perfect as always. The clothing needed a bit of straightening out…

There was a terrific smash against the glass front of the station. A trolley, from who knows where, had been rammed into the glass. It was full of stuff; black boxes, shiny things. Two guys were at each other's throats, one being forced unnaturally backwards across the trolley's handles. The fighters soon broke up, as both were lifted off the floor and into the air.

James ran to the windows, his wide eyes following them up.

What is this? What the hell…?

His thoughts were interrupted by the sight of others in the street outside the station. People were running amok. It was Hell. He glanced back into the empty lobby, the voice of Debbie coming to him from the speakers down the corridor. She was crying.

Unprofessional bitch, he thought.

He was deciding whether to stay or go.

Inside there was relative safety (the trolley had only cracked the glass), a limited amount of food in the staff canteen (should last a few days) and water in the drinking fountains (plus a supply of bottles in the fridges). And clean toilets, even a shower. It wasn't a bad place to seek refuge while waiting for the cops to come.

They're not coming.

He knew that was right. But there was something missing, something he couldn't live without.

Gina.

Unless he stayed and fucked Debbie? Maybe on-air! He laughed, the sound echoing around the lobby. No, with Gina was where he needed to be.

CHAPTER 29
JAMES

A deep breath, he tapped the security pass against the outer door and, holding his breath

(It might be in the air…)

he ran out onto the crowded street.

He couldn't resist glancing into the trolley to see if there was anything he could use. Looking around, seeing the chaos, the looters, the fighting, the panic, the running, he decided that if he wanted to, he could simply steal something himself.

Best not. Might get recognised.

He glanced up, seeing the two floating guys were still trying to attack each other, but finding it impossible to move their arms and legs. One was facing down and the other facing up toward the sky. Both spread like reverse starfish. As if they had been pinned on some maniac God's specie board.

And they weren't the only ones up there.

Women, kids, some looked as young as ten or…

Someone pushed him violently from behind, driving him to the floor, knocking the wind out of him. He saw it burst from his mouth in a vapour and thought he momentarily saw a blueish tint to it. It seemed to fuzz, buzz…

Must be a trick of the light.

The Floaters were forming a human storm cloud, blocking the daylight.

What if they do stop the light coming through? We'll all die then.

Get up. Get home.

Wise words.

He had time to think that he may be one of the lucky ones, having not instantly been taken into the sky himself. The thought was stopped short as a blast of pain came as someone trampled on his fingers.

'Aarrgghhh!'

'Sorry man!' said a middle-aged guy in a business suit. The guy stopped, crouched, and James thought he was going to do the gentlemanly thing and help him up. The guy looked at James quizzically. 'Hey, love your show!' Gave a thumbs up, turned and ran, flickering as he did. James thought how it looked like the man was running into rain or a strobe.

People.

James gave a quick glance around and got to his feet, brushing at his trousers.

I need a window, gotta check my look. People are still recognising me despite all this.

He turned searching for a window.

What are you doing? What are you actually doing?

A woman passed, kicking up some papers that had been dropped. The Big Issue. Ah, Keanne. James always took time out to talk to Keanne. He'd been working his patch selling the magazine for the last six months or so and James always gave him time. Never cash. It was good to be seen talking to the homeless. Made his fans like him even more.

Being generous and all that.

James suddenly found himself unable to put a face to Keanne's name. How long had he known him? Was it six months? Or was it far less time? Maybe only a month or less?

Maybe only a couple of weeks.

James became aware of his thoughts, feeling himself losing control.

That would never do.

Underground. Go!

That made sense. He needed to get away from the outside. From people.

'James! James! Help!'

He stopped dead, turning 360. Had he imagined that. There was noise all round him. How could he possibly-

'James!'

He looked up, recognising the face, as if waking from a dream.

Keanne. Hanging from the sky like the others.

Can't stop now, sorry Keanne. Busy today.

The words almost came out of his mouth. Another odd thought; he could throw some cash up. Catch!

Got to get a grip.

'H…h… How?' his mouth felt dry. This wasn't pro. Not at all.

Get a grip!

Keanne was drifting, moving away from him, part of a growing human cloud. James followed underneath, manoeuvring between people and obstacles, trying to keep sight of Keanne. Trying to keep him tied, like a boat to a dock, through vision alone. As if he could attach a thread between their eyes.

I never gave him a penny. I could've helped him. Why did I never…

'Where's Benny?' he found himself saying. His voice, the thing that had made him his millions (well, not quite, but Gina's dad would sort that out eventually when the old bastard popped his clogs) was doing the thinking for him.

Benny. Good call. One last favour I can do for him.
Keanne was now drifting toward the larger building opposite the radio station. He and several others were level with the 3rd, no 4th, floor.

If I can get up there fast, I can open the window and…

'Benny!' James turned, breaking the eye-thread he'd thrown to Keanne. 'Benny!' he whistled, a good one. Two fingers in the mouth. Proper job. 'Benny! Bennnyyyyy!'

A dog came bounding out from the public toilets on the small patch of grass to his left. James squatted on his hunches. 'Here boy!' Benny ran to him. No lead. Benny was never on a lead. James held the dog briefly by the collar. He turned, searching for Keanne, to show him he had done this One Good Act.

Keanne and the others had reached the taller building that was blocking their path. They were now crushing up against each other, against the building itself… and then they simply began to swarm around it, like water around a lamppost.

Need to get into that building, I can grab him from the windows on the other side.

No. They'll drag you out, you know they will.

I've got to at least try.

'First things first,' he said, dragging Benny by the collar to the nearby Tesco Extra. People were gathered in there, many filming on their phones (had they been filming him? What if he looked disheveled? Wouldn't matter, he thought, he'd been saving a homeless guy.) 'I'm a hero,' he muttered. The smile was spread like melted butter back on the mask before he even knew it.

Ever the pro.

Back in control.

CHAPTER 30

JAMES

The onlookers from the supermarket were holding out their hands (the ones not holding the phones) egging him on. 'Come on man, almost there. You'll be safe here.'

'It can't get you in here,' shouted another.

James took a second to realise he was actually now one of the last few wandering outside of cover. Out in the open air.

I'm a hero.

'This is Keanne's dog, Benny. You know Keanne? The homeless guy who sells that mag?'

Shit, should've bought a copy, can't recall the damn title.

'Don't bring him in! He might be infected!' shouted a voice from within.

'Can't be dude,' said another. 'Otherwise, he'd be up there with the Floaters.'

Floaters.

Hadn't he called them that? Did he coin the name on-air? He couldn't remember. But what a claim to fame that'd be. What the heck, he'd say it was him anyway after all this had ended.

This… occurrence.

'The dog's cool guys,' said James flashing his smile. It worked as always.

'Hey, that's James Whitbourne! Let him in, he knows shit!' More mummers greeted this.

Fans, thought James. *Not critics. Please not critics.*

The held-out hands, pulled him in, not that he needed any assistance. And then they simply gawked and applauded. Many were still filming.

'Can I have a selfie, James?' asked a young black guy.

The smile was back. 'Sure, although, got to be quick. See, I need to get back out there (he said these words slowly emphasising the danger he was putting himself in) and up to the top of that building (was it an accountancy firm? He couldn't remember. And what was the name of that blasted mag?) and save Keanne. Him and some others have drifted around to the other side, so if I'm quick I can get a window open and save them.' He paused dramatically, the timing perfect allowing his audience to ooh and ahh. Theatre. Life is one big theatre. Now who said that?

'Would you mind looking after Benny? I'm scared he'll run off searching for Keanne and get…' he allowed himself another masterful pause before continuing, '…lost, or even run over.' That was well delivered. He even thought about wiping an imaginary tear from his eye.

Superstar Presenter Saves the Homeless with No Thought Given to His Own Life.

No, the tear wipe would be a step too far. Right now, he had them eating out of his hands and was pleased to see many still filming this.

The selfie done, he turned to flee.

And hesitated.

What if he really did end up joining them? What if he did get dragged out of a window by the hands clawing at him for safety? What if?

He'd already set the scene. He had to go now. He waited a second longer, hoping, praying someone would force him to stay – 'against his will'.

No such luck. Instead, they applauded once more.

'Go for it, James!'

'Man, this dude is one brave mutha!'

A hand thankfully fell on his shoulder. James breathed a sigh of relief. Someone, it seemed, was going to hold him back. He turned, smile perfected.

The young black kid, Mr Selfie, was staring intently at him.

And then his fate was sealed.

'I'll go with you.'

CHAPTER 31

JAMES

The kid introduced himself while hoisting his hoody up around his nose and mouth.

'I'm Jordan. I'd shake hands, but we've a job to do.'

James nodded back. No need to state his name.

The kid gave one last glance to James and nodding, ran out into the open space. James reluctantly followed, hoping his run didn't give him away. His legs felt like jelly. He had beige trousers on and prayed to Any God Who'd Listen to cleanse him of all sins and please, please don't let him piss himself.

Not now. Not on camera.

Heroes don't cry. Or piss themselves.

Sin.

Maybe that's why they're up-

Jordan shouted. 'No, dog, come back!'

James turned as Benny ran past him and into the entrance of the building he and Jordan were heading toward.

'Benny!' shouted James. He paused, suddenly unsure if he wanted to run straight into the building after the dog. He felt a deep feeling of dread. Gut instinct. He took a deep breath and walked across the pavement, against his better judgement.

(Judgement… they'll be judging me from behind the safety of the shop fronts with their phones, their all-seeing-cameras…)

As they reached the entrance, still calling for the dog, a window opened on the second floor.

And from it dropped Benny.

The dog was dead before it hit the pavement.

CHAPTER 32
ADAM – DOUG'S CAR

Adam had long let the paperwork fall from his lap into the footwell.

'Jesus Christ! Did you guys see that?' He was still staring out the back window. The receptionist's body was fading into the mist.

Adam turned back, searching first Nick's and then Doug's face in the rear-view mirror. None of them had answered him. Both were staring as if lost, waiting to be given directions.

Waiting to be woken.

Was this a dream? Adam felt like slapping himself, testing if he were really awake. No, he was here alright. He felt… alive. And then began to laugh. 'Guys, seriously, like what the fuck?'

Nick was holding his hands clasped, squeezing them between his knees as if in deep prayer. In reality, he was trying to stop himself shaking. Doug was focused on the road ahead, his eyes like those of a bird of prey, searching for the kill. He seemed static almost, as if Adam expected to see his life force running over his body. Like electricity or magnetism.

Magnetism.

The thought seemed too obvious. Were humans magnetic? Weren't there certain blood types?

The car veered violently to the left, back the way they had come. The lanes around the golf club were narrow, and the mist that had been here on the drive in was clearing, improving visibility but making them more likely to have a head-on crash should a car be coming the other way.

'Doug, slow down. We all need to get home yeah? But driving like this will only get us all killed.'

Doug chose to ignore him, again. The hierarchy of the car had shifted. Before the meeting, Nick was clearly the boss and had now gone into a childlike trance. Doug was driving like a teenager in a stolen car, all sense of vulnerability gone. Adam wondered if it was going to be the mist or the car which killed them eventually.

Maybe it was something in the mist?

CHAPTER 33

ADAM

They swung out at high speed onto the dual carriageway, Doug being the perfect Hollywood get-away driver. If only they had something to get away from.

'Aren't we still looking for a phone signal?' Adam said, holding on to the door handle and edge of his seat for dear life.

Doug took the bend at full speed, pedal to the floor, the car lifting slightly on Nick's side, Adam grateful Nick had far more pounds than him to help weigh it down. Nick's beer-gut could have just possibly saved their lives.

Maybe skinny ones get taken?

The thoughts continued to flood his over-worked brain, searching for a reason. For some way to find a cure.

How can you cure something you can't even diagnose?

Another bend.

'Doug, for fuck's sake! Let's just calm down, pull over and make a call. I'm sure Nicky and the kids are fine.'

Adam thought briefly of his mum, alone in the house. Not as fortunate as the other two, Adam was still a long way from being able to put money down on his own pad. Until today's meeting that was.

If it had happened.

Adam thought that in later life he'd have plenty of cash. He imagined himself in his mansion, feet up on an oak desk, puffing a cigar. Quite the Drug Lord of the Manor. Something about that vision felt real, like he'd experienced it before. Déjà vu.

Another bend was approaching. Doug took it. Fast.

And straight into the back of stationary traffic.

CHAPTER 34
NICK - THEN AND NOW

Something had simply switched off in his brain. A primitive survival mechanism or simply a fault with the programming, he neither knew or cared. All that mattered was he was not there when it happened. Not in the car. Not even in his body. The girl, that pretty receptionist that even a guy of his mature age could imagine bending over the front desk and giving one, had been panicking. And he couldn't help her.

Why didn't we let her in? Why?

No that wasn't right. Why hadn't *he* let her in. He was the boss after all.

He could have helped. Instead, he had left her there to die. He had turned, seen her bleeding, seen her raise her arms…

And saw no more. Couldn't take it.

You're not tough. You've gotta be tough, Nicholas or you'll never get anywhere in this life, you hear me?

Yes, dad.

Yes what?! Another slap.

Yes, sir.

What, was this the 1930's? Nobody, but nobody called their father 'sir' anymore, did they? It seems Nicholas Holmes Senior insisted they did.

His kid anyway.

And now, over fifty years later he was still having 'daddy issues'. The therapist was little help.

Oh, but these things take time, Nicholas. You have all these issues that have been building your whole life and they won't vanish overnight.

She had moved closer then and took his hand in hers. Soft and warm with brightly painted nails. Always biting her lip. Not being coy, just trying to sort out her own issues. Weren't all psychiatrists?

So, he'd gone into his zone. The one where nobody could hurt him. His body, sure. But not him, the real him. He'd hide inside his body. His father would reign blow upon blow on him, his mother in the kitchen pretending not to hear. Let him beat the body all he wished. He'd never get to the boy.

Nick's hands were trembling, so many memories coming back. He couldn't deal with them. Not now.

But she just floated up? She asked for help and I didn't help her.

Like mother. He couldn't help her either. It seemed his father had finally snapped her body, her spirit unable to find refuge further, deeper down inside.

And where had he been during this? In his room, hiding under the bed. His baseball bat by his side. Just in case.

You keep this here to scare me, Nicholas? His father had found it propped up against his bed that fateful night. He'd lifted it, spinning it between his hands. *What are you gonna do? Huh -*

the first shove with the end of the bat - *huh, you're no man -* second shove. Nick had begun to cry. He'd promised himself countless times after every fight they had, that he wouldn't cry ever again. It only made his father angrier.

Retreat, go down Nick.

And he had. Finding solace somewhere deep inside himself.

His father hadn't used the bat on him, just kicked him, each kick punctuated with the words 'disappointing', 'pathetic' and 'weakling' and then left him alone, blood seeping into his bedroom carpet. Nick's hands would cover his face, seeking the dark. Begging it to come.

After that beating, his father had killed his mother that night in October '77 when Nick was only eight years old. Nick had managed to get himself up and out of the back door, running from the house, running until he'd collapsed on one of the quiet roads the other end of the village. A passer-by had found him, almost running him over. At first Nick thought the car headlamps were those of his father's. He'd come to finish the job.

Nick spent years being moved from foster home to foster home. He wanted to stay in the same village and often would wonder how somewhere so affluent, so sought-after (words he picked up as he matured), so quiet, could contain such dark secrets. Behind the walls, his idyllic lifestyle much yearned for by others, was not quite as one would imagine. Not by a long-shot.

Be careful what you wish for. That was something he had learned a long time ago.

As he grew up faced with moments of fear, he'd change the childlike hands covering his face to a slightly more adult choice; the hands placed between the knees. That way he could stop them from shaking. In such situations, his mind told him to be strong, but his body would give him away.

The body could deceive.

Seeing the receptionist float into the air, Nick's mind had snapped. He went back into himself, down deeper than he had for a long time.

The bliss was welcomed.

It made the impact of the car smashing into the traffic something he barely felt.

CHAPTER 35

DOUG - NOW AND THEN

Nicky. Luke.

They're home. Have to be.

Gemma.

School by now.

All indoors. Must be.

Please be!

He didn't believe in any god or deity. What was, was. Simple as that. Doug knew he was driving fast, but he had to get home. Had to check they were safe. He'd almost lost Luke once before.

Not again. I can't go through that again.

We *can't.*

Nicky had blamed herself for the birth going so very wrong. But Doug had been with her every step of the way. Luke had simply been around the wrong way, entangled with the umbilical cord and came out blue. It was touch and go for the first few hours. However, by the second day he was still critical but looking likely to get through.

They said he had a strong heart. When Nicky had finally been allowed to hold her child, their baby, she had cried more than Doug had ever heard anyone in his life. Tears of blame, of letting go. And Luke had been so warm.

Luke warm.

They'd already picked his name, but the joke was left unspoken by Doug as he first took hold of his son…

Doug was aware of Adam behind him laughing, screeching, panicking. Tough titty. He was getting home. Adam hadn't sown his wild oats yet, still living with his mum, his bad luck.

Nick was silent, a possible heart-attack flashed across Doug's thoughts.

Tough tits too. There was only one priority right now. Getting home.

The corner was taken a little too fast, Doug feeling the wheels beneath him and Nick lifting slightly.

Slow Doug. Slow.

He breathed out.

Adam was still moaning.

The next corner he took a little slower, but still way too fast.

The impact of the crash killed him before he even had time to realise what was happening.

His last thought on this confusing day was simply 'Home'.

CHAPTER 36

DOUG

A jolt. A memory. A golf course. A car… and he had been driving.

A wife and kids. His?

The glove box and sex toys. The other women he'd lured into his car.

Between worlds, Doug felt himself falling forward.

New voices.

Arms waiting to catch him as he fell.

CHAPTER 37

ADAM

Bending to collect the fallen paperwork from the rear footwell of the car (it might yet come in handy when all this shit settles down, he had told himself) had saved Adam Fletcher's life. The impact was terrific. His body, still seat belted, slammed forward into the back of the passenger seat. That in turn slammed forward and then everything was thrown backward. The car was concertinaed.

He could see people in the traffic ahead leaving their vehicles, with many floating into the air, others holding onto anything within sight for dear life.

CHAPTER 38

NICK

Someone was trying to unclasp his seat-belt and get him out of the wreckage.

Nick was gone, retreating into his safe place. Deep down where no-one can hurt him.

You must get out! A voice. His mother's?

Can't mum. Can't. There's something wrong with the air.

No, there's not. His mum's reassuring voice.

How do you know Mum? We need to stay in the car. It's…

She was dragging him out of the vehicle, his eyes screwed tightly shut.

Got to get you out.

No, Mum, we can't! It's in the air. It'll lift us. It'll take us.

'Listen to me… if you can hear me… you're too heavy for me! You fat bastard!'

Mum?

No, not mum. Another voice…

Help him. Move yourself.

Confused, hurt and lucky to be alive, Nick fainted.

CHAPTER 39

ADAM

The car door sprang open

(He thought they had locked it back at the club before the receptionist had tried to get in…)

as if by some saviours hand. Adam had seen it fling open either just before, or a split second after

(After… what?)

the impact.

Must have been before. Must have.

Several other things must have happened before he knew what he was doing next.

He must have unclasped his seat belt. He must have crawled out of the wreckage. Must have not floated up to join the others in the sky. Must have crawled around to the other side of the car. Must have opened Nick's door…

(How? Look at the state of this thing! Must have been someone else…)

'Listen to me,' he reached across Nick and felt for the seat belt clasp. Nick grunted, muttering. Adam couldn't make out the words.

No time. Got to get him out.

Every film he'd ever seen rushed into his head forming one narrative; crashed cars blow up.

'Nick… if you can hear me…' Adam tried to pull Nick out. He took Nick's hand

(Sweaty, no good for a handshake at our meeting with the new clients)

from between his knees and pulled with all of his strength, falling back onto the road, taking Nick with him.

'You're too heavy for me! You fat bastard!' Adam breathing hard, Nick hanging half in, half out of what was once a Mercedes. Others were running to help him now.

'Stay down, stay in if you can!' screamed a man.

'There's another, front seat…' Adam panted, still gripping Nick's hand in his.

'He's…' the man trailed off as he looked frantically for a body in the front seat. No-one was there. 'Alright, your mates out, now grab him under the arm yeah bro, we got to get you both inside and quick.'

'The trees, quickly,' said another voice.

Panting, lifting, sweating. Adam disorientated but feeling some sense of being led. Oh God how that felt good. Someone else taking the lead now. He was struggling to cope here. Doug was silent, Nick was unconscious and Adam was…

'Just the golfer really. I bring the papers, get the coffee…'

'What? Yeah sure bro. No worries yeah. Just help me get him up.'

The stranger was trying his damnedest to lift the bulk of Nick off of the road, encouraging Adam to take the other arm over his shoulder and help drag Nick to safety.

'Golfer? I meant gopher.' Adam laughed out loud. Nick's arm dangled over his shoulder, the stranger walking ahead dragging Nick's other arm. Lop-sided they took him to cover under the trees alongside the road.

'The golfer, he was floating!' laughed Adam. 'That was why I said golfer.'

The stranger dropped Nick to the grass verge, breathing hard. He reached out, putting his hand on Adam's shoulder.

'Get a grip yeah, mate? You survived that, so I guess you're one of the Chosen Ones today too, yeah bro?'

Adam had no idea what the stranger meant. He turned to look back at the Mercedes. The car wasn't there, only a massive pile of crushed metal.

And broken glass.

But no blood. Thankfully, no-one had been killed.

Had they?

Adam felt a huge headache coming on.

There had been someone else in the car with him and Nick.

The more he tried to think, the more his head hurt.

Falling to his knees beside Nick, Adam fell back, laughing hysterically, his face to the canopy above him. He could make out a shape floating above the trees.

A human shape.

PART FOUR

CHAPTER 1
SAFFI & CYRUS

Everyone had mocked their choice of lifestyle, highlighted by their choice of vehicle. There wasn't really an option when it came to the perfect vehicle, the one that was the epitome of their lifestyle, only a financial limit. And those who had mocked them were, in the main, envious of their VW Camper Van. Traditional, original, a classic. No new engine, just replacement parts. No high-end spec interior, just some incense and dream-catchers.

'If we're gonna do it, then we do it properly!'

That was Saffi's thinking when they had made the decision to a care-free lifestyle. So, no new engine. Which meant plodding along at the usual 50mph (on a good day) whilst the rest of the world sped past you to their heart-disease and early graves. At the start, seeing them (or rather comparing others' speeds to their own), was heart-warming, as if Saffi and Cyrus had been touched by God himself. They were special.

They were chosen.

They had the secret knowledge. Life wasn't a race. It was humans being. Not humans doing.

Another of Saffi's sayings.

And that camper van, with the low speeds that others had mocked, had been the thing that had saved their lives that morning.

Not that they were in any danger of being involved in a pile-up. Cyrus, he of the World's Smallest Bladder ('bladder like an egg cup,' his dad was fond of reminding him, usually when in company) had stopped for the mandatory side-of-the-road pee.

Which meant two fortunate things; one, they weren't in the vehicle that the Mercedes slammed into, and secondly, they were in the perfect position to run and help (and bladder free, another small mercy in Cyrus' world).

'Help Cyrus!' Saffi had shouted when the car had shot round the bend into the traffic.

Cyrus had looked down from the tree he was half-way up, already planning to try to help those who were in trouble above him. Floating as if on ice.

The sound of the impact was sudden, loud and short lived. Cyrus couldn't see it from his position, but felt it. He was certain that whoever was in that car wouldn't get out alive. All the vehicles in the traffic had people either hiding within, or had abandoned them, risking either the cover of the trees or the possibility of being taken upwards.

What a choice.

What a day! And it wasn't even breakfast time yet. Cyrus was well aware he hadn't even been up long enough for his first spliff of the day. Not good at all.

He'd dropped out of the tree, running to where Saffi was standing. Both of them had not been too stressed by the goings-on above them. Whatever force it was wasn't here for them. And they knew it. Somehow, they knew it.

'The Day of Reckoning I reckon!' Cyrus had said, digging Saffi playfully with his elbow.

That was after the first cars had begun to brake, gradually coming to a stand-still from where they had pulled over (and, mercifully, after he had forced his tea-spoon full of piss out. Nothing worse than straining to drip with an audience).

The first passengers had been happy (as happy as any driver can be, Cyrus assumed) to sit in the traffic. But after a while many faces had begun to look upwards, out of their windows, frightened faces turning to each other. At that time, Cyrus wondered what they were looking up at. One had wound down a window, seeking an explanation from the hippy on the side of the road.

'Is… is it a joke mate?'

Cyrus had looked at Saffi. 'Is what a joke?'

'What they're saying on the radio?'

They exchanged another puzzled look, before Cyrus had walked over to the stationary vehicle. Another window had opened then, further up in the queue of cars.

'Stay in your car mate! For Christ's sake! Look at them!' the driver had leaned out, pointing to the sky. Cyrus had walked toward the driver, searching the sky behind the canopy that was blocking his view.

That was his first glimpse of the bodies.

Only a few at first, stretched out as if they had been gutted and stuck there by magic.

Black magic.

Saffi.

Cyrus had turned, running back to the safety of the trees. Back to Saffi.

To safety.

Other drivers were now honking horns eager to get away, so many ghost faces on their mobile phones.

A motorbike had been snaking through the two lanes of cars when Cyrus had been running back into the trees. The bike rider had almost taken the head of a car driver off as he had sped between the cars. Passengers were leaning out of their cars, some brave souls getting out. It looked to Cyrus as if dog and master had changed places, so many heads lolling out of windows. And then the bike rider had been lifted off his bike, dangling in the air. His body continued to move forward at the same speed as his bike had been going. It was like watching a great stunt but one where the rider wasn't going to descend and land back on the saddle.

Those who had braved the outer world away from the safety of their cars soon dived back in. Some weren't quick enough, also being lifted into the air.

One woman was holding her kid's hands through the back window, urging her daughter (if it was her daughter, Cyrus was too far away to tell and wasn't going back out there himself, Chosen or not Chosen) to help her back in. Selfish really as the kid's hands were small, so if anything, the mother was going to drag the poor kid up too. Cyrus reminded himself that you never know how you're going to act in these kinds of situations.

'What would you do if like, your Saffi right, was like, raped by a mate?' Or, 'What if your mum was murdered by an immigrant?' Other hypothetical shit Cyrus was often asked by his usually drunk or stoned friends. His band of thieves. You never knew how you'd react.

Like to the question; what would you do if you saw a woman being dragged up into the sky and was asking her kid to save her? Over a drink, Cyrus would argue that he'd run and help of course. No questions asked. But in reality, his reaction was far different. He hid in the trees.

'Let her go woman, for fuck's sake,' he whispered.

The kid was now being dragged out of the back window too.

'No, no, no! Let her go woman!' Louder this time.

The woman had slid momentarily, her hand leaving her daughters. In desperation she reached for her child's long hair. The girl was screaming now.

'For the mercy of Christ. Let Her Go!' Cyrus was shouting now.

The woman finally had. It was perhaps her daughter's scream that had done it. You sacrifice yourself for your kid. Every parent knows that.

Which is why he and Saffi had chosen to never have kids.

The woman had just floated up, joining others who were now hovering overhead, moving slowly like the most bizarre cloud.

'Pareidolia,' Saffi said from behind him. She stepped forward taking his hand. When they connected the feeling was even stronger. It buzzed between them. Like electricity.

'Yes,' Cyrus replied. 'I couldn't think of the word.'
'Although you're not making the faces out in these clouds Cyrus,' Saffi put her head on his shoulder. 'They're real.'

And so, they stood, hand in hand, staring as the human clouds drifted over them.

CHAPTER 2

CYRUS

I can help somehow. But who to help? The girl or her mum?
He didn't want to leave the safety of the trees.

He looked up.

The trees.

To the trees! Was that from Robin Hood? He couldn't remember. God, he loved that film. The Kevin Costner one. Not the other one with those guys in tights.

He'd begun climbing, thinking of other lines he loved from that film. 'Well, at least I didn't use a spoon.' Another classic. Alan Rickman that was-

'Help Cyrus!' said Saffi from below.
The deafening crash from beneath him stopped his thoughts. *Back down, Cyrus. Back down.*

A man was crawling out of a car. Or what might have once been a car.

'Stay down, stay in if you can!' shouted Cyrus, hands cupped around his mouth. Man, if I have to go back out there then…

CHAPTER 3

CYRUS

His legs were carrying him before he knew it.

'There's another, front seat…' the crawling man panted. Cyrus glanced into what was left of the front seat. There was nobody there. Had the driver already gotten out? In his minds-eye, Cyrus felt sure he could see something in the front of the car. Not a person, more a fuzz. Almost smoke like. His eyes couldn't quite make out a solid form. He had a bizarre image flash into his mind of the posters that were all the rage a decade ago; you looked at them and only after a while could your eyes make out the actual picture. It would suddenly come into focus. This felt the opposite: Cyrus felt like he had seen a form of someone but now it was gone.

'He's…' not there, thought Cyrus, not wishing to make matters worse right now. He bent low, took the other guy in the back seat under the arms and dragged him out of the car.

'Alright, your mates out, now grab him under the arm, yeah bro, we got to get you both inside and quick.'

'The trees, quickly,' said Saffi from behind him.

The thinner guy was bleeding heavily but at least he was conscious. Rambling, but awake. Cyrus heard him uttering about golfers. Maybe they had swerved to avoid a golf ball or something.

'What? Yeah sure bro. No worries yeah. Just help me get him up.' Christ the guy was heavy. Cyrus wasn't sure if he could lift him on his own. *If my heart goes now… no, can't do. We're too stress-free like. We're Chosen.*

'Golfer? I meant gopher.' The guy laughed out loud. 'The golfer; he was floating! That was why I said golfer.'

Cyrus and the guy had managed to get the fat man to the verge, Saffi squatted down looking at him in her caring way. Cyrus knew there was nothing she could do. Or knew how to do. But she had a good heart. He searched the other guy's face, seeing hysteria lying dangerously just underneath. He'd break soon. Cyrus reached out to steady him.

'Get a grip yeah mate. You survived that, so I guess you're one of the 'Chosen Ones' today too, yeah bro?'

CHAPTER 4

SAFFI

The man was heavy set, breathing but not conscious. Saffi put her ear close, closing her eyes, feeling and listening. Not for breath, she could see the man's chest rising and falling steadily, so knew he was alive. She was listening for *him.* To see if he would speak to her. Maybe a name. Maybe a medical condition she should be aware of.

Nothing.

She raised her head, touching the side of his face with her hands. The man spoke softly.

'Thank you, mum,' he said.

Saffi smiled. The man was going to be OK. His mum may no longer be alive, given his age (she had put him at around 60) and would need a good talking to about going vegan given his stature. But first things first. Saffi had to speak to him.

She placed her hands gently on his chest, breathing with him, allowing her breath to synchronise with his. Next to them both, the other man from the crash was staring open-eyed, his laughter now gone. Saffi wasn't as concerned about him yet. He could wait. She'd looked over at his eyes. Yes. He was waiting already. That was good.

Another mutter from beneath her.

'Can't.'

Saffi smiled, she closed her eyes, sending her energy down through her arms, through her splayed fingers, channeling it into the man. *Heal. Feel. Be. Still.*

Her mantra.

She began bucking, gently at first, as if having a joyous romp. Doing it in public had never bothered her. Another of those things others made comments on, frowned upon, but whom she knew, in their deepest hearts were so envious to give it a go. To break free. To fuck freely. Wherever. Whenever.

Saffi moved, swaying more rapidly now, speeding her breath, muttering her mantra faster and faster.

Heal.

She swayed; eyes tightly closed. A vision came; a girl. In uniform.

Feel.

The first beads of sweat began to form on her brow, under her head scarf. Another flash; two girls. Waitresses?

Be.

The man was muttering now. His breath also increasing. Flash; new vision. A woman. No girls.

Still.

She stopped dead. Her eyes opened; her hands left his chest.

She leaned forward, her mouth close to his, eyes inches from his own.

'Nicholas,' she whispered.

CHAPTER 5

NICK

It was almost like being screwed. Ah, that golf club receptionist. Young and so very courteous. And he was a member. A special member. She had to treat him right. The thought had made him aroused. And then he had felt her. Impossible.

No, not her. He was wrong.

What was this?

Just imagine who you want.

Can't.

Course you can! Just think of her if you want. What was her name? Sandy? Cindy? One of them. He often mixed them up. Embarrassing when they weren't wearing their badges.

Then have them both, Nick. It's a fantasy after all!

Yes, have them both, how delightful. How… delicious.

Can't. Not yet. This isn't them.

'Can't.'

Fuck them, Nick. God's sake man, enjoy yourself. Who's going to know?

'Mum.'

And then he heard her voice. And she had whispered his name.

CHAPTER 6
PAULA – ON THE BREAKER

She awoke without the feeling 'oh, what a nightmare' or 'ah, it was all a dream.' Instead, Paula's sleep had been unintended, deep and without dreams. Where had she been heading? Towards the men. One was a policeman and the other…

'Reminded me of my dad,' she said.

But that wasn't quite right. Paula shook her head, trying to clear her thoughts. Trying to remember. She hit the back of her head on the Breaker and even this didn't surprise her. She was up here, that was that. Not afraid anymore, not in fear of falling, or of being swept away. Paula awoke feeling a kinship with the Breaker above her. It gave her time.

'To think.'

About what exactly?

The men. The ones she had been trying to reach before she… before she dozed off? Passed out? Didn't know. Didn't care. Things were different up here. Things were-

'Calmer.'

That was a good word for how she felt. Things were calmer. Paula smiled, a genuine one, perhaps her first for a long time. And she felt something else too. She felt safe. She felt-

'Happy?'

Had she a right to feel this way? Was this happiness? If so, how could that be given her situation?

'I could fall any minute. I may never get down. I could die up here.' The smile widened.

No, this isn't happiness. This is a breakdown. This is the first sign of madness.

But she felt different. She didn't feel mad. She actually felt like laughing.

Dad.

Him.

'Need to find those two men.'

She'd had many men come in and out of her life. And what good had any of them done her? None. Her first encounter of the male species was one of utter hatred. Her father. Paula felt like spitting.

Do it girl. Enjoy yourself.

And then another voice. Somewhere deep inside her, and at once outside of her too.

Be free.

It didn't frighten her. She honked a good one to the back of her throat and then, feeling it gather on her tongue, enjoyed the release. Paula's act of public defiance made her smile even more. She pictured a gull, shit-bombing the public. The thought crossed her mind; if she were up here for a while, she'd need to go herself soon. Could she really see herself doing that?

'Not up this way, baby!' she said, laughing.

Paula thought things beneath her were growing quieter. She stared ahead; her eyes restricted by the movement of her head against the Breaker.

For the first time in a long time, she felt like she was no longer being judged.

Being blamed.

She felt free.

CHAPTER 7
MIKE

The case was open, the pictures falling.

He was above the school playground when it happened. And there - Oh God no - was Casey with her friends below. Playing hopscotch. They looked up as the papers fell like large snowflakes. Casey glanced up, shielding her eyes to the sun. The first print-out landed right in front of her on the floor.

'Casey, no don't look at it!' Mike screamed.

Casey looked. Bent down. Mike saw everything in perfect detail. Her hand reaching out, turning the paper over. Revealing its horror in all its graphic detail. A child, like her. Same age or thereabouts. Could even be her in another life. And an adult. Could be him in another life. But in this life, he'd never, ever do that.

Then why is it OK for you to see someone else doing that?

'Casey, it's not mine. Screw it up now, you hear me? Stop looking at it!' Casey was either not hearing or chose to ignore him. Other papers were falling all around the group of girls now.

'No. This can't be.'

Bang. His head hit the back of the Breaker.

Darkness.

No, *some* light.

'God?'

Don't be stupid. It was just a dream.

But it wasn't. It was more than that. It was-

'Another reality. This thing… the reason for this, for what I'm going through

(What *you're* going through? What about the kids in those

pictures, Mike? What were *they* going through you sick

'I… I don't know them. And I don't know you.'   fuck?!)

He glanced to his left. Briefcase still there. Clasps still thankfully closed. He turned to his right. He caught his breath, banging his head against the Breaker once again.

The policeman was still right alongside him. His mouth was moving, but Mike couldn't hear a word.

'W… what?'

Again, the copper's mouth moved. No sound.

The silence was-

'Welcoming.'

Mike didn't know what was happening. Not physically or mentally. He felt an eerie calmness. He needed the silence. He needed to think. His life wasn't supposed to be like this. Mike wanted rid of the case and every fucking thing within it. He felt repulsed by it. He tried to let it go, send it off along the glass ceiling. He didn't even give a fuck if it now fell to the floor. He just wanted it gone.

It and its dirty little secrets.

Mike shook his hand violently, his knuckles banging up against the Breaker.

'Why won't you let me go!?' he screamed at the case. No matter how hard he shook, he couldn't uncurl his fingers from the handle. It was like they were stuck there.

Held by an invisible force.

Someone wants me to suffer. Someone wants me to feel the pain.

'Life's not supposed to be like this,' he sobbed. He stared at the ground, still drifting beneath him. 'Why won't you let me go!?' he screamed again, his voice breaking. Tears poured from his eyes, his knuckles bleeding against the Breaker, the blood spreading out, smearing as he shook more and more violently.

'Please…' his pathetic sobs grew weak.

The policeman was almost touching him now, his mouth still opening and closing, like a goldfish gasping for air.

Mike turned his head staring into the policeman's eyes.

'Help me,' he said.

The policeman didn't reply. His hand reached out and he touched Mike's arm.

The shock that ran through them was electrifying. The sound incredible, a screech so high Mike thought his ear drums would burst.

'HELP ME!'

This time the policeman heard him.

CHAPTER 8

PAUL.

'Chaddy.'

He shook his hand.

'Chaddy, let go of me. We can't hold hands like this in public. You know what they'll say.'

They. The others in the force. The jokes at their expense would be never-ending.

'Let me go!'

A sharp intake of breath and Paul Ross awoke from one nightmare immediately into another.

He was back in the air. He didn't like this. Not one bit. The dream of Chaddy was fading fast. Thankfully. Paul swallowed; his mouth dry. He needed a drink, not a stiff one (Chaddy, don't even say it!) either, just water. The purest kind. Straight from the tap. None of that bottled crap. It always amazed him that people actually paid for bottled water in the supermarkets - shelves of the stuff! - when they also paid to have it on tap at home. Like you'd buy booze if you had that on tap at home!

Get with it, Paul. Sort your shit out.

Good advice. He was often his own best counsel. That's what kept him in check with his feelings for Chaddy. That was what drove him to be fit, to be the best he could be. And that was what would now get him off of this thing.

The briefcase.

The thought was the first that brought him back into professional mode.

First the briefcase. Something's wrong there.

Then the situation.

It should have been the other way round he realised; the priority was all wrong. But somewhere in his heart he knew there was nothing he could do about the situation up here. He knew, felt it deep in him, that this was bigger than him.

Maybe bigger than the human race itself.

But I can do something about that guy.

He glanced to his right. There was movement. A lady. Did he recognise her? He strained to think if he had seen her somewhere before in another time and place. A sketchy memory tried to surface; a white room, circle of chairs, the smell of freshly cut flowers.

Had he arrested her before somewhere?

The memory wouldn't come.

He turned his head awkwardly to the left. He could see a foot. About two meters away. He traced the outline of the foot, up to the hips, to the torso and an arm, poking out like a starfish. Paul shifted his head, he couldn't quite see his face, but was sure this was the same guy. The one with the briefcase.

Paul called out to him.

'Sir, we need to talk. I need to know what you have in the briefcase.'

The guy didn't reply. Paul didn't feel safe coming to him from the bottom, so shifted his weight, trying to gain purchase against the Breaker. He saw himself in his mind's-eye from above, like a fish swimming around a fallen leaf on the surface of a pond, trying to get to the other side of the leaf.

He could move very little but could change his position. After a lot of effort for little gain, Paul began to slide up alongside the guy. Had they exchanged names? He couldn't remember.

'Sir!'

No reply. He was almost at the same level as the guy now, their heads facing the same direction.

If the guy would just turn to his right he'd see-

He did.

'Sir! The briefcase. What's in it?'

The guy looked as if he didn't know Paul was there. As if they'd never met before. A flash of recognition may have flicked across his eyes then. Paul was unsure.

The guy replied, his mouth opening, forming words but no sound came out.

Paul tried to reach down to get his nightstick. The effort it took to barely move his arm was incredible.

No chance. Watch him, Paul. Something's going on.

He tried talking to the guy again.

No reply.

Then the guy began to freak out, his head banging back and forth on the Breaker. His hand with the briefcase shaking violently.

This is it, Paul. It's a bomb. You smelled the danger, but you were too late.

Paul had a sudden pang of regret.

Chaddy.

Maybe they *should* have been open and honest. It could have worked.

Maybe in another life. A more tolerant one.

He closed his eyes, a silent prayer.

Nothing.

The silence was overwhelming.

One eye opened cautiously.

Paul looked toward the guy.

(Mike. His name's Mike. How do I know that? Did he tell me?)

He was crying. Sobbing. Mumbling. Paul couldn't hear him but saw these things.

Why can't I hear him? What the fuck has he got in that briefcase?

Paul reached out with great effort. His fingers almost reaching Mike's arm.

Almost.

Just a little more…

Contact.

The surge was violent, electricity charging through him, right to his core.

His hearing cleared.

'HELP ME!'

CHAPTER 9

PAULA

The two guys were just ahead. Paula tried to shimmy again, trying to encourage the Breaker to force her along at a quicker pace. She needed to reach them, still unclear why. The guy with the briefcase was shaking violently. The other (Policeman, watch out, he might recognise you…) was trying to get closer. Paula saw the policeman shimmy himself, seeing him move alongside the briefcase guy, like a faster swimmer in the next lane.

I can do that.

She tried. Not quite as fast, but she had more bulk to move that was for sure.

I expect he's gay. All the fit guys are it seems.

'And in a uniform!'

The conversation with herself made her laugh once more.

Madness?

Who cares! Enjoy yourself.

Be free.

Paula stopped suddenly. That voice again. She looked about her. It was as if she was channeling someone else's thoughts.

Free from what exactly? Free to gob? Free to move?

'I'm not free of this… thing,' she said.

Paula had a vision of herself in another time. Dressed in a dark uniform. She saw a small bed, small room, tiny desk. She didn't feel free at all.

She shook her head, clearing her thoughts.

Glancing ahead, she saw the policeman now reaching out for the other guy. And. for a reason she didn't understand, she had the overwhelming urge to shout a warning.

But it was too late.

CHAPTER 10

MIKE

It was like watching a film on fast forward. What felt like a million images passed through his mind, each leaving a mark. Flashes of events. Some kids. Others of grown men. Teenagers too? They were too fast to process an order or make sense of them. Feelings and emotions surged through him, seeming to eat into his very bones. Mike felt uplifted, alive, exhausted, depressed. Everything at once. He wanted it to stop, but the visions kept speeding through; Christmas trees, animals (was that a dog?), award ceremonies, kissing, fucking, eating, shitting. The images, playing like video, seemed to slow. Now he could see the pictures clearer. A policeman. A car ride. A partner. A feeling; love? And then seeing himself floating ridiculously in the sky above his house, but from another's eyes.

From his eyes. *I'm seeing myself through the copper's eyes.*

Impossible. But true.

The video continued, all from the policeman's perspective.

White corridors, locked doors, a white room, faces of people he seemed to know somehow. And a smell.

The smell of flowers that reminded Mike of Spring. More memories. A man, short, chubby. A woman, dressed in white, holding a clipboard.

Recent memories… Floating up toward Mike, being impaled on the Breaker, speaking to Mike and then…?

Blackout.

CHAPTER 11

PAUL

It happened the moment they touched. They merged, his life with Mike's every waking moment, every dream he'd ever had. Every thought. Every sensation, every feeling. Paul felt as if he were being filled with another life, felt like his body should simply burst from the weight of it. As if too much blood were being pumped into him.

Surely a body can only contain one soul?

The tendons in his neck stood out, his teeth gritted, Paul felt as if he were being electrocuted.

Visions hurtling through his consciousness; balloons, food, people, hugs, celebrations, more food, drinking, growing pains, girlfriends, intercourse, even more food - Christ, did the guy ever stop eating? - shaving, the bumps, a broken leg, a promotion, a parking ticket, arguments… all too fast and too much to make any coherent sense of.

Paul felt like slipping away into the darkness, welcoming death, but the policeman in him made him pay attention. Made him look for something.

These memories hold the key to all this, I know it.

Feelings coursed through his veins; sorrow, joy, envy, love… too much information. Surely his brain would simply melt? He couldn't take his eyes from the video. (He was vaguely aware his eyes were actually closed, the video playing internally for him in all of its 'Must Be Viewed' clarity.) And still he forced his mind to stay focused. Stay sharp. *There must be something that gives the game aw-*

There.

People sitting in a circle. Another group, standing behind the sitters, black clothes. A man and woman in white.

A clipboard.

Rewind! Can't.

Damn.

The faint smell of flowers.

The video was mercifully slowing.

New visions…Getting a tie from the cupboard, checking the mirror. Some papers… a briefcase.

Focus, Paul.

Snapping it closed… a young girl in the doorway. Pigtails. Smiling.

She was a cutey.

The briefcase put down on a bed. A feeling of wrong. Something wrong.

Cutey running to him.

All seen from the other's eyes.

And then leaving the house… car keys… walking into the air…

Something wrong. Very wrong.

Focus, Paul.

And then…

Blackout.

CHAPTER 12

MIKE & PAUL

They both had a sense of what had happened to them. They had become fused. In body and mind. Like Siamese twins.

Paul knew that whatever he thought, Mike thought. And vice-versa.

They didn't need to be told. They knew.

Paul knew of the porn pictures, felt both excited and upset at the same time.

Was he the upset feeling? Or was he the excited one?

Didn't matter. Both were feeling both at the same time.

They were one.

And they both had a true understanding, of such deep clarity, of the true meaning of Hell.

For them, there wouldn't be any redemption.

CHAPTER 13
ANGELA & TASHA - ABOVE THE BREAKER 9:55AM

Silence.

Like watching an explosion on a TV screen with the sound muted.

The fire from Ahmed spread out on the underside of the Breaker engulfing a body or two. And then it ceased, seeming to drop away from the invisible floor beneath the helicopter. A fireball now going toward the ground. And then, simply, nothing.

A pulse of blue shimmered in all directions, emanating from where the explosion had occurred. Angela tried to follow it with her eyes as it evaporated into the distance. She glanced back to the source of the blue. Two charred bodies were sticking to the underside of the Breaker.

For the moment, although she didn't realise it, all thoughts of panic were forgotten.

'Whatever just happened, whatever that blue ripple was, it won't let us land,' she said.

Tasha sensed that this could be the remaining few moments of her life. If only she could get the camera down somehow. At least then her final act of reporting would make her infamous. Nobody would be getting these shots.

As if the Breaker had read her mind, the camera fell out of her grip.

'Shit!'

She fumbled, watching the camera hop, bounce and skip in her hands, like she was juggling a hot potato. Angela turned the chopper slightly, which was the final part of the camera's dance; it fell to the Breaker.

Tasha felt a pang of jealousy wondering what her final pictures would have looked like, one's she'd now never see.

The camera continued to skit and bounce, as if thrown on ice, its shutter clicking, flashing as it hopped along. It finally came to a stop, facing upwards.

She began to cry.

'We're going to die, aren't we?' The words coming slowly, clearly. Hauntingly.

Angela wasn't replying, just facing forwards, hands gripping the controls in a death-like grip. She was racking her brains, trying to find a solution to landing safely before they ran completely out of fuel. She lowered the chopper, gently.

'Tasha, baby, listen. See if you can put your foot on it. But carefully. Don't hurt yourself.'

With fierce concentration, Angela maneuvered the helicopter down, hovering a few meters above the Breaker.

'Can you reach it?'

'A bit lower,' Tasha replied.

Angela was sweating. She descended a fraction.

'Ah, fuck this,' said Tasha. She wanted the camera back, wanted to see the pictures. She jumped the last few meters.

CHAPTER 14

ANGELA

'No!'

Too late. Tasha had jumped. Angela thought she heard her scream. Maybe she'd broken an ankle?

'Maybe she's dead.'

Angela refused to cry. She felt terribly alone, isolated. It seemed utterly despairing. No way to land. No way out.

And now no Tasha.

Her lover.

Gone.

Maybe not, take your chance.

She felt strong. Her knuckles white, feeling the desire to rip the joystick out of the floor, letting fate choose where and how the machine would finally crash.

Wake up. This is not you.

The voice was quiet, but there. Trying to get through.

Like a body under ice.

Angela turned, her neck muscles creaking, as if her head were made of iron. The air increasingly difficult to breathe. She remembered a supply teacher back in her primary school telling the class about all of the horrible tortures that were used in the Middle Ages. One in particular came to her now; the piling of weights upon a person's chest until they breathed their last. Angela felt as if the air was crushing her from every direction.

Wake up.

She felt that wasn't quite right.

Stand up!

Her eyes glanced down as the machine tipped to the left. Beneath her, she saw the Breaker with countless bodies on its underside. More and more of them now floating up to the surface, to her as if from the depths of a murky river.

Stand up. This isn't you, Angela.

She unclasped her harness.

Let it happen. Jump. Take your chances.

Angela continued to fight her internal struggle of whether to risk jumping or await the last of the fuel and go down with the chopper. She'd have to jump from a higher altitude, otherwise the fucking thing may well just crash and burn right next to her, wiping both her and Tasha out if they survived landing on the Breaker anyway.

'Can't… stand… this.' Barely a whisper.

And then, a stranger's voice.

'Nicholas', it breathed.

CHAPTER 15

CYRUS – UNDER THE TREES

An explosion.

'That was big.'

A daft reaction, but the only thing that Cyrus could offer at the sound. All eyes went to where the sound had come from. Cyrus ran to the edge of the grassy verge, still offering unhelpful analysis. 'That might be something crashing into the thing from above.' Cyrus was both horrified and excited at the prospect of a plane that had tried to land but had smashed into whatever the thing was that was taking people.

People began to get out of their cars again, many thinking better of it, shutting the doors before temptation could take them too.

I'm Chosen.

He glanced back at Saffi. She was still kneeling by the big guy he'd dragged from the rear of the car.

We're Chosen.

Stepping onto the road, faith maintaining his calm, Cyrus walked between the cars, avoiding the scared gazes from the windows all around him. Like ghosts, faces swimming beyond the glass. He had a flashback of a film he'd seen where a gang of kids playing on an icy lake had given way, and one of the boys had slipped in. As the gang panicked and searched for him, he came to the surface, trapped under the ice. The kids grew silent as they walked along the top, following their friend's screaming face, until he screamed no more and sank into the depths of the lake.

Cyrus shuddered.

Was that a film? Something about that vision felt wrong somehow. *Did that happen to me?* Before he could consider the oddness of the memory further, he saw the fireball being thrown downwards towards the ground. He crouched down, hands covering head, waiting to be engulfed.

What a way to go. I'd rather have the peace of drowning in the lake.

Heat but no pain.

After a moment he glanced up.

Directly above him, Tasha fell silently onto the Breaker. Directly above her, Angela was grappling with her own inner battle.

He was unaware of either of them, unable to hear a sound from above the Breaker. It had sliced the world in two.

A guy who had braved stepping from his car was gesturing to the sky.

'See that? He just blew up!'

Cyrus ran to him. 'Who?'

'Dunno. I saw shadows over there. More of these Floaters, I guess. And then one of them just…' the guy made a motion with his hands, open palms moving away from each other. A clap in reverse. Boom.

'Well… like, where's the fire, bro?'

The guy continued to stare into the sky. His shrug said it all. *Dunno.*

He turned to Cyrus and smiled as if greeting an old friend. 'Hey, how come we can be out here then?' It was Cyrus's turn to shrug. *He can't be Chosen too. He… he doesn't look right.* The guy smiled; a flash of silver twinkled off a tooth. Cyrus backed away as if the guy was the Devil himself. *It's Him man. He's trying to butter me up. To sell me a better life of sin and shit.* Nonsense, but given the happenings already this morning, nothing was impossible on a day like today.

'You know one of those days where you wish you'd just stayed in bed?' the guy was still talking to Cyrus, still smiling and still shrugging. Cyrus didn't answer his question.

Get away from him, man.

He ran back to Saffi, turning away from the guy only when he was sure he was not going to throw a knife in his back. As he did, the man shimmered.

Cyrus passed under Mike Hegessay, Paul Ross and Paula Asketh. All were in their deep sleep. The blast of Ahmed's bomb causing the Breaker to react.

And react it did.

CHAPTER 16

ANGELA - ABOVE THE BREAKER

Her hands loosened on the joystick in front of her. A sharp pain came as she straightened her fingers, releasing the tension of her grip, allowing the blood to rush back in. Someone had released the spell. A magic word was uttered. Angela thought hard to recall the whisper she had heard in her mind. It had made no sense.

'Nervous?' No, that wasn't it.

'Was it you, mum?' No reply.

It was a name! A man's name.

Yes, that felt right. Angela maneuvered the chopper back across the sky she had just covered, circling around so she could pass back over the charred bodies, over the others floating

(beneath the lake)

over Tasha. Her friend and lover.

'Nicholas,' she formed the word, feeling it echo from her mouth, feeling a connection with the very sound as it passed through her lips. And then it was gone. Like a magician snapping the hanky away to show the rabbit has vanished.

CHAPTER 17
NICK – UNDER THE TREES

He was with her and she was keeping him safe. How he had loved her. How he missed her. He didn't think the human heart could hurt so much. The fantasy of having his wicked way with the two receptionist girls from the club house was now a distant wave, cast out for survival but ignored over the power of the one behind it. The one of his mum.

And then he heard her again. She was whispering his name, calling him. But how could he go to her? How could he find her?

I'm wandering in the dark, Mum.

Don't hide my dear. He can't hurt you anymore. Come out of the dark.

Where are you Mum?

He was now aware of running down a long white corridor, trying the door handles as he ran. This one locked, the next one locked, the next one open. He glanced inside. She wasn't there. This was a bedroom. Except it wasn't.

This was the *bad*room. This is where he hurt her.

'Mum?' he called as he ran further along the corridor.

And then his name again, coming from above him, but further away this time. He stopped in the corridor, knowing that this was a dream. He gazed up, awaiting the voice again.

And then his eyes fluttered open.

The face of a beautiful woman looked down at him, smiling. She was stroking the side of his head. He didn't know her.

'I've been calling you,' she said.

CHAPTER 18

SAFFI

She felt the energy coursing into him, aware that she only had so much she could give at this time. Who knew what would lie ahead for her the rest of this day? She may need her energy for others. And for herself.

With her hands on his chest, she had sensed more about this man; a stranger gradually revealing himself before her, without a word being spoken. Like peeling the layers of an onion.

Another vision; no girls now. A woman. Gone. Then a long white corridor seen through the eyes of a boy. Small hands were trying the door handles, reaching high to turn them. Locked, closed, shut, one by one. Then one swung open. Beyond it lay a bedroom. A word; bad. He was lost, seeking Saffi in his dreams. She had to guide him.

'Nicholas,' she spoke softly, gently touching his cheek with a caring, steady hand.

Another flash; the boy leaving the room, running scared. Words: Him. Hide. Hurt. The boy stopping. She saw through his dream-eyes, staring to the ceiling.

And then she said his name again. As she did, she saw another in her mind's-eye. A woman. This woman was in trouble. And she had heard Saffi calling for Nicholas.

Stay true, she told herself.

He's coming now, he can feel me.

And with that Nicholas opened his eyes.

Saffi smiled down at him, her hand still working its magic on his cheek. A gentle touch. A motherly touch.

'I've been calling you,' she said.

Nicholas breathed in a stuttered breath, his eyes welling up.

'My friends?' his voice dry, broken. The effects of trauma manifest.

'Shhh…' Saffi stroked his face, urging silence. She had a bit more work to do. She needed to know which other was trying to come through.

Closing her eyes, reaching with her mind, feeling her energy being forced up, through the floating people, through-

Screaming, Saffi clamped her hands to her head, squeezing hard.

Cyrus turned, leaving the roadside, running to her. Nicholas sat up, propping himself on his elbows, struggling to come to.

Cyrus acted fast, knowing it wasn't the big guy who had hurt Saffi. It was another. He crouched at her side, gently easing her hands from her temples.

'Saffi?'

Tears were threatening at the corners of her eyes. She turned her face, moments ago full of her love and light, now ashen grey. She looked twenty years older.

She read the concern on Cyrus' face. Raising her arm, now trembling with the effort, Saffi pointed up into the trees. 'Above them,' she whispered, 'there's trouble above them.'

Cyrus had no idea what Saffi was referring to. Lifting her gently, helping her to her feet. He glanced down at the big guy.

His eyes now fully open, he was looking with concern at his mate who lay alongside, eyes closed.

She'd brought him back, that was good. But there was always a price.

'Come, lay,' offered Cyrus. He'd never seen her so tense. So shaken.

So lost.

She was whimpering now, struggling to control her breath. 'Calm, Saffi, calm,' he urged.

Her eyes, bloodshot, sought his. It said all he needed to know.

CHAPTER 19

NICK

Confused and aching to buggery, Nick turned sideways, feeling his suit jacket straining at the neck. *Need to lose some weight mate,* he told himself. *Perfect time for self-deprecation you plonker! The world is falling apart around you, and you want to look good for it!*

'Adam!' he grumbled, the word not sounding as he thought he had spoken it. Christ, he was tired. He rolled over onto his belly, mildly aware that his pristine white shirt, ironed only that morning for the important business meeting, was now covered in grass stains. 'At least there's no dogs,' he laughed to himself. It sounded odd to him, in the circumstances. Behind him the strange lady *(I've met her before, I'm sure of it…)* was deeply upset and alongside him Adam was laid as if dead.

'Adam, you muppet!' he called, struggling to haul his mighty ass along the grass like the world's biggest slug. Adam's eyes opened; his head turned to Nick. Nick smiled. Adam laughed. Nick got close enough, collapsed, his arm over Adam's chest. They were alive.

And for now, that was enough.

CHAPTER 20

CYRUS

He tried to tap into Saffi, to see what she had seen, but she was closed off to him.

'You're exhausted. Get some rest.'

He lowered her head, went into the back of the camper and retrieved a blanket. He covered her as she rested on the grass.

Cyrus stood, considering his options, scratching the back of his neck the way he always did when was he was unsure.

Trust the Light.

He centered, his eyes closed, feeling for the grace flow to through him. To guide him.

Above. A threat from above the people floating.

His eyes snapped open. He turned and ran to the edge of the grass verge. He walked into the road, among the stationary traffic. Somewhere in the distance, sirens were wailing. Cyrus thought that today most of the emergency care needed would be provided by him and others like him (Chosen Ones) the traffic and sheer scale of what was happening before their very eyes becoming all too clear. He jogged between cars, the ghost faces still looking out at him. Radios were playing, people were on their phones, all trying to make sense of what was unfolding. As he moved, he kept his eyes turned to the sky, occasionally glancing down to make sure he didn't fall over something or someone.

Above, something above them.

'Dude!' He called to the stranger he had spoken with earlier. The guy who had made the bomb motion with his hands, as if he were playing Charades.

'Can you see anything above those people? In the sky?'

The guy stood, still smiling at Cyrus.

He tried shouting again.

'Above them! Can you see something above them?!'

The guy smiled. His hands moving in and out. He stared at the sky.

Cyrus slowed, suddenly wary of the smiling man. As he watched the man appeared to fade in and out. In a heartbeat like he was pulsing.

Cyrus was distracted by movement above. Something visible between the bodies of the Floaters. Something above them.

A helicopter!

He pointed at it, running back to the others on the grass, shouting as he went; 'There's a chopper!'

He stopped abruptly, still in amongst the traffic. He tapped into his inner voice.

He was seeking something, some clarification on the chopper and the people in it.

Were they here to help or were they part of the problem?

Cyrus looked into a car window, saw people inside. Saw the phone on the back seat. He had a sudden urge to steal it. Something told him he was pretty good at stealing stuff.

PART FIVE

CHAPTER 1

NIGEL

Odd. Usually, it's those trapped behind the bars asking to be let out.

Nigel considered this whilst shaking the mesh of the shutters which kept them out - kept them from being safe inside the station - with all of his strength. Being a typical middle-aged fat-bloke didn't help, his energy levels low. *If only I was like Slim,* he thought. A hand touched his, smooth, silky.

(Maggie)

Lihua, tears standing in the corners of her eyes, threatening to break, gently eased his violence. He was scaring her baby. Maybe she'd got the wrong idea? Nigel's only aim was to get behind those bars, so she could be with her baby again. Not out here where it's-

'Unsafe. We need to go,' she said, her eyes convincing him of the truth. If she could get away from these people and leave her baby behind, then he could find the strength to do the same.

Only it wasn't strength, it was anger. Pure and simple.

'How dare you,' he hissed through the bars to those faces standing pacified, non-judgemental behind their metal prison. His jaw clenched. 'How dare you judge me.' He glanced at Lihua. 'Judge *us*. We've just as much right to be safe inside there as you do.' His voice was controlled. Slow. Steady. A sure sign violence was boiling just beneath the surface. Lihua the only one trying to keep it that way.

Easy, Big Bear.

Nigel sighed. Maggie. How he missed her.

He checked his watch. 9:38am. Christ he'd only been on shift for less than 40 minutes. What a shit-storm of a day this was turning out to be.

Get home, Big Bear. Get safe.

Hands still hanging on the shutters, Nigel dropped his eyes to the floor, controlling his breath. Steadying the beast within. His gut was sticking out, partially obscuring the pavement from view below him. All the cock jokes came flooding back; 'When's the last time you saw your cock, Woods?' followed by the usual roaring laughter. Good natured laughter. Back in the changing rooms. Back when he had a chance to become something. Anything.

I'm not a murderer. I didn't kill her!

He forced the thoughts away, wondering where the hell they had come from.

He turned to Lihua, her hand still resting lightly on the back of his.

'How has it come to this?' he begged her to answer, his eyes seeking some kind of comfort.

Lihua turned, her head gesturing to his hands. 'Go?'

He let go of the mesh. Staring back through the shutter once more. Seeing Slim stroking Business' head. She still looked unconscious. He saw the bundle.

Must protect her.

Spring Flowers.

He closed his eyes again, picturing just that. A deep breath, he imagined he could smell the petals.

He had a vision of being in a room with a man and woman. Everything was white apart from the vase of flowers.

Not now.

Go! Maggie. Lihua. Two women urging him on.

'I'll be back for her,' he hissed through the bars. The faces behind floated like ghosts, as if he were a thing to be watched on their TV screens.

No emotion.

'Fuckers.'

CHAPTER 2

NIGEL

The car was still smoking, nothing yet blown.

Maybe I shouldn't have got out of that. The Uber driver hadn't. Poor bastard.

Business had got out physically but maybe not mentally. And Chunhua? Who knew? For now, he had other things to consider. The main one being not to get sucked up into the air and join those already up there.

'Can you run?' he asked Lihua.

She nodded and kicked off her high heels. 'Where?'

Bloody going to run a damn sight quicker than I will, Nigel realised, regretting taking the hero-saviour role now. And where?

How the fuck should I know?

She answered him in her usual way deep inside his mind; *Home.*

He turned his eyes towards heaven, regretting the decision as he saw more desperate bodies calling for help above him.

Jesus died on a cross. So, what have all these souls done? To be hung in the air for all to see.

There was no mercy.

Nature doesn't care about you.

He'd heard that somewhere. A lecture back in college? Maybe.

His legs were working, his mind running in circles.

Calm, Big Bear. You're already outside. So, you're not going up to join them. Otherwise you'd be there already. You've saved a lady. You've saved her baby. Now, get somewhere safe. Somewhere you know. And take her with you. She's your responsibility now.

Good advice. 'And when this shit dies down, I can get her reunited back with Chun.'

Lihua stopped, gripping his hand tightly. 'Chun?'

He'd barely realised he'd spoken. 'My home. We're going to my home. I'll get you back with your baby once this (he pointed to the sky) has died down.'

Or once they've died.

She took a deep breath, composed herself and then dropped her grip.

'Home,' he said.

Lihua nodded.

Good, thought Nigel. She understands. Now just one problem. How to get there.

CHAPTER 3

NIGEL

Carnage everywhere.

Cars? No good. Roads blocked worse than usual.

Motorbike? No good. He couldn't ride one. As a kid, he'd struggled with a push bike with stablizers. Lord knows what a fat bastard like him would do on one with an engine. *And* a girl on the back.

'Ark at you, Big Bear! Girl on the back of your bike. You stud. He could hear her laughing. All in his mind.

Push bike? No good. He'd need two. She'd have to follow him and could get lost. Or get hit off. Or mugged.

Raped.

'Christ man, control yourself,' he muttered. No, it'd have to be something…

The tandem was leaning against the wall of the building opposite the station, alongside the crashed cars. It was unchained and looked new. As if it had been left just for them.

'Lihua, come,' he hoped it didn't sound too much like he was calling a dog. She followed obediently, he a middle-aged, overweight Superman, her an Asian Lois Lane. What a combo.

He put his hand on the bike. It was red, his favourite colour.

A shout came from behind him. He instinctively dropped the bike frame, it falling back against the wall. He also began to raise his arms, as if he were about to surrender. Anger seeped in, his arms lowered, he swung around. There were people flocking all around him, running this way and that. Many were now forcing the shutter he had just vacated, with far more force than he. But nobody, it seemed, had been shouting at him. He looked around, taking in everyone. Nobody was claiming the bike.

'Should've locked it up,' he mumbled. 'Get on.'

Lihua was unsure, taking time to glance round. Nigel was busy raising a leg, trying to force it over the bike's frame. *Wrong day to wear jeans eh, you fat bastard?*

He tried to lower the bike over, leaning the handlebars more toward the floor, half expecting to be caught, half expecting this moment to haunt him on some internet exposé show; The Bumbling Bike Thief. And his Oriental Chick.

Oh, so she's a 'chick' now is she, Big Bear?

He grinned and to his surprise, Lihua burst out laughing.

And so he stood, one leg straddled over the leaning tandem, trying to force it back upright. He could see the funny side.

'Get… get on!' he said, waving awkwardly with his free hand to encourage her to sit on behind him. 'Quickly!'

She did as she was told. And then Nigel laughed out loud. A real honker this time.

The bike was facing a dead end.

CHAPTER 4

LIHUA

Oh, this guy was mad. Brave maybe. But crazy.

Lihua had considered running from him with her baby, but realised that although he seemed - what was the word? Brash? As good as any - he also seemed caring. And he knew his way around north London. That was a good sign. He'd tried to look after her baby, she was sure of that. Seeing him skim Chunhua under the falling shutter had stopped her heart. Had he been trying to kill her baby she would have felt it. Of that she was certain. But he'd only tried to save Chun. And now she needed saving too. And this guy was her best bet.

She'd seen the bike before he did, hoping that he wouldn't consider it. The Gods were against her today it seemed, for he ran to it, calling her over. Lihua was searching the surrounding buildings, hoping for a door, an open window, anything that they could use to take shelter until this storm passed, but somewhere she could keep an eye on the station entrance. She had to stay near her baby.

Home.

That was what the guy had said. Damn, what was his name again? She tried to think back to the cab journey. He had said it, but the other lady, the pretty blonde one, she had been in a frenzy.

Nigel.

That was it.

He was trying to mount the tandem. She was trying hard not to laugh. Had he not realised it was facing the wrong way with no room to turn it around? It seemed not, as he turned, waving behind him as if he had broken wind. She played along, allowing herself to be rescued. All the while thinking how she could stay close, stay near to Chun.

Home.

The word kept haunting her. The one place she had spent her life savings on escaping. Risking her life and Chun's just to get away from…

Home.

And now Nigel wanted to take her back.

There was no way she could let that happen. She'd kill him if she had too. As she'd killed the others.

CHAPTER 5

NIGEL

A decision needed to be made. Either stay here, flop over these goddam handlebars and laugh himself to death or…

'Nigel?'

'What love?' He didn't have the sheer effort to even consider turning round to face her. 'What?'

Patience, Big Bear. She's vulnerable this one.

'We… stay… near Chun? We… stay… safely?'

'Right, you're going to have yourself another wet panty's moment now love,' he said as he began to try and dismount the tandem.

The encouragement to move quickly came when a gunshot rang out, accompanied by a whistling sound alongside his ear. The wall to his right puffed into a little cloud of smoke.

'What the…?'

Some language he didn't understand, a dialect he was quite sure he'd never heard, came from above him.

CHAPTER 6

LIHUA

There's three ways people handle extreme abuse; they fight it, they commit suicide or they retreat into themselves. Lihua Kwok chose the latter of the three, albeit unconsciously.

At times in her violent life, she often wondered what the point of living was and if suicide would be the better option.

Put an end to the suffering. Around the age of twenty, Lihua couldn't find peace even in her sleeping world, her dreams had become nightmares, reflecting her waking life.

It was finally Aabid who gave her the one reason to live. He had broken the rules, had raped her and gotten her pregnant. Despite not being able to speak Albanian, Lihua understood only too well that Aabid was now an enemy of the gang himself.

Running away was never an option for her, as if they caught you, it would be worse than death. At least in death you'd finally have peace.

There was no way the gang would allow her that. Not after the effort they had gone to, to have her trafficked across so many countries and continents.

Aabid was now fighting his own battle; either she had to go, or he did. And he would never leave his brotherhood, his family.

Lihua could barely remember hers, having been smuggled away from her parents at such an early age. She had vague flashes at times, hardly worthy of being called memories. Just an image here and there of an elderly woman - maybe a mother figure, or perhaps a grandmother (maybe just visions in her imagination; a coping mechanism of her mind conjuring up an idyllic mother figure to help her through this life. That was of far more comfort than the thought of her parents actually giving her to the traffickers, if that *was* the reality of her situation) - and a simple kitchen, her viewpoint below what would have been a dining table of sorts she guessed, which gave her pause for thought that maybe she had really been in the parental home at one time.

Maybe.

The rule was simple; only the girls who were fresh in could be raped by the gang and only then for a few days. As if they weren't human, just a new piece of machinery being given a review and checked for broken and damaged parts. Mentally all the girls were broken and, after the first few days with the gang, parts were soon damaged. Some of the girls managed the bliss of suicide, but that was not easy. They were under constant watch by the gang, transported here, there and everywhere. Forming friendships was not allowed (and impossible anyway - the girls were never in a room together, even sleeping, for more than a few hours at a time).

But word got round, the human spirit ever capable at adapting in even the most terrible of circumstances. Lihua envied the ones who got away.

That was what they called it; 'got away'. Never suicide. Lihua guessed that it gave the tiniest sliver of hope, a glint in the broken mirror of life, that you could, maybe, just maybe get away.

One day.

And that day had finally come for her. With her belly swollen, Lihua knew her good looks would only keep her alive for so long. Clients still fucked her, despite her evolving bump. Lihua did her best to control the situation, but most of her clients liked it rough, so she was often brutally forced onto her front, or slapped, punched and kicked by men who had paid to have their way with her. But never the face. Should a client ever touch her face, the gang would have words, usually accompanied by a gun or bat.

Lihua knew she was somewhere in London that morning, about two weeks ago (or was it? Her sense of time had lost all perspective. Everything seemed wrong. Out of balance). She'd been hiding as best she could, a shadow living among the shadows, staying as close to her gang as she could, for fear of Aabid killing her off, destroying the evidence of his rape.

She'd been woken early, slapped across the face by Rei, an Albanian she'd only been with in her latest hovel for the last few weeks. Told to get dressed, shoved toward the shower room (with the blood stains still on the tiles from a beating another girl had sustained the evening before, Lihua had covered her ears from the screams as they had echoed around the halls) and then told to dress in the smart clothes laid out before her.

That meant one of their wealthier clients.

Heavily pregnant, she had been taken in a blacked-out car to a hotel, where she, on the arm of Rei (himself dressed in his cleanest, most-pressed shirt) walked into yet another classy hotel.

Lihua knew the drill by now, being in the game since she was around 17 or maybe 18 years old. Her mind had blocked most of the time in between. Her body told the story her mind tried to forget in a mixture of fractures, scars and a slight deafness in one ear, where one guy some time ago had gotten too excited and punched her in the side of her head. Hard.

She smiled at anyone who looked at her, all the time feeling Rei's tight grip on her arm, secure and threatening. Lihua knew what he was capable of. Had seen it many times. She was with a murderer.

Once they had departed the lift, Rei led her to a door. Knocked and waited. A voice called from beyond. Rei muttered, pinched her hard, then gently stroked her belly. Lihua preferred the pinch. She tried not to squirm, tried not to flinch, hoping in some small way the baby inside would kick just to see if the bastard had any feelings in him at all.

Rei gestured to the door. 'He. Need. Baby Woman. Hard Fuck.' He was looking intently at her, seeing if she had understood.

Living as a shadow, Lihua had picked up some of the various languages on her journey. She communicated through nods, whimpers and tears. But yes, she could talk. Another weapon she was keeping secret waiting for the day…

Rei turned and walked back along the corridor. She knew he would be only a phone call away from the client. Despite being a big man, he would soon become invisible in the hotel, waiting the full hour before he came back to collect the girl and cash.

And Baby Women were more expensive it seemed.

Her days were limited, the closer she came to giving birth. But now she had a reason to live. And the reason was another image from her distant past. A field, full of long grass. Lihua was running through it, a blue dress short at the sleeves, long at the ankles, catching in her legs as she ran. Laughing. Feeling the sun on her face. Feeling alive.

Feeling free.

And in that field, there were flowers of the prettiest colours. Spring Flowers.

CHAPTER 7
LIHUA

The client was someone she hadn't met before. He opened the door, ignored her, leaned out and glanced down the corridor both ways. He looked agitated, frightened even. Lihua didn't know if he were checking for passers-by or to see if Rei had gone. He stood back, finally acknowledging her with a weak smile.

Guilty, that smile said.

Smiles can be sad, Lihua knew that. The mask of a clown, put on to hide true feelings. She'd been wearing her mask for as long as she had ever known. Mirrors were not in the gang houses, as girls may use them to end their life. Or that of a gang member. The only glimpse she had of the mask she wore was in situations like these; in hotel rooms, car rear-view mirrors, and the occasional reflection in a shop window when being escorted to clients.

The door was now fully open, the client blushing, eager for her to be in so he could close the door on the outside world. Close the door on his being judged.

Lihua stepped in, stopping to give him a quick kiss on the cheek.

'Not yet,' he said hastily wiping any mark from his face.

The door closed softly behind her.

It was a nice room. A penthouse by the look of it. Many doors and further rooms.

The client was wearing a dressing gown, hiding his obviously obese frame. Lihua no longer had any impulse to be impressed or disgusted by the human body. Lust was an experience she would never enjoy in this life. Nor love.

She stroked her belly.

'I'm Luke, although, as you know, that's not my real name.' He was rambling. She let him continue. The longer she could drag this out the better. There had been times when she had managed to avoid any sex completely, the client often finding it almost impossible to get it up on demand, their guilt causing them to suffer. It didn't really matter to her whether they fucked her or not, she was numb.

But with Chunhua now in her belly (she knew, just knew it was a girl) she did all she could to not have to fuck. The gang never knew, as long as the client paid, they couldn't give a damn.

Standing by the drinks bar, Luke was sipping a glass of champagne. The bottle next to it appeared almost empty. He was wealthy, able to pay and make his fantasies a reality.

But experiencing something in the mind is a far, far cry from doing it in reality. Maybe Luke (Lihua didn't give a fuck what his real name might be) was having second thoughts. Rei was a guy not to be messed with and Luke would have been vetted by the gang well before they ever left a girl with a client alone.

And for an hour.

That was over £2000. Lihua knew that. Probably more for a Baby Woman.

He held out a glass for her, his hand shaking. He saw the trembling and put the glass down.

'Please.'

She accepted and walked slowly over, picking up the glass, her painted nails tapping the stem. Crystal. Expensive.

By now Lihua would usually have opened her overcoat, revealing her body, the make-up concealing any recent bruises and covering her worst scars. She would have slipped off her shoes, sexy, high-heeled and be working on the man, getting him aroused. But for some reason, something dangerous was in her mind right now.

The most dangerous thing there could be. The thing that could get her killed.

Hope.

CHAPTER 8
LUKE

He'd never, ever done anything like this before.

Didn't they tell you from the youngest age to study hard, work hard and success will be yours? Well, if they meant financial success then he had achieved that. But on the path had sacrificed so much more. His wife gone. His daughter gone. His friends, true friends, not those two-faced wankers at the bank, gone. He had all of the ingredients the western world decried were vital for true happiness; the big house (three actually), fast cars, a yacht, tons of money. More than he knew what to do with. And with each purchase, with each million made, Luke felt a piece of him dying.

It wasn't supposed to be like this.

The highs had to be sought from elsewhere; gambling soon bored him, speeding made no difference to him, he could afford to pay off any fines and if he lost his license, he wouldn't give a shit. He had a chauffeur for work. Cocaine had presented itself early on in his career, but the 'study-hard, work-hard' ethic in him hilariously stopped him from partaking of that particular enjoyment. Cocaine equalled death in his mind. And he was too successful to die.

What a thought. He was too scared to die, that was the truth of it. It takes courage to kill yourself, to admit your wrongs, to end your miserable life. And successful people don't drop out that way.

Study-hard, work-hard, kill-yourself.

No, that wouldn't work in his world. But God how he felt it in him. It felt so right.

So, he'd gotten into girls. The last chance at a high. To feel alive once again. He'd had many fantasies of fucking girls, threesomes, Orientals, replaying the fantasy over and over in his mind, tugging his cock under the duvet like a guilty teenager every night. He finally made the choice to act and get it out of his system.

Study-hard, work-hard, fuck-hard.

For now, that would work in his world.

But how to find a girl? Damon had sorted that one for him. He could get him anything. Drugs, girls (even the younger kind he had told Luke one evening and Luke preferred to convince himself that Damon was joking), even a firearm.

Luke had considered asking for the gun over the girl. But no, ever the coward had gone for the girl. Better to ruin another life than end his own.

He was lost. A failure. But if he could get this fantasy out of his system, then maybe…

The final two parts of his ultimate fantasy were two Oriental girls (Asian chicks always made him hard when watching porn), a bathtub full of cash and one of the chicks had to be pregnant.

In the end Damon had sorted most of it, claiming on the morning of The Fantasy (as it had now been codenamed between them) that he could only get one girl, but the good news was she was pregnant.

And so, Luke had gone. Not in his car, but by public transport. He'd even bought a new suit for the occasion. Not to impress the girl, just so he could burn it after. Remove all trace of The Fantasy. He'd purposely got a different colour and cut to his usual style, to disguise him.

The Fantasy had given him a buzz, given him a reason to go on, as he had planned it over the last… Christ, had it only been a week or two? Damon moved fast. God alone knows where he got the girl from.

Luke had planned most of it, giving Damon his request list. Verbal not written, couldn't risk a 'success' like him having evidence come back and bite him on the ass. Chinese girl. Had to be clean. Happy to do anything. Happy to put the johnny on him (he had tried many times when he was with Kirsty but it always removed the passion from the proceedings, putting a rubber raincoat on your cock in the heat of the moment) and happy to let him fuck her in the bathtub of £50 notes. He offered to let the girl keep the cash, but Damon told him to keep the cash his own special secret, as he could end up with prying eyes if they knew he had that sort of money lying around. Luke had asked what eyes may be prying, but Damon had assured him all was safe and above board, just to keep his mouth shut about the cash.

He'd checked into the hotel prior to her arrival, just to get things ready. He hadn't had any pictures of the girl; only knew she matched his requirements.

Like ordering a pizza.

He'd hardly slept recently, the bags under his eyes adding years to his face. The lines were deeper, the cheeks more flushed, broken veins beginning to show through the translucent skin here and there. Christ, no wonder Kirsty had left him. As he'd stared into the bathroom mirror that morning, he'd begun to wish he had asked Damon for the gun. And one bullet.

Then the knock came at the door.

CHAPTER 9

LIHUA

Her heart was racing and she felt her cheeks beginning to grow hot. This was not good. Maybe it was the baby? She was only a week away from giving birth, maybe even days.

No, she had convinced herself to hold Chunhua in, defying the laws of nature, not letting her be born into the gang world.

Never.

She'd kill them both before that ever happened.

But now, that idea she'd been holding onto, that persistent vision, of being free, allowing her and her daughter to live in peace and safety, suddenly seemed as if it might soon be a reality. That was *her* fantasy.

Here she was about to live out yet another man's fantasy.

Yet, her fantasy seemed hot, like she was walking right into it. For real.

But why now? Why this man?

Because he's guilty. She felt it. She must have been in the room for a good ten minutes already and still he was pacing, trying to get himself under control.

Maybe he'll have a heart attack, she thought. Then she could somehow get out of the window or-

'Please, um, sit down. Anywhere you wish really.' He interrupted her thoughts.

Lihua smiled, glancing around the room, pulling her coat tighter around her. Another very unfamiliar move on her part. It should be on the floor in a pile by now along with the rest of her clothes.

'Do you like money?' he slapped himself on the forehead, making her jump. 'I'm sorry, I didn't mean to scare you,' he laughed nervously.

Hope began to bloom in her chest.

Easy, she told herself. *Breathe. Let him talk.*

'Come, see. I hope you like it.' He got up, walked to yet another door in this vast apartment and stood holding it open. He smiled and waited for her.

Lihua placed her champagne glass down, as yet untouched.

Good, keep your head clear.

Smiling, she walked over to join him at the door

(Push him in, lock the door, go to the window and… Penthouse. No good. Too many floors up.)

half expecting him to shove her inside and begin doing whatever he had planned.

The bathtub was huge, one of the biggest she had ever seen. Gold taps protruded halfway along one edge. Lihua took a moment to realise it was money that was filling it. Red bank notes.

'I… I did this all for you. I hope you like it.' Luke was stammering again.

Good, she liked to hear it in his voice. Gave her time to think. To plan.

A sudden pain gripped her stomach, forcing her to double over

(Mind the baby! Mind the baby!)

Luke was at her side. 'Are you OK? Is it… Christ no! Not now. For fuck's sake!' He suddenly left her, storming back into the main room. She could hear him swearing.

'Fucking Damon! I thought he'd know not to get one who is about to fucking drop. For fuck's sake!'

Got to calm him down. Before he calls Rei.

She stood, reaching out for some support, only to burn her hand on the heated towel rail. She felt that surge of hope begin to close, like a flower as the day's sun dies.

I'm foolish. There's never a way out. Never.

Stand up.

She glanced at the bathroom mirror. If she could break it, she could get away. Get away for good. From this life. And take Chunhua with her.

Her thoughts stopped as she saw the face looking back at her. Her reflected self. It gave her strength. She looked hard, wondering if it were an illusion. A tear fell from the corner of her eye. For the face that stared back at her, for the first time in a long time, was smiling. A smile of hope.

Her mask was gone.

CHAPTER 10
LIHUA

'Luke. Please?' she called.

He was still ranting. She prayed he hadn't picked up the phone. There was at least 40 odd minutes of their time left. And she needed it all if she were to act out her plan.

He ran into the bathroom.

'I'm sorry, it's just I had this idea, this fantasy…'

'Stop. No bad. No baby coming. Please.' She held out her hand. He saw the red mark. His eyes flicked to the towel rail.

'Oh my god! My fault. I put it on so you'd be warm, we'd be warm when we… if we, you know, if you wanted to. The money is yours by the way, no worries!' he laughed. Damon would kill him when he found out he'd given the girl all of the cash. It took nearly £300,000 to fill the tub. He'd actually used towels in the bottom of the bath, hiding them with the spread of notes over the top. His handiwork had looked pretty good. It reminded him of a lost hobby he used to have. Art and photography. He'd given them up as they weren't part of the 'study-hard work-hard,' success formula. He'd wondered what his life may have turned out like had he followed his heart and not his head.

A starving artist probably. But a happier soul. Of that he was sure.

He went to take Lihua's hand, then flinched away as if she were damaged goods. He opened his mouth to speak, then raised his finger instead. Inspiration had struck. He took a hand towel from the basin, soaked it in cold water and then handed it to her.

'I can wrap it for you if you like, if it's easier, if it helps? I'm so sorry, I didn't think.'

This was not going anything like he'd imagined all those nights under the duvet.

'It's OK. Thank you.' She knew she could speak the words more fluently, but something told her to speak slow. Play dumb. Something clicked inside of her mind right then; the images, the smiling woman's face, the dining table, running through the field of spring flowers - they weren't memories. They were dreams. Visions of Chunhua. Seeing the world through her baby's eyes.

The flower in her heart opened again.

Hope was back.

And she had around half an hour to make those dreams come true.

CHAPTER 11

LIHUA

She stood upright, feeling the pain in her belly die down. And then she felt it; a kick. She yelped with surprise and joy.

'What?' asked Luke.

'Please. Feel.' She was working on autopilot now. Something larger than her was guiding her. And she knew that this was the day. She was going to be free and give birth to her daughter.

The sweetener was that she would have a coat full of cash when it happened.

****

Whether it was feeling the baby kick, or simply his health, her client stood up, smiled, then began to sob. He sat on the edge of the cash-bath holding his head in his hands. He muttered something, Lihua unable to hear precisely what he'd said. Later she often thought back, trying to capture his words in her mind's-eye. They were to be his last in this world. (Later still, she had found out that Luke had repeated the exact same fantasy with many different girls of all shapes and sizes with vastly different outcomes.)

She had tried to soothe him. The expanding flower of hope in her heart was growing with each beat, giving her strength. She wanted the sun, to feel the sun on her face, warming her belly. She wanted to give herself to the light.

Not being a religious person (she had long abandoned any thought of a god in this sick world) the bathroom itself began to glow, as if radiating from her. Lihua knew this was all in her mind, but the feeling was sensational. Her entire body began to tingle, her nerves alert. She'd never felt more alive. And then a presence, something bigger than herself, bigger than her client, came into that room.

Lihua lived a long life and she never forgot the grace of God that came to her that day. It saved her life, saved her baby's and in return took another.

She felt no pity for him. Saw it as a fair trade.

He was guilty after all.

CHAPTER 12
LUKE

In the end he hadn't needed a gun. He hadn't needed to worry about getting it up, or whether to give the girl the cash or not. Didn't need to fret about Damon or the big guy who had come with the girl.

At 10:32am, half-hour after Lihua had arrived into the penthouse, Luke Brown had simply stood up from the bath tub and vanished into thin air.

Taken by God.

****

He woke in a familiar place.

A white place, everything white.

They were smiling. They'd been expecting him.

He'd come home.

It hadn't turned out as he'd hoped.

Luke understood. He'd be with them forever.

CHAPTER 13
LIHUA

Getting out of the hotel had been easy.

She had slipped out of her high heels and hastily dressed in Luke's clothes. A well-pressed suit was hanging in the wardrobe. It hung around her but gave her what she needed; a disguise. Not a great one, but one that would work in the ensuing panic.

The fire was easy to start. Luke had a gold flick lighter in the jacket pocket. The towels in the bath went up easy. The sprinklers kicked in within moments and, more importantly, so did the fire alarms.

Her new suit and complimentary hotel umbrella up (a perk of being a penthouse guest and convenient to shield her from the sprinklers now going off across the top floor) adding an extra layer of invisibility, Lihua had been helped by staff down the fire escapes. She'd kept an eye out for Rei, knowing he'd be watching out for her either inside the lobby, or just outside the main doors waiting to pounce and re-capture his investment. His property.

And that was when God saved her once again.

CHAPTER 14

LIHUA

Although she'd never be told in what was to be her short life, Chunhua was born during the chaos of the fire at the hotel in Regents Park.

The ambulance was already waiting as the staff led a strange lady in a man's suit out of the building, the alarms ringing in her ears. Whether Rei ever saw her or not, she had no idea.

The doors of the ambulance finally closed and still Lihua wouldn't believe she was free, half expecting the driver, or the paramedic in the back with her, to suddenly transform into Rei. A mask was placed over her face

(a new one… I'm free…)

and smiling Lihua drifted into a welcome sleep.

In her heart the flower still spread its petals. The sun had shone on her that day.

CHAPTER 15

NIGEL - NOW

Decision made. He wasn't the fittest of men by any stretch of the imagination, but the foreign accent, the high-pitched whizz sound passing by his ear and the cloud of smoke (not to forget the bang that preceded those events) could only mean one thing; someone was shooting. At him!

Must be an accident.

Accident or not, Nigel had no intention of trying to escape on a tandem facing the wrong way in a dead-end.

Dead. End.

Not him. Not today.

And he would not, would *not*, in these days of social media with every goddam bugger living their entire lives out online, end his life being filmed by some sicko after being shot dead leaning over the handlebars of a fucking tandem.

'No, Nigel. No!' Lihua stuttered.

He turned and with athleticism that defied his age and body type (fat bastard) fell off of the bike. Without any dignity at all, he flopped onto the pavement, in his mind's-eye looking like the fat kid in gym class trying to do a roly-poly.

Get up, Big Bear.

Lihua was behind him in moments, either trying to use him as a human shield or-

Another bullet, another scream of anger in a language he didn't understand. And now she was helping him up.

'Nigel. Please. Come.'

He stood, awkwardly, the breath gone from him.

Fat Kid Gets a Merit for Trying. Class Goes Wild. Guaranteed Years, repeat YEARS of Torment Now.

Lihua was dragging him toward a doorway. It would provide some cover, but not enough. The door was locked shut. To top it off, the doorway stank of piss.

'Who the fuck is shooting at us?!' he managed between breaths.

More shots. They weren't completely safe, the bullets chipping into the stone around them. Nigel replayed the moments. Counting... had that been six bullets fired? He wasn't sure. Instinct kicked in. He leaned out, shielding his face, trying to see who was taking the shots.

Get back, Big Bear!

Too late. The pain was excruciating. His right hand now had a hole in it. Through it he could momentarily see the sky. And the bodies floating there.

After that, nothing.

CHAPTER 16

AABID

Thursday 19th January was a day Aabid would have never forgotten even without the crazy weird shit that was happening

all around him. People were floating into the sky. Aabid was mightily pissed at whatever God had caused this. Today was his day to shine. His day. He'd been months preparing Ahmed, guiding him, counselling him and ultimately arming him to carry out God's will. And now God himself had appeared and taken over the show.

If not Allah, then a terrorist cell had decided to stage an attack and this one would take some beating. Years ago, the towers came down and the folk in his country danced in the street. But to make the enemy go *up*? That was some attack.

Some trick.

He'd not known if Ahmed had managed to carry out his suicide bombing due to being overshadowed by the Floaters. Ahmed may not have even bothered going through with it once he'd seen all of this shit unfolding.

And for Aabid, he had finally tracked down the bitch, the perfect end to his day.

He was going to take her back, her and his baby, and kill her. Slowly. He even considered killing the baby too and making the bitch watch. Maybe make the bitch do it herself. She'd deserve it. Tricking him into fucking her.

Bitch!

But things hadn't gone to plan. The gang was already talking behind his back. Paranoia was rising in him day-by-day as Rei had lost Lihua at the hotel just over two weeks ago. Every time he saw a hooded girl, he had to fight the urge to run up, pull back the hood and put a bullet between her eyes.

Maybe even not bother pulling back the hood. They all deserved to die.

Could it have really been two weeks ago? Aabid felt time slipping. It was all becoming a blur. Everything appeared to be happening *now*. Impossible but somehow true.

He'd been waiting at the hotel in a stolen car, knowing his time was limited to kidnap Lihua and the baby. How she'd gotten the money to stay in such a quality hotel he had no idea. He couldn't walk into an establishment like that and just take her back. That would cause way too many problems. And there was already a target on his back, he felt sure of it. His brothers had only kept him alive this long, due to his commitment to their Jihad and the fact he had personally trained and mentored his baby brother Ahmed to carry out the first of their planned strikes in London.

No, she must have been fucking around behind their backs. Pocketing the money. The pregnant bitch had fetched more money anyway since he'd given her that gift.

And by God, he wanted it back.

If he didn't get her today, then his life would be over. He'd be on the run himself.

She came out of the hotel quickly followed by another bitch. Blond hair, smart suit. Some corporate type. Nice legs. Aabid considered what she would be like to fuck. His eyes returned to Lihua. She looked so lost, so innocent. So *vulnerable.* The thought made him hard.

Look at her, in a new suit of her own.

Spending more of their client's money. Money that wasn't hers.

Their eyes had been to the sky throughout, as the first people had begun to float up and off into the sky. Aabid found it hard to stay focused on Lihua, with pandemonium erupting around him.

Just what the fuck was happening?

He had the radio on, listening for news of Ahmed's attack. Ahmed's sacrifice. On his seventeenth birthday as well. He'd be in Paradise soon.

Lihua had run to a cab and had the back door open. The suit woman with nice legs had seen an opportunity and taken it, jumping into the back of the cab too. Another guy had tried to hold the door, but he'd been taken by the force into the air. And then the cab was gone.

Like a fucking bullet.

Aabid had followed, not caring if he killed anyone en-route. He had no worries of being caught by the police, given the shit storm going on. They'd be busy fishing for the floating fuckers, he told himself.

The cab driver knew the back roads, swerving here and there, expertly maneuvering around people screaming, running amok in the ensuing chaos. He could make out Lihua's head through the rear window. He considered leaning out and taking a shot from here, but he wanted her to know it was him that had gotten her back. Wanted to see it in her eyes.

Bitch!

He'd promised himself he'd give her one last hard fuck before putting the bullet into her brain anyhow. How he looked forward to that.

She'd been carrying a bundle, so he guessed she'd finally given birth. Was surprised she hadn't sold it to make more money for herself.

He'd finally lost the cab near Cockfosters station. The roads were manic.

Aabid's hand went to the door handle to pull it open, to see if he could spot them on foot. A woman ran into the side of his bonnet, her nails scratching the paint work, as she was dragged into the air before his eyes. His hand fell from the handle.

Best to stay inside for now.

His eyes darted to and fro, searching out the cab, or Lihua amongst all of the chaos around him.

Why today?

He began to edge the car forward slowly, hitting people in the legs, not caring. It seemed they didn't too, as most just carried on hysterically. Gradually the streets began to clear, many having been taken into the air, others hiding under cover.

Either way, death was in the air today. Aabid could smell it. Could feel it.

The car had edged forward more, his eyes alert, determined to have one success today. The commotion at the tube station entrance was incredible. It appeared as if those inside had pulled the shutters down condemning those still on the street to their deaths.

And then-

A flash, just the tiniest flash of a woman and a guy. The guy was leaning into a cab. Could it be the same one? Not likely given the number of black cabs on the road.

But Aabid felt that this was right. He didn't know how. He mounted the pavement in the car, still edging it forward, aware of the people still crushed up against the tube station shutters.

He could see a red bike against a wall. And smoke coming from the cab or maybe just in-front of it.

Didn't care. It was the cab. The one carrying his bitch.

He knew it.

And then… there! Mounting the back of the bike. There she was!

Without thinking, he leapt from the car, screamed her name, cursed her in his native tongue, aimed and fired. The manic crowd by the shutter were sent into panic over-drive, many rattling the shutters with their full force to get inside, others ducking and running for cover.

He realised the error of his ways. He should have fired first, then shouted. Now he'd given them a warning.

Them? That guy. The driver. He must know her.

Then he'll die too.

It was all the same to him. Infidels.

It wasn't the order of those actions, whether he should have screamed then fired, or vice-versa, that was the real error of his ways. It was forgetting to stay inside the car. Within moments of being outside of the stolen vehicle, the radio still blaring from inside (the DJ going berserk about what was happening all around him), Aabid was stepping into the air. He didn't even acknowledge this miracle. He was still ranting, still firing, trying to kill the bitch and her fucking saviour.

Missed, missed, missed, missed and missed again.

Fuck, fuck and fuck!

He calmed himself, still only vaguely concerned he was now being pushed up against some kind of invisible ceiling, being forced to turn himself over, facing the street below.

Vaguely aware of others around him, moving, shifting, squirming.

One bullet left.

Lihua's saviour put his head out of the alcove they had dived into for dear life.

Ha! Bad move fucker.

The last shot was well aimed. Aabid wasn't certain but felt the bullet leave the gun, felt it fly into the head of the hero below.

At least one good thing had happened to him today.

Now he was just waiting for Ahmed to blow himself up. By tonight they might just be in Paradise.

Together again.

CHAPTER 17

LIHUA

This couldn't be happening.

She had been so careful over the last two weeks since escaping from the clutches of the gang.

Or… had she? Lihua had the peculiar sense that the last couple of weeks were a blur, like she'd experienced them on autopilot. Like they weren't real.

Probably her body's way of coping.

She knew they'd be looking for her. Aabid would either be dead or out for the kill. Luke's bath full of cash

(Had that really been two weeks ago? It seemed like it had happened only this morning…)

had provided enough to keep her from sharing her story. Money talks.

Handing over cash had gotten her a nice hotel room, new clothes, a personal shopper. All without a credit card or any form of ID. His intentions may have been bad, but in the end, Luke had done one last act of goodness before leaving from this world with that bath full of cash. Lihua hoped that if there was a God, he would take pity on Luke.

But an hour ago, all that temporary safety had changed.

The first body floated up outside her hotel room while she was idly brushing her hair, considering what she'd do that day. She'd been keeping a close eye on the street around the hotel and the lobby. After years of being hidden from society, moving in the shadows, Lihua was used to hiding in plain sight.

She'd die before she let anyone take Chunhua. Lihua had half expected to see Aabid in the child and even briefly considered killing the baby shortly after birth, so she'd never be reminded of him.

Of what he'd done to her.

But through suffering had come joy. From darkness came light.

Chunhua gave Lihua her reason to live, her reason to begin seeing the beauty in the world.

Her reason to begin to outlive her past.

Earlier that morning, the first person floated, screaming, up past her window.

Lihua grabbed Chunhua, wrapping her in the blue luxury blanket at the foot of the bed and then, dressed in her new clothes, she had stashed the remaining crisp notes into her suit pocket and fled from the hotel.

People were panicking.

Hell was visiting Earth.

Lihua looked behind her briefly, wondering if Rei was still on the prowl. She heard a voice, small, scared in her mind, telling her to stay put, stay in the hotel.

Stay safe.

Before Lihua could make a decision, she was pushed out of the hotel doorway by a businesswoman, dressed in a smart suit. Smarter than Lihua's. Chunhua mumbled, her eyes flashing open, rolling around trying to comprehend anything. Lihua put the baby's face to her chest, shielding her as best she could.

She ran.

A black cab sat at the curb, engine idling. Lihua ran toward it.

CHAPTER 18

LIHUA - NOW

All that seemed so long ago. Yet it had not even been an hour.

Nigel had fallen back into the doorway, his body slumped against a blue door which had three padlocks on it. The peeling paint was now speckled with fresh blood. The red absorbing into the blue.

Drops on the pavement.

Nigel held his hand up again, trying to comprehend what had just happened.

'Fucking. Bastard.' Each word uttered slowly. Precisely.

A hole passed through the palm of his right hand, smaller at the front, larger at the back. His little and ring fingers were already turning blue.

Lihua knew who had shot him and that they had got the wrong target. She knew the bullet was meant for her. Either he'd run out of bullets, been apprehended or the sky had taken him. The only other option she didn't want to even consider.

Yet knew she must.

Must check he was gone or, at the very least, no longer a threat. A danger to life.

Chunhua.

Suddenly the enormity of the day was pressing on her, threatening to overwhelm her senses. She felt dizzy, felt the fingers of darkness trying to shut her down.

Chunhua. Lihua had to get back to her baby.

She slid past Nigel's body helping as best she could whilst trying to stay covered in the doorway. She eased him back to rest against the door. Something told her there wouldn't be any ambulances available to help today.

She glanced around the corner, seeking him out. He gave himself away, shouting, screaming at her from above. She saw the gun still clamped in his right hand, now no longer a threat, his arms being pinned to the sides as if he were being crucified.

Maybe there is a God after all.

Her thoughts of a divine creator responsible for all this continued to see-saw in her mind. Lihua forced her mind to stop thinking of philosophical matters. The meaning of life could wait. If she didn't get herself under control, she'd have no life to give meaning to.

Chunhua.

She had to get into the station and get her baby.

CHAPTER 19

NIGEL

The pain threatened to knock him out, but he wouldn't give in to it. Maggie spoke to him, her healing words giving him the strength to carry on. She told him he had a girl to save and a baby to find. And he could do that as long as he wasn't dead. In pain, sure. But not dead.

Nigel held his battered hand before him, grateful that it had saved his life. A hand for a head. Wasn't that a saying? He brought his hand up, able to see right through a hole in his palm.

'Fucking… Bastard,' he said in disbelief, both angry and in fear of what someone had done to him and why they had done it.

Got to keep it up, Big Bear.

Yes, blood flow. Keep it above his heart level. His watch glinted in the dim sunlight threatening to break through the clouds (and Floaters). Maybe he could use that as a tourniquet.

Chinese was now shifting behind him, helping him back against the piss-smelling door. He wanted to warn her not to put her head out there, some cunt was shooting at them, but no words would come out of his mouth. Only a line of drool. And that wasn't pretty.

He turned his hand back and forth like a patient admiring having a new arm fitted in surgery. Amazed he could still control it and repulsed at the damage done. He could see bone, sinew, tendon, muscle. And blood.

Lots of blood.

He put his head back against the door, thinking how he'd have to wash his hair as well as his hand now. Wash well too just to get the smell of piss off of him.

And then he felt his hand being taken lightly. He could barely open his eyes, pain giving way to darkness. A lady was gently holding his wrist, examining his hand.

He opened his lips, whispered.

'Maggs?'

CHAPTER 20

LIHUA

It was nearly 10am. She could read his watch clearly. Aabid was no longer a threat. She felt it, but didn't want to hang around out here too long. There may have been others with him.

Rei.

Focus. Fix Nigel, get Chunhua.

The damage was dire, yet she knew that he wouldn't die from this. Nothing vital had been hit. His only danger now was loss of blood and infection. (And the threat of the sky taking them both, of course.)

Nigel had a long line of drool forming from his lip to his jacket.

Lihua looked around for something she could use to stop the blood flow to his hand. She briefly thought of filling the hole with £50 notes, but realised that probably wouldn't work.

He muttered something. She hadn't heard him clearly. Bags?

She looked around, wondering what he may have seen. There! A plastic bag was on the floor. It didn't look too dirty or well used. Lihua ran and picked it up. A simple white plastic bag. As she did so, it momentarily flashed in and out of existence. She blinked, causing the fuzziness to clear. Perhaps she needed water. She grabbed the bag, placed it over his hand, as delicately as possible. Nigel was looking at her through half-closed eyes, a strange smile on his lips.

'Nigel? Stay awake. Please,' she urged him.

He winced as she pulled the bag over his lacerated hand, being careful of the fingers which were swelling and turning purple. Not good.

She needed something to keep the bottom of the bag tight to his wrist. Glancing around, Lihua felt the panic returning.

Calm. Be calm. Steady.

His watch.

The strap looked like it had a few more holes his large wrist would not reach. But if she could get it higher up, around the small handles of the bag, then it might just work.

She loosened the watch.

Nigel's left fist came up and caught her on the side of her face.

CHAPTER 21

NIGEL

Maggie was placing a white sheet over his hand. God bless her. He thought she was dead, but here she was in his hour of need.

It's only a scratch love, he tried to tell her.

No good, she was being stubborn as usual. He closed his eyes. Christ it hurt. He felt like his hand was the size of a car tyre and about to burst.

Got to keep it up.

His eyes flicked open again, now swaying between consciousness and the welcoming darkness looming just beyond.

Who was this? This wasn't Maggs! Some Asian guy with long hair was trying to steal his watch.

He took a deep breath, summoning his remaining strength and clenched his left fist by his side.

Bastard.

With a grunt, he brought his fist up with a swing, feeling the satisfying crack of knuckles on jaw. The Asian guy let go and fell to the floor.

Nice.

Nigel smiled. He slid down against the blue door, a padlock digging into his back. At last, he let the dark wings envelope him.

PART SIX

CHAPTER 1
JAMIE - INSIDE THE TUBE STATION

Being healthy in mind and body was supposed to prepare him to handle disruptions in his everyday life. But all of his meditative and gym training hadn't prepared him for this. He wondered if anything could have.

First, there was the Floaters to think about.

Floaters.

Wasn't that something you couldn't flush? Maybe God had decided to pull the flush on humanity and the detritus wouldn't quite go.

Then there was the woman whose head was in his lap. She looked familiar. Scars on her wrists. Blood streaks on her face. Even in her semi-conscious state her face wore a mask of distress. The lines looked deep, wrinkles forming at her eyes despite her youthful age. Jamie reckoned it wasn't only the occurrences of today that had given her much to worry about in life.

He cocked his head, trying to picture the woman without the blood streaks on her face. She looked a little like his sister. Actually, now he was thinking about it, she looked a lot like her. Like Lucy.

And for some reason the most important thing, the most biblical, was the baby. Slid to him like a puck across the floor by the cab driver.

Before they locked him out.

They.

It was always a *they*. A *them*. Maybe the government were behind this? Another atrocity to look like terrorists. Another reason for invading another foreign country and inflicting a way of life on them. All for commercial gains, of that Jamie had no doubt. He wasn't a conspiracy theorist. He preferred to think of himself as more of a conspiracy factualist. The real threat to this country wasn't from homegrown terrorists, converts or immigrants. No, the real enemy, the real *they*, were paid for and protected by the taxpayer, living the high life in their higher social circles.

The puppet masters.

He reached out and gently lifted the wrapped bundle seeing the beauty of the tiny face hidden within. He felt like crying. He didn't have a girlfriend, never felt the urge to have children of his own. Always saw them as something of a curse. An expensive curse at that. But this one, well, she was just about melting his heart.

Soppy sod.

He brushed a tear from his eye.

The area was growing increasingly crowded, people coming up from the station below, others trying to get down, to get away from here. From this hell.

From his position on the floor, he couldn't see through the shutters, just a blur of legs and feet. Had the cab driver gone? Had the mother made it in? Jamie assumed the oriental lady must be the mother.

The crowd at the shutter were growing violent. This wasn't good. He may be fit, but strength wasn't his strong point. The pun made him feel like laughing, but he couldn't bring himself to utter a sound. Part of him felt like staying here, silent, still, waiting for the others to either beat each other to death or simply leave.

Chaos hates patience.

He closed his eyes, picturing himself somewhere warm. Somewhere safe and under control. And… what was the other key ingredient his therapist had asked him to picture to retain his calm? Ah yes. Imagine he was with someone he loved.

The face of his sister flashed before him again.

Lucy.

They were inseparable. Until she met that Bastard, of course.

This wasn't good, he was feeling agitated. Thoughts ran like a reel of film, speeding past frame by frame in his mind.

Warm, safe. A beach, listening to the sea.

With a loved one. His head on Lucy's legs, her playing with his hair.

Interruption; the Bastard, smiling. Hiding the shit he really was.

Agitation. Breathing hard.

Not good.

More frames, now forcing the calmness; sunshine, suntan, ice-cream. Feeling safe. Lucy smiling at him. She loved him dearly. Protected him. Promised to never leave him after his parents-

Interruption.

He couldn't protect her. Not from the Bastard.

Interruption.

Parents. Crash. Car. Drunk driver.

Not good.

He opened his eyes, seeking solace from the chaos unfolding around him. He was back feeling as anxious as ever, the techniques to calm him, the *expensive* techniques, only adding to his emotional state. Some help that did.

Thanks Buddha.

Jamie had no idea why he blamed Buddha. His mind always connected calmness with Eastern philosophy.

Someone stepped on his fingers.

'Ouch. Don't say sorry will you!' he shouted after a set of legs, which soon blurred with the rest. He pictured a watercolour he'd seen in a gallery somewhere, greys and purples running down a canvas. They looked like legs.

The woman in his lap began to moan.

Her eyes opened softly, then closed again.

Lucy.

The roles were reversed, her head on his lap (and no beach, warmth or calmness here).

She briefly opened her eyes. Blue. Just like Lucy's.

Not good.

He gently reached and caressed the scar on her left wrist, her hands resting on her chest. Had he put them there like that? Like she was already dead? He couldn't remember. The baby was still cradled between the woman's head and his thigh. As safe as he could make her for now.

He glanced down at the tiny face again. Yes, she was a girl. And she was beautiful.

His finger traced the woman's scar, gently lifting her suit jacket sleeve back, revealing more. Covered in make-up, but there. Had she done this to herself? Or had-

The Bastard jumped back into his mind. Jamie felt he was going to bawl his eyes out. Why hadn't this been triggered in one of the endless hours of therapy? He was paying for that to happen there. But this woman, this Lucy doppelgänger, was threatening to bring it all out. Right here, right now.

Not good! Not good! Not good!

'I'm sorry…' Jamie began to sob, stroking the woman's hair from her face. 'I… couldn't protect you… Lucy…' A tear fell onto her lip. Her tongue flashed out, tasting it.

Her eyes re-opened.

She began to panic.

CHAPTER 2

BUSINESS

No, no, not again.

He was above her. She was bleeding again, could taste blood on her lips. Salty.

Blood's not salty…

No time to think. Just react. *Go for his eyes.*

She reached out a hand, claw-like nail, bright red and shimmering like a miniature knife poised to dig into the bastard's eye. Only…

It wasn't him. This guy was shocked. Alert. Sad.

'What… where… who?' The basic questions of life.

'Shush Lucy, it's OK,' Jamie said, still trying not to have a complete melt down, stroking her hair, gently touching her cheek. Despite the scratches that marked her face she was still beautiful.

'How do you know my name?' Business tried to sit up.

It was like someone had reached into his chest and put their hands around his heart and squeezed. Hard. His breath left him. Jamie suddenly wanted to be away from this woman. Was she a ghost?

'Y..y..you can't… be. You're… dead,' he was now pushing her head off his lap, the baby falling to the floor. He used his feet to scuttle further away from the ghost of his sister, wanting distance between them.

Lucy sat upright, looking around her, seeing the panic and people. She was used to seeing people rushing in London and seeing crowds. But this was different. There was death in the air. She glanced back, her eyes on the wrapped blanket.

'Oh,' an unintended squeal of surprise. She turned onto all fours. 'That's… that's the blanket the Asian girl was holding. It's a…'

'Baby girl,' Jamie finished for her.

Lucy slid her knees under her, tilting her head to one side, weeping at the sight of the innocent baby. 'Where's the mother?'

Jamie shrugged. He was still coming to terms with the fact that this wasn't his Lucy. Wasn't his sister. The face looked so similar, the mannerisms identical, but the voice? No, that was wrong.

And that was good.

Lucy looked around, checking faces, reaching out to touch a trouser leg nearby. A man turned, shock on his face, not really comprehending her. She looked back at Jamie, still not daring to pick the baby up. It looked too delicate. Too fragile. What if she might break it?

'Have you seen the mum?' she barked at Jamie.

'She was outside when they began to pull the shutters across,' he managed.

Lucy looked over her shoulder, her knees now growing numb from her position on the dirty tube station floor. She felt like a junkie.

'Did she get in in time?'

Another shrug.

'Is she even alive?'

Before he could answer, a gunshot rang out.

CHAPTER 3

JAMIE

Terrorists. Had to be.

More gunshots.

A man, screaming hysterically in a language he couldn't understand.

He was a few feet from the crowd at the shutter entrance, which dissipated on both sides when the first shot was fired.

Jamie closed his eyes, allowing his head to rest back against the wall.

Within moments, exhausted, he slept.

CHAPTER 4

AABID

He felt the shudder rip through the glass ceiling above him. The sound echoed through his body, making his teeth clench. Something had exploded and not too far from here.

Something had finally gone right on this day.

A tear fell from the corner of his eye. He watched it fall, losing it at the last moment, as it vanished into the air. Watching it fall, he thought of the Wile-E-Coyote cartoons when he fell off the cliff, vanishing into a puff of smoke as he hit the bottom of the canyon. That had made him and Ahmed laugh when they were children.

The tears began to flow.

The explosion meant one thing.

His brother was at peace.

Aabid resigned himself to his fate.

It wasn't to be as he had expected.

Within the hour he was far from the Paradise of which he had often dreamed. But he was reunited with his brother.

For life.

CHAPTER 5

JAMES

The dog hit the floor with a sound like a lump hammer hitting a joint of ham. It burst like a giant fun-shaped water-balloon, spraying blood, guts and teeth on the pavement.

James was amazed at the number of teeth that were lying around the dead dog. He tried to look up, to see who had thrown the dog from the second story window but couldn't take his eyes off of the mess at his feet.

He used the toe of his shoe to pull a tooth out of the carcass, smearing blood onto the curb. And then the worst of all; Benny's eyes lolled in his head and looked right at him.

He can't be?

The initial shock subsided and James was sure the dog was dead. The rolling eyes had been a natural reaction, the dog having died on impact. Those eyes continued to stare at James, making him feel guilty. Feel watched. Why the shame? Had he not stopped regularly and talked to Keanne? Stroked his fucking dog?

Yeah, it all looked good for the cameras though.

No, fuck that. NO! He was a good person.

He was breathing hard. His mind flashed to Gina. He'd make her bite the pillow fucking hard tonight.

Jordan tugged at his arm. The kid's voice becoming clearer as if he'd water in his ears.

'James? You with me bro? We got to get in there, yeah?'

James continued to look at the dog-mess. He imagined himself cleaning up. Isn't that what the posters say? Clean up after your dog or risk a fine?

Well, fuck that, this wasn't his dog, but Christ he felt such an urge to pick the fucking thing up with his bare hands and dump each and every part into the dog bin. Just to stop those fucking eyes staring at him.

Judging him.

In anger, James leaned forward and kicked what was left of Benny's head. More teeth scattered over the pavement, twinkling like diamonds.

I'm having a breakdown, he thought.

Jordan had backed away, alarmed and confused.

James looked up to the sky, wanting to scream, wanting to vent the anger he felt. Was this his judgement day?

It's not always about you, y'know James!

Now, who's voice was that? He didn't know. Didn't care. Just wanted the dog out of his sight. He saw bodies up there, floating above him. They were squished against the top of the building, like froth on a seashore. Litter in the corner of a park pond.

Filth.

And Keanne was up there with them.

Keanne.

Fuck! Had he seen him kick the dog? Had anyone?

His social awareness suddenly kicked back into place. He looked around him, eyes wide. Looking for the phone camera that would give him away. The footage that would soon appear online with the wrong headline; DJ Kicks Dead Dog's Head. No, worse; DJ Kicks HOMELESS Man's Dead Dog's Head. He could see the tweets below; 'I used to listen to him but always thought he was an arrogant prick.'

'Complete cunt! Let's kick his head till he's dead!'

And worse; 'DJ never to work again after PUBLIC breakdown.'

And then he imagined a reply, a tweet. Such hurt in so few words; 'I'm glad. Wish he was dead. He hurt my head too. And my heart.'

Gina.

CHAPTER 6
JORDAN

The guy was clearly having a breakdown. He'd gone from hero to zero in a matter of minutes. Granted, the falling dog had shocked Jordan, but given the nature of everything getting fucked up today, this was the least of his worries.

Jordan also thought the dog was dead before it hit the pavement which made him think twice about entering the building.

Maybe, whatever the fuck-up in the sky was, began from this building. This was the epicentre. Like an earthquake, but somehow in the air. Was that even possible?

Fuck knows.

He grabbed James' arm.

'James, you with me bro? We gotta get in there, yeah?' Although he wasn't sure they really *should* be going in there.

James relaxed and Jordan thought he had taken a moment to grieve over the dog's death. Hadn't he known the homeless guy too? Probably saw him every day. Being a big hitter, probably gave the guy the odd £20 note too. Maybe even the occasional £50 at Christmas. How the other half live-

James leaned in and kicked the dog's head as if he were taking a penalty.

Jordan jumped back. He wasn't afraid of James, years of being on the estates had made him tough. But this guy was losing it.

Jordan considered his options (he couldn't believe it had been only that morning, he'd had the same conversation with his mum, considering whether he should go to Uni or overseas to study medicine. He loved the workings of the human body. Maybe he'd become a vet after today's gift from God?); he could run back to the store. Or knock this guy out and drag him back with him. Or… go into the building, with or without James.

His legs made the decision for him.

Tugging his hood collar close (another habit from growing up on the estate) he walked into the building. His curiosity was getting the better of him.

It seemed the saying about the cat was wrong.

Curiosity killed the dog.

CHAPTER 7

JAMES

Get. A. FUCKING. Grip!

Good advice. He could always count on himself for that.

The smile returned but needed practice as it felt wrong somehow. Felt like it belonged to some other him. He felt the corner of his lips twitching.

P*laster that grin on firmly*, he told himself. *Nobody was likely to have filmed you, their cameras are all pointing at the sky. The human clouds.*

Were they - the people behind this attack - just taking the scum? The down-and-outs? Was this nature's way of cleaning out the shit? It would explain why he was still on the ground, safe and sound. Well, safe… or maybe just sound.

Or not.

He closed his eyes, breathed deeply, held it. Counted to ten. He heard footsteps alongside him, but forced his eyes to stay shut.

Control the smile, man.

It was his lifeline. If that mask cracked then it was game over. His mind would soon follow.

Eight… Nine… Ten.

He opened his eyes, purposely avoiding looking at the mess that was once Benny. Just in case those eyes came back round. Came back to judge him.

He turned; smile welded firmly in place. It felt better. Still not natural, but better. It felt strong.

Good, he was calm, he was back. Now he could deal with things.

Jordan had gone.

James glanced behind him, smiling widely at the shoppers in doorways, behind windows, staring, judging. They'd seen him kick the dog.

Shit!

'It… it was raging! It looked mental! I think it was going to attack us!' His audience wanted to hear from him. To know their hero was safe. He cleared his throat and raised his voice.

'Whatever turned that dog mad, is in that building!'

First act set. Now build the dramatic tension. Christ, he was good. Ever under pressure he was a natural. 'And… it is the reason for them being trapped up there!' he pointed to the

(scum)

Floaters.

Pregnant pause. Build the tension.

He could feel it. It felt good.

The smile was back.

Now, go for the kill.

He puffed out his chest.

'And I'm going in!'

Put that on twitter cocksuckers.

He smiled wide, half expecting them to applaud. He followed Jordan into the building.

CHAPTER 8

JORDAN

James was out in the street, now yelling something about rabies. Whatever. He didn't care. He just wanted to find out what was in this place.

The lower level was all security doors with number pads on them. He stepped lightly over the blue carpet, making his way up the stairs. He could smell cleaning products, some fake flowery scent, but there were no signs of life. The only signs were on the wall, directing him to the various businesses on each level.

JC Casey Solicitor, level one.

He stood at the top of the stairs listening. There were moans from above, Jordan unsure if it was from people trapped in the building or coming from those poor souls trapped outside in the sky.

The mere thought of their predicament made him feel like this was some bizarre dream. A trip or something.

A voice came from downstairs.

'Jordan? Listen, sorry man? I thought the dog might have attacked us or something, y'know?'

He was coming to the bottom of the stairs; Jordan could hear his footsteps.

That's right, walk loudly and shout you muppet, he thought. *Great way to sneak up on whoever, or whatever, is in here.* He felt like punching James right in the face, wiping that smarmy grin off.

Now, now Jordy. You're not likely to get into medical school with that on your record are you.

He smiled to himself. It sometimes felt like his mum was actually living in him. He even thought twice about masturbating to porn, in case she spoke up. In case she could see through his eyes. Crazy thought, but she had a hold on him. And after today's events, who knew what was possible.

And there was somebody else in his life too, besides his mum. A girlfriend? Young, pretty figure. He couldn't place her face or name, only a deep sense that he had some special relationship with her. A dependence.

James was coming up the stairs, still shouting and interrupting his thoughts.

'And so, I was just trying to save us!'

Jordan decided he wouldn't knock him out. But he would put the record straight - namely that the dog had been dead before it fell - once they were out of this building and back on the street. In the meantime, it might be handy to have an extra pair of hands.

'James, hush. It's fine man. Look, I'm up here yeah? Now keep your voice down.'

James appeared from around the top of the first flight of stairs. He was stroking the banister with his hand, as if he were about to ask who had done such a good paint job.

'Yeah, right, quiet man. Sure thing. Listen, I think we need to get up to the next level and see why Benny turned mad?'

This joker has all the lines. Jordan nodded. Agreeing was easier at this point. But there was no way he was going to let this joker lead him into who knew what.

'You lead, yeah?' Jordan played to James' weakness.

James didn't even realise, grinning broadly, convinced he was now back in the driving seat.

A sign on the wall informed them that JTW was on the second floor. The sign didn't offer any further clues to what JTW did or was.

'Maybe they're detectives?' offered James, as if reading Jordan's mind. 'Keeping a low profile and all that.' The joker was still talking. Did he not understand what SHUT THE FUCK UP meant? Jordan doubted it. The guy made a career out of talking after all.

'Y'know I will save Keanne, yeah? And you too. Trust me, I know you volunteered to help me sort this matter out yeah, but you'll be safe with me.'

Jordan walked softly, staying two stairs below James as they ascended to the second floor and the mysterious JTW business.

'Jump Through Window!' James turned, grinning. 'JTW geddit?!'

Ever the joker. Jordan forced a weak grin, becoming more and more convinced the guy was scared out of his mind. He was rambling now. Trying to act like everything was cool. This guy was a control freak.

'Benny jumped through the window.' At least he whispered that.

'He didn't. He was already dead.'

Shit. He'd said it out loud. James stopped, his back to Jordan.

There were three more steps to the top of the second floor. He saw James slowly shake his head before continuing up the stairs. Jordan let out his breath, unaware he was holding it. He held his hands out in front of him checking for trembling. Checking he was staying in control himself.

He suddenly felt dizzy. His hands appeared to vanish; one moment there, real, crystal clear. The next, gone. Then back again, as quick as a blink.

What the hell?

He was shaking, probably normal given the circumstances…

His throat was dry. When had he last had a drink?

James turned onto the second-floor corridor.

'Shit!' he screamed and ran out of sight.

CHAPTER 9

JAMES

It didn't take long to convince the kid that he had saved him from being attacked by the dog. And then, before he knew it, the kid was letting him lead again.

Fucking dunce. Probably a druggie or something.

James kept him talking, leading up the stairs. He only wished the kid was filming this, so they could later show how brave he was. He'd probably had someone film him from far off when he had attacked the dog, so guess that if the angle and distance were just right, it would back up his version of events. And then there was his speech. Someone must have recorded that. He'd be on every news channel in the UK by this evening. Fuck, even by lunchtime. He felt good. This was going to be a great day after all. Maybe he'd let Gina ride on top tonight.

And then the kid ruined his day.

'He didn't. He was already dead.'

Fucking kid. He'd now tell everyone James had lost control and kicked the fuck out of a dead dog.

James paused, considering his options. He shook his head. Decision made.

Whatever happened now, only one of them could walk out of this building alive.

CHAPTER 10
NANCY - INSIDE THE BUILDING

It was her second day on the job, answering the phones for a fledgling publishing company. James Thomas Wentworth had borrowed money from friends, raising far more than he had anticipated, in his ambition to become a publisher of adult fantasy books. His latest flirt, Xia, was away today modelling for new photos to then be illustrated for their next book. Some bondage thing. Domination and sadism. Nancy didn't know much about any of that. She'd tried to read 50 Shades but felt so disempowered by the girl in it and ashamed it was written by a woman. If she met a rich billionaire who wanted to slap her naughty bits and call her a bad girl, she'd kick him right in the bollocks. And hard.

JT, as he had asked her at the interview to address him as, wasn't anywhere near a billionaire but had that same kind of attitude. I have the money so you'd better do as I ask. Xia fell for it. Had the figure, tattoos and always dressed in such tight clinging black material that Nancy thought, one day the poor cow would actually stop breathing. Maybe that was another of their S&M routines.

Asphyxiation.

Nancy got out of breath just walking up the two flights of stairs to this love dungeon, without needing to be clamped with a black dog collar, tight around her throat (she thought Xia probably liked to be led around the office on all fours once Nancy had gone home, at her master's beck and call). The choker Nancy wore even had a metal loop in it, presumably that was where her lead went. He probably made her drink from a bowl too. Like a dog.

She shuddered.

That was one thing she simply couldn't imagine. Acting like a dog. Even being near a dog freaked her out. Always had done. One of her earliest memories was being chased by a golden retriever who had ran out of a neighbour's garden. Nancy had screamed, cried and wet herself all in one go. Her water element had simply burst, trying to vacate from any orifice.

But to put a collar on and then let some weirdo guy (whom she guaranteed had an extremely small penis) lead you around the room… what was that about? She often had to bite her tongue when Xia was in the office, giving it 'yes JT, no JT, you got it JT' and giving him a high five. What was she, some kind of slave? Women. Only had themselves to blame.

And Nancy was not a girl you could shove around. Literally, she weighed close to 15 stone. Never had a boyfriend in all of her 23 years. Never even had a kiss (except from her parents, but that was different. And no tongues).

That made her titter.

Tits.

The words were even creeping into her everyday vocabulary. She'd only been here for, what, two weeks or so? Time seemed to be a blur of late. She suddenly found herself struggling to recall what Xia looked like. She knew the name but Xia's face escaped her. Strange but true.

Must be tired, she thought.

She had to get out of this place and find another receptionist job.

The commotion outside had begun, as far as Nancy could remember, shortly after 9am. She'd come in as usual, always punctual, if the job started at 9, she'd be there at least ten minutes early. Which meant giving herself plenty of time for tube journeys (even skinny girls had a job squeezing onto early morning trains, without some perv pinching their butt and claiming it was an accident. Although, she rarely ever had them pinch hers. Just heard other girls moan about it happening. She lived in hope), and then extra time to get a double espresso (usually followed by another coffee on the hour, every hour until 5pm) and the extra few minutes to waddle her fine ass up the stairs.

She'd been ticking off lists, having done the 9am catch up with his Holiness, who sat in his own office (the only single large room on this floor) as she had to make do with the entrance vestibule of their office space, crammed behind a desk, facing the doorway. Her back to the outside world. She was aware that the desk made her look even larger than usual.

But she had to give JT one thing; he was smart. There was a lot of people out there who wanted to read more of this stuff. And the majority of their direct clients were women. Nancy didn't think she'd ever come to terms with that.

The latest paperback was on her desk and she flicked through a copy, her eyes catching the odd word here and there; butt-fuck, butt-plug (was everything butt-related in this one?), cock, cum and the usual splattering (she tittered at herself for that one - another tit! - she felt like this was going to become an illness. Porn Tourette's) of spank and wank. She flicked to a page which showed Xia, Nancy instantly recognising her face once again. Xia was a good-looking girl. Nancy had to give her that. Slim body, legs up to her armpits. But tits that belonged on the body of a twelve-year-old. Nancy had bigger ones when she was eight. She laughed again.

JT had called her from his office (no need for an intercom, he sat next door, about 3 feet as the crow flies - or as the slave-dog crawls - she thought) asking if she had read the latest copy of their published works yet. Nancy blushed feeling guilty for even looking at the book, dropping it onto her lap, almost knocking her coffee over in the process (I expect he'd have spanked me while I lapped it up like a dog, she mused). And then he'd screamed.

Nancy wondered if he had gotten his manhood caught in some kind of device he was maybe testing out for review, or just for his own sick amusement, not knowing whether to run to his aid, or stay put. The last thing she needed was to see her new boss with his trousers round his ankles and his cock in a bracket.

A bracket? She had no idea what that might even look like. She hoped she wouldn't be called on to write a review with those sort of terms-

And then JT burst into the reception, all five-foot square of it. His mouth was going up and down, his fingers jabbing at the window. Nancy slowly turned in her chair (there was no other option for her, speed wasn't her strong point) and saw a lady simply float past her office window. The lady tried to grab hold of something, anything, to stop her ascent, her nails clicked and clacked against the glass. Nancy simply stared, mouth and eyes wide open. She had time to see the lady's bright red nails, and thought they'd be good for raking the skin on a man's back and chest, feeling his curly hair part between her soft, exploring fingers…

She closed her eyes tight.

She had to get out of here.

JT leaned past her, almost pushing her out of the chair into the corner, on top of the tiny waste bin (which had suspicious tissues in it). He opened the window, reaching out to try and grab red-nail's hand. Trying to help.

Nancy simply sat and watched, her breath coming hard and slow.

Before she knew it, JT had followed the lady, falling *up* and out of the window, himself dragged by invisible arms. Nancy's response was to simply shut her eyes.

She wondered if she'd be next.

For once in her life, she was grateful for her girth. Let the force try and rip her out of this goddam chair.

CHAPTER 11

NANCY

One eye opened.

The window was still raised, giving her an uninterrupted view of the chaos outside. People were sailing into the sky, like human balloons without tether. Some were screaming, others crying. A few were simply silent, resigned to their fate.

Got to stay away from the window, she thought. *Whatever it is girl, you might have the weight to stop it from in here, but who knows if you get too close.*

JT was slim (he also showed her his well-toned arms, not purposely she supposed, but given he had a gay-guys crop top on at the interview, she guessed he had really wanted her to see) and well sculpted. Some girls liked that, but not her. She liked enough to squeeze and get lost in. Folds were fabulous.

No, this isn't right. I'm not fat. I like slim men. What's going on here?

The thought confused her.

Have to close the window.

She reached out, hand shaking, almost touching the top of the lower part of the window frame. All she had to do was slide it back into place. JT had lifted it with ease, so it mustn't be too stiff. She had a flashback to the book she had been reading but moments ago.

'There's too much cock in this place,' she said, leaning forward, both hands now on top of the frame. She slid it partway down, then it jammed.

'Shit and tits!' She'd pushed too hard on one side, causing the window to not fall straight. It was now slightly angled within the frame.

Get it up again. Another flashback to the novel. That was it, she decided she definitely had Porn-Tourette's.

She rummaged through the desk drawer and found a knife. It had a beautiful black handle, shiny, sleek. The blade was edged and looked extremely dangerous. Nancy wondered if it may have been for one of JT and Xia's after-office hours games. She stroked the knife, it felt so soft and silky in her hands. Wow, this was a real piece. She considered nicking it. Maybe using it to touch herself-

'Girl, you listen. There's shit kicking off outside, so get your (she was going to shout ass, but changed her-) mind in gear and get thinking. Or you'll be joining JT up…' she let the sentence trail off, not knowing quite where JT had gone.

She stood, angling the knife, ready to try and unjam the window in its frame.

And then her heart froze.
Behind her, a dog barked.

CHAPTER 12
JAMES

His eyes cast around the white corridor. Whoever had glossed these walls and woodwork had done a great job. It was so smooth, clearly it'd had a good sanding before applying the paint. Job's only worth doing if it's worth doing well.

A black woman stopped his thoughts. She was squatted on the floor beneath an open window. She held something in her hand. Her eyes were open but glazed over. Even from where he was stood, her eyes looked like glass.

And then he saw the light catch the object she was holding. A knife.

'Shit!'

He ran, ever the hero, towards the woman. She was a big girl and James saw what she meant to do. He couldn't let her die. He'd need a witness for the other death that was soon to happen on this floor.

And guess what, *he* was also black.

CHAPTER 13
NANCY

She'd lost time. There were no other words for how she felt. Everything seemed to be happening around her, but she wasn't part of it. As if she were viewing the world as a solitary goldfish in its bowl. Suspended in space, floating, feeling light, free. Feeling that she was no longer a part of life.

She saw the dog, she felt herself sliding back against the wall, her large thighs giving her little choice of where to move, except down into a ball. The nightmare had frozen the part of her mind that allowed her to think rationally, clearly and decisively. The animal instinct, the one she read somewhere that the Freudians called the id, took over. The dog had jumped, she had tried to protect herself (had she?) her arms covering her head. And then… well then, the dog was just gone. Not there anymore.

She felt something hit her arms (had she really?) almost taking the knife out of her hand.

Had the dog even be real? At one point she was sure the dog had flickered in and out of existence. A trick of the mind. A coping mechanism maybe.

And then… Nancy was gone too. Just gone.

A blurry figure had come into her focus, maybe a man, maybe a woman.

The light from the window and ceiling bulb cast odd shadows over Nancy, glinting off the object in her hand. Had she tried to do something? What was happening now?

She no longer cared. Couldn't bring herself aware enough to care.

The blurry figure was moving fast, coming at her. *Was he one of the fallen ones?* That felt wrong somehow. Had he been rising instead, toward the sky? If so, how did he get here? Was he dangerous?

She heard herself trying to call herself forward, trying to bring her very being back to the forefront. If this guy meant danger, she needed to protect herself. Or maybe just resign to the fact that her time was up?

A small voice inside burst forth, echoing around her mind the regret that she hadn't tried in some way to live a more courageous life. A life perhaps like Xia had. Maybe she should have tried to live more…

CHAPTER 14
JAMES

…Dangerous.

The woman looked dangerous. Something about the look in her eyes, it was like she was possessed, a ghost living within the shell of a woman. He was at her feet now, aware that Jordan was close behind. But now he'd got here, he had no idea what to do next.

What if she suddenly lashed out at him? He was aware of his angles, knowing Jordan wouldn't be able to see clearly past his body, blocking most of the view.

He could shape this story too.

Shit, had she killed Benny?

Her eyes rolled and she appeared to be swimming in and out of consciousness.

Don't look at me like that, he thought.

He felt that urge again, that rising anger. Felt like kicking her eyes into the back of her head too.

Outside the window he could hear moaning coming from the Floaters and commotion below from those hiding in doorways, crouching under trees, huddling together, not wishing to be dragged up, or miss the spectacular events unfolding before their eyes.

He wished he had an audience to see his next part in the play.

In the James Whitbourne Show.

The knife, get the knife.

He leaned over, gently putting out his hand, his best smile now firmly plastered in place. His eyes twinkled. He closed in on her fist, aware he was trembling ever so slightly. Just one more inch and the knife would be his, slipping easily from her grasp.

CHAPTER 15
NANCY

She tried to focus, seeing the blurry figure of a man, definitely a man, leaning over her. He kept flashing his teeth, although she was barely able to register the image, lost as she was. Did he mean her harm? Had he been a dog a few moments ago?

The man leaned closer and then he fell, impaling himself on the knife.

Snapped from her trance, Nancy began to scream.

CHAPTER 16
JORDAN

James was fucking clever. Jordan had to give him that. No audience, but by Christ he'd put on a great show, even sacrificing himself to get the most out of it. The bad news for James was that Jordan was not born yesterday.

And he had a good working knowledge of the human body.

He'd sprinted up the steps, after James vanished out of view along the corridor, half expecting to be involved in some kind of fist fight. But then James was too cowardly to run headlong into that kind of action. So, Jordan had reached the top of the corridor, only to see nobody but James moving slowly toward an open window. Jordan could see a desk and something, a pile of bags or… he shifted, putting his head to the corridor wall, like he was trying to listen to the neighbours.

Not bags, but clothes.

It was a woman.

She was squatted down, but Jordan couldn't make out anything else, James was shielding her from his view.

Jordan ran closer, calling James' name.

'Who is it, James? Is she OK?'

James glanced back over his shoulder, muttered something and then Jordan was sure he saw him smile. Almost a smirk. Fuck you, it said.

Before Jordan could reach him, James staggered forward and fell onto the woman.

Then all hell broke loose.

CHAPTER 17

JAMES

He knew he was a coward, knew that he wouldn't really be able to murder Jordan. In his heart of hearts, he was a nice guy really. Always believed that. And then an idea struck him. One so wicked that he couldn't help but grin. He didn't have to murder the kid. Someone else would do it for him. After all, Gina's old man was seriously connected and if he knew that some black hooded kid had caused his daughter to almost lose her man, then he'd move Heaven and Earth to get the little bastard who had done it.

James knew he had seconds to decide. The woman was near comatose, so that was good. She'd remember diddly-squat. He scanned through his body in his mind's-eye, checking off the vital organs. The knife looked sharp, so he'd better stay away from the biggies. Don't want to puncture a fucking lung when trying to frame a nobody. Christ, he was going to be the ultimate hero after today. Saving not only a highly vulnerable black woman from attack, maybe even a rape, but also taking one for the team in the process. The sympathy they would afford him would be overwhelming.

He made a mental note to practice the tears in front of the mirror in the coming days, make them as sincere and as powerful as the award-winning smile.

He leaned slightly to one side, hearing Jordan approaching from behind, calling out.

He had probably 3 or 4 seconds now.

'Who is it, James? Is she OK?'

Three…

He glanced back over his shoulder wanting to make sure the kid was real close.

Two…

Yep, there he was. James couldn't resist a smile. This had worked out perfectly.

One…

James twisted slightly as he fell onto the upturned knife. He felt a sharp and intense pain in his upper shoulder, realising he'd almost missed landing on the fucking thing in his attempt to not hit any major organ. But the pain felt like this would be enough for his purpose.

Oh, and beige trousers! How that would work in his favour. Blood on beige would show up excellently.

As he felt the blade slide in, like a hot knife through butter, he rolled over, taking the blade with him. The woman began to scream, coming out of her coma.

It all added to the idea he hoped was forming in the minds of his audience waiting outside below. He would convince them, just had to stay aware and make sure all of the pieces fitted the timeline.

This was manslaughter.

And then Jordan came forward and added an extra gift for James, making the pieces of the jigsaw fit perfectly. Better than he could have imagined.

The kid grabbed the handle of the blade, adding his fingerprints to the story.

Perfect.

This was turning out to be his best day ever.

CHAPTER 18

JORDAN

He knew James was up to something. Knew it from when they first met back in the Tesco Express. James hadn't liked the way Jordan had encroached on his space. Jordan felt it. And then, when Jordan had volunteered to go after the homeless guy, the DJ had hated that. Jordan could see through his plastic smile, no problem.

The guy was full of shit.

And he was now trying to get even.

Jordan dragged James off of the woman, quickly assessing the situation. She was near hysterical. Blood was spurting from James' shoulder, the woman already covered in blood. Had she harmed herself?

Jordan's mind tried to put the pieces together in the correct order, aware that James was perhaps planning a different series of events.

The woman was here, the dog came up. She must have somehow attacked the dog, hence the blood over her. And then… just fainted? A possibility.

'You… you pushed me! You fucker!' James was breathing harshly; the accusation already being levelled his way. Jordan knew to stay quiet, knew his plan.

He grabbed the butt of the knife, already convinced the blade was well away from the top of James' right lung. It had gone through several layers of muscle, but nothing that wouldn't be healed with an operation. The blood loss was significant but not life threatening.

Man, the fucker had done a good one.

'You've been lucky. No major damage. Leave the blade in until we get outside.'

James' face was a masterpiece in acting. He looked at Jordan with incredulity, wide eyes, strained tendons in his jaw and neck.

'You… you… get away from me!' Jordan realised James' neck was being strained as he had cocked his head to allow his shouting to be heard outside, through the open window.

Clever bastard.

'James listen, you're confused. And also, there's so much shit happening today that the chance of an ambulance is, well, I'd say pretty slim. You're lucky, I'm studying to be a doctor. A surgeon actually. And this isn't life threatening. You'll be fine. Just keep it still.'

James hadn't expected Jordan's calm, calculated response.

The woman had stopped screaming and was simply looking at them with wide eyes.

Thinking he'd foiled James' plan; Jordan hadn't expected what happened next.

CHAPTER 19

JAMES

The pain was amazing. He thought he may pass out. That was what he had expected. He caught himself actually enjoying this in his own sick way. And the pain was feeding him, keeping him alert and aware.

Good.

But then Jordan began to talk. He couldn't believe the kid's attitude. No fear. No anger. And what was this? Claiming to be a med student?

Bollocks! There was no way a hooded druggy like him was going to be a surgeon. Utter shit. James thought the kid might have a knife or two of his own on him.

And that could make matters a lot worse.

He stared into Jordan's eyes, saw there *was* fear there. And that was good. So, the kid might be just smart enough to realise he'd better play this well or he could be in deep shit. And there goes any chance of med school if the little fucker was telling the truth.

The woman had stopped screaming, another good sign. She'd be his only witness.

Jordan had given James the final bit of knowledge he needed, to make the attack totally convincing. Jordan had advised him to keep it still.

James, always knowing best, grabbed the handle.

'No, don't pull it out!' James yelled, purposely tilting his head so his words would carry on the air to the ears below.

James grabbed the handle and yanked it free.

The pain went to the next level.

And then, he passed out.

CHAPTER 20

NANCY

This was all she needed. Only a fortnight into the new job and her boss had been taken up by aliens and two weirdos were now in her office taking their gay bondage shit to the next level of downright queerness.

There was blood everywhere. This was masochism on another level.

Nancy was aware that she had been here for a while, squatting on the floor. Her butt and legs felt numb. She had no idea how she'd get up.

Just need to stay away from that window.

Her only other way out was blocked by these two guys.

She had definitely had enough of this job, all this porn, sleaze and now this! But then one of them said something. Was it the hooded guy? *Did he just say he was a medical student?* No, the other guy had been attacked, so that didn't make any sense.

Just need to get out.

But maybe that wasn't such a good idea. Who knew what was happening out there? She was stuck between a wall and a head-case.

The stabbed guy screamed, the knife now on the floor (was that her knife? Had she gotten that for something?) and there was blood spurting everywhere.

Fucking weirdoes.

CHAPTER 21

JORDAN

He'd done it. The dopey prick had actually done it.

Jordan had given himself the sound advice at the outset; don't speak. But now he'd given James the leverage he needed to make this really serious. The guy would bleed to death unless Jordan sorted it.

Man, the Oath. He'd try to save James despite him being a mean, cruel, egotistical prick.

Jordan took off his hoody, pressing it to the wound.

'Your name?' he asked the woman. Man, she was a size. He wondered if he'd be dealing with a heart attack victim next.

She stared back at him, *through* him. James was gurgling beneath him, his body starting to convulse.

'Listen, my name is Jordan. I'm here to help. Do you have a phone?' He spoke each word softly, confidently. Slowly. The woman appeared to be letting each word sink in, nodding at each syllable. Jordan wondered if she understood English. He was about to repeat the question when she spoke.

'Nancy. Yes. Desk.'

'Good, well, nice to meet you, Nancy. Please call 999.'

Nancy burst out laughing. And that seemed to give her energy. At last.

'Really? Look mister, my boss just fell ass-upwards outta this 'ere goddam window. And you two rent boys or whatever you are, have come waltzing in here playing your fuckin' weird sex games. Well, I didn't sign up for this, so I'm gonna go now and you can both sort your own shit out. Ya hear me?'

The woman was shouting now.

'Listen, Nancy,' Jordan tried a calming smile, 'there's no weirdness going on inside this building. Outside, yeah sure. But this guy, he asked me to come in and help save the homeless guy, and probably your boss too, who are stuck on…' Jordan paused trying to comprehend the words he was about to speak, hoping he didn't convince himself that he sounded crazy, '… sort of, around the outside of the roof. They're on the outside, but if we can get up there, we can get the windows open…'

'No more dogs!' the woman brought her massive thighs up to her equally large bosom and hugged her knees, head falling into her arms. Jordan thought she looked like a ninja sumo warrior, curled up ready to spring upwards and attack. If that was even possible. Given the events so far today, he was starting to believe anything was.

'No, Nancy. No more dogs.' Slow, like speaking to a child. He had to move fast or James was going to die.

Then let him.

The thought shocked him, made his heart skip a beat. He could never do that. That would be giving James exactly what he wanted. No, he wanted the bastard to live, to face the consequences of his actions.

Slippery fucker.

'Please, call 999. Please.' Jordan pleaded with his eyes.

Nancy took a deep breath and then reached out without looking to the desk top. He could see her hand tapping around, searching without sight. She spilt a cup of coffee, the smell strong but welcome. It was getting stuffy in here, even with the window open. And then she grabbed the phone. Mobile. Good.

Nancy brought it slowly down into her lap. Her hands were shaking but she appeared to be getting herself composed.

'Shit flaps! No signal.'

'What?'

She turned the phone shoving the screen to his face. No signal.

Blackout. They'd caused a blackout, due to what was happening, he guessed.

'Do you have um… a landline?'

Nancy simply laughed at that. It was all the answer he needed. Nobody had a landline these days. Jordan thought people would soon re-install one after today's events had worn off. Landlines don't lose signal.

'We've got to move him or he's going to die.'

Nancy appeared to consider this.

'Chuck him out the window,' she giggled.

Jordan realised he was more or less on his own.

'Is there anybody else in the building?'

'Only downstairs. The upper floors are empty. Some accountancy firm went bust JT told me.'

Jordan had no idea who she was talking about and didn't care. He needed more people to help.

'Xia might be back soon. She'll be slut modelling somewhere local.'

Another bit of pointless waffle.

'Alright, I'll leave him here. You need to keep the pressure on the wound. Push down hard.'

'I'll sit on the bastard,' she giggled.

Jordan shook his head, wondering if she were serious. 'No, look, just pressure. Stop the blood flow. I'm going to go downstairs and see if I can find someone to help me move him. He needs blood.'

Jordan took Nancy's hand and put it on the hoody, encouraging her to push down hard.

'You can't do him any harm pushing down hard there, OK?'

'What if he wakes up?'

Jordan looked in her eyes.

Do I know you?

'He won't.'

He stood, holding onto the edge of the desk, dizziness creeping over him. For a fraction of a second, he felt the world around him ripping apart at the seams. He heard distant voices. And in a heartbeat, the feeling passed.

Once steadied, he ran back along the corridor.

CHAPTER 22

JORDAN

He took the stairs three at a time, the final six in one leap, holding on to the banister for support. A memory of a man teaching him this when he was a boy. The man's face flashed out of focus, perhaps just the remnants of a dream. Jordan made a mental note to maybe broach the subject with his mum when… if… this nightmare ever ended.

And if he were still alive.

Scratch marks on the wall at home, running down the stairs, a broken banister clip. All tiny details that backed up the memory. Had it been his father? That was one subject his mother would not broach. Ever.

The glass front door was facing him, nobody on the street outside. He lunged at the handle, pulled but the door would not open. *Must be push.* Still no give.

'What the…?'

He looked left and right searching for a door release button. He had used them in his mate's block of flats. His hands slapped bare walls, nothing helping him. He glanced up; a security camera. Good. Really good. Fucking excellent in fact.

He hoped James hadn't realised that his entire act of sabotage might have been recorded.

That'll teach that smarmy prick.

Although, if Jordan didn't act fast and get him some help, then there'd be no James to answer for his stupidity.

You never mind about that white guy my boy, you hear me? You came in here to do good and good you will do. There are people up on the top floors outside the window that need your help. And they need it now. So, you shift your whining ass!

It was like his mum was standing next to him, he even looked round half expecting her to be there.

She was right. He came to help. He had to get upstairs.

He leapt up the stairs, pausing on the second floor to shout out to Nancy and see how she was doing.

'Still breathing,' came her reply. Followed by 'I guess.'

He ran up the next set of stairs, another short corridor. Nobody around. Another flight hid behind the corridor's dividing wall. Each floor being a mirror of the one beneath.

He bolted up the next flight, his heart hammering hard, knowing every second counted. James would bleed to death soon. He was torn between getting him help or helping those he had originally come in for.

The homeless guy.

Jordan reflected how the guy had lost his dog now too. If there was a God then he was a mean-spirited bastard. Maybe the homeless guy had fucked someone over in a past life.

Or in this life.

A fire door, locked, stood at the top of the stairs, making the decision for him.

CHAPTER 23
NANCY

She had called out after him but didn't want to raise her voice too much in case that somehow affected the guy bleeding beneath her.

'The fire door will be locked! You need the key…' Too late, he was already hurdling up the stairs. Nancy could feel the vibrations of his feet on each step. Then he was above her running along the corridor. She considered leaving the bleeding guy, getting off of her ass and getting the key from JT's office. Every office space had a key. Although Nancy was pretty sure locking a fire door was illegal. Hadn't a ton of poor folk died in a factory somewhere in India because a fire broke out and the doors were locked?

She glanced up, the fire alarm and sprinkler system safely blinking their respective red and green lights above her head.

'Nah, he'll realise and be down just as fast. Although…' she glanced at James' face, turning a pale blue. 'This guy might not have much longer.'

Having a person die on her didn't fill her with the dread she thought it might. Not that she had ever considered it until now. Death and bondage were closely linked it seemed and something told her that if she got out of this alive, she should do something good. Something she could talk about. Something she'd *want* to talk about. And be proud of. Funny, she'd been there a couple of weeks and already it felt like a lifetime.

A lifetime. What was that really? The guy beneath her was abruptly ending his and she was powerless to help.

Maybe I could give him the kiss of life?

She felt repulsed at that. It was too close to S&M again for her tastes.

She turned her eyes to the ceiling, closing them, praying to a God she had never believed in to help her through this.

In her arms, James' body shimmered.

CHAPTER 24

JORDAN

He could try kicking it, but the chances-

A shadow passed by changing the light.

'Shit! They're at this level!' He ran into the big room at the front of the building, seeing feet, hands and clothing dangling just beyond the top of the window frames. The sea of people was easily in his reach, he just needed to get the window open.

A screeching sound came, like metal on glass, maybe someone's key chain dangling down. He unlatched the window, these being older sash frames. He yanked the lower half up. Taking a breath, he leaned out.

A hand grabbed him by the collar and pulled.

CHAPTER 25

NANCY

I can't leave them like this. I can help. Sure, I can. I may be big, but this beauty knows how to act.

She opened her eyes.

The blood was congealing around the wound. She didn't know if that was good or bad. At least she could let go.

She gently lowered James' head to the carpet, taking her back-support cushion off of her desk chair and then lifting his head to raise it slightly. She checked his mouth, something in the back of her mind about people swallowing their tongues. He was still breathing, shallowly. She had an urge to take her vanity mirror from her handbag and hold it under his nose just to make sure he was still with her.

Not usually one to move fast, Nancy finally began her New Year's Resolution, albeit three weeks too late, and ran into JT's office. She grabbed the fire door key from the inside door of a cupboard and then smacked herself hard on the forehead with the palm of her hand.

The First Aid box.

Now, why hadn't she thought of that?!

'Might have something to do with a dying guy laid in your lap, honey,' she told herself.

She took the box, placing it next to James, not knowing what, or if, there was anything in it she could apply to help him right now.

No, go get the medical guy.

Sticking a plaster over a knife wound would probably get her put inside a mental institute more than anything else.

She felt an overwhelming desire to laugh at that, but restrained it, somehow feeling it unfair to the dying guy.

She fled from the room, breath coming hard and tackled the next flight of stairs.

'Jordan,' she tried but her breath stuck in her throat.

Don't you die girl, you hear me?

She grabbed her throat with both hands, feeling mucus rush into her windpipe. She blinked twice and, realising she couldn't do both shouting and running, went back to heaving her ass up the stairs into the large office.

A pair of legs and a hand holding onto the inner window seal greeted her.

'Jor-'

She lunged forward and part dived, part fell onto Jordan's legs, hugging them with all of her strength. Grateful again of her weight.

CHAPTER 26
JORDAN

The hand was strong. It came so fast, as if the body it belonged to was expecting him to lean out right there and then. He was almost taken off his feet. Two things occurred to him in that fleeting moment, before his natural survival instinct kicked in; one, life was fragile and two, he wasn't going to go up with the others. All he felt was gravity, his weight shifting. His other hand darted out and grabbed the window-seal with full force. He felt his weight shifting into his torso, felt himself beginning to topple out of the window.

And then he felt pain as his knees cracked into the old radiator beneath the window. Something had rammed him from behind and hard. The weight shifted back, the hand grabbing him from outside the window releasing its grip, a fingernail being ripped off in the process. Feeling faint, Jordan fell back into the room and landed on something soft.

CHAPTER 27

NANCY

Two guys rolling on her in one day. She didn't know whether to laugh or cry.

Jordan had spilled back on top of her, bending at the knees, using her like a human bean bag.

'Get off me, man! As long as you're inside, get… off!' Her words were muffled due to her chin being forced down; her mouth full of her clothing. Whether he understood or not Jordan rolled to the side, awkwardly, his legs coming free of Nancy's huge arms.

He lay on his back, his breath coming hard, eyes to the ceiling.

Nancy uncurled, making a promise to herself that that was enough exercise for one day.

Breathlessly Jordan said, 'We need a mirror.'

CHAPTER 28

JORDAN

He'd hear people say it, your life flashes before your eyes.

That wasn't true in his case. What he had seen was the pavement below and then a blueish tinge around the bodies stuck to the sky. But the faces… they weren't human anymore. They seem to shift, to move… to *squirm.* Like many ghosts running underneath the human face. He felt nauseated, eyes tight shut trying to control the desire to be sick. The faces formed a montage in his mind, blurring, running one into the other.

'They're more than one person,' he found himself saying. It made little sense to him.

Jordan was aware that if he could handle the sickness, then he would gradually have time to work these things through when this was all over. For now, all he knew was what he saw. What he felt he saw. Those people up there, they weren't just people anymore.

And he wanted a better look.

This time without the risk of losing his life.

'We need a mirror.'

'I've got a compact in my handbag.'

He turned his head, feeling the sickness settling. Laying on the carpet was good. Just one more moment. He needed rest.

Eyes tight shut once more. Yes, he could have died. Seeing those bodies, that face, made Jordan once again promise himself that if he were to die this day it would be through falling down. Hitting the pavement. A quick death. Game over.

Going up was madness.

Utter madness.

CHAPTER 29

NANCY

She had one, of course she did. But it meant more exercise. More stairs. And going back down to the other guy. The bleeding one. He might even be dead by now.

Nancy already felt sick in her stomach, what with the events unfolding around her. And the exercise, of course. That didn't help. Up and down these stairs was like being on a treadmill.

'Fuck that. I 'aint no gym-bunny,' she told herself.

Jordan was glancing at her, then closed his eyes again.

He'll be just fine, she thought.

It looked like she was on her own to get the mirror. What had ever happened to chivalry? She thought back to the books she was actively now being an ambassador of in this weird publishing house. No chivalry there. Just bull whips and cock straps.

She wasn't even totally sure what a cock strap was. Or if it even existed.

'I have got to get out of here,' she said, struggling to her feet. That was effort in itself. First one arm, locking the elbow, hand planted firmly. Then onto one knee. Then two knees and then… well, then came the Big Push. She had to throw herself upwards, massive chest shifting with her and, as if that wasn't embarrassing enough, she often had the fear - the utter horror - of farting right at that moment. The icing on the cake. And in front of this kinda cool dude too. That would really piss her off.

She lunged up; grateful Jordan still had his eyes shut tight. Still trying to deal with his own issues. What had he seen out there? He came back in looking like a ghost.

'You sit there honey, I'll go get your mirror, yeah?' Sarcasm wasn't going to help anybody today and she immediately regretted her tone.

Do a good deed girl, go get the mirror.

Wise words. Probably not hers.

Nancy re-traced her steps back down the corridor, down to her floor. Hark at her, her floor! She'd only been there a few weeks and already had decided this job was done. D.O.N.-

She turned at the bottom of the stairs and her thoughts stopped dead.

The body, the bleeding guy, was gone.

CHAPTER 30

JAMES

His eyes fluttered open, just to see the massive rump of the mad cow with the knife lumber away.

Great, everyone's leaving me, bunch of heroes that lot are.

He felt like calling out after them but didn't have the energy. All he knew was he had put considerable expense into this little stunt, which had now become possibly life-threatening. He had to get his reward for the effort he had gone too. He had to win.

That was what it was all about. Always was.

Always will be.

The smile, the ambition, the awards. It was all about winning. Even down to Gina, he had to win her over. And then her parents - them being loaded was a bonus bit of information he discovered at the time of his first shag with her. They had to be won over.

And now he was in danger of losing.

And that wouldn't do. Ever.

He rolled, pushing himself with his legs against the wall, trying to sit upright. His shoulder hurt like a bastard. Someone would pay.

He saw his clothes matted with blood. Seeing the amount of it all over him, on the carpet, everywhere it seemed, had caused a mild panic to rise in his chest. He didn't have the effort to control it. If his body wanted to panic then so be it. He was on autopilot now.

With strength he didn't know he possessed, James struggled up the wall, bringing himself to an upright position of sorts. He took a moment, head spinning, eyes blurring everything in sight. He had the beginnings of a massive headache.

This was shit.

His beige trousers were now a dark brown. He had to make it clear he was bleeding having been stabbed by a black kid while trying to save a lady in danger and save a homeless floating guy. Had to make it clear that he hadn't shat himself. That wouldn't make for any good PR, smile or no smile.

Thinking was good. It kept him occupied, kept the pain at bay.

He stumbled along the corridor, hearing shouts from upstairs, Christ only knew what they were up to. He suddenly found himself hoping that the black kid - what was his name? Josh? Who cares! - Hadn't been able to rescue the floating guys. That wouldn't work well with his own story.

Got to be quick, before he can do any good and steal the limelight.

Got to win!

James almost fell down the first flight of stairs, oddly conscious to get as much blood as possible on the glorious paintwork he had so admired on the way up. It would all look good for his story. They may even leave it for others to see. The hero's last trip.

Last trip? Fuck that, he wasn't going down here. Not now. Not like this.

Fuck. That.

Now at the bottom, breathe wheezing in his chest, feeling light. Oddly light. He reflected that it couldn't be a spiritual feeling. He didn't believe any of that crap. No, this was just light-headedness, the result of losing several pints of blood now on the floor upstairs. Enough to make anyone considerably lighter.

A glass door stood between him and the outside world.

That was open when we came in.

James suddenly felt a little more aware. A little more alert. Was someone down here? He glanced around aware he was now maybe minutes from actually passing out. Or even dying.

No. Get to the door.

Each word in his mind taking effort to form as if his consciousness was dying with him.

You're. Not. Dying.

He had reached the door. He looked for the handle. There wasn't one. His eyes began to dart to the walls, seeking a switch. Something, anything. An axe to break the fucking thing down with. A creeping realisation began to take over. This was it after all. He was trapped.

And he was dying.

Outside he could see the dead body of Benny, the dog with the blaming eyes. James began to cry, hot tears falling onto his damp, sticky clothes. He was dying.

And nobody was there to see him.

****

On the pavement outside, what remained of Benny the dog flickered in and out, like a strobe lighting effect and then was gone.

CHAPTER 31

JORDAN

His eyes open. This was the wrong floor. He needed to be far away from those… things… up there in the sky. Best get down to the next floor, then lean out with the mirror. Maybe that would help him.

Help him do what? He didn't have an answer for that. He didn't like this situation. He wanted it all to stop.

Got to stand up.

Got to stand up.

Got to stand up!

He dragged himself upright, the sudden change in position pushing vomit up into his throat. He could taste it. Metallic. He gulped it back down, feeling a burning sensation in his windpipe.

What a day.

He stood slowly, breathing in on the way up, something his first aid training had taught him. Stops the brain from being starved of oxygen. Therefore, less likely to faint.

Jordan steadied himself, seeking his centre, composed for what may now lie ahead. He didn't want to look out at those floating faces ever again. He thought that image he had seen would haunt him forever. He'd never escape it.

Jordan had a wave of anxiety rush over him. He'd never felt anything like it before. It was as if his very soul wanted to burst from his body. He suddenly felt trapped inside his own skin. He turned back and looked at the window.

Just end it. Just jump.

Jordan had never felt suicidal, hadn't even considered it as an option at any time. He'd heard of people doing it, didn't know anyone who had. But this feeling. He couldn't tolerate it. He just had to go. End it now.

No. He needed to take a stand. To stand up for what he believed in. He was being tested.

Get away from the window. Get down, away from the sky.

A tiny voice struggled to be heard, his anxiety levels rising fast. Jordan was aware of himself being his own worst enemy. Felt himself urging him to end it all, break free from his mortal prison.

Inside this building, this room, he felt like he was trapped in a glass box, everything seemed unreal.

He wanted to break free.

What the fuck?

With incredible will-power Jordan turned, roared and ran back along the corridor, descending the stairs three, four at a time. With each fall he felt the feeling retreating.

By the time he reached Nancy, who was looking at him in mild amusement like he was a sideshow carnival freak, he felt relatively calm again.

And in control.

'You OK honey?' she said.

CHAPTER 32

NANCY

Well, fuck only knows where that one's gone, she told herself. *Maybe those creepy floaty fuckers have taken him up to their Mother-fuckin-ship or something.*

That had made her laugh.

(Titter)

She rolled her eyes, letting the Porn-Tourette's flow in her mind.

Mirror. That was what she was now after.

She grabbed her handbag from the coat rack, grateful she'd hung it up given the blood all over the carpet. She had tried to step around it, but her office was smaller than most disabled toilets she'd ever seen (*hey man, size is a disability right!*) but gave up when it looked like it would involve more exercise. Instead, she'd just trodden through it. In some ways she was glad she was making the little office dirty. Peddling those books was dirty business, so this was giving JT a taste of his own medicine.

Dirty little fucker.

'Clean that lot up you sick mutha,' she laughed again. From above her Jordan let out a primal scream and came hurtling down the stairs.

Great, she thought, *seems like more exercise is coming girl.*

CHAPTER 33

JORDAN

He stopped short, collecting his breath and thoughts, feeling the suicidal urge leave him like an evil spirit lifting away over his head.

'Don't… go…' he gulped, finding it hard to breathe and talk. His finger pointed to the ceiling. Nancy nodded. She understood him.

Jordan looked down at the carpet. Another point. Where?

Nancy shrugged and continued to rummage in her handbag. 'Maybe he jumped,' she said, gesturing with her thumb over her shoulder to the window behind her.

Jordan dived past her, about to lean out and then stopped. No, that wasn't safe. Not after what he'd just been through. They may take him again. Or that feeling… that feeling…

(The need to stand… stand up!)

He turned, saw Nancy unbelievably doing her make-up in the mirror and snatched it from her hand.

'Lip gloss! Really?' he managed. She frowned but stayed quiet. He looked at himself in the small compact mirror, sensing her about to give him what-for now that he was checking his appearance out.

'I'm looking for…' he didn't know how to finish. He was going to say himself. That he was looking to make sure he, his very self (or what he assumed that to be) was still there. And not some ghost behind the surface. Lurking. Waiting to possess him of that feeling again. He shuddered.

'Yeah, I'd shudder too if I had a mug like yours,' Nancy teased.

Jordan looked back at her and smiled.

Once again, he had a strong feeling that he knew Nancy. Or she reminded him of someone in his life. Someone important. Similar personality. But slimmer. Much slimmer.

CHAPTER 34

JAMES

His head had smacked against the door, as he crumbled down, collapsing in a pile at its base.

Human doorstop.

His breath was fogging the glass, spreading out. Each breath producing less vapour. The small circle of breath on the glass was shrinking, James watching his life ebbing slowly away before his eyes. *This is what it feels like,* he thought. *This is what it looks like.*

I'm seeing myself die.

Not long now.

The circle of breath hardly there, maybe bigger than a coin. James noticed it had an odd tint. Almost blue.

A loud noise, followed by a scream came from somewhere overhead. Or maybe it was behind him? He was vaguely aware.

Then came the gunshot that didn't kill him, but shattered the glass over him, a million shards of icicle rain.

CHAPTER 35

JARED - NOW

He could only deal with one problem at a time.

His training had made events fall into an order. Those in the sky he filed under category 'fucking weird, maybe terror-related. Deal with that once the threat has been substantiated.' For now, the answer to what was happening overhead was somewhere near him. At street level. Maybe in one of the many windows staring at him like square glass eyes all around.

(Squares. Glass boxes… why did that seem familiar?)

He felt the comforting hardness of his gun tucked into the waistband of his jeans. Off duty, not really allowed to be carrying, but today wasn't a normal day. So, he'd taken it with him as he left the house. His radio he'd left behind, regretting it once the scale of the problem became clear. Or clearer. He still actually had no idea quite how big a problem this attack was.

Or even if it was an attack.

For now, he treated it as one.

People were screaming, shouting, huddling together, making the usual London crowds look even more hectic, such was the rush for safety under any shelter. Away from the force dragging people into the sky.

Jared had been hiding in one of those doorways himself, like a smoker on a routine 10am break, when all hell had broken loose around him. As fast as people were trying to get into buildings, others were trying to get out. There seemed to be a mixture of reactions. Fight or flight. Those inside were perhaps re-living visions of 9-11 and wanted to be out of the buildings, fearing they may collapse. Others outside, seeing the hands of God take many into the sky, wanted to be inside.

And for Jared the feeling was worse. He didn't ever take the flight option. But fight was impossible if you didn't know who (or what) you were fighting against.

Jared had edged himself out of the doorway, unable to focus, not wanting to bring attention to himself in all of this panic. One, people may look to him for answers. Two, people may think he is responsible. Especially if he draws his weapon.

And the paperwork for doing so? He didn't even want to consider that.

He could see himself standing in the dock, but part of him felt that, after today, things weren't going to be quite the same as they once were.

Things were changing today.

Was it the Mayans who had predicted this? Was this the End of Days?

All he knew was he had to help, had to make sense of this.

His chance came when he saw a guy, bleeding heavily, trapped inside a building.

The guy stumbled, seeming to consider if he should step outside of the building or not. And then he had collapsed by the glass door.

Jared always tried to see their eyes. He prided himself of knowing whether they were a genuine threat, what he called a 'Class A' or not, just by seeing their eyes. Seeing *into* them.

The guy trapped behind the glass door had caught Jared's eyes, just for the briefest of moments and Jared saw fear there. Absolute fear. Whatever had happened to him, had taken place within that building and he was trying to escape from it.

And then Jared saw what may have been his first Class A of the day. Stood by a half-opened window on the second floor. A black guy. A glinting object in his hand.

Jared's eyes had already clocked other parts of this story; he thought he'd seen some kind of thing, maybe a dog (although given the blood around it was hard to tell) on the pavement under the same window but whatever it had been was now gone. And another person - maybe a suspect - in the room with the black guy.

Jared's mind processed everything with incredible speed, he was already running, no concern for his own safety, drawing his gun in mid run. He'd have one shot and it had to be not only accurate in its precision, but also in his judgement.

The pieces seemed to fit; dead person, maybe animal on pavement beneath window (*where had it gone?*), bleeding person trapped inside front door of office block and a pair of suspects, maybe terrorists, on second floor. A glinting object in the guy's hand.

Jared felt eyes looking at him as he moved, softly, almost without sound (but with the chaos all around him, he couldn't judge how quietly he was actually moving), scared faces in hidden doorways, others at the windows of their offices. Coffee shops crammed with humans, like some kind of modern-day concentration camp.

He raised the gun, aimed and made his split-second decision.

INTERLUDE

A human life.

An amazing creation, coming from nothing and ultimately, becoming nothing. Yet between those periods of non-existence lay everything. Between those first and final breaths lay meaning. Between those moments, the blink of an eye in the scope of space and time, lay all we can ever know, all we can ever be, to make sense of the gift of being.

And, like the extinguishing of a candle flame, the light of life can be taken from a human in the briefest moment.

CHAPTER 36

JORDAN

Nancy had given him the mirror almost reluctantly.

Jordan took a moment to consider his own reflection, searching his face for an inner strength, hoping - praying - to see it there in his eyes. But more than that. He hoped to feel it.

A breath. Drawn in long, eyes closing. Seeking strength. Whatever lay outside that window was too far up to have any reach, any pull on him, from down here.

He put his arm out holding the mirror, head titled back, trying to get the best angle before attempting to put his head into the outside world.

Just in case.

CHAPTER 37

JARED

Whatever the guy was holding was now being pointed out of the window.

He had to act.

One moment there was a man in the window.

The next there wasn't.

Jared had extinguished another light.

****

The next bullet shattered the glass door, Jared shooting with perfect aim, still in mid-run at the door's weak spot in the top corner. The guy behind was covered in glass, but Jared had leapt through as the glass fell, trying to shield the guy from as much of the falling shards as possible.

That was the thing he always relied on, but never knew if it would actually show up when he needed it. That inner daredevil. The automatic pilot who saw no danger, just a series of targets to be accomplished. He'd taken out what he hoped was the threat here (albeit a tiny one in the bigger picture of today) and was now working to save another.

An eye for an eye.

As the glass fell, everything seemed to slow down for Jared, in the familiar welcome way he had experienced many times in his career. He used to beat his girlfriends, then his pets, thankful he never had kids or he may have beat them too. And as he had beaten them, time had always slowed down.

Sure, he could tell himself it was because of the stress of his job. A shrink would probably find something to do with the fact that some creepy carer in one of the kids homes he spent his childhood in had touched his penis or something when he was a toddler. Some shit like that. But he felt he knew the truth of it.

Jared Gibson was just a mean-spirited, black-hearted bastard. God probably made a fuck-up in every few hundred, or maybe every thousand, people.

And he was one of God's fuck-ups.

He saw his hands around the throat of Stacy, his last girl. Not always during sex, sometimes just because. It may have been a look, or a word. Or perhaps it wasn't anything. Just him. And as he'd squeezed, just enough to see a tear come from her eye, just enough to know he could do a lot worse; time had slowed. He'd slapped her several times before she finally left him and each time everything slowed. He had time to see his hand descending. Time to make tiny adjustments to where it would connect with her, which part of his hand, even down to the smallest patch of skin. He'd had time to smell the air, taste the room, savouring the presence of something in there with him.

And now, with glass falling around him, Jared had time to see his reflection in so many pieces. Each being him, yet not. Each reflection accusing, judging him. Like a million spirits hovering in the glass.

His curse.

That was the hand he had been dealt. One of God's Rejects.

But lately he'd been trying to make the best use of that anger. That skill. That gift.

And with his job, Jared had the best of both worlds. He could be angry, could hurt, could even kill. Yet also try to do some good. Enjoyment through cleansing the world of other fuck-ups like him.

He'd often thought that if there was a God and Heaven let him in, he'd even make his last act the one where he'd put his hands around the Almighty's throat and squeeze. Let the bastard have his comeuppance for making him this way.

But, more likely, Jared assumed he'd go the way of the guy he'd just eliminated upstairs. And the way the guy beneath his feet would soon go unless he got help fast.

Like a burnt-out candle flame, they'd just cease to be.

Forever.

CHAPTER 38
KEANNE

Everything was so confusing. He saw Benny, then Benny was dead. He saw others, that radio guy who always stopped to chat, then he was gone.

Had he attacked Benny?

Then Benny was gone.

And then Keanne was gone too, merging into another Floater. Fusing.

INTERLUDE - FUSION

The horror which lay ahead for those in the air, was at once terrifying and merciful. The terror was long-lasting. The mercy came from the individual becoming something else, something more than themselves, so they didn't suffer alone.

The Floaters became a fusion of their body-parts and of themselves. Souls became merged, as the atoms of their form swam into each other, exchanging complex information.

The Floaters experiencing the fusion were aware of themselves as they fused the first time with one other. As more bodies floated into each other, like boats unanchored on a harbour, they became less and less of themselves. Memories and DNA carried in cells and atoms began to merge with others, carrying pieces of the self to other bodies.

Physically, arms merged with legs, torsos with heads. Loved ones became living monstrosities. As the number of Floaters increased, the solid form of Floaters adrift in the air became less and less, with those below who had the stomach to observe the fusing, unable to pin-point the precise location of what their loved one had become. The person who had been their loving husband, wife, sister, brother, mother, father, grandparent, aunt, uncle… were no longer there. Parts of them were and occasionally they called down, their pain and torment trapped in their calls of distress.

It was a sea of living hell.

The worst part was the faces. The bodies merged but the faces remained. A human canvas of skin, joints, sinew, muscle, interspersed with faces. Spirits swam over those faces, like fish beneath ice in a pond.

As the number of Floaters grew, so did the canvas. Stretching as far as the eye could see. An oil spill of spirits.

PART SEVEN

CHAPTER 1
PAULA - FLOATING

She had been so close to the cop and briefcase guy when the two had collided in the air. And then she had witnessed something that cast a new thread of terror through her, piercing her skin and nerves like a hot needle. The terror tingled across her entire body, Paula thinking that she might pass out once again. Willed it even. But, unfortunately for her, that never happened.

Paula found herself pushing backwards, like a fish against the tide, trying to get distance between herself and the abomination that was forming before her very eyes. She expected to smell burning - was unsure why - must be from an old movie or something. A smell like sulphur, like the welding they insisted she did back in senior school. Like she'd ever need, nor want, to weld anything in her life!

But this mixture of the two people, morphing into each other was unexpected, ugly and smell-less. As if caught in a riptide, Paula found the force increasing with the two bodies becoming one.

Got to get back. Got to get away.

Away? Well, she couldn't go down, nor up. Panic began to fill her heart threatening for the umpteenth time that day to override her and take control. She would not let it. Going that way was certainly going to be the end of her.

And Paula Asketh was stronger than that. Fuck yeah, she could weld if she had wanted too. 'I could have made an entire fucking caravan if I had too!' she shouted through gritted teeth, knowing that she was relying on the old trick of diverting the mind so as to prevent a full-blown panic attack.

And she had every right to have one of those, she did give herself that. What she had put up with so far. And all for what? Because she had been a petty thief? Had the odd behind-the-back shag? Well, so what. *Sorry for not being a complete God-Bothering Holier-Than-Thou Citizen of the United Kingdom,* she thought.

It was a good feeling; it gave her strength. Made her feel like she was standing up for herself.

If only I could stand up.

She'd never felt more like stretching her legs than now. She turned her head down, feeling a wave of nausea creep over her, as she tried to look along her body (lying upside down on the underside of this ceiling thing, or whatever it was) and wiggle her toes. Another pang of panic suddenly made her feel she might even be paralysed. Could she even feel her legs?

'Wiggle you bastards, come on now! Make those piggies come to momma.'

Movement. She couldn't see it, her head stuck to the Breaker. But she felt it.

Now stretch, go for it girl!

She clenched her jaw and pictured her body stretching, like being on a medieval rack, the bones separating in her minds-eye.

It felt good. She supposed she had stretched but being up here stuck to this thing made it difficult to actually ensure she had achieved her objective.

And all of this was a distraction, of course. A way to cope with self-control and not think about the unthinkable.

Becoming part of that abomination lying ahead.

Despite her best efforts, within the hour Paul Asketh had fused with the others.

CHAPTER 2

MIKE/PAUL

The two bodies continued to morph, stretching themselves into and around each other, like lovers. A black widow trapping her mate. It was hard to tell who was actually the more dominant being, such was the mishmash of arms and legs.

Mike's last sole coherent thought was knowing that, for him, the game was over. He was done. Finished. And with that, he no longer had to hold onto his secret. He could let the others try to piece that together. By the time the briefcase was found, he expected nobody would be able to tie it to him. Would they?

A final vision came to him of Katie and Casey standing in the porch of their house, policemen at the door, neighbours looking on. They held the case up, locked but seeking verification. Katie, one arm on Casey's shoulder, trying to stay composed, holding back the tears. Another officer holding a bunch of white papers sealed in a transparent bag, the contents obscured by an opaque envelope, like a teasing image of a porn mag on a newsagent's shelf, the juicy content hidden from any easily offended eyes (but never from the mind, no, that could always see what it wished). And thankfully, before seeing anymore, before seeing the devastation on Katie's face as the contents of the briefcase became clear, Mike Hegessey was gone, swimming in a pool of atoms with what had once been Paul Ross.

Within minutes, more and more Floaters had been drawn into the fusion. Fragments of memories, of selves, of lives, mish-mashed together, a Picasso composition; his black period.

The bigger the fusion of Floaters became, the more it generated its own pull. Like a black hole, the outer bodies were trying to push away from being sucked in, to no avail. Many simply gave up, allowing themselves to join the mass.

The combination of minds, the devastation of bodies, continued to grow and spread. A cancer of human clouds.

CHAPTER 3

JORDAN

He was determined that nothing else was going to threaten his life today. He'd gone through too much and now saw this as some kind of personal challenge. The Gods, or whatever, had decided to test him today. And this was it. All of this was an elaborate stunt, a prank, just to test his inner strength. To cast a judgement on his character.

And by God, he'd make it through, doing the right thing.

Gotta stand-up for freedom.

He'd so needed to see the faces in the sky, so desperate to understand what was happening. If he could just understand it, then he may stand a chance of diagnosing it. And then possibly curing it. An ambitious goal for a first-year medical student.

Nancy had given him the compact mirror as he'd asked. He knew that whatever was happening up in the air today was bigger than him. Maybe bigger than the whole human race, the greatest minds, best theorists. Beyond war, beyond religion, beyond comprehension.

But still, he had to look. He thought the same was probably true for anyone who decides to give their lives to helping others. Like rubbernecking on a car crash. It's wrong to look. But you just have to. That in-built desire to see, to know.

All in the guise of an attempt to understand.

Remember Jordan, what you see can't be unseen, right? So, you remember that when you and your posse start using knives on each other. Get the hell out of those gangs my boy, or you're gonna be carrying those shadows for the rest of your life. Y'hear me?

His mum was right even back then. You can't un-see.

He saw his own reflection in the compact mirror, all the time the inner conversation back and forth between him, his mum, other voices. Trying to find the one right reason to take a peek. Even just a glance. He'd already seen the horror up there anyway - albeit unintentionally. So what harm was there in now getting a proper look? Studying it.

It seemed the Gods had other plans.

He'd leaned out of the window, only for Nancy to drag him back in within a second of the wall to his side erupting into dust.

Someone had just tried to shoot him.

CHAPTER 4

NANCY

Jordan hadn't even offered an explanation as to where the the body of the dead guy had gone. One moment he was laying there, Nancy pushing down on his wound, trying to stop the bleeding, the next she was handing over a mirror so the kid could now save the world.

Jordan had leaned out of the window, a strange expression on his face.

Whilst in her handbag she'd checked her phone again, but it was useless. No signal. Everything was down. Completely.

Social media the way forward? Yeah, right. Today put that idea in its rightful place as being absolutely useless in a full-on attack.

Her eyes had been opened to a lot of things in the last fourteen days with the new job. A lid had been lifted on the stranger parts of the human condition. But this? Well, this was a whole new level.

She turned, ever the athlete, at her usual slow graceful pace. Leaned, trying not to add any extra weight to Jordan, who was slowly putting his arm out of the window, as if he half expected it to be ripped off, or him dragged with it. And then her eyes saw movement outside, coming across the pavement. A guy, dreadlocks. And something…

She reacted instantly.

And saved Jordan's life.

CHAPTER 5
JARED

Hunched down, shoulders rounded, glass everywhere; in his hair, trapped in the straps of his leather jacket, shimmers of it on his combat trousers. That was all fine.

However, the guy wasn't.

'My name's Jared. Can you hear me? If you can, just move anything. Can you open your eyes?'

The guy was ashen looking. Almost grey.

Jared moved fast, rolling over, taking most of the glass with him. He jumped up, the glass shards falling from him like glitter. He was back down by the guy in less than a second, hand on pulse.

A beat. Very slow. But there.

Next step, check out the damage.

Jared cocked his head hearing commotion on the floor above. If there was somebody else, they may also have a weapon and be working with the shooter.

If it *was* a shooter.

Not now, man.

At times like this, in the midst of the job, his mind always catastrophised every sound.

Not now.

He peeled the shirt back from the guy's shoulder. A wound. Probably a knife. Jared looked around, searching for the weapon. Nothing.

A split-second decision. Jared couldn't let the guy bleed out. That wouldn't be fair game. On the other hand, if he'd had the opportunity to kill him directly himself, from a standing start…

No, he's part of the core group. He'll lead you to the others.

'You've lost a lot of blood, but you're gonna be OK. It looks like no major organs were hit, lungs seem OK, but we gotta get you some blood, my man.'

Footsteps above, powerful, heavy.

He pictured a monster.

Not now!

Jared lifted the guy, propping him against the inner wall, allowing the wound to get some air. His gun was back out and, keeping low, Jared moved along the corridor to the bottom of the footwell. Whoever was upstairs were now coming down, breathing hard.

Two voices.

Shadows appeared, Jared once again having to make a split-second decision.

He raised the gun.

And prepared to fire twice.

CHAPTER 6

JORDAN

Thankfully he had fallen on top of Nancy as she had grabbed him from the window. It took the wind out of him. But she had saved his life in two ways; pulling him back before he got shot and then him landing on top of her. The other way round could have killed him.

He found himself smiling, eyes once again on the ceiling. Had he ever spent so many times in one day looking up at so many different ceilings? He made a mental note that ceilings were dull. Who looks at them anyway? He vowed to make his own flat, if he could ever afford it, have remarkable ceilings. Ones like that place in Rome, with the touching hands. Creation of Adam or whatever it was called.

Funny how the mind worked. Here he was led on top of a lumpy stranger who had just saved his life and his thoughts were preoccupied with architecture.

Panting from beneath him.

'Get… off… now!'

Jordan rolled off, completely unflatteringly.

'W…w…what the fuck just happened?' he stuttered.

Nancy was trying to get herself composed, not an easy task given her struggle to get up. He felt like offering a helping hand but thought it might add insult to injury given he had fallen on her hard.

'Some dude out there running around with a gun, tried to take a pop at you.'

Jordan wondered if the shot had been aimed at those in the sky, but had gone awry. He had visions of the sky monsters now deciding to come back down to earth now their transformation was complete; hideous insect-like human abominations, crawling down the walls and coming through the window any second.

Get a grip Jordan. Get. A. Grip. This ain't no horror story, he told himself.

Yet… he couldn't bring himself to put the mirror outside again. Not that he could see the mirror anyway. Maybe he had dropped it outside. Maybe that too was now floating up there with them.

And maybe someone really was trying to kill him.

What a day.

Nancy was holding onto the edge of the desk, forcing herself up, clearly exasperated from all of the physical endurance she was going through. He made a silent promise to take her out for her favourite meal when this horror was all over.

Jordan had a sudden strong vision of Nancy and him. They were at a restaurant sharing a dinner. A candle burned brightly between them. Soft reds on the walls. Safe. Like being in a giant womb. Nancy was Nancy but not this Nancy. She was slim, attractive. More than that… She was beautiful. And she was licking her dinner knife, smiling and he was making a joke. She liked him, loved him. They were happy. They had plans.

Before this horror.

What's happening?

He'd used that word again. Horror.

Maybe this is *a horror story?*

They had to get out of this place. They'd not managed to achieve any of the things he and James had come in here for. The homeless guy had become something other in the sky, more were joining him. And James himself had attempted some bizarre kind of suicide with Nancy's knife.

Jordan stumbled, reaching out steadying himself on the wall. That feeling of being overwhelmed, of being trapped inside his own body, coming back.

Nancy lightly touched his shoulder.

She's not really like this, he found himself thinking.

A strange thought. Weird. But somehow right. Somehow so right.

'We need to get out.'

Nancy nodded.

They walked along the second-floor corridor, hearing a voice from below. Something about blood. Jordan had heard more noises during the commotion of being dragged back from the window into the office with Nancy. Another loud bang (gunshot?) and smashing glass.

And here he was leading Nancy down to the noise, down to the unknown. To whatever lay beneath their feet.

They descended the stairs; aware everything was now quiet. The light, growing increasingly dull (he assumed due to the gathering storm cloud of freaks in the sky) cast their muted shadows on the white walls. The walls of which James had pointed out the standard of paint work. Another strange memory in this ever-increasingly weird day.

Nancy was right behind him.

And for the third time that day, Nancy again saved his life.

CHAPTER 7

JARED

Two shadows. Two people. Maybe the gunman from upstairs, but maybe hostages now free. He took the chance and fired two warning shots, hopefully making it clear he could easily have used both bullets to end their lives.

The shadows froze on the stairwell.

'Whoever you are, I want to see hands, open and empty. And I wanna see them now, y'hear me?!'

The shadows moved quickly.

'Ah-ah, sloowwly now.'

The shadow puppets continued to raise their arms, distorted on the wall. From Jared's point of view, they looked like they had arms that went to oars at the tips and had a perfect bend in them.

Maybe they aren't human, he thought.

Not now!

Whatever came around that corner, he wouldn't hesitate to blow the fucking head off it if it didn't do as he asked. Or strangle them. Or just give them a beating with his belt.

Hands raised in surrender, two people came around the corner. Two black kids. Girl and boy.

Jared kept the gun aimed steadily at their head level. He could take them out easily.

He even felt like giving it a try just to see if he was right.

'I… I…'

'Shut up. There's only one *I* here and that's me. *I* say, *I* speak and you don't. Understood?'

Jordan glanced over Jared's shoulder.

'James!' he immediately regretted speaking and put his hand over his mouth, trying to stop the words from coming out, like a three-year-old caught in the telling of a lie.

'You know him?' Jared asked.

The black boy and girl nodded. Clearly afraid. Good, he had them under his control. Jared tucked the gun into the back of his pants and turned back to James.

'OK, so you guys need to help me get him out of here and get him some blood.'

Jordan moved fast. 'What type is he; do you know?'

Jared looked at Jordan as if he had been something on the bottom of his boot a moment ago. Shit walked in off the street.

Jordan thought of Benny.

Jared looked hard at the black girl. Did he know her? No, impossible. He'd never been to this building before, unsure if any of them ever had. Why was it almost empty? This was central London, yet the building was empty. He hadn't thought of it before, but seeing into the ground floor offices, all were empty. Jared had a compulsion to go into them and check them out.

Why am I feeling this? Just deal with the bleeding guy. He glanced back at James, wondering whether to just let him die now he had two more to lead him to the others. But something about those empty offices bothered him.

Jared stood, staring through the glass door leading into the lower office spaces. 'Have you guys been in there?'

Jordan and Nancy looked at each other and shrugged. 'No,' Jordan replied.

Jared squared up to the door, checking the edges as if it may contain a device, an alarm. Or worse; a bomb. 'Something's not right here,' he said to no-one in particular.

Jordan stood alongside him, flanked by Nancy. They felt it too.

'Those offices…' Jared continued, 'they should be full. Every fucking doorway, every inch of space is packed out there,' he gestured over his right shoulder to the outside world.

'So why are these spaces empty?' He pushed the door, thinking it may be locked which would give an answer to his query.

The door swung open easily on its hinges.

He paused at the doorway, taking in the room. Office cubicles (workstations, he thought they termed them) lay out in a haphazard way. Jared guessed some management consultancy had been paid a shit load to get the layout just right; maximising productivity and profitability, all the while lowering the morale of their staff.

Poor fuckers. Caged like hamsters from 9 'til 5.

He had a fleeting vision of glass boxes again. Saw himself sat, no strapped, into one. Trapped.

Caged like a hamster.

He shook his head, cleared his mind.

I've felt this before. It's OK.

'I'm going in.'

'Wait, what about James?' asked Jordan.

They all looked, the body of James slumped against the wall. Eyes shut. Drool hung from his lips, snagging his shirt like a spider's web.

Jared said what they already knew; 'Too late. He's dead.'

CHAPTER 8

JORDAN

As soon as Jared had said the words, Jordan knew he was right. Wasn't even worth checking. James was gone. *Stupid fucking idiot. All because he wanted to be the hero.*

Jordan still hoped there would be some video recording on CCTV somewhere. Anything that proved conclusively he was not responsible for James' death. He had Nancy's word of course, but which court would trust two black kids in this modern climate? *Racism's dead, my ass,* he thought.

He could see the white judge passing sentence now. See the headline; BLACK TEENAGER STABS LEADING MR. NICE GUY. SINGLE PARENT MOTHER SAYS 'HE WAS GOING TO BE A DOCTOR'. Jordan felt like laughing. He *was* going to be a doctor and no showbiz-radio-chat show-fuck-up was going to change that.

Jared was already in the offices, stopping every so often to listen.

Jordan couldn't hear anything over the beating of his heart.

He looked back at Nancy. She was staring down at the body of James, tears standing in the corner of her eyes. She looked up at him, searching for an answer. He nodded.

I know, it wasn't you and it wasn't me. It's OK.

She nodded back, the thought passing between them.

Jared sunk down to his haunches, looking beneath the cubicles. Jordan entered behind him, gesturing with another nod for Nancy to follow. *Stay close.*

Jordan thought Jared was going to pick something up off the carpet, maybe a hair and sniff it, like a tracker in the outback following their prey.

Instead, he stood, knees cracking and brushed his dreadlocks over his shoulder. A door stood beyond the offices leading into what Jordan surmised was more of the same. Empty cubicles where workers gave up their hopes and dreams for a pitiful paycheque to sustain their miserable existence.

Not a fair swap.

He was more determined than ever to make something of himself now.

But not like James. That was false.

Jared paused a moment longer, Jordan assuming he was giving consideration to going through into the next room. He did have a point after all; where the was everyone? It was a Thursday morning around 10am. This room should be packed. Even more so given the chaos on the streets outside (although most of the chaos was now in the air, granted).

Jared made his decision, he turned and left the room, gesturing for he and Nancy to follow. They stepped over James' body, through the shattered door frame and out onto the street.

****

Had they gone through the other office door leading off the ground floor they would have found another set of cubicles; the layout and every detail an exact duplicate of the room prior to it. Even down to another door leading off. And that too would lead to a duplicate space. Everything the same. On and on.

Infinitely.

Impossibly.

CHAPTER 9

NANCY

Things were becoming mixed in her mind. Not only the bizarre situation she found herself in, but something deeper. Something tugging at her heart, trying to get her attention.

Those cubicles… that office…

Had she even seen it before? She'd only worked at JTW's for a fortnight, but already she felt as though she hadn't walked past the lower offices and seen anybody in there. Had she?

And Jordan. Something about him too. She had met him before, she felt quite sure of that now. Not in that way when you first meet a stranger yet it feels like you've known them years. This was a deeper connection. They'd met somewhere she couldn't quite put her finger on. It was like she was leaning over the side of a boat and could see a treasure chest at the bottom of the lake. The chest was open and she could see the treasures inside; memories like framed pictures. But the harder she looked, the more they drifted out of sight, deeper into the water.

Deeper in her subconscious.
And this guy; Jared. He too was familiar. In a stranger-I've-already-met way.

They walked out of the shattered glass door and onto the pavement.

Not that Nancy would have noticed, but the dog was gone. The body no longer there. No blood, no guts, no trail. Nothing. Like it had never happened.

Don't look up, she told herself.

Whatever Jordan had seen when he had looked, was not for her eyes. She felt if she even chanced a glance, it would drive her mad. Insane.

You can't un-see.

Nancy felt as if she was on the verge of a great discovery. Something was soon going to click and make everything fall into place.

And then Jordan stated the obvious and thrust her back into confusion once again.

CHAPTER 10

JORDAN

Of the three things, Jordan noticed only the most obvious one. It was of such profound disruption to his cognitive process that it paled the rest into insignificance. In fact, it made the other two changes obsolete. Benny was gone. Had Jordan turned he would have seen James was gone too. Simply gone. As if he'd never existed.

But over-shadowing all of that was a bigger disappearance. Or rather an appearance. Central London was gone. They were in North London. Near a tube station; Cockfosters.

'What the fuck?' he scanned 360, looking up but wishing he hadn't.

The buildings had changed, the scenes, the people. All changed. But not the Floaters. They were still there, growing, merging, gathering, moaning.

Dying.

Try as he might, Jordan couldn't put the monster back under the bed. It was here in full daylight. Demanding to be seen.

We need to get inside, somewhere safe.

He spied Jared running toward the station, thinking ahead, taking action. The change of reality didn't seem to have affected him in the slightest.

Who is this guy?

But Jared wasn't running to the station. He was by a lady. And lying next to her, with blood around where he lay, was a fat man, something white on his hand.

'Get over here, quick!' called Jared.

Jordan couldn't get his body into action, finding he was holding his breath in… shock? Anticipation? Nancy broke the spell, slipping her hand into his.

'Come Jordan, he needs us.'

CHAPTER 11

JAMES

He'd had enough.

Everything had gone wrong.

He always had a plan. Plan A, Plan B, Plan C.

But this time, the events had beaten him.

He was supposed to win this!

Aware of three others stepping over him, running away *(cowards, fucking cowards!)* he managed to stand.

As he did, he fell into the arms of an angel.

****

His eyes slowly opened. Faces leaning over him. He thought he recognised one of them. Thought he was somehow responsible for all this.

James tried to speak, his mouth dry, no words coming out.

Everything around him was white. Immaculate. Even the people hovering over him were clad in white.

Angels, he thought.

A hand rested on his forehead.

'Sleep James, sleep,' said the angel.

CHAPTER 12

NIGEL - NOW

Shaking Maggie. Shaking her hard, her head flopping back and forth like a rag doll. He wanted to shout, to scream, to slap. Anything to wake her. The cancer was biting deep, taking his wife with it. And he was powerless to act.

'Wake up, come on man.'

Shaking. Shaking.

The voice became clearer. Nearer.

'Come on.'

And then came the slap.

Nigel shook his head, feeling a stinging sensation on his own cheek. Had Maggs slapped him? He blinked once, twice, everything swimming into focus.

'Yeah, there you go! He's with us, he's OK,'

A black guy was squatted alongside him, holding Nigel's shoulders. Nigel looked at him quizzically, trying to put a name to the face. No good. He'd never seen this guy before.

Lihua!

His head turned, searching for Lihua, the pain in his hand hitting him like lightening, making him scream.

'Yeah, dude, I wouldn't move that if I was you. We've tried to stop the bleeding as best we can, but man! We thought you might be dead, bro!'

Nigel looked at his hand, a white plastic bag over it. And then it came back to him. The foreign guy shouting in some funny language. And then a gunshot. Nigel held his hand before his face, turning it slowly, as if he had X-ray vision. There was blood on his sleeve, jacket, everywhere.

'We need to get you up. We've got to get away from here. From that.' The black guy pointed up. Nigel's view was partially blocked by the doorway he had tried to hide under, but could just make out some kind of dark shape up there.

'Lah,' he tried to force the words but they wouldn't come.

'Not yet. Save your strength. Did the girl shoot you? Just nod.'

Nigel looked at Lihua sat propped up against the far wall opposite. Another guy was hunched down near her. Nigel shook his head. His hand hurt like a bastard.

'I know man, I know it hurts. I've done what I can with what we've got right now. But we need to move on.'

'Baby,' Nigel managed, almost a whisper.

The guy put his ear nearer to Nigel's mouth.

'Baby,' he tried again.

The guy looked into Nigel's eyes. Nigel felt the incredible urge to laugh. Felt like laughing harder than he probably ever had in his life. Maybe this was the tipping point into madness? If so, bring it on. Anything better than this pain and what was gradually becoming a new reality. *Not you,* he wanted to say. *I'm not gay, right? I meant her baby. Have you found the guy with her baby?*

No use, nothing would come out of his mouth at the moment.

Nigel shifted and a strong over-powering smell filled his nostrils.

God no. Not that. Please, I wanted to help, not shit myself!

The black guy - not much older than a kid really (Nigel put the kid's age at maybe eighteen, or just slightly older) - gave a small nod as if to say he knew.

'I think it's the doorway people use late at night when they've had too much to drink, y'know?'

Ah yes. The pissy doorway. Thank Christ.

He helped Nigel to his feet.

Stand-up and it's over.

A dizzy spell rushed over him, but he held strong.

You're alright, Big Bear. Lots to do. Now come on.

I know Maggs, give me a second.

He raised his eyes, putting a hand on the kid's shoulder.

'Who's that,' he mouthed the words, gesturing at the guy with Lihua.

'Oh, his name is Jared. He's definitely the sort of guy we want around with us today.' The kid smiled. It was a nice smile. Put his face into a whole new light.

Funny, Nigel thought, *I wouldn't stop for this kid on the street if he flagged me down, especially if he's with that dreadlocked guy. But there you go. They turn out to be the nicest folks.*

Big Bear! Tut tut.

He managed a smile and, using the kid as a crutch, hobbled over to Lihua and Jared.

'Keep your hand up and as steady as you can,' said the kid.

Nigel nodded. He saw his wristwatch was tight around the bottom of the bag. Thankfully nobody had nicked that. Maggs had given it him as an anniversary gift, engraved and all.

He vaguely remembered somebody had been trying to mug him. Or had that also been a dream?

'How…?'

'Try not to talk,' said the kid.

Nigel shook his head, jaw tensed. Stubborn refusal to be told to shut up. The kid smiled again.

'Hey, he's OK!' said another voice. Nigel saw a fat black girl standing by the red tandem. He tried to imagine her riding it with him on the back. What a sight.

In his mind, he heard Maggie laugh.

'How… do you know…?' Nigel managed, barely audible. He used his head to gesture to the bagged hand.

'Ah! I'm studying medicine,' said the kid.

CHAPTER 13

ANGELA - ABOVE

10:00am just gone.

Angela knew a decision had to be made and fast. Had done for the last fifteen minutes or so now, watching the fuel guage drop ever lower into the red zone. That slither of red, her mind breaking it up into millionths it seemed, all in the hope of somehow having just enough fuel for one more circuit, one more chance to find somewhere to land.

She'd tried to land on the invisible Breaker again but was bounced right off it just as before. She'd thought of getting as close as possible, getting near to Tasha and just stepping out onto the surface of the thing. But that would be suicide.

You don't know that. Not for certain.

True. She didn't. But she didn't feel like trying. Her thoughts kept going back to Tasha, lying there. She may even be alive. And here she was, her lover, flying around and around going nowhere fast.

Just need to get down.

Same thoughts, also going nowhere.

Angela had tried the radio repeatedly; nothing, it then dawned on her, she hadn't seen a single plane.

Not one.

She was up here alone.

And that didn't make sense. Made no sense at all.

CHAPTER 14
CYRUS - SIDE OF THE DUAL CARRIAGEWAY/UNDER THE TREES

He had the gift, but beyond sense and channelling had no actual way of doing anything about the threat he could now see. A single helicopter was circling right above them. More people were gradually being lifted from their car windows, the force taking them into the air to join the others already there. Cyrus had to keep moving, darting between vehicles, just to keep the chopper in view. It drifted in and out of vision, passing between the human clouds forming above. Cyrus' forced his thoughts away from the horror lying overhead, instead thinking, trying to devise a plan - a way - to do something beyond stare hopelessly at what flew overhead.

Had Saffi been right? Was the chopper the actual threat? What if it was sent to help? Maybe even a journalist? Surely the more news that was spread about what was happening here the better for everyone. It would mean help must finally be on the way.

A guy shouted through his car window at Cyrus breaking his train of thought.

'Put your window down, I can't hear you clearly!' Cyrus yelled back, feeling his patience run thin. Something told him they didn't have long now to solve this… puzzle?

He stopped, mouth at an angle, a frown creeping over his brow. Now, why did that feel right? And yet… so far removed from what was actually happening?

They're trying to divert you from achieving the goal.
What?

Cyrus began to think he may be losing the plot. He needed space. Solitude. Somewhere quiet to think, to gather his thoughts. Impossible out here in the chaos.

The guy was still shouting, banging his steering wheel, desperate to get Cyrus' attention.

'It's not just here! It's everywhere!'

Cyrus ran to the car. He felt like smashing the window, dragging the guy out. All in frustration, just so they could talk civilly. Was that a sign of madness? Could he justify violence to achieve a civil outcome?

The guy partially lowered his window, Cyrus taking the opportunity to put his fingers into the gap.

'It's not only here,' said the driver. 'It's global! Whatever this…' he pointed to the sky through his windscreen, '…is! It's happening across the country. Before the radio quit there was reports of it coming in from all over Europe. It's spreading man! It's the end. Y'get me?!'

With that the guy closed the window, trapping Cyrus' fingers. The pain was immense.

The driver released the handbrake, floored the accelerator and screeched the full three feet he had available between his and the stationary car in front.

The noise of the impact far exceeded the situation. It shouldn't have made that much noise, not in the short bit of road the car had available to it. Cyrus' fingers had been trapped throughout. His arm yanked from his shoulder, the pain ripping like a wave of fire across his body. He was lunged forward, his head banging hard against the car door.

'Bast-'

He lay, dazed, hanging by the hand from the window. His butt not quite reaching the floor, legs bent, flopping, not supporting him. All the force was in his hand, arm and fingers. He was sure they'd soon sever.

This can't be. I'm Chosen. Not like this. This can't be.

The words circled in his mind over and over.

Stand. Got to stand.

His legs, trembling beneath him, tried to get some purchase. He felt so weak. With force, he got his knees under him, releasing the incredible pull on his arm. He was panting heavily, eyes just above the driver's side window. The driver's airbag had not gone off - maybe not enough speed, Cyrus thought - but the guy had done maximum damage to his face. His forehead was rested on the steering wheel, Cyrus grateful the horn wasn't on constant as happened in almost all films. The driver's head was facing Cyrus. His nose was crushed, his eyes closed. A yellow gunk forming at their edges, already crusting up. Not a good sign. Cyrus felt a moment of pity and a moment of envy. At least the guy was free now from whatever lay ahead for the rest of them.

With a grunt, Cyrus used the anger he now felt to stand fully. His fingers were bleeding, the nails feeling as if they may have come free or splintered. He yelled, standing on tiptoe, his efforts to drag the window down and release his fingers proving unsuccessful.

Come on you bastard! I need a tiny space just to free my hand…

Nothing. The window felt jammed. The doorframe was intact, but the impact may have buckled it. Cyrus wondered how the window had stayed intact. Surely it should have shattered?

The driver's head moved. A sickly smile rose on his lips.

'Christ! He's not dead!' Cyrus muttered, now more than ever wanting his fingers away from the thing now driving the car. He began to shake, rattling the window in its frame, determined to break it. He screamed, scared at the power of the shrill roar coming from him. This was survival now.

'Come… ON!!!' Such violence in him.

The driver's eyes still shut, yellow gunk crusting in his nostrils, around his eyes, even coming from his ears. His mouth flopped open, several teeth falling. Cyrus continued to force his hand free, happy to sever his fingers at this point.

'I… I… can't see… them… anymore…' the driver muttered, Cyrus halting his exasperated attempts for freedom, suddenly completely transfixed by the driver trapped inside.

'It… it's… better… when… you… can't…'

Again, that sickly toothless grin, blood like fine threads between both lips. The driver laid his head back on the wheel. The horn now activated.

Smoke was pouring from the engine. The combined noise of the horn, the fear of the car suddenly exploding (*don't they always on every film?* Cyrus thought) combined to allow him access to his hidden energy reserves. He shook, pushed, tore at the window, now trying to free his wrist from his hand.

Let my fucking hand stay trapped if it wants to hold the window that fucking badly!

Why wasn't the driver of the car in front coming out? Doesn't that happen in every crash?

Another yell, another rip sending pain like electricity up his arm. Where was everybody? Afraid to step out in case they joined those above?

Cyrus looked, searching for the big guy, the one with the 'bomb' hand gesture. He was still there, still gazing up, smiling. Cyrus shook his head, disbelieving what he'd just seen.

The guy - bomb hands - was shimmering. As if filled with light. Cyrus could see through him.

And then, like a magician's trick, he was back again, solid, full. Human.

Powerful arms grabbed him from behind and yanked him to the side.

And then a metal pipe shattered the driver's window. The relief was overwhelming. Cyrus's hand felt cold, numb. He was sure he'd never be able to use it again.

And then there was no more. Just darkness.

A distant voice spoke to him as he fell into the void.

Stand up!

CHAPTER 15

NICK

The yell didn't sound human. The crash sounded too close for comfort.

Not again!

Nick was up off the floor in a movement of such grace it defied his size. Adam followed just as spritely.

Nick was always a bigger-picture thinker, Adam more the detail guy. So, whilst Nick took in the scene around him; the healing lady laid down, the stationary traffic on the dual carriageway, the shadow being cast by the Floaters above, Adam would have been able to tell you what everyone was wearing, colour of the cars and…

The cars. Nick sensed something wrong with the traffic. He saw the guy screaming, trying to break into a car by the looks of it and smoke too.

Better be careful.

But… something else. Further up the road, a man stood in the road between the cars and was somehow dancing with light, as if he were an illusion; an oasis on the horizon. Nick shielded his eyes from a sun that wasn't shining, trying to focus on the shimmering man. On the cars.

'Adam, we need to help that guy, right?' referring to the yeller dangling from a car window.

Adam was already ahead of him, noting the true situation. The guy who had helped him get Nick out of the crash earlier now had his hand trapped in another car. And worse, the car was smoking badly. Adam pushed Nick forward, urging him to move toward the smoking car. Nick saw Adam bend, picking something from the floor. No doubt he had a plan.

Nick bounced, his heavy gut being its usual hindrance, squeezing between cars, seeing the faces of people trapped within. Nick guessed they were staying inside given that people were being sucked into the sky. Many were on phones, holding them, blue screens dancing in car interiors. Nick thought back to their phones, they'd been no use. Whatever was in the sky was interfering with the signals.

Maybe they're all just trying to phone home?

As Nick got closer to the yelling man, the shimmering man was still the object of his attention. His primary focus. One moment the man was there, then he wasn't. Nick recalled a trip on a ghost train when he was just a boy

(Corridors, endless doors, locked, locked, locked…)

seeing a ghost in front of him, something he later found out was actually a reflection of a real actor projected onto glass. Peppers Ghost the technique was called.

Funny what you think of when you're stressed.

The shimmering man was solid once again, looking up at the sky. Why wasn't he helping? Nick was about to call out, but his attention shifted back to the cars. Something wasn't right. That sense of wrongness returned.

They're all the same.

Now, where did that come from?

He shook his head, trying to clear his thoughts.

Sensory overload. Too much happening.

No, I can feel I'm slipping again.

Not now. Not now.

He had to stay here. Stay present.

He forced himself back into the moment.

But he was right. Unable to look and confirm for fear of slipping into the dark, Nick had noticed something very odd. Beyond the shimmering man, every car was an exact replica of the car next to it. And on and on it seemed to go.

Infinitely.

Impossibly.

CHAPTER 16

ADAM

The girl was lying down, holding her forehead, clearly suffering a headache of some kind. She was kind of cute (he made a mental note of asking her out for a drink when this was all over). She had saved Nick who was excitedly moving toward a guy in pain. Adam could see the guy had his hand trapped. Blood smearing down the side window. Adam took a moment to wonder how he could actually see that from this distance. There was smoke too. And the bang must have been a crash. But… there wasn't room for a crash.

Adam began to move toward the hanging guy, stopping to pick up a pipe. It was metal, solid and brand new. He thought briefly how it hadn't any rust. Not even a mark. It was as if it had been left here for him. Left for this very purpose. To smash the window and free the guy.

So many questions were running through his mind. He saw Nick stop briefly in front, hand to his head. Adam prepared for Nick to slip away again, something he was apt to do in extreme situations. It had happened when he and Nick had gotten trapped in an elevator once a few years back.

No, that had been real.

Adam stopped, holding his breath. The thought had interrupted the memory and made little sense.

Real? Of course, it had been.

He put a reassuring hand on Nick's shoulder and urged him ever forward. Toward the yelling man. Nick stopped again, shielding his eyes. There was another man down there, stood in the road between the cars. He was staring into the sky, a broad smile on his face.

How can I be seeing this? These details from this distance?

He decided it must have been the crash, perhaps it had made a part of his brain speed-up or improve or… he thought of John Travolta in a film he'd watched in the cinema years back with a friend of his and his girlfriend. Travolta played the part of a guy who you assumed was having a paranormal experience, suddenly being able to move shit with his mind and stuff. But turned out he had a tumour.

Great thinking, that'll cheer you up! Dick, he admonished himself. But still, he had a point. How could he possibly see the blood on the car window from here, so clear, so red? Too red. And the grin on the shimmering guy's face?

Maybe this is all a set-up? An elaborate hoax?

Adam knew that was wrong the moment he thought it. His mind was desperately clinging to any hope that his world wasn't falling apart around him. And one quick look into the sky and he'd see what was happening up there. That was all he needed to convince himself that this was happening right here, right now.

Then why aren't I up there with them?

Another question without an answer.

He was at the window. Nick had the guy under the arms trying to hold him up. Smoke was bellowing out of the bonnet.

It's going to blow up any moment!

Adam thought to tell other people in the surrounding cars to get out and run. But then thought better of it. Run, where? They might not be as lucky as him. They might end up in the sky.

Better to be blown apart.

Maybe.

'Mind your eyes', he warned Nick and the screamer.

He bought the pipe down with devastating force, far more than was actually needed. He needed to be rid of that blood. Those red, vivid streaks driving him mad. As the pipe swung in its arc, Adam saw the metal shimmer, flick in and out of realness.

Must be a trick of the light.

Then the window was no more.

The blood was gone.

The screaming man was free.

CHAPTER 17
CYRUS

He fell, sliding out of Nick's arms, concertinaed on the road. Cyrus had no idea if he'd look up and see his fingers still gripping the driver's window, white bones glinting like a Halloween prank, protruding from their skin fingers; horror gloves. He was dizzy and needed water. He swallowed what felt like a lump of lead in his throat, wondering if he'd swallowed his tongue. If so, his life would end here, on the road, bleeding. He could imagine such circumstances in a war-torn country, even in a desert, but here? Hertfordshire? Surely not. Especially as he was a Chosen One. As was Saffi.

Saffi.

He tried to struggle up, Nick hunching over him, offering him kind words. 'You're going to be alright my friend, you've lost some blood, but not as much as we first thought.'

'Fingers,' managed Cyrus.

'Yes, your fingers. They were stuck in that window, but…' Nick trailed off, having caught sight of the driver lying inside, head still on the horn. Nick felt like he was going crazy. Had he signed up for this?

(A flashback; white walls. A smiling woman. Papers. Lots of papers. A pen handed to him. His stomach somersaulting… was he really going to do this?…)

Adam was already ahead, looking in the car in-front and shouting to the shimmering man. Searching for water.

Nick looked back down at Cyrus. 'As I was saying, your hand is injured, but if we get it patched up with a first aid kit, we can get you to a hospital as soon as.'

Always bigger picture. Getting Cyrus to a hospital was not part of Nick's immediate plan. Had he been able to speak, Cyrus would have declined anyway. Saffi could heal him. She just needed to recharge her own energy.

His main concern was the helicopter. Everybody sensed it.

'Water?' Cyrus begged.

Nick called to Adam.

'Any luck Adam? This guy needs water!' Adam raised an arm without turning, now walking towards the shimmering man.

Nick stooped, back cracking. Christ, he needed a long hot soak in the bath. And his pipe. He'd not smoked his pipe for Lord knows how long. But he needed it now.

'C'mon man, let's get you up.' Cyrus tried to smile and, cursing his damaged hand, struggled to his feet.

CHAPTER 18

ADAM

The car the yelling man had smashed into had a driver. Same deal; dead, leaning on his horn. Again, no air-bag. Adam thought air-bags were standard requirements in this day and age.

What day and age?

An odd thought, but he had lost track of time. He forced himself to think; 'Nineteenth. Yes, nineteenth of January. 2017.' Good, he wasn't completely losing his mind.

Above him, the noises were increasing as the floating bodies merged into each other. Adam couldn't bear to watch. Didn't even feel too comfortable being out on the open road, knowing he could be taken up at any time.

'Hey, mister.' The shimmering man turned to respond. Adam walked closer. 'Have you got any water?'

The shimmering man smiled and flickered in and out of existence again, like a mirage.

He's not really there. It's me who needs water.

The shimmering man looked back up into the sky. Adam turned, following his gaze. The helicopter was still buzzing above the Floaters, like a giant insect looking for somewhere to land and feed.

Maybe it's the army, he thought.

Adam turned back, mouth opening to ask the shimmering man about water once again. Only… the shimmering man was there, but further away. Still standing in the same pose, just further than he was moments ago. *How can this be?*

Adam put his hand on a car bonnet, needing support. Behind him the car horn continued.

'Hey, do… you… have… any… water?'

The shimmering guy looked at Adam and moved his hands apart, as if trying to explain something. Movement? The expansion of something?

'This isn't time for fucking Charades, my friend!' Adam yelled, immediately regretting the curse word for fear of kids being in the cars. Further down the road a ginger haired girl stepped from a car into the middle lane, behind the shimmering man. She immediately was swept off her feet, legs to the sky, her dress falling part way over her head. She clung for dear life to the car door, screaming for someone to help her.

'Help her! Where the fuck are the parents?' Adam shouted to the shimmering man.

'For fuck's sake man, behind you! Help her!'

But the shimmering man simply turned his face back to the sky, that same broad grin.

He's lost it, Adam thought.

Adam looked back to see how Nick was getting on with the guy they'd rescued, hoping he wouldn't see them also now heading into the sky.

Nick was leaning into the driver's window. *Hopefully trying to disengage the driver's head from the horn,* he thought. Adam turned back, the girl now only fingertips from floating. Her ginger pigtails hung down. She screamed, begging for help.

And still the shimmering man stood gazing into the sky.

'Dude, I swear to Christ, if you don't help that girl, I'll…' he didn't know how to finish, the shimmering man flickering once again in and out of existence.

Stay away, Adam. Stay the fuck away.

It seemed like good advice. But the details… the details were making Adam more and more curious of the shimmering man and less and less scared.

The details.

Adam stopped, going against his nature, against the will to rush forward and save the girl. Instead, he studied the shimmering man. He began counting.

One, two, three, four…

Still staring at the sky…

Five, six, seven, eight…

Ah! Now he looks!

Nine, ten, eleven, twel-

He begins making that expansion gesture, hands moving apart from each other. What was he trying to say? *Keep counting.*

Fourteen, fifteen, sixteen, seven-

The shimmering man flutters in and out of existence, one moment solid, then liquid, then solid again. Almost as if he was a projection. Pixelated. The image not quite catching up with itself.

Nineteen, twenty…

The shimmering man looked at the sky once more.

He's on a loop. He's on a loop!

Adam moaned, a small sound of shock escaping him.

Adam thought back to the events he'd seen so clearly. Too clearly; the receptionist at the golf club. Her bleeding nose.

Her blood had seemed too red. As if it was trying to be real and failed in the process. His mind jumped. The crash, coming around that bend into these cars. Doug…

'Fucking hell, Doug…' he said in a whisper, already having put that horrific event out of his mind. There'd be time to think about that later. For now, he had to focus.

The details. They'd tell him all he'd need to know.

And then, out of the crash, with hardly a bruise.

(Doug…)

And then helping Nick. The healing girl. The hippy guy

(the yelling man)

seeing his blood, so real, so clear. Yet he was quite a way from Adam at that point.

Blood. Too real. Too fake.

Adam looked around him, a complete 360. The ginger girl had given up her grip, now floating into the sky.

We're not supposed to be standing still.

The thought didn't connect with him but told him something instinctive. He needed to stay calm, not panic. Not rush. He needed to see. Clearly.

'Really see,' he told himself.

The shimmering man. The smile, so clear, so plastered on, so fake.

'Trying to be real. It's all trying to be real.'

Adam moved toward the shimmering man, occasionally glancing into the cars as he passed.

'They're all the same.'

Saying it out loud helped convince him he was *really* seeing. *Really* looking. Stating the facts. The details.

He looked back at Nick, now walking back to the grass verge, helping the hippy guy. He looked up at the sky, finding it hard to locate the helicopter, through the growing mass of swirling, trapped bodies.

Move then, you bastard, he thought, his attention back on the shimmering man willing him to continue his cycle.

And he did.

Adam walked faster down the middle of the road, cars flanking him on each side. He had stopped checking in them now, knowing the faces inside were more or less the same. Same actions too; kids in back-seats holding phones to faces. Blueish glow lighting frightened faces. Either one or two adults in the front. The women all the same. Men too.

Adam was walking faster, faster, but not gaining on the shimmering man, who had reset into a solid form after twenty seconds, now back in his eternal loop of searching the sky, expanding his hands and smiling.

'I'm not going to reach you am I, you bastard?' Adam muttered, now breaking into a run.

'Adam?!'

A yell from behind.

He stopped, the shimmering man now just as far from him as he was at the start. Adam wondered how long before a car door opened further down, a ginger pig-tailed girl taken into the sky.

'It's all on a loop.'

Turning, Adam ran back to the grass verge, feeling he'd made a great discovery but unsure quite how to tell the others without them thinking he'd lost his mind.

Above him, the shadow of the helicopter passed low.

CHAPTER 19

ANGELA

She was on the brink of giving up.

Fuel was almost out.

Angela had gone through every conceivable emotion in the past few minutes - seemed like hours - but had managed to keep the panic just beneath the surface.

The surface.

Angela was now close to Tasha's body. Knowing this was probably the last moments of her life, she was choosing how to end it. Down in flames with the chopper? Or lying alongside her lover?

The choice was easy.

Angela bought the helicopter as low as she dared and began to fly over the surface. Tasha was just a few meters away in front. When the time came Angela would jump, rolling, hopefully landing next to Tasha. One last embrace before whatever happened happened.

She just prayed it wouldn't be painful.

Prayed it would be quick.

The helicopter should have just enough fuel and momentum to fly on a few meters, before crashing down on the Breaker. After that? She didn't care.

Tasha was less than 50 meters now…

Let it burn, let it blow the fucking Breaker to smithereens.

Let me die like they did. Dad and the Wicked Witch. Consumed by fire. It's what I deserve.

30 metres…

'I'm coming Tash,' tears blurred her vision. The speed she was descending at was sure to kill her if she jumped. And even if it didn't, the Breaker would. It had killed Tasha.

In her heart she knew it was her mum she'd see first.

Her mum.

Would she recognise her? She'd committed suicide when Angela was just a baby. Angela pictured her mum, the one she'd fallen in love with from photographs growing up. Wanting to remember her face so she could find her on the other side.

On the other side.

If she'd only been able to land back on the ground, on the other side of this thing, life may have been so different. But would she really want to live without…

Tasha.

Angela jumped.

And landed perfectly.

CHAPTER 20

ADAM

As he ran back to Nick, momentarily cast in shadow by the helicopter flying low overhead, Adam saw Cyrus point up through the trees. Nick and the girl stood alongside, all staring into the sky.

Adam was considering how he'd tell them his discovery when a ball of fire erupted overhead.

As it happened, Adam pictured the shimmering man, his hands moving apart like a clap in slow-motion.

CHAPTER 21

NICK

As he stared into the sky, glimpsing the explosion of something above the Breaker, images came rushing back to the forefront of his mind. Memories from childhood; a cold night. The frost clinging to spider's webs in the corners of the patio doors. Beyond, the fire, built proudly by his father, burned bright. Moisture ran down the outside of the window. Nick was huddled indoors close to his brother and sister, like the perfect firework night family photograph. The fire outside burning brightly, but soundlessly. Nick couldn't even hear a crackle. His father was poking at it with a stick, still trying to show that man has power over everything, even fire. Nick, wrapped in his scarf and gloves, still shivering from the cold from playing outside before the big fire was lit.

Man conquering nature, his father had used a lighter, some caveman.

The explosion overhead was the same; seeing fire through glass. If the Breaker was even made of glass.

Soundless.

There wasn't even a noise when whatever happened that side of the glass ceiling had happened. He assumed it was the helicopter they had seen.

The only one in the sky.

Saffi was up now, still massaging the back of her neck with her hands. She was squinting, the light hard on her eyes. Nick remembered that she had somehow been speaking to him minutes ago. She had helped him. Or had she? She *had* invaded his thoughts, been there in his dreams somehow.

He shook his head, aware that the beginnings of paranoia were slowly beginning to wake. Not good. He had enough to deal with.

Another image; the corridor. Long. White. So many doors. Each locked. Turning Handles. Locked. And then one standing open. One. And inside…

'That was real…' That sentence slipped out without Nick even being aware.

Adam was now panting, joining them on the grass verge.

'It's not…' he panted, bending over, either about to be sick or collect his breath. Or both.

'You're getting seriously unfit there, Adam,' Nick joshed.

Adam stood, steadying himself with his hand on Nick's shoulder. He was shaking his head.

'Real,' he managed.

That word. Nick felt himself falling, as if his soul was being untangled from the inside. He saw himself as sinew, millions of threads, each with electrodes rushing along their length. He held his hands out before him, half expecting to see little sparks of light - life - rushing along him, as if he were made of electricity, muscles now wires. Cables.

What is happening to me? his frightened mind enquired.

'None of this is real,' Adam managed at last.

Cyrus was perched on the grass, his hand held before him, Saffi now taking it in hers. Nick saw Saffi had her eyes closed again, and - he must be dreaming - a white light was emanating from her.

'Electricity,' Nick muttered.

Nick stumbled, his hands now searching Adam for support.

'Hey, whoa… you OK there, Nick?' Adam steadying him.

Nick lifted his head, eyes meeting Adam's, horror and madness hiding just beneath the surface.

'It was real. The corridor and the doors. They were real. And I wasn't… I wasn't a kid, Adam. We were there. All of us.'

Adam felt like hugging him. Felt like holding onto Nick and never letting go. He was a lifeline. If they just embraced, just stayed like that, maybe all this would simply cease to be.

'Reality is only what we tell each other it is,' said Cyrus.

Nick turned, still holding onto Adam.

'What?' he puffed.

'It's true. Sane and insane can easily change places, if the insane becomes the majority. And then we'd have a different reality.'

'But… this isn't real,' said Adam.

Nick felt like retreating again, just collapsing to the floor and going into his safe space. Into the dark where nobody can hurt him.

Saffi was still glowing white. Cyrus had his eyes closed, looking like he'd already died.

'Are we… are we insane then?' managed Nick.

Cyrus didn't answer, he lay propped against the tree trunk, his mangled hand safely clasped between Saffi's healing palms.

Adam piped up adding to the confusion; 'Look. That guy standing down there. He's not real. He's…' Adam was unsure how to finish. Unsure if he should even try. Had he really seen what he thought he'd seen? The mind was renowned to play tricks, especially in dire circumstances. A survival thing.

He took a deep breath and ploughed on, realising with each word that he was sounding more and more insane. If what Cyrus had said was true, Adam realised that with each word he was crossing the line, shaping their new reality. An insane reality.

How much can the human mind take?

To add another layer to his unasked question, Nick collapsed on the grass at Adam's feet.

It appeared his mind, at least, had taken all it could.

CHAPTER 22

ADAM

He bent low, his hand resting on Nick's chest. Adam wasn't too concerned. Nick was gone again, that was all, back into his safe zone.

He could feel the steady rise and fall of Nick's body as he continued to breathe. *Lucky bastard*, Adam thought.

He glanced across at the two hippies, those strangers who had been thrown into this chaos with him. Nothing about this day was sane. Nothing.

How had it come to this?

Adam remembered how he had been so upbeat only an hour ago.

Was it really only an hour?

How life can change so fast.

Sane to insane.

They had been in Doug's car, driving to their big meeting, all full of hope, nervous excitement about the opportunities that may lie ahead.

And then everything had changed.

Adam thought back to before the car journey, trying to bring sane thoughts into his mind, channel his family to give him strength.

Only… his mind was blank. He couldn't recollect his family. A sudden rush of panic bloomed in his chest. *This is it,* he thought. *This is where I'll die. Heart attack. Here, on this dual carriageway verge. Here, with these two hippies. One glowing. The other dying. Here, with the shimmering man.*

Here.

He lay back on the grass, struggling to breathe, but aware it was he who had ultimate control over this. He wasn't dying. Knew that from the panic attacks he had suffered-

There! See, a memory. Good.

He took deep breaths, eyes closed, hand still on Nick's chest, timing his breath with Nick's. Adam suddenly felt more alive than he ever had. Felt a connection with everything. Felt part of something bigger.

No longer felt alone.

What a fucking rollercoaster, his anxious mind screamed at him. Welcome to the rollercoaster of Massive Emotional Outpouring. Roll-up, roll-up, ride if you dare. Look out for the Shimmering Man. Look out for the twists and turns. The explosion you can see but cannot hear! The Hippies, one glowing white, the other The Yelling Man. And don't miss the Ginger Pig-Tailed Girl who rises to the sky over and over again. See them. Picture them! The cars, all the same, all going on forever into the distance. And the loop! Oh, don't miss the loop-de-loop! The best bit of the entire ride! The loop-de-

'Loop.'

He opened his eyes.

CHAPTER 23

CYRUS

How can this be?

He, a Chosen One, injured like this. He was on the brink, or so he believed, of finding out who was causing all of this. He'd seen the helicopter. Seen the damn thing flying overhead. And Saffi, she'd sensed it too. Sensed its danger. *Must be a terrorist attack.*

And then another explosion; seen, felt, but not heard.

Had he felt it?

Cyrus didn't know. The pain in his hand was now subsiding. A numbness was taking its place.

Have to stay awake. Have to stay awake.

That thought, repeating over and over, forced him to stay in the moment.

The big guy had collapsed and Cyrus had neither the energy or care to help. The skinny guy, the one with the tendons forever standing taut on his neck, looked like he was about to join his mate.

Cyrus pitied them; remembering their car crash not long ago. How had so much happened in such a short space of time?

Cyrus had drifted, his eyes closing and opening, giving himself moments of deep relaxation, with glimpses of awareness. With each opening of his eyes, he saw another changed scene. Saffi massaging the back of her neck healing herself. Easing her headache. She'd saved the big guy. Then the big guy lying down. Then Saffi, next to Cyrus himself, cupping his hand.

Eyes closed.

Open again; Saffi beginning to glow, her magic now working on him. He loved her more than ever at that moment. She'd suffer, always putting others first. A true spirit.

Closed. Open; the skinny guy now going, Cyrus seeing a glimpse of his shoe on the grass. He must have fallen behind the big guy.

Closed. Open; head tilted back. The leaves standing perfectly still above him. Cyrus smiled.

Closed. Deep breath. Open; fire, specs of orange and yellow flickering between the leaves. Like intense sunlight. The other side of the Breaker.

Closed.

A word from the skinny guy. Loop.

It's all a loop.

Open.

CHAPTER 24

ADAM

He sat bolt upright, like a vampire from a coffin.

'I can't recall them because they're real. This isn't!'

He got to his feet fast, a look of jubilation on his face. He didn't know what to do first. A line from Dickens' *A Christmas Carol,* came to him (not that he'd read it, only seen the Muppet's version one Christmas); Scrooge delighted that he'd been given a second chance by the three ghosts and unsure what to do first.

Adam laughed out loud, his hand stroking his blond hair.

'You see!' He jumped Nick's body, squatting before Cyrus, alongside Saffi.

Saffi had dropped Cyrus' hand, her white glow had faded. Both were looking at Adam, clearly believing he had finally flipped to the minority; the insane.

'It's not real. I can't recall my family.' He looked off to one side, 'Nope, not even where I live. Or what I had for breakfast today. Or…' He was grinning like a madman. He looked to their eyes, hoping to find understanding.

Instead, he saw pity.

Saffi reached out, her hand touching Adam's. She tilted her head.

'Don't you dare,' his voice was breaking. 'Don't you fucking dare.' Still she held firm, her touch soft, healing. Caring. Adam shuddered, knowing his breakdown was almost complete. First the jubilation. Now the tears.

'I can't remember them. I can't. No matter how hard I try. And that's because…' he looked over his shoulder, Nick now lying in a fetal position, his coping mechanism complete. Further behind Nick, the road. The completely caved-in car - Doug's car. The two lanes of traffic, shimmering. And the man himself, still standing between the lanes. Gazing into the sky. The Shimmering Man.

Tears ran down Adam's cheeks, a silent cry, refusing to provide the soundtrack to his mental breakdown.

'Shhhh…' Saffi.

Tending to him. Man, how he loved this girl. He didn't even know her. But how he loved her, right then. His heart felt like it was breaking inside his fragile chest.

'I… thought… I just thought…' the tears stinging his cheeks. 'I thought I had it figured out, y'know? None of this is real. It's all working on a loop. It's all re-setting and…'

'It's OK. Shhh…' She had moved closer, lightly stroking his head, bringing it to her shoulder. A mother's embrace.

'Dude, it's cool bro. This is one fucked-up day!' Cyrus tried to help. A poor second to Saffi's naturalness.

Adam could smell her. He relaxed, giving in to his emotions.

And then the memory came back, one followed by another, each a snapshot in his mind. A flick book of his life, shutter-click, shutter-click, shutter-click, photograph by photograph sweeping into his consciousness. He pulled back from Saffi.

That smell.

It had triggered the realness. The reality.

His reality.

He pushed her away from him, studying her face hard.

'I know you,' he said. 'I know you!'

CHAPTER 25
SAFFI

The feeling was everything she expected it to be. Everything she'd ever hoped it would be. From her earliest dreams as a child, that powerful super-human idea. The healer. Not someone who fronted comic books, no, this was more hidden. More secret. And more powerful. Could even be real. In another world maybe.

Another time. Another place.

Cyrus had come to her with such pain, battered hand, bleeding, feeling on the edge of despair. Saffi knew she could do it, but this time she had turned the volume up a notch. Just to see.

Just to feel.

And how she had.

Clasping his damaged hand in hers, she had entered into a trance. One of power. One of completeness. She felt whole. Felt at one with everything, the life force itself coursing through her veins. She felt electric. Felt light. Saw light. Bright, white, energy, coursing over her, through her. And with it came love.

It was orgasmic. She hadn't wanted it to end.

She was aware of the others around her, aware they were watching. But it didn't matter. This was her moment. Aware too of the chaos above, the floating people, trapped in torment; a modern Gates of Hell. Dante would not be amused.

Aware of the helicopter (or something) above the floating people. Aware it had fallen. Aware another had fallen with it.

Angels above the sea of misery.

And it had all been taken away in an instant as the skinny guy had looked at her. Looked into her.

I know you. I know you!

He was right.

It clicked right then, the final piece of the jigsaw fitting neatly into place.

None of this was real.

CHAPTER 26

CYRUS

He leant forward, gently curling his undamaged hand into a fist. If this guy was losing it, then he'd best be prepared to take him down. In case he gets violent. He wouldn't let him touch a hair on Saffi's head.

'OK bro… take a deep breath, my man. All's OK. It's just your way of trying to deal with this chaos, yeah?'

But the guy - what was his name? Adam, that was it. Always have their name if you want to get control of a situation. Who had taught him that? Didn't matter.

'Adam, yeah? We need to sort your friend out, Saffi can help. Then we need to *calmly* (Cyrus was mindful to drag the word out with emphasis. NLP or some shit he recalled) put our heads together and work this out. Calmly. Yeah, bro?'

Saffi had her back to him, but when Adam had claimed he knew her she had almost leapt away from him. Like she'd been tasered.

'Saffi? You cool, yeah?'

She didn't reply.

Cyrus rolled onto his hip, as careful as he could, mindful of his mangled hand. He pushed himself onto his knees, wincing at the pain that shot up his arm. *Breathe,* he told himself. Calm. He'd be OK, he was a Chosen One.

Saffi and Adam both stood, holding each other's hands, like lovers before a first dance. Cyrus was not impressed.

He hobbled over, wondering why he felt his legs had taken just as much punishment as his hands.

'Guys, break it up, yeah. We need to…'

Adam turned, staring with such intensity into his eyes that Cyrus felt the sudden urge to run. Something big was going down here.

'Adam bro, you look tired.' Cyrus was right in that observation. Adam's eyes were incredibly blood shot. He looked like he was about to morph into something from 'the other side'.

Werewolves.

That was all Cyrus needed now to add to this already messed up day.

Cyrus glanced briefly to the heavens. *This must be a test. A test from God.* He couldn't see the heavens, just the Floaters through the tree leaves and glimpses of the flickering flames above them. Thank God for the leaves. Without them, the scene would have been horrific.

Saffi looked at Cyrus, her eyes now sharing that same intense look. Cyrus felt suddenly afraid. Zombies? Was that the next stage of this unfolding nightmare?

'He's right Cyrus. He's right.'

'Okayyyy,' he added, slowly as if addressing a madwoman.

'It's not a dream, it's like a dream, but it's not. We're here. But we're…'

'Not,' Adam finished for her.

Cyrus backed away from them, wanting to run. Wanting to, but at the same time realising how pointless that would be.

'What's round the bend?' Adam asked.

You two fucking loonies! Cyrus bit his tongue, the words almost out.

'What do you mean?' asked Saffi.

Adam dropped her hand.

He saw Saffi shudder almost imperceptibly, a magic gone between them. Cyrus was jealous. And a jealous man pushed to the edge… *and*, with injured fingers? Well, who knows what that kind of anger could manifest into.

Adam was suddenly all smiles, pacing from foot to foot. 'See, I've always been a details guy. That's how I know that he,' Adam pointed off into the lanes of traffic, 'isn't real. He was flicking in and out of existence. That was the first flaw in their plan.'

'Whose plan?' Cyrus' question fell on deaf ears. Adam was on a roll. Another sign of his increasing breakdown. And Cyrus was dammed if Adam thought he was taking Saffi over the edge with him.

'And so, I know, I remember, what was around the bend when we came flying round. I remember Doug driving way too fast. I remember being in the golf club. I remember it all. But I don't remember what happened before that.' He was speaking fast now, his voice rising.

That's because you're having a nervous breakdown bro, Cyrus thought, choosing to let it remain unsaid. Better safe than sorry. His good hand was still balled into a fist.

'And so, I know that if we all go round that bend, I know what I should see. Even down to the last tree. And another thing! Look…' he ran excitedly, like a kid entering the lounge on Christmas morning to see what Santa had brought, '…where's any other cars? Where? We were the last car to come round that bend! The *only* car to come round that bend!'

Cyrus frowned. That was the only sensible observation the skinny bastard had said. Saffi was looking at Adam, her hands clasped to her chest, like a teenager excitedly watching her boyfriend score the winning goal at the school's football tournament. He expected her to break into a cheer-leading routine any second. Give me an A… Give me a D…

A-d-d-i-c-t.

Ah, that was making sense to Cyrus now. The guy was obviously an addict! The bloodshot eyes. The extreme changes in mood. Emotional outbursts.

And seeing things.

Seeing people shimmering. Yeah, likely! Cyrus glanced down the dual carriageway, scratching his cheek as he saw the guy still standing, there, between the lanes, explaining something to someone who wasn't there. The guy's hands gesturing apart, as if he were describing the explosion overhead. A bomb.

OK, so maybe that bit was right. But the rest?

The cars… he had that point too. They did all look the same in the distance. But that could be a trick of the light. And the cars this end? Another point. Why had no other cars…

'Because the Police have stopped the traffic, man!' Cyrus yelled a little too enthusiastically.

Adam was still pacing back and forth, an excited teacher telling his pupils of his favourite battle scene in history. Still grinning.

'That's why!' continued Cyrus. 'Go round that corner and you will see the Police signs, see the tape. We're in the middle of all of this shit!' Cyrus' hands echoed the Shimmering Man's, moving apart from one another gesturing to everything around them. His arms dropped to his side, the fist clenching routine increasing in pace. The pain shooting up his damaged arm almost forgotten.

Adam laughed. Another notch toward madness. 'So, let's go round there then! What is there to fear? If there's help, then let's get help!' Saffi clapped. Cyrus blinked unbelievingly. She had fallen for this crap.

For *his* crap.

The ramblings of a madman. Round the bend. It was even in the guy's speech for Christ's sake!

Cyrus stepped forward, clenched fist (fortunately, it was his good arm). This guy was dangerous. There was only one course of action. Cyrus smiled, forcing the grin. He needed to take back control. And he knew the first step.

'Adam,' he said.

Always use their name. Always.

CHAPTER 27
ANGELA - ABOVE - LYING NEXT TO TASHA

She thought time may slow down, something often depicted in movies when the hero jumps in-front of the car to save the screaming kid, frozen like a deer in the headlights. But this was real. And time didn't slow down. Angela fell from the helicopter, making a last final effort to ensure the helicopter was forced onwards and slightly upwards, so it didn't end up whirling down on top of her.

She fell, rolled and landed next to Tasha's body.

'Ummph.'

Angela lay there, unsure if she were dead or alive. She felt a tingling all over her skin, like electricity charging along the fibres of her body. Had she heard something? She scanned herself mentally, trying to gauge if she had broken anything.

Step one was good, possibly. She was alive. Her cognitive thoughts proved that.

Step two was better, nothing appeared to be broken. The Breaker had saved her fall. Breaker? Ironic really. Nothing was broken.

Step three, best; Tasha was groaning.

Angela rolled onto her side, hand extended wondering if she should touch Tasha. She may be electric or hurt.

This must be a dream.

'Ungh.'

'Tasha?' a whisper.

She dared not speak louder, in case the dream was shattered.

Angela put her arm over Tasha, bringing herself into a press-up, her body hovering above Tasha.

The helicopter exploded on impact only meters from her.

The helicopter made no sound, gave off no heat. Just exploded on impact. It should have been close enough to incinerate her and Tasha.

Who cared? The helicopter was metal. Metal was already dead.

Next to her was life. Tasha on her back.

'Tasha?' another dangerous whisper. The fragile dream tested again. Everything was holding. Maybe, just maybe…

'Omg… Angela?' said Tasha, her camera lying alongside her. It looked like a mechanical extension of her shoulder. A futurist human cyborg - part lesbian, part camera.

Angela had tears in her eyes, of joy, sheer joy. Despite everything they were alive.

Angela breathed the air, clear, clean. She pushed off one arm, rolling onto her back, snuggling up against her lover. Facing the endless blue sky above, Angela counted her blessings.

'We shouldn't have got through this,' she muttered.
She was crying, tears falling onto the Breaker beneath, wetting her hair. Angela felt incredible guilt. She was alive. They were alive. But beneath them, almost to the touch, were the other humans she had seen floating at the start. Bodies, people with names, with lives.

Another soft thud came from underneath; another floater had joined those already there.

Maybe we'll soon die up here anyway.

She had tried to get down past the Breaker in the chopper and that had failed. It appeared to go on forever, infinite. If she couldn't find an edge to it, to pass back under it while flying, she had no hope on foot.

No water, no food.

Trapped. Above the ground.

Another tear fell. She was alive. Tasha was alive.

But for how long?

CHAPTER 28

SAFFI

A vision.

Two women. Huddled together like lovers.

They were close yet not close enough to get to.

She thought of the shimmering man.

He's telling us. He's a sign.

One thing at a time.

She breathed out through pursed lips, calming herself.

Saffi walked a little way from the group now under the canopy of the trees. She needed time to think. Space to clear her mind. To order things.

As she did, her dress flickered impossibly, like a rainbow through a waterfall.

One; the shimmering man is a clue. She felt sure of it.

Two; there are people above the Floaters. Directly above. She saw them in her mind.

Three; the shimmering man. His hand gesture… in and out. Expanding. Contracting. Like breathing.

Four; the shared memories when she touched another. Saw their thoughts, their fears. Saw *them*.

Knew their names.

Five; the one called Adam *(It's not real, nothing is real)* and Cyrus acting strangely toward him.

She sat on the grass, legs crossed, eyes closed.

Focus.

Another vision; a man with a bright white hand. An oriental lady. Young.

Yet more…

Two black people, young man and woman.

A tube station. A man and smartly dressed woman. Scars on her wrists. Blood streaks down her face.

She hurts herself.

A package.

The smell of flowers. Spring flowers.

And… a face she couldn't quite make out. Dreadlocks. Holding something. Black. Shiny.

Dangerous.

She opened her eyes.

'Jared,' she said.

CHAPTER 29

BUSINESS/LUCY – INSIDE THE TUBE STATION

Lucy gently lifted the baby to her chest. The guy who had freaked her out when she became conscious was propped up against the opposite wall, head lolling, either asleep, dead or passed out. She didn't care which.

Her bottom lip quivered as she looked at the tiny face asleep in her arms. A tear fell onto the baby's cheek, yet still she didn't wake.

'I always wanted you,' she whispered. Her tears became sobs as she recalled the miscarriage. The one caused by him. Her ex. She bit her lip hard, causing blood to swill into her mouth. Another familiar taste from life with her ex. The pain caused her to stop sobbing and get a grip. She pushed the sadness deep down, back under the floorboards of her heart.

God had given her a gift. This baby.

A second chance.

Lucy stood, her knees cracking, wondering what to do next. Should she wake the guy who seemed to know her? Or should she-

The guy.

There *was* nobody else.

She put out her hand, steadying herself against the wall of the station, fighting nausea, careful to keep the baby huddled close (safe) to her chest with her other hand.

Where had everyone else gone? There was no-one else around.

'What…?' her words trailed off, confusion and dizziness overcoming her.

Next to her, the guy opened his eyes.

CHAPTER 30
JAMIE

Where was he? What time was it?

The noise of the station bought him immediately back to the chaos. There were people everywhere. How did it get so crowded? He felt like he was suffocating.

He gulped; his throat dry.

His eyes felt sore, like he was trying too hard to simply see.

The baby. Lucy.

He glanced up, seeing his sister's doppelgänger holding onto the wall, steadying herself. She had her back to him, but he could see a bit of blue blanket in her other arm.

The baby.

He had a fleeting vision of a man, grinning, rocking an invisible baby in his arms. Had he dreamt that?

Jamie struggled to his feet, his legs cursing him.

As he rose against the wall, the noise of the crowd diminished.

Jamie stood fully, his back against the wall, eyes closed, steadying himself. Everything went quiet. He heard his heart beating in his ears.

He opened his eyes and what he saw took his breath away.

The station was almost empty.

There was just one other person.

Lucy was still holding onto the wall. Still holding the blue bundle.

'What the…?'

CHAPTER 31
LUCY

She turned upon hearing the voice from behind her.

Her legs still felt like jelly and her stomach was racing with butterflies.

She checked herself, biting her lip again hard.

Yes, the pain was real. This situation was real.

The man was facing her. She mustn't let him hurt the baby. *Her* baby. Not again, no matter what. She'd fight him with all the strength she had left.

Instead of coming at her, the guy slid back down to the floor.

CHAPTER 32
JAMIE

This must be an illusion, he thought. A great magic trick bought on by drugs or something. His body must be elsewhere, lying in bed. Had he taken an overdose?

He closed his eyes, trying to think about what had happened. All he could picture was running, running, running. People ascending like balloons.

This wasn't a trick.

The girl with the baby turned to look at him. She looked like he felt: Exhausted. Terrified. Lost.

He sank back down to the floor and as he did, the illusion returned.

People re-appeared all around him, a sea of legs, briefcases, handbags.

Smells returned, odours, filth.

The baby woman remained as she had when he was stood up. She was still looking at him.

Summoning his strength, Jamie urged himself upright again.

And just as before, the people vanished. The noises, smells, chaos; all disappeared.

He shook his head.

'Give her to me,' he gestured to his sister (*it's not her, only looks like her. She's dead. Died when I-*) No, his mind wouldn't let him go there. Not right now. He had enough to deal with.

The lady took a step back, instantly guarding the baby with her body.

'No,' she said. Blood spilled from her mouth.

Is she a vampire? Jamie thought. *Is she going to eat the kid?*

He was going mad.

'But you've got to see this,' he said. 'The people, right? They're… they're…'

The lady took another step back, turning her body three-quarters on, body language making it clear the baby was to be protected from him.

'I'm… I won't hurt her… or you,' His voice sounded unconvincing. 'You just need to see the people. Just sit down and tell me what you see. *Please.*'

Lucy was scared. What people? This guy was dangerous. She looked about her, desperately seeking others for support. For help. If this guy went for her, she knew he'd easily over-power her. She couldn't lose another baby.

Please, God. Please. Not again.

Jamie smiled, feeling his face starting to crack. His reality was rapidly falling apart. She must trust him. He'd never hurt her.

'I never meant to hurt you… it was an accident. I only ever planned to hurt him.'

Lucy felt panic rising. She didn't know whether to run or not. Fighting wasn't an option. She was weak. Running was a possibility. But something told her this guy would easily catch her. He looked agile.

'Who… who do you think I am?' she said, voice quivering.

'You're not her. I know that. But you look like her. My sis… her name was Lucy. She…'

He was clearly confused. She thought it best to let him continue. Gave her more time to think of an escape plan.

Jamie continued. 'She… died. It was… it was my fault.' What was he doing? Confessing to a stranger! This was madness. Tears coarsed down his cheeks, cutting through grease and dirt. Lucy admired the way it created clear track marks on his skin. Reminded her of her marks. Her scars.

CHAPTER 33

LUCY

Scars. Track marks.

Boom!

The memory flooded her totally without permission or restraint. Emotionally. Physically. Spiritually.

She was engulfed.

Overwhelmed.

She was in a hospital. A special one. Everything white. Everything shining. Not a trace of dust or dirt. Her arms were heavily bandaged. A doctor and nurse were with her. Both dressed in white. Behind them stood two others. Wearing black. They were here for her. The doctor looked at her sympathetically. Had she been injured? Attacked?

The nurse's expression wasn't as kind. She felt anger coming from her.

What had she done?

Another vision: a needle. Her arm in a tourniquet. Veins. A man. Him. Her ex. His teaching her, showing her, helping her, *grooming* her. The overdose. And then waking here, in this place. And the news. The devastating news.

The miscarriage.

Then her being led away by the arms. No cuffs applied due to her bandaged wrists.

Why hadn't they let me die?

She deserved it. She'd taken her baby's life.

A nursery rhyme: Ring-a-ring o' roses. A pocket full of posies. A-tishoo! A-tishoo!

We all fall down.

A click bought her back to the present.

CHAPTER 34

JAMIE

He'd lost her. She went somewhere, he saw it in her eyes. He had to get the baby from her before she did something stupid. He couldn't let her lose another baby!

Stop, Jamie. No! This isn't YOUR Lucy. That was an accident for fuck's sake.

'I'd only meant to kill him. That was all.' He was crying now.

He wiped at his eyes with the sleeve of his jumper.

'Listen, please…' he clicked his fingers in front of her, trying to bring her back into focus.

Ah, there she is.

'Look, I know it all sounds crazy, but I promise you I'm not going to hurt you or the baby. Promise. Cross my heart and hope to die and all that.' He made a gesture, crossing his heart. He didn't hope to die. Not just yet. He wanted to figure this situation out first.

'Just, please, put the baby down and see what I saw. There's ghosts…' he regretted the word as soon as he had said it. Ghosts. No better word for convincing someone that you actually are crazy. Seeing dead people.

'… I mean, ghost-like people… oh, fuck it, JUST SIT DOWN… *NOW!*'

CHAPTER 35

LUCY

He was clicking at her. Rambling. He was crazy. If only there was someone around to help.

Now he was shouting.

Her only choice was to humour him, keep him calm.

Do as he says. No. I spent years doing as he said and I became a drug addict. I lost my baby. It was all his fault.

She silenced her inner voice.

'OK. Just stay there, OK?'

Lucy bent over, keeping her eyes on him. She lowered the baby gently, so gently, to the floor. As she did, she heard noises. Voices. She saw legs. Lots of legs.

Lucy snapped bolt upright so fast, she almost passed out and dropped the baby.

Jamie rushed forward, steadying her, taking the weight of the baby.

'Did you see them? You did… you saw them, right?'

PART EIGHT

CHAPTER 1
NIGEL – OUTSIDE THE TUBE STATION

Quite where the dreadlocked guy had gotten the bottles of water from, Nigel had no idea. Jared the Magician. Ultimately, it didn't matter as everyone was desperate for a drink.

The relief washed down Nigel's throat, he thought he'd never tasted water so good…. so pure… so…

(*Everything is too clear, too… perfect. Like it's trying too hard to be real…*)

A strange thought.

Nigel stopped swigging from his bottle, suspicious of who was now gathered round him, of what he was drinking.

'We need to get inside. It'll be safer,' said the fat girl. Nancy, wasn't it? Nigel didn't remember names at the best of times, let alone with a seriously damaged hand *and* the events of the morning so far.

He chanced a look up and was astonished at what he saw. A human mishmash of body parts. People, no longer whole, melting into each other, like paint on an artist's palette. People of all colours and ethnicity, dissolving into each other.

Nigel felt sick.

The vision was bad. The noise was worse.

Whether it was in his mind or not, he was unsure. The whaling. Moaning. Nigel closed his eyes hard, squeezing his water bottle.

This can't be real.

Maggie's cancer. That had been real. The way she gradually disintegrated

(dissolved)

before his eyes. She'd gone from walking to bed-ridden in weeks. No, days. And what had the doctors said? Nigel couldn't remember. He couldn't actually recall any doctors or nurses coming to the house to see her.

Must be all that's going on, he convinced himself.

You're alright, Big Bear. You did your best by me. As you kept saying, we didn't need doctors.

Nigel shook his head. Yes, that was right. He didn't need doctors, specialists or nurses hurting, prodding, cutting, dissecting his wife. His Maggs. He could take care of her just fine, thank you very much.

But people did come in the end, Big Bear.

'Yeah, I think they did Maggs.'

CHAPTER 2

JARED

Jared smiled. He had the two black kids in tow and now he had the fat guy with the bad hand and the Asian girl too. His gut told him, this time it seemed easier than ever before. Although, he only had fragments of other times.

'Who has maps?' he said to white bag hand man.

Nigel glanced up, shaken from his trance. 'What?'

'You just said someone has maps?'

'No, it was my wife… I… no, sorry. You misheard me,' said Nigel.

Jared made a mental note to take Nigel down first.

Once he'd got the baby.

CHAPTER 3
LIHUA

Tired. Stressed. Struggling to hold it together, especially since losing Chunhua.

She's not lost. She's in the train-station. With them.

She turned to face the station entrance behind her, unclear how they had gotten back here.

And equally baffled why the streets were now empty. Hadn't there been loads of people around only moments ago?

Lihua was sure she'd soon have to drop the 'I don't speak English' pretense and start guiding these people.

She looked back at her group; the young med student who helped sort Nigel's gunshot wound; Jordan. The other girl, Nancy, who looked like she wouldn't be much help if they all had to suddenly run or fight. Lihua momentarily felt envious of Nancy's weight, perhaps the one thing helping to anchor her to the ground and not join the other Floaters.

She glanced up; the sight nightmarish.

Her eyes focused on a face, floating among the masses now straddling the sky, moving in one big mass, like rubbish on a river. One face, one pair of eyes staring back at her. She couldn't tear her gaze from those eyes. Their distress. Their anguish. Their guilt.

Their shame.

She thought back to Rei, Aabid and the endless rapes. How she would focus her gaze on something, anything, that happened to be in the room when it occurred. Looking at the object with such intensity, seeing its detail, colour, shape and size. Anything to keep her mind from feeling what they were doing to her body.

Nancy interrupted the spell.

'There is a map, inside the tube station, if you think that'll help?'

Nigel was about to say how he knew the roads and backstreets like the back of his hand - the one that hadn't been shot (Christ alone knew what the back of his shot hand would now look like) - but thought better of it. They did need to get inside. To get safe.

'They have my baby,' said Lihua.

The group turned to look at her.

'Who?' said Jared.

Lihua pointed to the station entrance, preferring to keep her secret of speaking perfect English quiet for now.

'We had no choice,' said Nigel. 'We just pushed her under the shutters before we could get inside ourselves. The bastards wouldn't let us in.'

'Well, there's nobody there now,' said Jordan. 'Let's just break it down and get in.'

Jared considered the group, weighing up his options. He could act now, but they might just over-power him. Better to wait until he could take them out one by one. He could lead them into the train tunnels. It'd be dark there. Easier to make them disappear.

'Good idea, kid. Let's do it,' said Jared, smiling to himself as they ran over to the station entrance.

CHAPTER 4
JAMIE & LUCY & CHUNHUA - INSIDE

He'd promised to keep her above waist level. To keep her above the sea of legs visible beneath that line. Lucy had trusted Jamie to hold Chunhua whilst she took a few trips lowering her body to a squatting position repeatedly, marvelling at the fact of the commuters disappearing every time she stood. It was like a camera edit, one scene moving seamlessly into the next.

'It must be something to do with the trial going on outside,' she said.

An odd word. Trial. Jamie frowned thinking about it.

'Why do you think it's a trial? I think we're under attack.'

Stood, Lucy paused her fitness regime, gesturing for the return of the baby (her baby).

Jamie handed Chun over. She was still fast asleep. Jamie was envious. If only he could sleep and block all of this out. This madness.

'Don't you feel it too?' she asked Jamie.

'Feel what?'

Lucy paused searching for the right words. 'Feel like we're being judged.'

Jamie considered what she said. 'One thing I do feel is that we need to keep moving. I'm not sure if we're sharing some kind of delusion or what. But I don't feel safe standing still.'

'I've read about that,' said Lucy, lifting Chun gently over her shoulder. The baby gurgled. Lucy and Jamie exchanged an anxious look. *Please don't wake now! A screaming baby is the last thing we need,* he thought.

Lucy patted Chun's back shushing her. She continued, lowering her voice, aware the tube station was deafly quiet. Eerily so.

'I've read about group thinking and how groups put under stress and deprivation can hallucinate as one, sharing the same experience.'

Jamie didn't know how to respond. He thought the notion was preposterous yet… they had both seen the legs beneath the waistline. The half-crowds going about their journey.

Their journey.

The idea hit Jamie like a lightning bolt. He once again squatted down to the floor, the voices, commotion and legs reappearing like magic. He studied what he saw, still overwhelmed by the sensory overload of the experience itself.

He was right. He stood, almost shouting at Lucy.

'They're not running away from the outside!'

'Shhh!'

He clamped a hand to his mouth and continued excitedly. 'The legs. The people beneath that line aren't running away from the entrance. They're going in all directions.'

'So… we're in some kind of time…' she couldn't find the right word.

Jamie stopped, thinking.

'Maybe we're dead.'

The moment he said it, it all seemed to make perfect sense. Lucy looked at him ready to burst into tears.

It was the commotion at the shutter that took their breath away.

CHAPTER 5
JORDAN – OUTSIDE THE SHUTTERS

He ran toward the shuttered station entrance. Nancy following in his wake.

'Jordan…' she panted, already out of breath.

Jordan turned in time to see Nancy fall over her own feet and hit the pavement bellyflop style.

CHAPTER 6
NANCY

As she fell, the little breath that hadn't already escaped her, was forced out of her body in a rush. She felt both embarrassed and ridiculous, seeing herself in her mind's-eye falling like a shit diver. A scene from one of the books she had been reading in the office (porn hub) came back to her; a woman clad in leather, dressed like a cat, crawling along the floor purring toward her master's feet. Lapping milk from a bowl, him stroking the leather ears of her mask.

Jordan was now next to her, his hand lightly on her back, checking on her. 'You alrigh…'

'Geddoff me!'

'Whoa, Nancy, calm down. I'm only trying to help.'

She felt stupid, trying her best to maintain some semblance of fitness. She rolled onto her back, eyes closed taking deep breaths.

'I'm… sorry… I…'

Jordan just nodded. 'You've scraped the skin off your cheek and forearms by the look of it.'

As soon as he said it, she became aware of a sharp stinging sensation on her face and arms. And a vision, as if from another world; a man, like a hippy, dangling from a car window. The car dragging him along. Behind him, a group of people stood under a tree. Among them a woman, burning bright. Glowing white.

Nancy opened her eyes.

And beheld the utter horror of the Floaters overhead.

She screamed, louder than she thought was possible.

Above her, the Floaters moaned in reply.

CHAPTER 7

JARED

Stupid bitch.

He had no sympathy for people who didn't look after themselves. Buggered if he was going to stop and help her up. He didn't mind being the hero when it mattered. Also didn't mind being the hit-man when it mattered either. To him, the two were almost the same. Just the circumstances differed.

He ran on, keen to be away from the mass of body parts whaling and moaning overhead. Keen to be inside the station.

The med student had gone back to help. Jared was fine with that. He pictured them holding hands, like they knew each other. And they were… what? Younger? And she was thinner. A lot thinner. He ran, shaking his head, clearing his mind.

And then he saw the man inside the station. And a woman.

And the baby.

His baby. His prize.

CHAPTER 8
NIGEL

He felt absolutely hopeless. He was supposed to be the hero here. He'd failed to keep mum and baby together. Failed to escape in the car. Failed on the bike.

(Tantrum? No, that wasn't right. *What are those bloody things called?*)

Tandem.

Yes, thanks Maggs.

And now Lihua was helping him, holding him up like she was a human crutch, his hand held high, the pain still incredible.

I'm a failure Maggs.

Hush now, Big Bear.

I'm a failure. I couldn't even save you.

Nigel held back the tears, not wanting to cry in front of Jared or the young guy.

In front of him, Nancy went flying. Usually, Nigel would have been the perfect gentleman and rushed to help. Instead, he looked at his bag covered hand (still brilliantly white and not a drop of blood had tainted it. Nigel found that most odd. Yet, his forearm was running with blood from his hand) and simply sighed.

Yep. Definitely a failure.

CHAPTER 9

LIHUA

He weighed a ton. But he'd helped her. So, she couldn't leave him behind.

She wondered how much blood he'd lost, his hand still held up before him to keep the blood from simply running out. She chanced a glance at him and realised he looked pale. She didn't think he'd last much longer.

Just got to get him into the station. Indoors. Get him safe. And get my baby back.

She stopped, Nigel humphing beside her. He'd been leaning heavily on her and had been stumbling in the last few feet of walking toward the station doors.

Her thoughts went to her baby. The one Nigel had bowled under the shutter doors. *These* shutter doors.

Yet, we got away from here? How can we be back here?

She momentarily considered she may have lost time. Somehow blanked out part of the journey, like she would when she was being raped *(stare at something, anything, look at the detail)*.

She saw Nancy fall down in front of her. Saw Jared glance back but run on toward the station. Saw Jordan, turn back and help.

And then her mind went back to Chunhua.

Nigel, the guy she was now helping, had given her baby away. He must have known there was no chance her or him could have gotten under that shutter, with all those people, with that closing gap.

He must have known.

No. He made a decision in the heat of the moment. Thanks to him, he'd saved Chunhua's life. She wasn't out here where the sky could take her.

No. He knew. He had given her baby away.

And for that, he must pay.

Nancy's scream forced her back into the present.

CHAPTER 10

NANCY

She had to turn over. Get that vision, those voices, that… *abomination* out of her head. She became convinced it would haunt her forever.

Stand up. Just stand up and it'll all be over, she told herself.

She tried to think of the leather Catwoman. Reading that stuff, she thought that was as low as things could get. But those bodies up there in the sky? That was unbearable.

I bet some sicko would whack off to that.

With gargantuan effort, she sat herself up and turned onto all fours (Catwoman flashed into her thoughts once again); her usual 3-point-turn from floor to standing position.

As she did, she looked toward the station.

And saw it crowded with people.

CHAPTER 11
JARED

Charm.

That was what this situation called for.

Many thought that those in the Armed Services only relied on violence. How wrong they were. The killers toolbox was full of all sorts of weaponry and charm was one of the most used.

It could totally disarm an attacker without spilling a drop of blood.

It could also get you laid.

Jared was a real-life James Bond, only black, with dreadlocks and without the suit. And he hated Vodka Martinis.

He slowed as he came to the closed shutter, its brick-like lattice all that stopped him from getting to the safety inside.

And to the baby.

He smiled at the smartly dressed woman inside (in other circumstances, Jared thought he'd certainly give charming her into bed a go) and a man holding what he assumed must be the baby wrapped in a blue blanket.

As he did, Nancy yelled out from behind him: 'The station is full of ghosts! Stay back!'

The smile vanished from Jared's face.

CHAPTER 12
NANCY

She couldn't believe what she was seeing.

The pain in her arms and cheek were momentarily forgotten, as too was the abomination floating above her (and the cat woman).

From her position on all fours, in the process of getting up, Jordan by her side, she was staring straight into the tube station entrance. And it was full of people. They were going in, coming out, commuters on an average day.

Where had they come from?

Jared was almost at the gate now; she saw him come to a halt just next to the closed shutter. His legs mingling with countless others. It was only thanks to his combat trousers she managed to keep him in sight. The irony crossed her mind; his camouflage pants actually stood out in the crowd, defying their point.

Jordan helped Nancy to her feet.

As she rose, an incredible thing happened. The commuters simply disappeared.

Nancy took a breath, her hands to her knees, her mind working overtime to make sense of everything. She glanced toward the shutters again; the legs had returned. As had the noise.

She stood up

(Just stand up and you'll be free)

the mirage of legs disappearing once again.

She shouted, warning Jared. In the heat of the moment, her vocabulary knew no other noun; they must be ghosts.

CHAPTER 13
JAMIE

Something didn't make sense. Or rather, yet *another* thing in this endless day of chaos and disruption wasn't making sense. Wasn't behaving in the normal realms of reality (or what he had previously thought of as reality).

He could see this man, running toward the shutter. He could see others behind him. Not many, just a small group. He could see them as clearly as he could Lucy.

Not trusting his senses, Jamie quickly squatted down, holding Chunhua carefully. The ghosts immediately returned; en-masse.

Ghosts.

One of the people outside the station shouted something at exactly the same time. Jamie was sure she had said ghosts.

Nothing else could explain something Jamie (and, it would seem, Lucy as well) had overlooked. The ghosts were passing through the closed shutters, coming and going.

But the guy who had run up to the shutter? He had stopped.

He's not a ghost. He's real.

Jamie stood, feeling the need to hold Chunhua close, protectively. Jamie knew he could run fast and far if he had to, but he didn't fancy running into the tunnels. One; he didn't know where he was. And two; he didn't want to mingle any more than he had to with the ghosts. Oh, and he didn't want to go outside and get sucked into the sky either.

But of all three options, for some reason, he felt he should be more afraid of this stranger at the shutter than anything e-

'Hi, I'm Jared.'

The dreadlocked guy put his arm through the shutter, extending his hand.

Jamie and Lucy exchanged glances.

Jamie was considering his options when Lucy spoke up.

'Jamie. Give her to me. Let's go.'

Jared's smile faded once again.

CHAPTER 14

JARED

Looks like I'll have to resort to another tool from the box.

Jared slowly pulled his hand out of the shutter.

He glanced over his shoulder. The rest of the group were still behind, huddled together, a few of them were hunched down like they were part of a rugby scrum. Jared had no idea what they were doing.

Got to get in.

If you can't break them down with charm, then just break them down.

He turned and walked a little way from the shutters, Lucy and Jamie taking it as their cue to go further into the station.

Nancy was hunched over, Jared thought she was being sick. Jordan was squatting, looking at Jared… no, looking *through* Jared, mouth agape.

What are they staring at?

Jared had intended to get a good run up and body slam the shutters, forcing his way in. But the look on Jordan's face stopped him dead.

CHAPTER 15

SAFFI – UNDER THE TREES

She stood, eyes seeing but not looking, her attention turned inwards.

She saw them: a smartly dressed woman, appearances deceptive (Scars, damage, baggage) glimpsed her name.

(Lisa? Lucy?)

Saw the man, flustered, running (always running, running, running) and saw the baby.

She spoke to them in her mind. *Go to the tunnels. Go to the escalator that is broken. Go up it.*

She didn't know how she knew, but Saffi guided them intuitively, knowing that they would soon be together.

And then she'd kill the baby.

CHAPTER 16
LUCY

Jamie was ahead of her, urging her on. Lucy felt an overwhelming desire to stop and glance below the waistline, to see if the ghosts were still with them. The invisible commuters.

Ghosts.

That's what the black girl had shouted from outside the shutters.

Ghosts.

The word chilled Lucy, making her cling the baby ever closer to her chest.

Ahead of her, Jamie came to a sudden halt, his head looking all around as if searching for something.

And then she heard it too. A woman's voice. A familiar voice.

Go to the tunnels. Go to the escalator that is broken. Go up it.

'Did you hear-?'

'Yes,' she said, cutting Jamie off.

'Let's go then!' urged Jamie.

'Wait… what escalator? The underground has loads of them, probably hundreds.'

Jamie paused, looking unsure how to proceed.

'And, I don't want to go into the dark, Jamie. Not with her.'

'It won't be dark. The power's on, look, there's lighting all around us.'

'But…' Lucy felt a strong part of her speak up deep from within, some primal in-built safety mechanism part of the brain, not used in modern times but still very much a part of being human, warning her not to go any further.

Jamie walked back to her and took her free hand.

'Look, we both felt that we couldn't trust that guy back there, right?'

Lucy glanced behind her, suddenly aware that she had forgotten about the dreadlocked man and the others.

'My legs. They feel heavy. Like I'm walking through treacle,' she said.

Jamie burst out laughing, forgetting the baby was sleeping, the sound reverberating all around them. Lucy felt like she was going mad.

'Treacle? When have you ever walked through treacle?!' He was aware he was making a joke to calm his own fears. Jamie had also found running more and more difficult, more tiresome, the further they had gone into the station. Like he was running with his lower half underwater.

'It must be… the energy of the ghosts,' said Lucy. 'Somehow, we're running against them, even though they're…' She was going to say invisible, but realised that was what ghosts are supposed to be. The very essence of being a ghost is that you are invisible. Most of the time.

'Fucking hell…' she began to cry. 'What am I talking about? Ghosts. What's happening to us, Jamie?' She looked into his eyes, searching for help, for understanding. Something to let her know that she wasn't going crazy.

CHAPTER 17
JAMIE

She's not crazy. I'm not crazy.
This is happening.

He walked back, feeling the path already easier to tread when facing away from the tunnels.

Maybe we're supposed to go back outside, he thought.

Choose the path of least resistance. Wasn't that the saying? But his instinct told him that was wrong. He needed to go into the station. To go to the tunnels. Go to the escalator that is broken. Go up it.

He put his hand on Lucy's shoulder and then gently turned her to face him. He felt like caressing her face, wiping away her tears.

You're so much like my sister. It's uncanny.

He felt like he wanted to fuck. Hard, violently. Like it was to be the last fuck of his life.

He felt desperate.

'Lucy, whatever this is, whatever is happening, it's making us feel… I dunno, depressed somehow. We've got to fight it. You heard that voice, yeah? We've got to find the broken escalator. I don't know how we know that, but I just know we have to.'

She nodded, her cheeks with white tear tracks that had cut through the grime, highlighting the blood red marks she had inflicted earlier.

'Maybe it was the voice of God,' she said.

Jamie bit his tongue. He wondered why the voice of God had been a woman.

He gently stroked the baby's head through the blanket. Without thinking, he leaned in and lightly kissed her. She was special somehow. She was key to all of this.

He felt it. Deeply.

CHAPTER 18
LUCY

The way he'd kissed the baby had reassured her. He was all she had to protect her.

She held out her free hand.

Jamie took it in his.

Together, with baby Chun cradled between them, they walked hand-in-hand into the station.

The lights flickered overhead.

Behind them a shout, a crash.

And then the lights went out.

CHAPTER 19
ANGELA

She stood, her legs felt like they'd been asleep or borrowed from a toddler.

'Fucking hell', she complained, hearing her joints crack.

'Tash? You OK?'

Tasha opened her eyes and held out her hand. Angela took it and tried to get Tasha to her feet.

'We've got to find a way down, baby.'

'My… camera.'

'What? Yeah, it's…' she looked around spotting it a few feet away. As she watched, a hand from the mass of bodies squirming beneath them rose up out of the cluster, like the arm of a dead person bursting through a grave.

'Impossible,' she whispered.

The zombie arm searched the smooth surface of the Breaker, hand grasping for something. Angela thought she could hear fingernails tapping on glass.

The disembodied arm grasped the camera and took it beneath the Breaker, back into the mass of bodies.

CHAPTER 20

TASHA

'Did you see that?'

Her hand was still being held by Angela, although her efforts to get up had proved disastrous.

'That was my camera!'

She looked at Angela, wanting confirmation it hadn't been a hallucination, hoping this was just a vivid dream and she'd soon wake up.

Got to stand up.

The voice spoke urgently, authoritatively.

Just stand up and it'll all be OK.

Angela heaved her up. She felt drugged.

'Oh, my head,' she said.

'Baby, I thought I'd lost you,' said Angela, her voice quivering. Tasha hugged her fiercely trying to remember what had actually happened. She remembered the helicopter, the bodies beneath the surface of the thing they were now standing on. She remembered leaning out for a good shot…

'I fell?'

Angela was sobbing on her shoulder. She looked up, their foreheads touching. 'You did, baby, but you're OK. We're both OK.'

Tasha took a deep breath, wishing they could stay in this embrace forever. It felt safe.

Angela broke it up. 'We've got to get down, and, if that arm could be on this side of this thing, then there must be a gap.'

Tasha, turned to look over at where the arm had come through. Only now did she realise what she was standing on, or rather, standing above, separated by the thinnest veil of glass. If it was glass.

The upturned faces, backs of heads, legs, arms, torsos. All squirming together. Tasha thought of a dead mouse she had found down the lane behind her house when she was a child. Every night after school, she'd purposely take a detour down the lane before going home, seeing what state of decomposition the mouse was in that day. By the third day the mouse had no eyes left. By the fifth day it was crawling with maggots. All of them squirming, fighting for their share of the mouse's body, its organs. Death giving life.

She was stood on human maggots. Feeding on each other. The upturned faces were horrific. She saw two heads coming close to each other. The ears touched. Saw the pure horror in the eyes of both faces. Saw one crying. The other mouthing something. There was no noise, only pure visual visceral horror. At once both stomach churning yet compelling.

The ears merged into one another, hair from one head merging, strands covering the eye, then nose, then mouth of the other. Just before Angela mercifully took her attention away, she saw the faces now conjoined, bloated, two noses, four eyes, two mouths, teeth spreading, tongues meshing, like acid poured over features. The faces dissolving, unifying, eyes and skin turning to liquid, melting into one another. Muscles and tendons being exposed, bone moving like jelly.

'Dear God…'

'Baby, don't look. Don't do it to yourself.' Angela was lifting Tasha's chin, bringing her eyes back to her face. Her beautiful face.

'What's happening? Those… poor people!' cried Tasha.

'I know baby, I know. Come, we've got to get down or we'll die up here.' She led Tasha by the hand toward where the arm had come through.

'No! No! I am NOT going through them Ange. NEVER!' She pulled back as hard as she could, releasing herself from Angela's grip, sending her skidding back onto her butt.

Tasha jumped up immediately as if she'd had an electric shock, not wanting to be anywhere near the people below her. Feeling dirty. Wanting to be away, far away, from them.

'Let's get off this fucking thing,' she panted. 'Where's the chopper?'

CHAPTER 21

ANGELA

She pointed to where the helicopter had crashed, to where the wreckage should be. Only, there wasn't anything there. Zip. Zilch. Not even a scorch mark.

'What the fuck?' she whispered.

Tasha's gaze followed Angela's across the vast infinite surface of the Breaker.

'It went down over there. It exploded Tash.' She looked into Tasha's eyes and took her hands. 'You've got to believe me.' Angela needed Tasha to believe her, feeling the threads of sanity gradually snapping one by one.

Tasha nodded. 'I do.'

I do. The one thing they had planned on doing. Before the

(Accident?)

Tasha shook her head briefly, clearing her thoughts. 'OK, so either way, there's no chopper. So…'

Angela read her thoughts. 'We get down over there. Through the gap that arm must have come through.'

Tasha dropped Angela's hands. 'No way. I'm not. I can't,' each word fighting back tears, her heart in her throat.

'It's our only hope, baby. I circled this thing we're on and there is no end to it. The bodies are stuck to it as far as I could see in every direction.'

Tasha felt panic rising. She felt trapped. *This is what agoraphobia must feel like.*

Angela tried to crack a smile. 'Besides, you can get your camera back from the thieving bastard who stole it.'

Tasha didn't laugh.

Hand-in-hand, they walked over the floating people, purposely avoiding eye contact with each other or those trapped below, closer to the place where the arm had come through the Breaker.

'What if there's no air below? What if it's deep, filled with bodies?' Tasha asked.

'They're only stuck to the underside of this thing. I saw when I was up there,' she pointed to the sky above, 'through gaps in these poor souls. There are still others on the ground beneath them. They seem to be alright.'

'Seem to be? Ange, I need more fucking proof than that!'

Angela dropped her hand, spinning round to face Tasha. 'Baby, look, I know you're scared. I'm trying to be strong for both of us,' her voice cracked, Angela didn't like the way it sounded. 'But I need you to be strong too, baby. We've got through… difficult things before… together. We can do this.'

Tasha took a few deep breaths, summoning the courage. She heard a low moan, coming from somewhere a few feet ahead. 'There,' she pointed. 'There must be a gap, I can hear them.'

Angela listened. She heard them too.

'What if it's not big enough for us to get through?' Tasha asked.

Angela thought hard. It was either try or die. They had to get through. They had to get down.

But once through the Breaker, how long a drop to the ground?

CHAPTER 22

SAFFI

She opened her eyes, aware that those who needed to hear her underground had done so. She had seen them in her mind, the smart woman and the man, holding the baby, moving into the station, into the dark. She felt the threat of the others behind them and the ghosts all around.

The dreadlocked man (the bad man) had broken the shutter. He was in, giving chase. Behind him, the others followed.

But now Saffi's attention was directed to others. Above them.

She looked up, preparing herself mentally for the onslaught of imagery that she would see. The mutilation, the utter horror of the Floaters, ones who had only hours ago, been like her, now suffocating, merging in utter despair. She felt them. Felt their anguish. She suffered with them.

But above them there was hope. Light.

Saffi walked back across the grass to where her group were waiting patiently. She knew they accepted her as their spiritual guide. They were waiting for her command.

My disciples.

Cyrus looked at her, keen to take some action. Before he could speak, she gave them all direct instructions.

'We need to climb that tree.'

She pointed to a large oak which hadn't been there moments before. The tree was an oddity, not only in its large size among the smaller roadside trees they had been sheltering under, but also its design. The side nearest them was bare, devoid of branches. Jutting out from the other side were branches, perfectly spaced, like a spiral-staircase. The uppermost branches of the tree were sparse, with only a few arms extending into the Floaters. The top of the trunk seemed to level out, creating a platform with the Floaters within arms-reach.

'Why do we need to climb that?' asked Adam. Cyrus was already running to the tree.

Saffi smiled. 'To help the women down. The ones trapped above.'

CHAPTER 23

CYRUS

Despite his throbbing fingers, he easily climbed the first few branches of the tree. As he did, he noticed how the branches seemed so perfectly placed, as if the tree was designed specifically for this reason. To be climbed by him right here, right now.

It was all too perfect. The tree seemed too real.

This is what someone who designs a tree would make it look like.

The thought made little sense to Cyrus, yet it caused him discomfort. Why should he be afraid - strange word to use but it fit - perfectly afraid of this tree?

'It's too real,' he said aloud.

Behind him Adam was already catching up. Cyrus glanced back seeing Saffi helping Nick across the grass to the bottom of the tree. As he stopped to watch her, he saw the grass shimmer, flicker.

Don't think. Just move.

He climbed higher, the moaning of those trapped above becoming louder.

CHAPTER 24

NICK

He was grateful for this beautiful woman. She exuded strength. He felt revitalised just being near her and now she was helping him stand, crossing over to the base of the big oak tree.

'You know, in many mythologies, a tree of life runs through the Earth. We climb it to reach the Gods.' Nick didn't know if Saffi was listening to him or not, but it felt good to talk. Made him feel more normal.

'Although, this one seems to be a stairway to Hell.' He forced a laugh.

Christ, am I flirting with her?

Saffi didn't respond. He knew he'd have no chance with someone like her. Yet he wanted to stay near her, to touch her. To feed off her.

He stopped, letting her walk ahead without him. As she moved away, the sense of peace she had given him wore off almost immediately.

She's special. She's…

Not knowing why, Nick suddenly became fearful. He felt a great sorrow rise in his chest, threatening to overwhelm him. He felt despair. He felt shame.

She's not who she pretends to be.

The insight was strong, powerful.

Saffi turned to smile at him. Nick wouldn't meet her eyes. Instead, he walked past her, purposely avoiding any contact. He began to climb the tree.

CHAPTER 25

CYRUS

He'd gone as far as he could, the branches had led him round the trunk so easily, a stick-like spiral staircase. The moaning from those now within arm's reach was at a pitch that caused Cyrus deep remorse. He felt the despair. It cloaked him like a heavy coat. Cyrus wondered if this was what it felt like to be chronically depressed. The sheer weight of their despair was forcing him to hunker down.

Adam was now almost alongside. 'My head hurts,' he said.

'It's them,' said Cyrus, gesturing to the Floaters.

When a white light shot up through the branches, parting the bodies above, creating a space.

Just wide enough for Cyrus' arm.

CHAPTER 26
SAFFI

It was all coming together.

As always, she let the universe do its thing, never fighting it, just listening and going with its flow. And, once again, it was attracting everything to her.

She sensed Nick had glimpsed behind her mask, but she couldn't see clearly into his heart. *That's OK,* she told herself, *he'll soon be gone.* The universe would take care of him.

She stood rigid, allowing herself to be used, her body a conduit for the energies beneath her. She visualised pure energy, the purest light, saw herself helping rid the sky above of the human detritus.

The feeling started the way it always did, but this time it was turned up to the max. A vibration from the soles of her feet, up through her legs, hips, up her spine and then out through the crown of her head.

The white light beamed, grew, an intense heat filling her entire being. The grass around her beginning to scorch black.

She had to make a gap in the Floaters. To rescue the women trapped above.

She had two angels to save.

CHAPTER 27
NICK

He'd never felt anything like this.

With each sluggish step up the branches of the oak tree, his heart grew heavier. He was vaguely aware of Adam and Cyrus already near the top. Had they been taken by the sky? He had no idea.

Didn't want to know. Didn't really care.

Everything was dying and he felt it all; all of the shame, sorrow, regret and despair. He was carrying it all.

'Adam,' his voice weak, barely audible.

He can't hear me above the noise.

The sound of the Floaters filled his ears, his head, his heart. Total and utter remorse.

'Adam… make it stop,' he moaned. His head lolled onto his chest, hunching more and more, barely able to lift his leg to take the next step.

This isn't climbing. This is a stairway to Hell.

Out of nowhere an intense heat shot past his head.

And a light.

Of the purest white.

CHAPTER 28
CYRUS

He shielded his eyes, getting his usual funny feeling in his groin.

She was doing it! She was actually doing it!

He wanted to jump for joy, rubbing his hands together expectantly.

In moments the light was gone.

Cyrus looked up and saw clear blue sky through the hole Saffi's energy had made in the Floaters. He smiled. They had a way out.

He put his hand through, realising the hole wasn't quite large enough for his entire body. But he could squeeze his head through.

Something told him not to.

Tentatively, he reached through, using his hand to scope out the surface beyond the Floaters. Their moans continued to haunt his ears, yet he felt empowered.

She will protect me. My guardian angel.

His hand hit something. A solid object. He snatched it back through the hole.

A camera.

CHAPTER 29
NICK

'Adam?'

He didn't know if that time he had even made a noise. His throat was beyond dry. It felt scorched.

What's happening now?!

Nick leaned forward, his mind and body struggling to cope, realising he no longer cared what happened next.

He fell from the tree branch he was on, his body flickering into non-existence.

****

A white corridor. A knock on a door. Handle turned. A woman. He didn't know her. Did he?

He walked in and sat across from her at the desk.

She smiled.

Do I know you?

She began to talk. She slid the paper toward him, nodding toward the pen.

He saw his hand pick it up, shaking slightly.

Do I know you?

He studied her face; the kind smile.

But her eyes.

They gleamed with power. He had no choice.

He signed the paper.

****

As Nick fell, he became aware of voices, hands, people around him, touching him. His soul was in free-fall but his body felt still. He was aching. With a sudden pain in his left arm, Nick's spirit was re-tethered back to his body. He felt whole again.

He opened his eyes.

CHAPTER 30
NIGEL – OUTSIDE THE STATION

It hurt like hell, but he was determined to catch a glimpse of whatever Nancy and Jordan were getting all excited about.

Keeping his injured hand as upright as possible, he crouched over, Lihua assisting as best she could.

When you're out of this, you need to lose some weight, Big Bear.

He silently agreed with Maggs that he'd give dieting another go.

The sight was worth it.

Below waist level, like an invisible water line, the world looked different. Sounded different. Even smelled different.

There were people everywhere, just like a normal day. He could see countless shoes, shapely legs, high heels, trousers, jeans, handbags, briefcases, sneakers, even sandals (the guy with white socks and trendy sandals stood out like a sore thumb in the mass of lower bodies, Nigel thinking how hipsters just *had* to stand out even if you couldn't see their annoying trimmed beards and tank tops).

He stood, catching his breath as he did, his eyes meeting Lihua's.

'You see them too, right?' he asked her.

Lihua nodded. 'Ghosts', she said.

Ghosts.

Nancy had been right.

Jared was now with them, listening. He turned, squatted effortlessly and stayed there for a while. Nigel wished he could see his expression, but he had his back to him. Nigel felt that nothing could seriously rattle this guy.

Watch out for him, Big Bear.

The pain in Nigel's hand was suddenly sharp and flowed through his body, his attention snapped back into the moment. He had to get some drugs.

Another voice, vaguely familiar came to him. *Get into the tunnels, find the broken escalator and come and find me Nigel. I'll heal you.*

He imagined a woman, a beautiful woman, dressed in red, long hair almost down to her waist (to where the ghost world begins) standing beneath an old oak tree. The tree seemed massive, too big for the others surrounding it, so high it reached through the clouds, through the Floaters. He thought of Jack and his mighty beanstalk. Nigel briefly wondered what ogre might soon descend.

'Can't be anything worse than those,' he muttered, glancing to the Floaters above. He'd almost forgot about them, what with his hand, the ghosts and this woman in red calling him. Guiding him.

Nigel noticed the light was strange, as if it was growing dark, yet it was still mid-morning or thereabouts. Wasn't it?

He had lost all sense of time. Even of place. He was outside the station but couldn't recall quite how he'd got here.

The big oak tree momentarily entered his mind again, flickered, like a strobe light had been shone on it, then he saw two escalators ascending from the underground; one had 'Do Not Cross' warning tape over the entrance. The oak tree world awaited him at the top of that escalator. He felt it.

Nigel took a deep breath, calming himself. All he had to do now was find the escalator.

CHAPTER 31
JORDAN

Whatever they were, when he was fully stood, they disappeared and for now, that was all that mattered to him. He sensed an urgent need to get into the station, breaking down the shutter if they had to. He knew he had to protect Nancy, even if her fitness slowed him down. Somehow, she was important to him, yet he couldn't quite place how and why.

Must be my duty of care as a med student, he figured.

No. It was deeper than that. In some way she was connected to him.

Maybe we knew each other in a different life.

A vision, so sudden and powerful, he reached out instinctively to hold onto Nancy's shoulder for stability; Nancy. Slim. Sat with him. A restaurant? He reached over the table and stroked her hand, so soft. Happy. She was happy. They were happy.

Another flash; then her calling his name. Screaming his name. Him seeing a reflection of himself in a rear-view mirror.

Flash. Another image. Blue lights. Him speeding away, lights off. A wooded area.

Flash. A comic book in the footwell. Cat Woman. Nancy in the passenger seat.

Flash. A woman, dressed in red, flickering, like a mirage, stood with white light emanating from all around her.

Flash. Two sets of metal stairs. One taped closed.

Jordan's breath escaped him as he was forced back into the present. His head throbbed. He felt like he'd just experienced an outer body shift, his soul leaving him and then violently returning. Even experimenting with drugs had never hit him like this. This felt so… real.

'There's a tree…' he said.

CHAPTER 32
NANCY

She finished his sentence.

'… At the top of the escalator. She waits for us there.' She turned to look at Jordan who looked like he was going to faint.

You're not how I remember you, she thought.

He looked at her, his brow creasing, lips quivering, eyes welling with tears.

We did something terrible.

'Not now,' she whispered. 'We'll talk soon. But now we've got to get to…'

CHAPTER 33
NIGEL

'…The woman in red.'

Lihua looked at him and nodded. Jared nodded too, everyone exchanging glances as if some secret unspoken pact had just been made. Whatever was going on, defied explanation. It appeared they had all shared the same vision, dream or mass hallucination. Exhaustion caused them to accept what was and move instinctively on.

CHAPTER 34

JARED

He turned, faced the station, yelled and charged.

His body cannonballed the shutter, it giving way, crumbling under the power of his attack. It bowed open, almost impossibly, creating a perfect arch, like an escape route under a chain link fence. Jared briefly considered how perfect the arch was, almost too perfect for the random attack.

He held out his hand, gentlemanly, helping Lihua through first, then Nigel (the white bag on his hand appeared to flicker in and out of existence as Nigel carefully crawled through, keeping his hand held high). Lihua screamed as she entered the gap.

'Close your eyes and stand up as soon as you're under. They're not real,' Jared shouted, referring to the ghosts that could clearly be seen when crouching down.

The ghosts were another acceptance of the group, tired minds being stretched to their limits, trying to keep a grip on reality.

'Just keep moving forward,' Jared offered.

It was wise words. Moving forward meant progress. Time for analysing could come later. For now, it was a matter of life and death. He felt it, was sure they all must feel it.

Time was running out.

Nancy and Jordan followed. Jordan stopped whilst ducking under the shutter, eyes wide. 'They look so real,' he said. He reached out to snag the leg of a ghost and his hand passed right through it. 'What the fu-?'

Jared gave him a boot up the ass. 'Keep moving!'

With the rest stood on the inside of the broken shutter, Jared took a quick glance behind him at the empty street. He looked up at the Floaters, still moaning and squirming into each other. He felt sick.

A deep breath, he crouched and crawled under the shutter, seeing the ghosts all around him as he did so.

CHAPTER 35
JAMIE - IN THE TUNNELS

The torch app was one he had always wondered about when it had first come out with the early smart phones. He was quite sure that he used to pay for the app, just to make the camera light come on and off. Now he suspected he paid even more for it, despite it being free on his phone, the cost of his monthly contract forever rising.

That usually worried him, the monthly costs of life. But right now, he was just grateful he had a phone, the torch feature and a nearly full battery.

The idea of running in the dark with ghosts alongside freaked him out. He was sure it was some memory from a Zombie film he had once laughed at, that made him think that should the lights go out, then the ghosts they had seen would be able to touch them. Consume them. He and Lucy (and the baby) running forever in the dark down here, ghosts themselves.

An eternity of commuters.

That was Hell.

Hell.

They were walking fast. It was too risky to run, although Jamie wished he could. He'd rather run and be out of here fast, than walk and be here for longer - forever - but he had the baby and Lucy to think about.

I've got you sis.

No. It's not her.

Christ, she looked like her though.

Holding Lucy's hand, he continued to lead her through the dark, torch held out in front, piercing the darkness. The station was silent, not a sound since the shout they had heard prior to the crash from behind them.

Jamie knew the dreadlocked guy was in the station. Chasing.

Hunting.

Jamie feared him more than the dark itself.

Step by step, urgent.

The darkness seemed to be getting heavier. Thicker. Choking.

He didn't know where he was going, blind and scared.

Lucy's hand felt sweaty in his.

Just check on her. Stop for a second and check. She may be your sister. Dead. Holding your hand. And her dead unborn baby.

'No, stop!' he said out loud, scaring himself and making the baby whimper. Lucy shushed it in the dark.

'Are you OK, Jamie?' she whispered, being dragged along behind him.

'Yes, sorry,' he replied, voice low. 'I'm not sure where we're heading, that's all.'

Come to me, Jamie. You're almost home.

The voice seemed to be all around them. Jamie thought it was the same one as before. The woman's voice. Soft, nurturing, reassuring.

Healing.

A dull white light appeared ahead of them.

Jamie and Lucy plundered on, hand-in-hand, toward the glow.

CHAPTER 36

ADAM – IN THE OAK TREE

'Nick? Nick?'

He called behind him, thinking he had seen Nick begin to climb the tree below him and should have now been far enough up the trunk to be with him.

'Nick?!' Louder.

No reply. He heard a rustle of leaves from the other side of the trunk.

He's either playing the fool or he's fallen.

I haven't got time for this, he thought.

He didn't hear a thud, so guessed Nick was just fumbling the other side of the trunk.

This tree is fucking huge, he thought. It seemed bigger now than it had at first.

Another trick of the mind.

I need water. I'm probably hallucinating.

When had he last had a drink? He couldn't recall. He had been going to a golf club for a coffee. Maybe a few drinks after. Him, Nick and… and…

Was there another guy? Adam couldn't quite remember.

Cyrus was a few branches (steps) above him. He was reaching into the white light. Reaching beyond the Floaters.

What's he doing?

He couldn't quite see Cyrus' face.

Adam hoped Cyrus' hand wasn't going to get trapped or ripped off. He'd not handled the previous injury well when his fingers were trapped in the car window.

'Aha!' Cyrus lowered his hand, gripping something.

'What's that?' asked Adam.

Cyrus turned, biting his tongue, a weird mix of mischief and excitement on his face.

His eyes beamed. 'It's from the angels,' he said.

CHAPTER 37
ANGELA - ABOVE THE BREAKER

The gap where the disembodied arm had come through the Breaker appeared to be widening. Angela didn't know if it was her eyes or a trick of the light, but a beam of white light seemed to be passing through, vanishing into the sky.

She rubbed her eyes. Opened them.

The beam was still there, appearing mist-like.

A woman appeared to be standing in the mist of the beam.

'Tash - is she… can you see this?'

Tasha looked where Angela was staring.

'Oh my God. Who is she?'

'More like, where is she?' said Angela, the ghost-like woman disappearing like a magician's illusion.

Then they heard the voice. *It's safe. Come to me. I'm Saffi.*

'Did you hear that?' said Tasha. 'It's safe, I'm safe?' Angela nodded. 'No, she said Saffi, I think.' She paused. 'Do we know her?'

Tasha frowned, trying to bring the woman's image back into her imagination. She saw red, a red flowing dress. Long hair. But the face was a blur. Hard to define. 'I'm… I'm not sure. I don't think so.'

'But her voice seemed familiar somehow,' said Angela.

'Either way, I think she's our only hope.'

'Maybe we're imagining all this. Maybe we're near to-'

'Don't say it Ange. Don't say that. We are not going to die up here. You… you…' Tasha's voice broke, the tears she had previously held back forming once again, trickling silently down her cheeks.

Angela smiled. 'No, baby.' She stroked Tasha's cheek, wiping away the tears. 'I was going to say that maybe she's a mirage, like a water fountain appearing in the desert. Come on, let's get closer to the light.'

They walked closer. The final few steps, almost a silent tip-toe as if they might disturb the monster under the

(glass) bed.

The white light pulsed. Angela thought of alien abduction documentaries she had seen but kept her tongue. She didn't want to alarm Tasha any more than necessary.

She peered into the gap which seemed to have been created by the light.

A man's voice greeted her.

CHAPTER 38
CYRUS

'Welcome to our planet!'

Cyrus held his hand up, the non-mangled one, offering it through the gap. Tasha screamed.

'It's cool guys, we're here to rescue you. I've got something I think might be yours. Adam, where's that camera?'

'Did he say he's got my camera?' asked Tasha the other side of the Breaker.

Angela looked back at Tasha, nodded and shrugged. The shrug said it all. She had made up her mind. Tasha knew it was pointless trying to talk her out of it now. Once she had made up her mind, she was not going to be-

Angela sat down on the edge of the Breaker, like a child dipping their feet in a pool. With one final glance at Tasha, she slipped through. 'See you on the other side, baby.'

'See, it's like being born again!' said Cyrus, taking Angela carefully, guiding her easily onto the wide branch on which he stood.

The moaning of the Floaters could be heard, albeit distant, despite their bodies being right alongside them.

Angela called up to Tasha. 'Come on baby, it's easy. You won't fall.'

First her feet, then her legs, Tasha descended through the hole. As soon as her feet touched the branch and she was safely in Cyrus' grip, the beam of light vanished. Like a light being switched off.

CHAPTER 39
SAFFI

Two angels.

Descending from the Heavens above. From above Hell.

Saffi always knew that spiritual guides existed, had written books on them, lectured on them and tried to tell the sceptics. Now she had living proof.

Sure, she had always thought that Hell was an underworld but she could live with that. It turned out Hell was floating about thirty feet overhead.

And here they came, back down the staircase of the tree.

Adam.

Angel One holding hands with Angel Two.

Cyrus.

Saffi frowned.

'Where's Nick?'

CHAPTER 40
ADAM

He looked at Saffi. Looked at the others. Where *was* Nick?

Adam sprinted off around the trunk of the tree, expecting to see a fallen body on the other side of the *(massive, how did it get so big, it wasn't here when we first got here… was it?)* tree trunk.

Before he realised, he was back with the group.

No Nick.

Saffi went to him, touching his shoulder. An electric charge ran through him.

'Nicholas. The fallen angel.' She looked crestfallen.

Adam brushed her hand away. 'What? What are you fucking talking about? Where the fuck is he?'

He looked accusingly at the newcomers.

Behind him, the grass opened like a rip in the Earth.

CHAPTER 41
JARED - INSIDE THE STATION

Despite being the last one through the broken shutter, he took the lead encouraging the others to stick close as he headed further into the station.

The others wanted answers (like he could give them!): Why were they following the other man and woman? (Jared didn't know if they were even aware of the baby.) Why there were a sea of ghostly figures all around them, only visible from a few feet off of the floor, why the people were sticking to the sky, why, why, why?

Jared realised he did have some of the answers. Not quite sure how he knew, but yeah, he knew. Or, at least, he had a strong instinct as to why things were happening.

(Commander, this is your first proper challenge so don't… mess… this… up!)

The voice clear in his mind. He shook his head, clearing his thoughts, marching on into the darkness of the underground.

CHAPTER 42

LIHUA

The moment she had first spotted them through the lattice work of the shutter, she knew that the couple had her baby.

Her Chunhua.

She had to play it calm. All the years of abuse at the hands of the gang had taught her to bide her time, wait for the right moment. She still had some cash left from the bathtub in the pockets of her coat, unsure if it would come in handy at some stage or not.

Patience. You may need a bribe.

Next to her, Nigel was starting to smell. Lihua considered it might be the wound or just might be him, being fat as he was and having to keep going through this… ordeal.

Ordeal.

Lihua had a strong memory flash before her eyes; her, another lady, white room. Some kind of contract. Stay here for longer or take the deal.

Remain or deal?

Next to her, Nigel collapsed.

CHAPTER 43
NIGEL

I'm done Maggs.

Ah, Big Bear. You did your best. Like you always do.

'Just leave me here. I'm… done.' He huffed and puffed, as the others gathered around him, sliding him toward a station wall, propping him up.

'They're… going,' said Nigel, smiling to himself, watching the ghost people around him vanishing into thin air.

He allowed his hand to finally drop, the blood spurting from the wound. The white bag

(Too white, too real, too white)

seeped bright red blood.

Jordan was hunched down, hands on Nigel's shoulders, trying to keep him conscious.

'Come on, man! You're going to be OK; we need to get you to a hospital.'

Nigel smiled.

'They're gone,' he said.

Jordan glanced around, the sight of the endless commuters' legs all around him, passing by him, through him.

Jordan stood, addressing Jared. 'You got any more water, man?'

Jared didn't have time for this. He had a baby to get, before they reached the light at the end of the tunnel. 'No, look, we'll come back for him when we get help,' he lied.

'It's too late,' said Nancy.

They looked back toward where Nigel had been sat.

All that remained was a white plastic bag.

INTERLUDE
NIGEL
BEFORE – INSIDE

1.

He wouldn't leave her side.

He wouldn't let anyone touch her, scar her, ruin her.

Invade her.

He would protect her now like he'd always done.

He gazed lovingly at his beautiful wife, a mere shell of the woman she once was, the girl he'd married thirty years ago.

The specialists wanted to zap her, drug her, plague her with radiation.

They wanted to kill her.

He wouldn't allow it.

She opened her eyes, the effort clearly taking its toll, whining as another bolt of pain shot across her fragile figure.

'Hey, Maggs,' he said, tears forming. He put a hand gently on her brow, feeling her temperature. She was boiling.

'Big Bear.' Barely a whisper escaping her dry, cracked lips.

Nigel retrieved the glass from the bedside table, positioning the straw carefully between her lips.

'You… have… to… let… me go,' she whispered, head lolling slightly, avoiding the straw.

'No Maggs. I can't. I just can't.' A tear tipped over spilling down his cheek. 'Drink, please,' he begged. 'Til death do us part,' he smiled through the tears.

Their daughters had wanted to visit, to stay over. They'd wanted their mum to go too.

To go *there.*

The hospital.

With *them.*

The specialists.

In the end, Nigel had changed the locks, stopping his daughters from coming into their family home.

'I can't do it, Maggs,' he said, still trying to get her to take the straw. She didn't have the energy to refuse, the straw clicking against her front teeth as he gently pushed it further into her mouth.

So dry. He could smell the decay coming from her as the cancer ate away at her very life force.

****

2.

He'd sat with the dead body of his wife for maybe a week or more, going out only once to re-stock the fridge. His black cab stayed on the drive, Nigel having no inclination to work. He'd survived on frozen dinners, sat alone next to her, watching TV, telling her about the various programme plot lines from their favourite soaps. The smell gradually became unbearable, so Nigel had washed her every day, being oh so gentle. By the end, her body had become so brittle and rigid, he finally accepted the truth.

He hadn't been able to save her.

****

3.

In the days that followed, Nigel's daughters had successfully orchestrated their plan, the one they had wanted to enact all along, or so Nigel thought.

They had the autopsy carried out by those bastards, finally allowing them to sink their knives into his beautiful wife's body.

Nigel was sure they were in cahoots, scheming to blame him.

Blame *him!*

After all he had done to protect his Maggs!

He didn't really pay attention when they arrested him, judged him, jailed him. He wasn't to blame. He'd made a concoction of pills to take away the pain. Anything to get her well again. Anything to stop her leaving him.

Anything to keep her alive.

He wasn't to blame.

He was her Big Bear.

But he'd failed.

****

4.

It sounded like the chance for redemption. Almost too good to be true.

Just sign the contract and he could participate and be given the chance to help. Maybe even save someone's life. Maybe more than one person.

He understood the risks. Understood that it was a test, a trial. Understood that it was therapy, algorithms, technology… another concoction. But this time, *he'd* take it.

It may just save him.

Or kill him.

After all, with his wife and daughters gone from his life, what did he have to lose?

PART NINE

CHAPTER 1
CYRUS - UNDER THE TREES

Even on one of his wildest trips, he'd never had a hallucination with quite the power and intensity - quite the realness - of what he was now seeing.

He'd pulled one of the new girls back as the ground near to the oak tree began to shudder, splitting, like a rip in a bedsheet.

Adam took the other girl and instinctively pulled her to safety.

Saffi remained perfectly still, a slight smile of her lips. Cyrus looked at her, seeing an expression of control on her face. A knowingness that this was supposed to be happening.

Cyrus suddenly realised he didn't really know this woman - hadn't known her. He felt scared of her.

CHAPTER 2
ADAM

He instinctively took the first girl by the shoulders and dragged her away from the grass that was tearing along an invisible seam right before his eyes. He couldn't bear to see anyone fall into the ever-widening gap. Enough people had already fallen *up* today.

'This must be an earthquake,' he shouted, his voice high pitched. His face flushed, realising he must sound more like a girl than the girls they'd just rescued.

Cyrus grabbed the other woman, Adam aware that they had intuitively kept them safe. Man protects woman. Primal brain. Only…

Neither of them had even thought of saving Saffi.

CHAPTER 3
SAFFI

They'd be coming soon.

They needed a path, a way up from the underground.

Once here, the final showdown would be enacted.

Where the winner would be the last standing.

Saffi smiled, knowing it would be her.

CHAPTER 4
TASHA

Her eyes bulged in disbelief. Whatever climate emergency they were experiencing was going from bad to utter fuck-up.

The ground tore open, like a giant zipper had been undone under the topsoil. As the mud erupted, she felt hands on her shoulders pulling her away from the edge.

She let herself be pulled, mesmerised by what was happening. First the people floating under the chopper. Then the vanishing chopper, then the white light beaming them back down to earth… and now this.

Something gleamed as the mud continued to spill out over the cracks of the chasm being created. The earth was revealing its metal treasure.

CHAPTER 5
ANGELA

In normal circumstances, she would have turned and punched any bloke who dared grab her. But this was far from normal circumstances.

The ground shuddered, leaves from the oak tree falling onto them. From within the earth, she could see something bright, something like a spaceship.

So, that explains all this!

Only, this wasn't a spaceship. It was coming more and more into view, the soil falling away as it rose up from the earth. She recognised it almost immediately, but the context wouldn't let her tired mind put two and two together.

Tasha solved the puzzle for her.

CHAPTER 6
TASHA

'It's an escalator, like in a shopping mall.' Even as she said it, it made little sense to her. 'Are we supposed to…'

'No. It's not for us,' said Saffi, her voice calm, sure, authoritative.

The shiny stairs faded into darkness as the escalator descended into the earth.

Tasha listened closely. She could hear something. A voice… no, many voices?

Footsteps running toward them.

She gulped, frozen to the spot, unable to turn and run away from whatever was coming up from the bowels of the Earth.

From Hell.

CHAPTER 7

JORDAN - INSIDE THE STATION

He couldn't believe what he was seeing. Or rather, what he was *not* seeing.

Everything in his logical world seemed to be falling apart, his perception of reality itself being tested.

Where the fuck had Nigel gone?

Jordan saw Jared walk over, crouch and pick up the white bag. As he did, it flickered in time, once… twice… and then that too was gone.

'Things don't just disappear,' said Nancy standing alongside him.

Jordan found he couldn't speak, couldn't put his feelings into words. His senses told him that there was a guy called Nigel, sat down near them one moment ago. And then, like a magic trick, he was gone.

Nancy was right; things don't just disappear.

And that bag. Something was wrong about that bag.

'It's all wrong,' he said, his words sounding like a stranger even to himself.

He thought back to James. He too had been with them one moment and gone the next.

He considered the constants. Him. Nancy. And Jared.

Jared.

As if reading his mind, Jared stood, staring directly at Jordan, his hand still held out gripping the space where the white bag was only seconds ago.

Jordan felt afraid. He felt the dire need to protect Nancy and Lihua. With Nigel gone, there was only him now. And he wasn't sure if he could take Jared should things turn nasty.

When things turned nasty.

As if sensing his thoughts, Lihua edged close.

Jared's gaze shifted between them all.

CHAPTER 8

JARED

Something told him that this could happen. That people will disappear once they die. He didn't know how he knew this, but felt it as being normal in these circumstances.

Even the feeling of knowing *that* was in itself a certainty.

Like Déja Vu. He didn't know how he knew, but he knew.

Sometimes they disappear.

The guy back at the office building, with the room of infinite desks.

And now this guy.

Jared had sensed that Nigel was flagging, had known he'd lost a lot of blood, but didn't realise he was that close to death.

To disappearing.

He crouched and picked up the white bag, marveling at how white is still was, not a trace of blood on it.

Almost too white.

He stood, aware of the others watching him. The black kid could pose a problem. Jared turned looking into the kid's eyes. Waiting to see who blinked first.

The oriental girl stepped closer to Jordan.

Jared saw everything, sensed their fear. He could smell it on them.

The fat chick and Lihua would be easy to take down. He was pretty sure it wouldn't come to that, but made a quick plan to take them out if he had to. Once they were in the tunnels.

In the dark.

But Jordan?

Jared shifted his gaze to Lihua, giving the kid a moment of triumph, a sense of maybe being alpha male. Jared was happy to let Jordan think he may have the upper hand here, oh Great Protector of the Women. Jared was concerning himself with another problem.

Whether to kill Jordan now or in the dark.

He didn't realise the white bag was no longer in his hand.

CHAPTER 9
JORDAN

That was a good sign.

Jared had broken eye contact. Jordan knew that it was a small but significant statement, far more truthful than any words. The body can't hide the truth. Jared was intimidated by Jordan.

Good.

Jordan took advantage, speaking up. 'Let's get going. I think we know where we have to get to.'

'The escalator,' said Nancy.

'The broken one,' Jared added, smirking, thinking that Jordan would be the broken one once they were in the tunnels.

CHAPTER 10
JAMIE - INSIDE THE TUNNELS

The light was almost overbearing.

He shielded his eyes as he blinked, trying to focus on the top of the escalator. He gave up, instead blinking hard, the purple after-image burned in his retina. Ghost shadows of a tall woman, surrounded by bright light. In his mind he saw her grinning, *leering*.

Was she the woman he'd seen in his imagination? The one who had spoken to him, guided him here?

Jamie ripped off the warning tape, and started to travel up the escalator, doubts plaguing his mind.

Behind him Lucy urged him on. 'Jamie, keep going… the baby's making my arms tired.'

Jamie turned, almost losing his balance on the metal stairs. 'Let me take her.'

'No!' Lucy snatched the baby from his reach. She didn't like the way she'd sounded then. 'Sorry Jamie, I'm just tired, but want you to stay in front and keep us safe from whatever is up there.'

Jamie looked deeply into her eyes.

He thought of his sister.

Christ, you look just like her.

What she had said made sense. He turned, suddenly fearful that the decision he was now making was of paramount importance; perhaps one of the most important decisions of his life. And it wasn't just for him. It was for her and the baby too.

He momentarily considered his options; turn back into the dark, or carry on up the steps? One seemed to lead to an unknown light (Heaven above) and the other back into the ghosts and tunnels (Hell below).

The scream from behind made the decision for him.

CHAPTER 11

JARED - INSIDE THE TUNNELS

They were ahead of him. He had seen Nancy and Jordan holding hands as they descended into the darkness of the underground station.

He assumed it wasn't too far before they would get the glow of the exit: the broken escalator.

He had to act fast.

He ran forward and pushed.

CHAPTER 12

JORDAN

Stay one step ahead, his gut told him.

Jordan had no choice but to lead the way, given the unspoken agreement between him and Jared had been for Jordan to be their leader. At least for this next stage of their journey.

He'd held Nancy's hand, another electric charge running between them and a surety that he knew her in another time and place. She looked different there. He looked different too.

No time for this now, he admonished himself.

Once they were in the dark, they had travelled down a slope, deeper into the underground. Jordan could make out a dim glow - or was it in his imagination - ahead. Almost non-existent.

He reached out blindly to his other side, feeling for Lihua. She moaned softly as he felt for her hand and encouraged her to hold him. The stability of three was easier should one of them trip.

The ground felt more level here and the dim light seemed more present. Jordan guessed they had maybe ten minutes or so to walk to the-

A rush of feet from behind, his arm was violently yanked as Lihua was flung forward.

CHAPTER 13
LIHUA

Just got to get to my baby. Just got to get to her. Got to.

That was all she could think about.

Nigel was gone. She didn't know how. He just was.

Her baby was with the others now and she was getting closer. Call it Mother's Intuition.

She had never feared the dark, often being hidden in car boots or cupboards when being shipped by the gang. The dark was safe. In the dark she could choose not to exist.

A hand touched her upper arm, making her whimper, interrupting her thoughts. The hand slid gently down finding her fingers. She closed onto them, feeling safe. Secure.

Her thoughts returned to her baby.

Got to get to her. Almost there. Almost.

The push was violent and rocketed her forward, her grip instantly coming loose of the gentle hand in the dark. She heard her spine snap. She screamed as she fell, the ground seeming too far away. Her shins hit something hard, metal. Her hands splayed out, hitting more metal and stone. Her head clipped something. The smell was instant: grease. The air tinged with electric, tasting iron in her mouth *(Blood? Am I bleeding?)*

and the noise was unbearable. People everywhere! Voices shouting, hands coming into view. She tried to look up, over her shoulder, the pain in her back unbearable.

(Am I dying?)

The light above the heads of the commuters was so strong, she had to close her eyes. Hands had been reaching toward her. She clearly saw one face; a woman, frozen, phone in hand. The woman had been staring beyond Lihua.

(I am dying.)

The wind rushed into her; the air hot to breathe. Lihua was aware that somewhere Jordan and Nancy were in the dark, in another place, looking for her.

In this world - the one of right here and now - Lihua's light was burning low. The dark tunnel ahead burst into bright light, the warning alarms crippling her ear drums. She tried to bring her hands to her face, to cover her eyes, a final instinctual (but pointless) primal gesture of protection.

Her last thought was how close she had been to finding Chunhua. So close.

Ghosts. They're all ghosts!

Of course! She was below that magical line, the one where the ghosts appeared.

The realisation made her drop her bleeding hands from her face.

She laughed, manically.

The train ploughed into her, killing her instantly.

CHAPTER 14
SAFFI - UNDER THE TREES

She bent over double, holding her stomach.

'The baby,' she whispered.

Adam ran to her side, Tasha and Angela looked on concerned. What now?

'Get away from me!' Saffi lashed out at Adam.

Adam jumped back surprised, more from the vehemence in her tone than the pathetic swinging arm. He knew she held some kind of power, a magic, and was both in awe and terrified of her.

Saffi stood slowly, her belly pulsing gently beneath her hand. Her sweet smile returned.

'I'm sorry, Adam,' she said, searching his eyes for understanding.

'It's… cool,' he said.

She smiled again, knowing the baby was safe. The mother was dead.

That she could live with.

CHAPTER 15
JORDAN - INSIDE THE TUNNELS

Everything happened so fast, it was mind numbing.

One moment they were wandering in the dark, (lost souls) the next, Lihua had been thrown from his grip. He'd heard her scream.

Then there were voices, shouts. He was jostled, shoved, almost losing his hold on Nancy. He fought to drag her closer.

The light was returning, bright fluorescent lights, as if the ghost level, the one beneath the waistline, was now rising, like a retreating tide on a watermark.

The underground was suddenly filled with bodies.

Jordan glanced at a woman, staring to where he thought Lihua had fell *(been pushed, Jared, Jared did this!)* and followed her gaze, seeing the terror in her expression. He felt the wind, knowing all too well the movement of air as a train approached the station.

Warm, stale air entered his mouth as he tried to call Lihua's name.

The crowd were pushing him and Nancy further along the platform, toward the exit.

(The broken escalator… must get to the broken escalator!)

He glanced back, neck strained, seeking any sign of Lihua. His eyes met Jared's. A sneer on his face.

There were only a few people (ghosts) between them. He turned, Nancy now in his arms, holding her close. He pushed forward, his arm around Nancy, like a loving couple, determined to get out of the station. To get to the show on time.

Ahead of him, the crowds were acting strange.

(As if this fucking day could get any weirder!)

Walking into the walls. Impossible but true…

Except… no, they were walking *at* the wall.

Jordan tried to see over shoulders, past heads, seeing what the people were doing. Why were they behaving so oddly? He was almost at the escalators. Two before him. The entrance to one had broken red tape dangling from it, as if someone had chosen to ignore the DO NOT PASS warnings.

(A vision; a woman in red, guiding him on. *Almost home.*)

He pushed Nancy ahead of him, determined not to look back, waiting at any second for Jared's hand to clamp down on his shoulder.

People shouting. A train blaring its horn.

Jared still pushed on. Lihua was gone. He knew it. No need to check and nothing he could do now.

Just had to save Nancy.

Almost home.

CHAPTER 16
JARED

He didn't know what the fuck was happening.

As they entered the tunnels the light diminished. He clearly saw the two lovers' hand-in-hand. So, he was on the right, she on the left. He counted… One… Two… Three… the light growing dimmer, the dark enveloping them…

…Four… Five… could just make out their outlines, almost too dark to see anything…

…Six …Seven … a whimper, maybe Jordan had pinched her on her ass. Her massive ass!

…Eight … Nine… he had almost lost all visibility; it was now or never.

Ten.

He'd lunged, shoved as hard as he could the shape of the person on the right. He knew the track was alongside, so they wouldn't need much encouragement to fall.

The body felt too light. Jordan was a skinny kid but it felt wrong.

And the scream was too high. Too… foreign.

Fuck!

He paused, a fraction of a second, evaluating his plan, dimly aware of a glow ahead.

(The woman waits there. At the top of the stairs. The broken stairs.)

And then all hell broke loose.

Within moments he was surrounded, suffocated by bodies. The ghosts, made real, fully formed, no longer hiding behind the mysterious half-way up veil.

The living and dead combined.

He sought Jordan and his fat bitch. Eyes darting to the group shouting at something (someone) on the track. Felt panic rising, wondering if he had been seen pushing, filmed by phones of ghosts, caught on CCTV.

No, it had been dark.

And anyway, you've been here before. It never goes to plan.

He locked eyes with Jordan, a few feet and several bodies between them. The kid turned, his arm around the wide shoulders of Nancy.

They're not even going to try and help Lihua, he thought. *Selfish fuckwits.*

He saw them push through the people, moving toward the stairs.

Toward the light at the top.

Out of this hell.

Jared hunched his shoulders and rammed his way forward, determined to catch them before they could get onto the staircase.

The empty escalator.

The realisation caused him to come to a complete stop. The escalators ahead were empty. Completely devoid of one soul heading either up or down. And yet…

Yet the commuters continued to shove and squirm all around him. He fleetingly thought of the abomination floating in the sky, what had been individuals at first and then a sewage of flesh and bone.

Why were they not leaving?

They're trapped here. It's their programming.

Jordan and Nancy were climbing up the escalator that wasn't moving.

It'll take her fucking ages.

Jared managed a smile, pushing through the last of the commuters. His attention taken again by an odd sight as he cleared the last of the people. Many were walking, butting against the walls of the station, trying to continue their journey, but the wall stopping them. He had a flashback to seeing a robot somewhere, maybe his as a child, when it had walked into a wall and kept marching up and down, legs trying to carry it forward. He had to turn it around for it to continue its journey. Jared had the mind to try and turn one of the commuters around to see if they'd behave the same.

No time. They're almost (home) *there. Almost with her.*

He gave one final shove, forcing his right shoulder through some of the wall walkers, knocking them aside but receiving no retaliation.

He was on the escalator.

His fatter, weaker prey already halfway up.

Jared gave chase.

CHAPTER 17
TASHA - UNDER THE TREES

'Arm yourselves, they're coming!'

Adam's sudden cry shocked her into moving again, her body still feeling alien, possessed by another, slower being. Everything seemed to take ages, even breathing.

Angela ran around to Tasha, jumping over the cracked earth where the metal stairs met the grass they were on. 'We need to run, baby.'

'No. Wait. It's all fine. They're no harm.'

Tasha, Angela, Adam and Cyrus all looked at Saffi as she smiled, staring into the hole, waiting for the hell which was about to be released from deep within the Earth.

'How can you be so certain?' asked Adam.

Saffi's only response was a gentle smile with eyes that demanded obedience.

Adam gulped.

Tasha held onto Angela's hand, hoping to provide strength and assurance but seeking it too. They'd got through the helicopter crash, through the Breaker, past the floating corpses, so surely their God would get them through… whatever was coming?

A head came into view. A man, his arm behind him, holding…

A hand appeared, then an arm, then the face of a woman, holding…

A blue wrapped bundle.

CHAPTER 18

JAMIE

He rushed out of the station, impossibly falling head-first onto grass. No pavement. No traffic. Just silence.

Lucy stumbled behind him, Jamie preparing himself to take her fall, but nothing happened.

The air was clear, clean and Jamie rolled onto his back, eyes closed, sucking in huge lungful's.

It tasted better than the sticky warm air in the tunnels. Yet, didn't taste truly pure here either.

Must be them, he thought, eyes opening, taking in the sight of the Floaters hovering above him, between the leaves of the tree he was near. *They must be trapping the air somehow, not letting it circulate.*

Not possible surely. Unless there were now thousands, if not millions of people up there?

Then, why not me?

He turned his head, aware of others stood around him.

Ghosts, no doubt. They'd vanish if he stood up.

'We've been expecting you,' said a woman's voice.

Jamie lifted his head to see the woman stood over him looking down, holding Lucy's hand. The woman in red. The woman bathed in light.

The woman he'd heard and seen in his mind.

'You're… real.'

She smiled. And, for the first time, Jamie realised she was holding the baby.

CHAPTER 19

LUCY

She was grateful to have him give her the necessary momentum, sheer drive to pull her the last few metres up the stairs and out into the fresh air. Jamie collapsed as soon as his feet cleared the top.

Lucy didn't rush to help him, suddenly afraid of the new people surrounding her.

Lucy didn't trust the men, the hippy one looked stoned, his hand was covered in blood. And the other guy looked like he was in shock. She took in the other three; all women. Lucy couldn't take her eyes off the woman nearest her. She'd seen her. In her dreams.

The woman held out her hands, smiling, so caring. Lucy didn't want to trust her but found herself moving closer, taking her hand and happily handing over the baby.

As soon as she was out of her arms, Lucy felt a huge relief wash over her.

She can be your problem now, she thought.

'We've been expecting you,' said the woman in red, a glow coming from her. Lucy realised the comment wasn't being addressed to her or Jamie. Only to the baby.

Maybe she's the mother? Thought Lucy. No, that wasn't right. The mother was oriental. *She'd got into the cab with me. With the fat driver.*

Yet… I know you.

Lucy frowned, searching her memories for where she may have seen this woman before.

Behind her, down in the tunnels, someone screamed.

CHAPTER 20

SAFFI

Everyone around her was paranoid, on the brink of panic. She had to maintain calm. Keep composed. She knew it would all come together here. Beneath the big tree. Before the cars with identical passengers. The man, still flickering, shimmering in and out of existence, stood in the road a little way from them. Still looking up, still expanding his hands.

Still on a loop.

And now she had the baby.

It was almost time.

It was almost game over.

CHAPTER 21
NANCY - INSIDE THE TUNNELS

Almost there.

Her legs had never worked so hard, Jordan dragging her up the steps of the escalator. She knew he was coming, chasing, and would soon be upon them. Jordan's hand slipped from her grip, his own strength tiring.

So close.

Nancy turned, huffing, struggling for breath. She had a crazy flashback of being on scales somewhere, a poster on a wall showing a human heart surrounded by drawings of alcohol, cigarettes, junk food, all on top of the heart, squeezing it, pressuring it.

But I'm not usually in this body, she thought.

Her hips took up almost the whole width of the escalator. She made a solemn promise to herself that should she survive this, she would exercise, diet and never take the lift or escalators again; she'd walk. Fuck it, she'd run! Anything to be fitter. Stronger.

To have the agility of a [black leather-clad] cat.

She stood her ground, Jordan begging her to come on, carry on, almost at the top now.

Jared came into view, stopping as he took in her girth. Nancy thought about simply running at him, cannonball style, taking him with her back down into the station. She could see the lights were all on below and could hear the voices, noise and smell the filth wafting up.

Lihua had died down there.

And we hadn't been able to save her. Hadn't even tried.

She grimaced, unsure what to do next. Turn and run or bowl the fucker down?

Jordan was still panting behind her. She turned her head, addressing Jordan, her eyes never leaving Jared still standing a few steps below. 'You go on now Jordan, go up to the top. I'll handle this.'

She suddenly felt empowered, strong and clear-headed.

She knew exactly what to do next. She had a plan.

What ruined it was the scream from above.

CHAPTER 22
ANGELA - UNDER THE TREES

'No, you'll kill her!'

Too late. The rock span through the air, whistling past Angela's ear. The hand which had held it, blood stained.

It struck Tasha on the temple. She fell to the earth, the green grass soaking up her red blood, looking like an artist's abstract painting.

CHAPTER 23
TASHA

It hadn't happened as she thought it might have. She had always thought her death would be painful, having seen her grandparents on both sides, plus her parents, all die with cancer, suffering terribly. In some deep way, Tasha assumed she would follow the same painful path.

Instead, something or someone, had struck her, hard around her head.

She felt warmth.

She gracefully fell to the grass, feeling only her spirit within the shell of her body. It was like being gently laid to rest.

And then the dark came, shrouding her, caressing her.

And then came the voices. Angels, clad in white, helping her.

She was alive.

And this was Heaven.

CHAPTER 24

CYRUS

Too many. There were now too many of them. He didn't believe they could all be real. He'd seen the shimmering man, watched him loop around and around, caught in his own smiling madness.

He'd seen the cars, filled with people all alike. All repeating behaviour.

He'd seen the ground open up. Saw the stairs appear, heard the noise of people from deep down within. Felt the warm air rush up to meet him.

He'd seen and climbed the tree, the one that hadn't appeared to be there when he'd first been stuck in traffic. In his camper van. The one he'd been in with Saffi.

Hadn't he?

And now he'd seen the final proof. The photographic evidence that this was all a sham, a mind-trip.

A game.

As Adam had descended the tree, along with the two women, Cyrus has considered looking at the camera he'd found. The one from above the floating people. The one from where the two women came.

He hadn't had the time right then, but once the ground began to open, he decided he'd wander off and have a look. He had been hoping to see images of reality - normal reality - something to keep him grounded as he became more and more unstable with the unfolding chaos all around him.

Saffi had become someone else.

Did I really ever know her?

Nick had vanished somewhere up the tree.

Had he climbed up through the Floaters? Was he in on the gag?

Adam had pointed out the looping man and the identical passengers.

Deep in his mind he kept hearing the words, stand-up, stand-up, stand-up… a constant loop begging him to take notice.

Stand-up to what? The women? Saffi? Adam?

The camera was to be his saviour, his salvation, his glimpse back to a familiar world, the one he knew only hours ago *(Was it? Was it hours? Days? Weeks? A fortnight? Yes, a fortnight…)* only… the camera hadn't revealed what he'd hoped. Instead, it showed images; views from up high, then of the first Floaters, landmarks being obscured by the bodies, then coming closer to whatever was holding them up.

And then he looked harder. He saw the pixelation.

The glitches.

The camera had captured photos of Tasha, eyes closed, but with parts missing, like pixels broken on a screen. It had captured Angela in a helicopter but not complete, more like a bad rendition in a computer game. There were pictures of the Breaker from above, again with parts missing, like pixels had been purposely removed.

None of it was real.

They were all in on it. Driving him mad.

It was him or them.

CHAPTER 25

JAMIE

He was up off the floor in seconds, witnessing the hippy guy smack one of the women round the head with something… a stone or ashtray? He couldn't see it clearly. As he rose, he expected these figures to disappear, like the ghosts down in the tube station. Only these people remained.

He squatted, stood, squatted, all to make sure they really were here, part of this reality and not belonging to a world which only existed below his waistline.

The woman in red, still cradling the baby in one arm while holding Lucy's hand with her other, looked on shocked. Before Jamie could react (deciding whether to stand and fight or do what he did best and run, run for his life) the other woman leapt on the hippy guy, tearing at his face, raking her fingernails across his forehead, cheeks, over his eyes. Blood seeped through. She was like a rabid animal, screaming, clawing, pushing. The hippy dropped the rock, arms flailing trying to stop the attack.

Jamie was breathing hard, unsure whether to help or (run) not, and if so, who to help; Lucy, the baby, the girl on the floor? (He thought she was beyond help, blood clotting, spreading, oozing from the gash in her head. Jamie thought how red it looked. Almost too red. Fake.)

Before he could act, two things happened; neither of which he expected. The bleeding woman disappeared and someone else ran, screaming, into their world.

CHAPTER 26

ADAM

'What the…?'

He was assessing his options, choosing whether to help or not. His instinct was to climb back up the tree, just get away from these people. Madness was happening all around him. He was long past thinking this was a dream, a nightmare.

But before he could, Tasha simply flickered and disappeared. Gone.

Poof!

A magic trick but without the smoke.

He had a brief flashback of someone driving the car he had been in.

Christ, what was his name?

Dan? No. Grant? No!

Whoever it was, that guy had disappeared too. Adam assumed he'd just run off, but as his mind tried to put a name to a face *(Doug! It was Doug!)* the two wouldn't merge, the name clicking but the face growing ever more distant, like a fading dream.

The new guy had jumped up from the floor, crouching down a few times, looking anxious just before Tasha had vanished.

And now Angela was going ballistic at Cyrus.

Adam turned to get her off when a young kid ran out from the crack in the Earth screaming.

CHAPTER 27

JORDAN

He didn't want to, but had little choice it seemed.

They were so close to the top of the escalator he could hear voices above, but couldn't quite make the words out. Nancy refused to move, her and Jared in a face-off on the motionless steps.

He took his chance, running up the last few steps (there had been more than he thought, perhaps an optical illusion bought on by the stress, lack of water, exhaustion) into the open. With his final breath, he called out for help, only the sight that met him took the words from him, so he uttered a primal scream instead.

A woman had her legs wrapped around a man, like a sex scene, only his face was running with blood. *How can these people help? They're crazy!* Was the first thing he thought in the seconds his feet hit the grass.

And he hadn't the energy to turn back round, run down the escalator and take on Jared.

He was done.

CHAPTER 28

JARED - ON THE ESCALATOR

He still had it on him. He could use it; surely, after all, it must be quite obvious to the others now what his plan was. His mission.

And, although he knew he couldn't recall all of the missions he had been on when he was in the killing zone, he didn't think he'd failed one.

Had he?

He didn't like it when his thoughts strayed too far from his objective. His eyes were still locked on the defiant eyes of Nancy.

'I'll give you a choice.'

His hand brought the gun that had been tucked in his waistband into view. Nancy's eyes widened but she remained resolute, blocking his way. 'I can either kill you, or you can turn your fat ass around, waddle up those stairs, thank me for the extra exercise, get to the top and live. Assuming your heart doesn't give out,' he sniggered.

Nancy opened her mouth to reply, but Jared had had enough. 'Ah, fuck it, I'll choose for you.'

He fired.

CHAPTER 29
NANCY

The last few moments were strange.

She felt so empowered, so strong, rooted to the escalator step, as if her legs were tree roots, extending beyond the soles of her feet, anchoring her to the metal staircase. Nothing could pass her.

In less than a minute, a small metal bullet would test that theory, passing through her ribcage on the left-hand side, puncturing a lung, clipping her heart and exploding out of her back, taking a chunk of spine with it.

She fell, those imagined tree roots instantly giving way, her body beginning to bend awkwardly, heading directly for Jared like a bowling ball down a lane.

CHAPTER 30
JARED

Like always, it was almost too incredible to describe.

Nancy tipped forward, the bullet well aimed and doing its job as efficiently as ever when he fired it. As she did, Jared saw everything happen in slow motion, the blood and pink matter covering the steps behind her as the bullet exited her chest; the look in her eyes as fear replaced defiance; the rolling of her shoulders; the flickering of her clothes.

Wasn't it always like this?

No, sometimes they disappeared instantly.

But sometimes they died twice. Slowly in front of him. And then they disappeared. Like he had imagined happened to that Asian bitch back in the tunnels. She definitely died twice; heard her scream when the train hit her, knowing she'd disappear shortly afterwards.

He savoured the moment when they died twice.

Before she crashed into him, Nancy flickered, coming in and out of existence. And then she simply disappeared.

CHAPTER 31

JORDAN

The gunshot rang out and up the escalator being amplified by the tunnel the steps had created in the Earth.

He saw the crazy woman had stopped clawing the guy's face, wondering if he were even still alive.

The other women retreated, stepping away from the stairs, carrying a baby.

Jordan briefly saw two other guys, both staring toward the escalator.

Jordan knew Nancy was dead. He felt her die. He closed his eyes, jaw clenching, knowing that this couldn't be the end. She couldn't leave him like this.

It's not her. She's elsewhere now, waiting for me.

He opened his eyes, startled, as a hand slapped him on the back. A man's voice: 'Quick, up the tree!'

Jordan turned, saw the women disappear stepping up the branches of a big tree. Jordan could have sworn the tree swayed, like a mirage, almost swirling with colour, before settling back into a solid form.

He steadied himself, reaching out to the guy for support. His hand swiped the air.

As he began walking unsteadily toward the giant tree, he glanced to the woman who was squatting down near where the bloody guy lay. Jordan didn't know if he had the energy in him to help them. Whatever shit was going on between them wasn't his problem. He'd already got involved in helping others today and that had got him to this.

This!

A fucking nightmare.

No, that had got me to Nancy. And now I've got to get up the tree and sort this so we can...

Can what?

He almost had it, whatever 'it' was. Balanced frustratingly on the tip of his tongue, the memory almost daring to snap into the forefront of his mind.

It's the first one... the first one to... to...

Damn. No time.

Behind him, Jared sprang out from the escalator, grinning wildly.

Jordan ran on shaking legs, begging them not to give out from under him, heading toward the tree.

As he stepped up on the first branch, a bullet whistled and hit the bark next to his leg. Another branch... one more... and he was on the other side of the trunk from Jared.

CHAPTER 32
ANGELA

Without Tasha she was nobody.

All they had been through. Together. Always together. She was her rock.

And now that bastard, that cunt, had killed her. With a rock. The irony didn't make her smile. Rather, it made her feel sick.

She looked at the mess she had made of the guy's face, looking at her fingernails, three now broken, as she had felt his skin tearing under her scratches, felt the gelatinous fluid of his eye gunk out as she clawed at him. She wanted to blind him, leaving him with the memory of her face, of what she had done to him. And what he had done to Tasha.

She vaguely heard a loud bang echoing from somewhere nearby.

Heard people shouting. Felt someone tug briefly on her shoulder as they ran away from her.

She didn't care. Tasha was gone. And now she had no reason to live.

Flash: the woman in red spoke to her. 'She's not dead.'

Flash: Tasha smiling, waiting, somewhere white. Angels hovering around her.

Flash: machines, monitors, sounds.

Angela crawled away from Tasha's killer. Her revenge had been swift.

A man ran out from the hole in the ground heading straight for the tree.

As he ran past her, she felt the air shift. The bastard on the floor reached out and grabbed his ankle.

As he did, she saw him begin to tremble, shudder and lift toward the sky.

CHAPTER 33

CYRUS

He'd been wrong. So wrong.

This was supposed to be redemption.

He could see it all so clearly now.

The camera was the proof, the thing he needed to see to make sense of it all. Only, he hadn't seen it clearly. It was like a veil had been pulled from over his eyes. A man no longer hostage.

He could barely see, but knew it didn't matter. He'd recover quickly. And soon.

Events no longer concerned him.

He'd had his chance and he'd blown it. Cyrus knew he'd have a long time to think about this, what he'd remember of it, in the coming years. Decades probably.

If only he could redeem himself in some small way.

One last act of forgiveness. For himself and for those who had given him this chance.

The guy carried a gun, Cyrus could make it out through his blurred vision. As he ran toward him, Cyrus summoned his last reserves of strength and grabbed the guy's leg. He quickly turned, using his injured hand, the one he'd jammed in the car window.

It's OK, that would heal soon too.

Yes, despite his blinded eye, he had perfect clarity now.

He hugged the guy's leg tight. Tighter.

I'm ready now. I've lost.

He felt his own legs become light, like puppet strings were pulling him.

Smiling, he began to float upward toward the sky.

CHAPTER 34

JARED

Motherfucker!

He had assumed the guy was dead. Now the blood covered prick was clamped onto his ankle like a dog in heat. Jared sneered, glancing at the tree, weighing up his options. He released the magazine chamber in the gun, checking on bullets.

Shit. One left.

He shouldn't have been so hasty to try to shoot Jordan before he was close enough to make sure he got him.

Jared cleared his mind, organising his thoughts. Chaos and stress didn't alarm him. He was trained to deal with it.

He had to get up that tree, but he would have a serious disadvantage. They were above him, they outnumbered him and they could throw things down easily.

But they were also trapped.

He could just wait and starve them out.

Or light a fire and smoke them out.

Options.

It all came down to time. He knew there wasn't long left before everything…

He couldn't think of the word or think how he knew. Sometimes this world made perfect sense to him, others it all seemed so new to him.

Reset.

Yes, shortly everything would reset.

Got to act quickly.

It might already be too late.

The ankle grabber was floating feet first toward the sky. And taking Jared with him.

CHAPTER 35

SAFFI

The branches of the great oak seemed too perfectly formed to be natural. Odd but true. It was more like climbing a steep spiral staircase rather than up a tree. Every branch was perfectly spaced, wide enough, flat enough to be the perfect step.

Too perfect.

She'd made the gap in the Floaters before, so assumed she could do it again, once she had reached the top of the tree. Make a gap just wide enough for her and the baby.

She glanced down at the baby. A girl. Tiny nose. Tiny fingers peeking just out of the blue blanket. Perfect. Too perfect.

Lucy was still behind her and Saffi felt she was still able to project into their thoughts, her healing power still with her, flowing through her as it always did.

Maybe time to plant a seed.

CHAPTER 36

LUCY

Since first arriving above ground, taking the hand of the woman in red, she had felt safe.

Safe.

Saffi.

The woman's name was almost the word itself.

Saffi had not let go of Lucy, had taken the baby so gently and now, as they began climbing once again, this time heading away from the safety of the ground - if that ever was safe - toward the Floaters above, Lucy had felt the energy fade as soon as Saffi had released her hand the moment they began climbing the tree.

Lucy's scars began to itch. She absent-mindedly began scratching the scars on her wrists, still keeping Saffi's red dress in view, trailing as it did on the branches as they continued their ascent.

She heard a gunshot from the ground, although it seemed to be in a different world to the one she was now in.

And then the voice of Saffi came to her, strong and clear.

'We're almost at the top. You can save them.'

A vision came to Lucy, seeing herself smiling, reaching out, arms spread, as if she were going to gracefully fall from the top of the tree.

Sacrifice.

Her scars continued to itch; her scratching furious.

No, she wasn't going to fall. She was a shield. To protect the baby.

The vision and reality began to blend as Saffi stood on a clearing near the top of the oak, the mighty trunk providing a shelf. Above them the Floaters moaned and whaled, almost unrecognisable sounds and bodies, a sea of human misery.

Lucy felt everything become dream-like, her wrists beginning to bleed.

I'm not going to make it through this, she thought.

Saffi was smiling, holding the baby so lovingly, tenderly, the blue blanket held to her chest, the baby quiet as a mouse. She stepped aside, giving Lucy room to step up to the shelf, leaves all around.

As she passed Saffi, Lucy began to smile through her tears, feeling all hope leave her. Her body was being moved for her, controlled by someone else. She felt like a trapped ghost.

I think, therefore I am. The phrase coming to her so clearly, the ghost in the machine.

She stepped to the edge of the natural platform *(nothing about this is natural, nothing!)* and turned to face the way she'd come, to face Saffi.

Saffi's eyes gleamed their own special magic, her voice clear in Lucy's mind, the words telepathic.

Do this for your baby.

Lucy nodded, raised her arms to her side, a female Christ on the cross. Bleeding wrists, she took a deep breath and then the bullet slammed through her, crushing her windpipe.

Sacrifice.

CHAPTER 37

JARED

He let himself be dragged up by the human hippy balloon, reorienting himself as he did so, wrenching his foot from the grip of the hippy. The guy's face was a mess, streaked with blood.

Jared gripped the hippy, entwining their arms, a human knot.

The hippy cried out in pain.

Branches and leaves passed by as the two bodies floated into the air to join the abomination above. Jared intensely focused on the branches, looking for the others. Five adults and a baby couldn't hide in the tree for long, they were too exposed.

He calculated that there might be room for them to hide the other side of the massive trunk, but either way, he'd get them and finish the job.

Have to be the last man standing.

The hippy's feet were now almost near the Floaters, Jared took a calculated guess that he'd have a second or two to jump for it.

And now the woman in red came into view, with a blue bundle in her arms. Jared smiled, aimed the gun.

Right then another woman appeared, blocking his view of the woman and baby.

Damn it!

This woman raised her arms, Jared thinking she was going to simply fall out of the tree.

The hippy was beginning to flatten against the Breaker.

It was now or never.

Jared fired.

CHAPTER 38
JAMIE

'We can't leave her.'

Jamie knew Adam was right. Yet, at the same time, he couldn't leave Lucy either.

I lost her in real life, so I can't lose her here. (She's not your sister she's not your sister she's not your)

A gunshot rang out from below.

Jamie and Adam stopped, first looking at each other then toward the base of the tree, Adam the closer of the two to the edge of the trunk.

Everything went quiet before a face appeared, sweat pouring, eyes wide.

Jordan.

'He's gonna kill us all, man. Keep moving!' the kid begged.

Jamie didn't need any further convincing, but Adam stayed where he was.

'Squeeze past me, go on to the top with the others,' he said making room for the kid to step past.

Jamie looked at Adam seeking an explanation.

'I can't Jamie. I can't leave her down there.'

Jamie nodded, torn between going back to help or carrying on to help.

Choices, choices.

Shit choices.

'Go, Adam. Go. We'll try to help the women up here.'

Jamie calculated that it worked out rather well; one man to protect one woman. He felt a weird panic that he needed to remember their names.

Lucy. The doppelgänger.

Saffi, the… the… magic mind fucker.

And… and the woman on the ground. The one who hadn't disappeared.

What was her name?

Before it clicked, another gunshot came.

This time it was from above.

CHAPTER 39
ANGELA - UNDER THE TREES

Her gaze followed the two men up, fighting like snakes, coiling around each other until one was hanging from the other's arm like a bizarre circus stunt.

She felt numb, not wanting to stare, not wanting to stand.

(Stand up, just stand up!)

She wanted to die.

To be with Tasha.

She tried to recall the fleeting vision she had had, seeing Tasha surrounded by people clad in white. A glimpse of Heaven? Already the memory seemed too fake, like her ideal vision of a perfect eternity, peaceful, clean.

Dangerous.

The sudden change in her brought some kind of feeling back into her soul.

It wasn't Heaven. It was… it was…

Before.

No. It was after.

'Fuck it, fuck it, fuck it!' She banged her fists repeatedly against her head, utter despair. She grabbed clumps of hair, pulling hard, wrenching strands from the roots, the pain instant and powerful.

Madness.

I've finally snapped.

She was aware of another gunshot but didn't care. Hoping in some way it was meant for her and she was now too numb to experience the pain.

Had she been shot?

A man appeared at the base of the tree.

I bet he shimmers, she thought abstractedly.

The man stayed whole, running toward her while looking toward the sky.

Toward them. The coiled pair of cunts.

The man was in front of her, squatting down, taking her hands.

She saw his expression change to one of sadness as he looked at the clumps of hair she had torn free, gripping them so hard, her knuckles were white.

He was speaking, but she didn't hear him.

She was done.

Let me die.

Let me be with Tasha.

The man looked up again, his face too difficult to read, emotions mixed.

He changed grip, taking her under the arms, he dragged her body across the grass. She let herself be dragged.

She briefly wondered if her punishment was not yet over, her suffering not complete.

Will he rape me?

She felt metal under her, her feet dropping down step-by-step as he dragged her further into the Earth.

I'm going to Hell, she thought.

CHAPTER 40

ADAM

He hadn't been able to save anyone so far.

He'd lost Nick. He'd lost D… the other guy.

Damn, why can't I remember him?!

But he could save this woman.

He didn't know why he needed to save someone. Maybe it was just a reason to stay sane, to give him a purpose as this day of complete fuckery continued to unravel in all of its chaotic ways?

Whatever the reason, he had to do something.

Save someone.

He ran to the woman who was still sat on the ground in shock, his eyes taking in another incredibly alarming sight; two bodies entwined, floating toward the sky. It was like watching a wrestling match, two men grappling, but in space where gravity was switched off.

The woman had harmed herself, holding masses of hair he could see she had torn from her scalp. He thought of a documentary he'd watched where animals in run-down zoos behaved the same, pulling their fur out.

Adam felt like the whole world was going to come crashing down.

He didn't have time to debate; he grabbed the woman from behind under her arms and dragged her back toward the escalator. It seemed the only possible place to be safe for now.

As he descended onto the steps, walking down backwards, heaving Angela's body, he couldn't resist looking at the sky one final time.

He saw the Floaters, saw the grappling men, saw one raise a gun.

And the last thing he thought he saw was a vision of Christ, arms spread, hanging way up high in the tree.

CHAPTER 41

ANGELA

She felt herself slipping, like falling to sleep.

Exhausted. Despairing.

Maybe you can die soul first, she thought. *Die of a broken heart.*

Her head tipped forward onto her chest.

She slept.

****

She woke.

White all around her.

People clad in white.

Tasha.

She tried to talk, unable to form words. A hand stroked her forehead.

A gentle voice hushed her, comforting her.

She'd be with Tasha soon, here in the afterlife.

She slept.

CHAPTER 42

SAFFI - UP IN THE TREE

She stopped cold, her thoughts instantly interrupted as she allowed herself to fleetingly leave her body, travel and see what was happening below.

Adam and Angela were going back underground.

Good.

Two birds, one stone.

A flashback to Tasha and Cyrus, the incident with the rock. The *murder* with the rock. She still couldn't believe he'd done it.

Some student he turned out to be.

Student?

She instantly returned to her body; thoughts of Cyrus parked for now.

She closed her eyes, summoning strength. The tree began to tremble.

In her mind's-eye she saw the ground below begin to contract, the escalator retreating like a silver snake disappearing back into the hell from which it came.

She smiled.

Now there was only Lucy, Jamie and Jordan to dispose of. Easily done.

She turned on the narrow ledge, ready to make a gap in the Floaters.

And came face-to-face with Jared.

CHAPTER 43
LUCY

She felt the force of the bullet tear through her throat.

She saw Jamie stepping up the last few branches to the ledge she and Saffi were stood on.

She saw Saffi freeze, holding the baby, assuming she was in shock at what was happening.

And then she saw no more.

Lucy's body shimmered as if confetti had been poured over her.

And then she was gone.

CHAPTER 44
JAMIE

He couldn't believe what he was seeing as he took the last few (steps) branches to the top of the tree. His eyes connected with Lucy, a look of horror on her face. It appeared she had a red tie on, as her throat and chest were running with blood.

'No!'

Not again, I can't lose her again. Her or the baby!

He was too late.

Whatever reality this was, he'd failed the woman who looked like his sister.

Jamie wanted to run, run away from this place, away from these people. He wanted to never stop running.

Lucy fell forward, her body turning translucent as she did so. Jamie poised, ready to catch her.

His arms collected nothing but a rush of air.

Lucy was gone.

****

Run, run, run away… and don't look back!

The voice was powerful, urging Jamie to move, to get away.

To escape.

From this tree. From these people. Reality was breaking down.

Jamie turned, his ankle twisting sharply, the pain shooting up his leg, through his hips, into his heart.

I'm finished.

Jamie lost his balance, crumpling like a discarded tissue, falling from the tree. A clear drop to the ground below with no branches hindering his fall.

He landed on his back; the wind knocked out of him. Above him, through the leaves, he could see the Floaters, or what remained of them.

He wondered if Lucy was up there with them, his Lucy. Not the doppelgänger who had invaded his life this morning.

Was she even real? She just disappeared…

Jamie was overcome with waves of pain, he felt broken, unfixable.

I couldn't save her. I couldn't save her.

His last thought before the welcome bliss of oblivion claimed him was of the Lucy in this world. And a realisation.

*She **was** real… I'd met her before. In the white room.*
The one with the flowers.

CHAPTER 45

JORDAN

He stopped part-way up the spiral-staircase-like branches of the tree. He was dizzy, head-spinning.

This is all so wrong. Everything: Nancy. The Floaters. This tree. All of it!

Jordan leant his back against the trunk, the moaning from the Floaters pressuring his head. He was being chased with nowhere to go. Jordan clamped his hands on his head, squeezing hard, trying to make everything go away.

A voice came to him. Strange yet somehow vaguely familiar; 'Just stand up.'

It didn't help his already confused and tired mind.

'I am! I am standing up!' he screeched, the veins in his neck standing taut.

Jordan slid down, the bark of the trunk scratching his back. He cried into his hands.

The face of a man came to him. Short, dumpy. Little round glasses. Jordan tried to place him. One of his medical professors at Uni? No, not there. Somewhere else.

Jordan thought hard.

Just stand up and it's all over.

Jordan took a deep breath, summoned his strength and, with eyes tightly shut, he stood. The dizziness vanished and, had he opened his eyes, he'd of seen that the tree, Floaters and everything that had been around him had vanished too.

****

He felt arms steadying him as he toppled into a glass wall.

Not again, he thought, the Breaker flashing back into his mind. The glass ceiling.

His eyes adjusted to the warm light around him. And he saw the faces of angels.

CHAPTER 46

ADAM - UNDERGROUND

The mud began to cave in.

He covered his face, no longer caring where the body of Angela had gone. One moment he was helping her, dragging her under the arms. The next, she was gone.

He wasn't a religious man, despite his name, but did give a moment to consider what he'd done to upset a God he didn't believe in. Maybe that lack of belief alone was enough to make him suffer.

And now he was being buried alive.

At first, a few crumbs fell into the hole the escalator had made, and then more until a landslide had erupted.

Adam turned, thankful for the lights which were still on in the tube station, and leapt down the stairs. He felt the escalator itself move with him, as if it was being recoiled back below the ground.

I've gone mad.

The sound was tremendous as the ground shook, mixing with the noise of the commuters below.

Adam paused halfway down the broken escalator, unsure if he wanted to go down there. For the first time, he saw the wall walkers marching their pointless march up against the brick walls of the station.

He turned, expecting an avalanche of mud to cover him. Nothing happened.

The hole had disappeared, the earth restored. The escalators led to nowhere.

Adam rubbed his tired eyes, tears and anger surfacing.

What was the point of all this? What was the fucking point?!

He sat down, head in his filthy hands, crying.

He was a failure. He'd failed Nick. He'd failed the driver…

And he'd failed the baby.

That was why I was here.

The insight was powerful yet didn't make sense to him. He looked through his fingers, seeing the commuters flicker.

They shimmered, faded and returned. One moment solid forms, the next ghostly apparitions.

The power's running out, he thought. *I'll just sit here and we'll see what happens.*

Below him, the commuters flickered and began to disappear. The noises faded.

After a few minutes, Adam was alone in the station.

CHAPTER 47

JARED

One down.

One to go.

The other bloke had fucked off. Jared was pleased with that.

He dropped the gun; not really wanting to, but his other arm was strained still clamping onto the hippy. Jared reached out and tried to grab a branch, seeking some purchase so he could get into the tree.

Get the baby.

The woman he'd just shot vanished. Another who'd died twice.

Above him, the hippy began to moan, Jared aware his time was short. If he didn't get into the tree now, then he might get sucked into the mess of bodies above. He was so close he could almost reach out and touch them.

Or they him.

He grabbed a branch, unsure if it was strong enough to hold him, but choosing to take the risk. Either that or join the Floaters.

He released himself from Cyrus, thankful the guy hadn't the strength to fight him and drag him into the Floaters.

The branch was not as strong as he'd hoped, it snapped under his weight, instantly lowering himself below the canopy and the tree's ledge.

Jared assumed the branch might snap but knew it wouldn't fall. As a kid he'd often climbed and swung from tree to tree, using branches as a rope, letting them snap as he swung on them, bending to right angles, but never actually breaking off from the tree. He was Tarzan.

And now he was going to kill his Jane.

As soon as his body hit the trunk, he used his aching arms to haul himself up.

Above him, a bright white light appeared out of nowhere.

CHAPTER 48

SAFFI

It was now or never.

She projected the energy, straight up, from her crown chakra, pure white light cascading into the Floaters, now only a few meters above her head. They screamed, moaned and began to sizzle as the light pushed them, melted them, dissolved them, creating a circle of light.

A gap.

Enough for her and the baby to squeeze through.

She looked for a foothold, something nearby, a branch – anything - to help her get up through the gap. As she moved toward a thick branch reaching up toward the Floaters, the white light moved with her, as if she were spotlighting the Breaker itself.

She needed to get a bit higher…

She stood awkwardly on the branch, lifting the baby up toward the gap in the Breaker. She needed a few extra inches…

She stretched, tendons in her arms and neck standing taut.

Just… a… few… more…

Someone grabbed her leg.

CHAPTER 49

CYRUS

He'd like to have another go at this life.

Maybe they'll let me?

It shouldn't have gone like this. As bad as this had.

He'd let Saffi down. After the time spent with her, studying her, learning from her, trying to harness the energies she knew how to tap into and all for what? To commit murder, to panic, to get hysterical.

To come apart.

Yet, this morning he'd seen her maybe as she always was; a fraud, a charlatan.

Had I ever truly known her?

His feet and legs were devoid of feeling now, merging with the others who had been here for longer.

His vision was blurred, one eye unable to see at all, thanks to the attack from the other woman.

It had all gone so wrong.

He felt a huge release of pressure from his arm as the man finally let go. Cyrus' other arm now blending with the Floaters, soon he'd be just a head and arm.

He saw Saffi searching, saw her incredible energy one final time. Saw through his one blurred eye her reaching, lifting the baby.

No, she won't get rid of her again. She won't harm the baby! Not again!

The thought was fierce and vivid. Something from his past.

He fought with every last ounce of energy, determined to make sure the baby was safely above this hell.

Cyrus was floating toward it.

It's not an It! It's a girl! My baby daughter!

The thought was out of context but powerful, almost overwhelming.

With force, he kept his blurred vision on her. The baby was within touching distance. A few more inches…

I'll save you this time. You'll be safe. You'll be above the clouds with the angels where no-one can harm you.

He reached with his remaining arm and scooped the baby up and into the gap.

He'd done it. He'd stopped Saffi from harming the baby girl.

Redemption.

His last thought, as his head and arm were fused with others, was that he'd wished he'd been able to return the camera too. That ever-watching lens, recording everything, capturing all truths. It had been those photos from above the Breaker that had driven him to murder.

And yet he knew, on a deep level, it had revealed the truth. None of this was real.

CHAPTER 50

SAFFI

Her body was dragged down with force, taking her attention away from the baby. Her arms dropped, Saffi thinking she'd dropped the little girl.

'No!'

She glanced up, unable to figure out quite what had happened, the white light dimming as the hand on her leg pulled harder, nails raking skin.

'No, No, No!' she screamed, eyes searching the Floaters for any trace of the baby girl.

Had someone taken her?

Saffi couldn't see any blue blanket among the mess of body parts above. She did spot a familiar face, momentarily thinking it looked like Cyrus, but then it too got submerged under a mass of what was once human beings.

'You!' She looked down, pure anger in her voice. The attacker was pulling himself up, using her leg and a branch as leverage.

Saffi raised her other foot and brought the heel smack down into the guy's face, cracking his nose and teeth.

'You nuckin bidge!' he cried, the words muffled by his crushed nose. But still he held on.

If he falls, we win. If he kills me, we lose.

She had to win, had to defeat him.

But how? His strength was awesome and still he held tight to her, threatening to carry her over the ledge with him.

Sacrifice.

The ultimate act.

She saw it clearly now.

Saffi looked down into Jared's watery eyes, looking up at him from below. She smiled.

I'm ready.

He sensed her motive, his eyes widening, the realisation of what was about to happen causing his legs and feet to kick in the air, trying to find purchase. His other arm still gripping the broken branch.

'No… no…!' he shouted, blood gurgling in his mouth from the force of her stamp on his face.

Saffi's eyes gleamed. It was her time now.

She bent low, stroking his face, still he held her ankle tight.

Jared was breathing hard, spittle foaming with blood at his mouth.

'You lose,' she said.

His anger was rising, veins in his temple standing out, pulsing.

Saffi dragged her leg backward, testing Jared's grip on her ankle. He tensed, knowing he was losing his hold on her. Her leg kicked free. Jared's hand scrambled for some new purchase, finding nothing. Saffi put her hand on his head, grabbing his hair. Jared snatched at her wrist, trying to break her hold but she was already moving.

She maneuvered her body, stepping over Jared, climbing onto his back; a human backpack. She let go of his hair, bringing her arm around his throat, choking him with all of her strength. Her other hand she used to rake at his face, seeking his eyes. She jerked, pulled and scratched at him, anything to make him let go of the branch.

Jared tried to fight back, thrashing at her with one arm, the other gripping their only means of connection to the tree.

She glanced below, a straight fall of around 20 meters or more, no branches on this side of the unusually designed oak tree.

It was made this way for us, she thought. *By us. We made it. All of us.*

The Floaters above continued to moan, forms coalescing, creating visions direct from Hell.

Saffi tugged, putting all of her weight into driving him down, forcing his hand. His fingers were bleeding, his grip on the branch weakening. His free arm now gripping the branch, arms trembling as he struggled to keep hold with both hands.

'You… lose,' she said through clenched teeth.

One final jerk on his neck and Jared's grip finally broke free.

CHAPTER 51

JARED

Like a memory from another life, he realised this time he'd lose. He was sure he hadn't lost before. Or had he? It was all confusing. Right now, he had to get the bitch off of him.

She clawed at his eyes, fingers forcing their way into his skull, the pain excruciating.

'You… lose.'

He'd never lost. He felt sure of it.

His grip was weakening.

There was maybe one last chance of winning.

She could break his fall.

Jared let go of the branch, purposely trying to turn his body, back first, so she would take the impact.

'Wrong bitch… you do,' he muttered, tooth and blood splurging from his broken mouth.

******

They fell like cajoled twins. The Devil and Angel in one final bout before coming to Earth.

Jared realised he'd made a mistake. But it was too late.

Saffi's body flickered, faded and simply ceased to be.

Jared's back hit the floor with tremendous force, he heard bones snap and something deep, deep within his skull echoed. Some primal life force that shouldn't be fucked with, broken.

His vision was almost gone in his damaged eyes. His last glimpse of this hell was as the entire mass of fused bodies and souls in the sky above fell to Earth.

CHAPTER 52
ADAM - UNDERGROUND

He didn't know what to do.

The station was now empty.

He sat on the escalator wondering what course of action he should take, or whether to bother taking any at all.

The tube station lights flickered. Once, twice…

They came on for one more pulse of brilliant light and then went out completely.

He was in the dark.

Above him he heard a thud.

Rain? No, too heavy.

And then came a torrent of thuds.

In his mind;s-eye, Adam pictured the Floaters, seeing them

all fall down.

BOOK TWO

PART ONE

CHAPTER 1
THE EDEN GAME - A CHANCE
AT A NEW LIFE

The Mordrake Institute of Therapeutic Rehabilitation was quietly closed down in September 2024. The work of this little-known organisation was never made public. The trial simulation before the facility was terminated involved a group of vulnerable prisoners including murderers, terrorists, rapists and paedophiles.

Dr. John Edward Mordrake and his team had begun the highly secretive and controversial project in collaboration with more dubious parts of the Government to use interactive digital stimulation as a therapeutic means of assessing a criminal's danger to society. The untested technology allowed prisoners to participate on the understanding that, if successful, they may be able to apply for parole; something the lifers involved would otherwise never have the opportunity to pursue.

The only fully immersive simulation the project undertook before closure was 'The Eden Game' which left one participant in a coma.

CHAPTER 2
MIKE HEGESSAY - BEFORE

Interview transcript:

The following excerpt from an interview transcript is with Prisoner 52514: Michael Hegessay, one of the first participants to join the programme.

Interviewer: Mike, I can see here in your files that you're serving a life sentence for the rape of young girls. You've now served 18 years of your sentence. If you choose to participate, we can look at the possibility of an appeal based on the outcome of the simulation and how you behave in it. That may mean you will be able to apply to be moved to a less secure unit for the rest of your sentence, although I stress it may not be successful.

Mike: What won't be successful? The appeal or the sim-

Interviewer: Well, to be honest, both.

Mike: So… why would I want to do this? Could I die?

Interviewer: [Pause] No. Of course not. Basically, you will be taken to another secure unit, outside of the prison, where you'll be monitored, given a full health check and you'll spend around two hours immersed in the simulation itself. So, for two hours of your time, given you clear all of the health checks, you could… and again, I stress *could*… ultimately be moved to a less secure unit allowing you more freedom. It's your choice.

Mike: When do you need an answer?

Interviewer: Well, as soon as possible really Mike. As you can imagine, places are limited, it costs a lot to logistically make it all happen and, with the chance of a lesser sentence for some prisoners, there's quite a queue.

[Silence]

Interviewer: It may also mean you could have more visits. [Ruffling of papers can be heard] I believe your ex-wife, Katie, is pregnant?

Mike: I'll do it.

END OF TRANSCRIPT.

CHAPTER 3

THE PARTICIPANTS - PART ONE
IN THE GOVERNOR'S OFFICE - BEFORE

They were always interfering, always making his job more difficult than it needed to be.

'Mrs. Henning, please show the Doctor in now.'

The Governor sat back, adjusting his tie, waiting for the man he had been pressured to see by the powers above.

He rose as the door opened and a stumpy bespectacled man was shown into his office.

They shook hands.

'Coffee, Doctor?'

The stumpy man smiled, nodded.

'Mrs. Henning, coffee please.'

'Yes, Sir,' she replied over the intercom. 22 years his PA and he knew she'd already have made coffee, along with her usual home-made cookies and would have it ready in moments. They were like a telepathic couple.

The Governor looked at the bulging belly of the Doctor seated before him, wondering if Mrs. Henning's cookies were really what he needed.

A polite knock, she entered, served the coffee and left.

The Governor spied two cookies. He offered one to the Doctor.

'Now, Doctor Mordrake, how can I help you?'

Half the cookie went in the first bite, crumbs falling onto the tie of the rotund Doctor. He absent-mindedly brushed the cookie crumbs onto the floor.

'Thank you for seeing me at such short notice, Governor.'

'Please, call me Jeff,' he said smiling.

The Doctor nodded, making the last half of cookie vanish in one mouthful. He began talking while chomping, making the Governor's dislike of the man only more intense. He hoped his expression of distaste wasn't obvious.

'I'm heading up an exciting opportunity between myself and several… benefactors who wish to remain anonymous.'

The Governor assumed these secretive benefactors were certainly in positions of power, given the pressure they had put on him to see the Doctor in the first place.

He nodded, urging the Doctor to continue.

'We are seeking some of your guests-'

The Governor smiled. 'Doctor, it's a prison not a hotel.'

'Of course. We'd like to select a group of category A prisoners to be part of this exciting trial.'

'And may I enquire as to what exactly this trial is?' asked Jeff.

The Doctor hesitated. His eyes glanced toward the last cookie. The Governor smiled, gesturing with his hand to the plate. 'Please, be my… guest.'

Maybe it was a hotel after all.

'Thank you! As I was saying, this project would require some of your prisoners, those who wish to volunteer, to be securely transported to our secure facility not far from here, where they will be with us for around three or four days to be inducted into our rehabilitation programme.'

Jeff stayed silent. Normally he'd ask a million questions; which is it, three or four days? How will you keep them secure? How will you rehabilitate them in less than a week?

He knew this was coming from the highest places in power, so already guessed much of the decision was out of his hands. This meeting was all just sideshow.

The second cookie vanished.

'So, if you'd be happy to perhaps talk me through some of the profiles of the… prisoners here, then we might be able to suggest to our mutual superiors who would work best for this exciting trial.' The Doctor beamed.

That word again; exciting. Jeff didn't like it. It hid BS. It covered the lie. It all sounded too good to be true, which, from Jeff's lived experience, always turned out to be anything but.

'Do you have permission to show me the profiles, Gov… Jeff?'

Jeff felt powerless. Normally he'd be asking them if they had a warrant to access such information. But he'd been told clearly that whatever the Doctor wanted, Jeff should provide. No questions asked.

'Of course, I am the Governor here, Doctor,' he replied hoping it didn't sound as sarcastic as he perhaps meant it.

The Doctor smiled again, a crumb on his lower lip. Jeff couldn't take his eyes off it. It seemed to sum this man up; walk in anywhere, whenever and take whatever he wanted. No questions asked.

'Please Jeff, call me John.' Jeff had no intention of using his name at all. He didn't like the man and wanted him out of his prison now. He hoped the smile the Doctor now offered would be enough to dislodge that crumb.

No such luck.

'Well, what are the parameters, as we have a lot of category A prisoners given our location.'

The Doctor's eyes went back to the empty plate. Jeff wasn't going to make that happen. Not while half of the damn thing was still around the Doctor's mouth and the rest now mindlessly cast on his usually spotless carpet.

'Ideally, we could look at them together and I can assess who may work best.'

Jeff demurred. 'Do they all have to be cat A's?'

The doctor considered this. 'Well, Jeff,' the Governor cringed hearing his name spoken by the fat cookie-eating monster, 'it could be people who you feel would best be served by being rehabilitated and gone from your prison… not that that would necessarily happen, of course!' he quickly added, sensing the Governor's surprise at his remarks. The Doctor frowned, his gaze retuning to the empty plate.

'Let me put it another way. If you had a magic wand to wave, who, from all your prisoners, would you like to see rehabilitated? Who would you like to see back on the street assuming you knew, 100% knew, that they'd never re-offend again?'

Jeff bit his inside lip, a subconscious tick he always did when thinking things through.

He thought of the two young black kids, both had potential to do something with their lives, but were in for a seven year stretch for supplying drugs. He thought of Ange and Tasha, both from diverse backgrounds who had found each other inside and were of such help to the other women. About the baby girl they were planning to adopt. He thought of Nigel who didn't really belong here. He'd killed his cancer-ridden wife as an act of mercy, yet the law of the land said otherwise. And then he thought of the others; Hegessay, serial paedophile. Ahmed, failed suicide bomber. What if the Doctor really could cure these ideologies, these corrupt morals, indecent practices, through whatever magical programme his institute had dreamed up?

He glanced back to the Doctor, who's eyes were once again back on the plate.

This could take a while, but yes, he had a list.

Jeff smiled, pressed the intercom.

'Mrs. Henning, more coffee and two more of your fabulous cookies please.'

CHAPTER 4
THE INTRODUCTION - PART ONE
AT THE INSTITUTE - BEFORE

1.

The chosen participants were taken to a large room, chairs in a circle. The room, like every other part of the institute was white, devoid of colour and feeling.

Except for the vase of flowers. The only colour in the otherwise lifeless room. They were beautiful, mainly blue. Their scent gave the room a sense of freedom, opposing the sterility and lifelessness of the white walls.

The smell of Spring.

Lihua Kwok became entranced by the flowers, her gaze rarely leaving them throughout the session. She would close her eyes and tilt her head, detecting their scent, their strong aroma bringing her a sense of peace. Of contentment. Memories of a world outside these walls.

A world of freedom.

'Chunhua,' she spoke softly.

Seated next to her, Lucy was scratching her wrists. She glanced toward Lihua. 'What?' she said.

'Chunhua. It means Spring Flowers.'

Lucy nodded, still scratching the white scars on her wrists. 'Chunhua,' she muttered.

Nancy saw Jordan and fought the urge to run to him, embrace him. They'd been imprisoned apart for nearly a year now, just one phone-call a week to maintain any kind of relationship. Her counselling sessions in prison had been helping a little but she still knew he was more to her than just a manipulator. More than just having used her for drug running.

There was love between them. They'd shared more than just needles.

Ushered into the spacious room, James's eyes roamed around everyone, admiring the rather attractive women dressed in what looked like medical uniforms. He'd always liked women in uniforms. Especially when he was in charge, telling them what to do. He felt himself becoming aroused, quickly averting his thoughts, plastering his well-rehearsed smile on for the benefit of all.

It was the first-time men and women had been brought together and James was surprised by the lack of armed guards. Surely the number of men and violent prisoners now in the room could easily over-power any of these bitches?

He glanced at the ceiling, seeing the familiar black domes, hiding the CCTV. He was here to hopefully knock years off his sentence, so an assault was probably not the way to go.

The doors at the other end of the hall swung open and in marched dozen heavily built men all dressed in black, fronted by a doctor and another woman holding a clipboard. The doctor was the only one of them dressed in white.

James's smile turned into a sneer, quickly corrected as the new woman alongside the doctor gave him a courteous nod. He wondered what she had written on her clipboard. The men fanned out, standing to attention around the room.

The doctor addressed the group. He invited them to sit.

2.

'Well, firstly, thank you. Thank you to everyone for being here. Now, I know many of you will have questions and this is what we are here for today. We aim to answer all your queries as best we can. You'll notice that we are also joined by our… other guests,' he gestured to the bodyguards stood to attention rooted about the big hall. 'I assure you they are only here for all our safety. They are not here to coerce you, so please, do not feel threatened.'

'Who the fuck are you?' said Ahmed.

The Doctor smiled at the interrupting youth, the youngest of all the participants.

'I am Doctor Mordrake and this is my facility. But please, let's refrain from any unnecessary foul-language, shall we?' He glanced back at Ahmed. The youth stretched his legs, slouching further into the chair, a look of nonchalance on his face. A full body shrug. Mordrake wondered if the simulation would help this particular person. Or, perhaps, show what his true intentions were should he ever be released.

Other voices piped up, demanding answers. Mordrake held up a hand.

'Please, now. Quiet. We've a lot to get through. I believe most of you have already signed the paperwork?'

Nicholas thought back to the day before when he'd been led down one of the endless white corridors in this place, into a room with the clipboard woman who now sat before him. Doctor Hampton? He couldn't remember. Couldn't care less.

'And this is my colleague, Doctor Hampstead,' said Mordrake, gesturing to the woman seated next to him, clipboard hugged to her chest. She nodded, her eyes scanning the participants. She glanced at Jamie, the two meeting for the first time less than 24 hours ago.

His story was particularly troubling and sad. She noticed that he was looking at another woman almost in a state of shock. Hampstead checked her clipboard. Lucy Peters. Ah yes, the wife of an abusive husband, who'd lost her baby when she'd tampered with the brakes on the family car. Husband and baby died instantly. Another sad tale. Hampstead frowned, realising the similarities between Lucy and Jamie's past: both had killed abusive men. Only Jamie had killed his sister *and* her abusive husband at the same time. The sister's death an accident. Apparently.

Hampstead consulted one of the women in white, while Mordrake continued to introduce the others in the room and explain about the history of the institute. The woman in white dashed off returning in minutes with two brown folders. Hampstead looked through them, still one ear on the ongoing conversation in the room. But something troubled her. Something she'd seen earlier but hadn't put two and two together until everyone had come together in this room, right now for the first time.

She was looking at the photograph of Jamie's sister, prior to the crash that had ended her life. Another similarity; both his sister's and Lucy's abusive partners had died in car crashes where the brakes had been tampered with. Yet, the two cases were months apart.

Evil minds think alike.

Hampstead closed the file and opened Lucy's. The photograph facing her took her breath away. Hampstead, flicked back to Jamie's file. The resemblance between Lucy and

Jamie's sister was uncanny. They could be twins. Hampstead made a mental note to talk to Mordrake in private later as having both participants in the game could be problematic. Each participant would already be overwhelmed with the simulation let alone having extra baggage to deal with. Hampstead laughed quietly, more in surprise than humour, when she saw Jamie's sister's name. Lucy.

Uncanny.

3.

Mordrake looked at Doctor Hampstead, her laugh had drawn the attention of the room.

'Something to share, Doctor?' he asked her.

She immediately closed the files, sat up straight and resumed her stern look. 'My apologies Doctor, please continue.'

Mordrake looked at her a moment longer before continuing.

'Yes, well… each of you are very special people. You have been individually chosen and will be, as I say, participating in a life changing immersive experience.' A hand went up.

Saffron Williams.

Cyrus was seated across from Saffi. The Doctor's words were not lost on him; he was done being a Chosen One.

Mordrake was fascinated by Saffi, her crimes and what she claimed to be able to do. But for now, he shut her down. 'No. Questions will come later, I assure you. For now, please let me outline exactly why you're here.'

Saffi lowered her hand, her eyes gleaming at Mordrake. He felt a trickle of sweat run down the side of his neck and into his shirt collar. It was hot in here.

He felt parched, glancing at the wall clock directly opposite. Only twenty minutes and it was tea and biscuits time. He had twenty minutes to explain the game.

'Thank you. The format of the day will be that I will introduce you to our incredible project here this morning. Then we will break in around half-hour for coffee. That will also give you all time to talk to each other. However, you will be asked to remain in your seats. Hence our… friends… to assist should they be required,' he gestured to the unmoving guards. 'Which I'm quite sure, they won't be,' he smiled.

Mordrake took a deep breath, steadying himself. The next part of his presentation would either be met with excitement or fear. Possibly both.

'I have created an incredible, thrilling adventure!' He'd chosen his words carefully when preparing and memorising his speech. 'And you,' he said, eyes wide, taking in everyone sat around the circle, 'are to be the very first people to ever experience it!'

'Sounds like a medical trial,' said Adam.

Mordrake smiled while Hampstead glanced at the clipboard. 'Far from it, my friend. Far from it. Think of it more like a grand day out.'

Hampstead looked up again at Adam. Adam Fletcher. He'd been part of a criminal drugs gang. His record was impressive and it took three combined police forces to finally catch him in the act. And over £5million from the public's purse. And then the bastard had almost gotten off. Bloody lawyers. They'd tried to exploit a loophole. Until the Minister had become involved and shut it down. Fletcher was slippery. He'd been the only one to sign the initial contracts who asked for a lawyer. Hampstead put a mark against his name. She'd be watching him closely. She knew Mordrake was excited by his participation in the simulation, wanting to see how he'd react. How he'd choose to behave.

Fletcher wasn't a killer. He'd never got his hands dirty. (If he had, then the prosecution had never found any evidence of him having done so.) But his drug cartel was responsible for more deaths than anyone else sat in the room. Hampstead wondered if the two black youths who were in for drug dealing were unknowingly part of Fletcher's vast empire.

Mordrake continued. 'Each of you will, if you decide to go ahead, be involved in what is basically a computer game. Like virtual reality. You'll be immersed in the game together and over the course of around two hours in the game, you'll have a chance to…' Mordrake realised he'd gone off script. Sweat continued to run down his cheek. 'You'll have a chance at redemption. Put it that way!' he smiled, his face reddening. He felt he was already losing them.

He looked at the clock. The minute hand appeared to be in the same place. Mordrake rubbed his sweaty palms together, wondering if he should open up the floor for questions now, rather than later.

No. He needed to maintain control.

'So, let me tell you a little about the aim of the game. We will be totally honest with you. This is a therapeutic experience.'

Groans went up from around the room.

'I knew it, it's a fucking test,' said Adam.

A guard stepped forward putting his hand on Adam's shoulder from behind. Adam glanced round, shrugged the arm off and remained quiet.

'Please, do let me explain,' continued Mordrake. 'It's not a test. It's a *game*. Once you're in the experience, you won't remember any of this session. You won't really remember any of your real life. Only temporarily!' he managed to get that line in before more groans drowned his words out. 'It's fully tested. As soon as you're finished in the game, you'll be back with us and normal life will resume.'

'So, what's the point of it then?' asked Aabid.

Aabid Wakin. Brother to Ahmed. His file claimed he brainwashed the younger sibling into wearing a suicide vest, thankfully the plot being intercepted by the anti-terrorist police. He, along with the Kwok woman, completed a trio of terror. Doctor Hampstead had voiced her concerns at all three of them being involved in the trial. It was after Mordrake made it clear that none of them would ever get the chance at early release no matter how the simulation went, that Hampstead had agreed to their participation.

'The point,' said Mordrake responding to Aabid's question and unintentionally opening the question-and-answer session ahead of schedule, 'is to see how you behave in a new environment. As mentioned, you won't recall this conversation, or very little of your actual lives whilst you're immersed in the game. But, as I say, you will remember it *all* upon exit from the game. What the simulation allows is for you to enjoy a virtually created experience and for us to determine how you may behave if allowed back into society ahead of your parole.'

Murmurs greeted this.

'And what if we don't have parole?' the softly spoken voice cut in.

Mordrake and Hampstead observed Saffi, her cool demeanour ever present. Mordrake glanced at Hampstead. 'Well, never say never, eh?' he offered.

Saffi smiled.

4.

After tea and biscuits, the conversation continued, questions coming thick and fast.

'How do we know if we'll be safe?'

'Can we get hurt for real in the game?'

'What is it you want to learn by watching us, like mice in a fucking cage?'

Mordrake answered them all patiently, one by one.

By lunch time all the participants knew what was being asked of them. They knew that they would be under observation throughout by a medical team, monitoring their blood pressure, heart rate and ensuring them of the Institute's commitment to their health and wellbeing.

The Doctor informed them of how they will be safely sat down throughout the experience, each person in a dedicated glass cubicle, with their own specialist observing them. He told them how, should they wish at any time, they can exit the game simply by standing up from the seat during the experience. Only Fletcher questioned how they were supposed to remember that rule, given everything they were being told was apparently going to be lost on them once they began the game. Mordrake put minds at rest, saying they would see and hear clues throughout which would remind them of the need to simply stand up, should they wish to exit the simulation.

What neither doctor told them was how they would be monitored within the game. The main purpose of The Eden Game was to observe whether any convict had truly been rehabilitated. Or would they simply assume the same subconscious bias on release?

Mordrake was intrigued to know if the murderers would kill in the game. The rapists rape. And the one who perhaps sickened him the most; would that paedophile Hegessay go straight back to his perverse, sickening habits once the game had commenced?

5.
Dr. Julia Hampstead
Lunch Break

She knocked on the door and entered without waiting to be asked.

Mordrake was at his desk, one hand absentmindedly eating crackers from a packet, while he wrote with the other. He didn't look up to see who had disturbed him, knowing full well only Julia would enter without permission. The cracker in hand was quickly devoured before another took its place.

'I guess you noticed?' she asked.

Mordrake continued to scribble, his face red from exertion and stress now his project was getting ever nearer to its first trial.

'I said, I guessed you noticed?' she asked again, raising her voice.

Mordrake stopped scribbling, dropped his pen and glanced up. She saw how tired he looked, his bloodshot eyes, beads of perspiration dancing on his brow. He automatically reached for another cracker.

'How can you eat those dry, John?'

Mordrake stopped the cracker en-route. He looked at it quizzically as if really seeing it for the first time.

'I ran out of cheese and pickle,' he said.

'Good. And when you run out of crackers, perhaps you'll finally start eating healthier, John!' she said.

Mordrake smiled. 'What are you? A doctor?'

Julia returned the smile. They'd been working together for years, purely professional with the occasion social meet-up outside of work, where matters other than work were rarely discussed.

She gestured with the folders she held before her.

'Anyway, I was saying…'

'No, I haven't noticed.'

'Well, it might pose a problem.'

Mordrake was reaching for his pen, but her sentence stopped him.

Problem. The thing Mordrake didn't like were problems. Most people-of-science enjoyed tackling problems. Not Mordrake; he preferred a life without problems. Ironic, given his entire professional life had been spent building his AI Simulation to help people who society had ordained *as* problems.

He remained silent as she opened the two files and placed them before him. Mordrake glanced down nodding back and forth between Lucy Peters' and Jamie Carter's file photographs like a referee at a tennis tournament.

He sat back and sighed.

'I don't see this being a problem,' he said.

'John, they're already going to be under huge stress and we're putting them both in the same simulation.'

'Well, so what?'

'So, what? Come on, John. Take a good look. She could be his sister!'

Mordrake didn't need to look again. Julia expected he already knew of the similarity of not only Lucy being a doppelgänger for Jamie's sister, who was also called Lucy, but the circumstances of their convictions.

'Both killed abusive men by tampering with the brakes of cars. Lucy lost her baby as well. Jamie killed his sister, who just happened to look very similar to Lucy Peters and was also called Lucy! It's quite overwhelming outside of the simulation as it is.'

Mordrake opened his mouth to talk but bit his tongue. Instead, he reached for another cracker.

'So, you think we should take one of them out of the trial?'

Julia hesitated in her reply. Mordrake continued while eating.

'Because, if we do, we may miss the opportunity for both of them to be rehabilitated.' Mordrake stood up, crumbs falling from his white coat onto the floor.

'I mean, think about it, Julia. If we keep them both in, their paths *will* cross - that's inevitable. And Jamie may get protective of her in the game in a way that means he can show all of us he is now a reformed prisoner. Who knows? He could end up being considered for early release.' Mordrake walked around the desk, clearly enthused by his argument to keep both Peters and Carter in the game.

'They may end up working together. They may even end up saving the day!' He took Julia's hands in his. 'I don't see any problem, Julia, only opportunity.' He smiled and squeezed her hand. She knew him well enough to know there was nothing sexual in his touching her.

Julia hesitated, her mouth squirming, unsure what to say. Mordrake beat her to it.

'I always value your opinion as you know. This isn't *my* project, it's ours. The whole team's. So, if you'd prefer I drop one of them, I will. But I ask that you do give careful consideration to the potential for their own growth in the game *and* our results. This series of coincidences in their lives could be a gift.' He nodded home his point.

She smiled. He had a point. This could be a gift. They were playing God. She nodded.

Mordrake released her hands and hugged her. As a man who hated problems, he had removed another from his life like magic.

Mordrake stepped back around the desk to resume his writing. Julia collected the two files off the desk, leaving Mordrake to his crackers.

As she walked out of his office she wondered if they were all crackers given the trial soon to unfold.

CHAPTER 5
THE PARTICIPANTS - PART TWO
IN THE GOVERNOR'S OFFICE - BEFORE

1.

Jeff looked again at his wristwatch. He had a million things to do. Yet, as annoying as the Doctor was, Jeff was fascinated by the proposal. Plus, he had little choice; the decision had already been made from the powers that be, so Jeff had to work with Mordrake as best he could.

The Doctor had been quiet while reading the latest brown file from the stack they had partly gone through. Jeff checked his watch once again, seeing the same time as only seconds ago. He resigned himself to spending the rest of the morning, if not the entire day, in the good Doctor's company. He only hoped Mrs. Henning had plenty of cookies on standby.

Mordrake sighed heavily. 'Terrible. Just terrible,' he muttered, putting the brown file down, removing his glasses and rubbing the top of his nose between finger and thumb.

You can't un-see it, thought Jeff. *No matter how hard you try to rub those images away.*

The file lay open. Lihua Kwok.

One of the prison's most deplorable inmates.

Jeff sighed. 'Yes, it doesn't make for enjoyable reading, does it?'

Mordrake replaced his glasses. 'Well, if we can help her, then in some way, it will be the ultimate proof of my design.'

Jeff simply nodded, eyebrows raising. He had little faith anyone could help Kwok. He didn't really *want* anyone to. Not after what she had done and the lives she had ruined.

Kwok was in for life. At her trail she claimed she had been a victim of sex-trafficking, claiming rape by Aabid Wakin. She went so far as to tell the police she had given birth to a baby, fathered by Wakin. The truth was even more sickening, if that were even possible.

Kwok had been the top of the tree. The boss. She had encouraged vulnerable young women into the sex trade. She had them housed by her gang, the Wakin's part of her entourage. She had been there while they'd been raped, drugged, beaten. She'd even carried out abortions without any proper medical intervention, using coat hangers, screwdrivers and other makeshift tools, killing both mother and baby on more than one occasion. At the trial it became clear that the investigation into the gang had only managed to scrape the tip of the iceberg. They never found out who Kwok's handlers or paymasters were. Or how many young women's lives she had destroyed.

'If there is an evil, then she embodies it,' said Mordrake.

'Doctor, listen, I don't know if there's any point in you considering prisoners like Kwok or the Wakins? What good can come of it?'

Mordrake smiled. 'Call it retribution Jeff, but there's a little bit of coding we put into the simulation for just such people.' He lowered his voice conspiratorially and leaned forward over the desk. '*We can make them experience their own crimes.*'

The Governor didn't know what to say.

The Doctor continued, 'so, if they haven't shown any remorse for their crimes in this reality, then we can put them through an intolerable experience in the simulation, which may be a starting point for continued therapy when they leave the game.' The Doctor's eyes shone.

The Governor clearly had reservations. 'I can't subject people to that. It's… it's not ethical surely?' He already knew he had no choice; his instructions were to give the Doctor what and whomever he wanted.

'Call it an eye for an eye,' said Mordrake. 'And remember Jeff, they'll only be experiencing it for a maximum of two hours, not two years or for however long those poor bastards suffered,' he said, brushing the paperwork in Kwok's file with his fingers. 'And she won't really be experiencing it. It'll feel real to her, but her body will be untouched.'

'And what about when they come out?' asked Jeff.

'From the game or into society?'

'The game,' said Jeff assuming no-one was really going to be offered early parole.

Mordrake knew that the Governer was referring to possible PTSD in the game, but chose to answer him literally.

'From our early trials, we've been told it feels like falling into the arms of an angel. When in reality they simply fall from their chair, slumping forward as our specialist medical team safely support them and transport them to a nearby bed.'

'So, it's like a near-death experience?'

Mordrake considered this. 'Think of it more like a re-birth. The chance for them to start life afresh. Absolved.'

2.

'They're exemplary inmates and have only recently applied to adopt a baby,' said Jeff passing two folders to the Doctor. 'Angela Pinkney and Tasha Davies.'

Mordrake took the files and opened them on the desk. He absentmindedly brushed crumbs from his top as he read them. Jeff made a note to have the folders shaken out once the Doctor had left to remove any trace of his visit.

'Pinkney and Davies…' said Mordrake to himself, his words morphing into silent, private thought. He glanced up. 'Exemplary, you say?'

Jeff leaned forward on his elbows, head tilting as he looked at the upside-down faces of his two favourite inmates. 'Indeed. Pinkney has been with us for over a decade. Davies arrived only two years ago and was immediately taken under Angela's wing. You see, Angela is a pier-worker. She acts as a go-between. A kind of middle-woman helping the newbies acclimatise and also keeping an eye on their mental state. When inmates are around officers, they tend not to show any signs of weakness. For that matter, they also shield it from the other inmates as best they can. But that leads to suicides. So, we have a healthy programme whereby one of the lifers who knows day-to-day prison life becomes a…'

'…Guardian Angel,' finished Mordrake.

Jeff shrugged. 'Yeah, I guess that's kind of what they are.'

Mordrake giggled.

'Something funny?' asked Jeff.

'No, not really. Just… well, they do say we are christened with the name that defines our destiny. And Angela is one letter longer than Angel.'

'Haven't ever really thought about that,' said Jeff. 'Yeah, I guess she is. She's saved many of the women in here from depression. She gives them new hope.'

'New light,' said Mordrake. 'Angels offer light. It's what they do.'

'Are you a religious man?' asked Jeff.

'Me? No, not really.' Mordrake continued to study the files before him. 'It's like our nurses and, well, even myself. We are dressed in white and many times, as patients are either going under or gaining consciousness after an operation, they later tell tales of having seen Angels who spoke to them. People dressed in white,' he said without looking up. 'People with haloes.' The Doctor looked up at Jeff and smiled. 'It's the overhead lights they are really seeing, with us leaning over the patient. It gives them the idea that they think they are seeing glowing astral beings.'

Jeff rubbed his chin thoughtfully. 'Makes sense when you think about it.'

Mordrake continued to read. 'Well, it's either that or they really are seeing Angels,' he said. Mordrake turned the pages of Angela's file. 'Says here, she's obsessed with flying.'

'She's always talked about one day flying away into the sunset in her own helicopter.'

'An Angel above the clouds indeed!' said Mordrake. He continued to read. 'Guess, she won't be going anywhere for a while. She killed two people in a house fire!'

Jeff sighed, considering whether to get into the full story. He decided to, figuring Angela deserved it after all she'd been through.

'She was convicted of arson which led to the deaths of her father and her step-mum. Pinkney confessed she only intended to kill her step-mum. She was abused by her step-mum for years. Her father was often away at work. From her earliest memories of her step-mum, she talked about the physical and mental torture, the beatings, the burnings, the scarring. When she was eighteen, she decided that she needed to escape or kill her. Turns out she did both.'

'So *she* says,' replied Mordrake never taking his eyes off her file.

Jeff bit his lip. 'I believe her,' he said.

'Well, you know them far better than I,' offered Mordrake.

Jeff decided to move on, feeling his anger rising. Who was this fucking man? He didn't know shit about his inmates. Jeff steadied his breath.

'Anyway, once convicted, she quickly proved to be one of the few prisoners I've ever met who was grateful to be inside. She never wants to leave. To her, the outside world is and was unsafe. In here, she's protected. Well, that's how she sees it.'

Mordrake was now looking intently at Jeff, absorbed by the idea. 'Wow! So, she went from a life of being imprisoned to a life behind bars… yet believes herself to be free. That's… that's beautiful,' he said without a hint of sarcasm.

Jeff merely nodded. *It is,* he thought.

'Anyway, so Davies gets convicted. She was your typical abandoned teen. Her parents were rarely there and when they were they were drunk. Her grandparents passed away when Davies was young. Her parents followed soon after. Cancer, I recall. Davies started with petty crime then eventually she got done for GBH. That's what happens when society lets them slip through the cracks.'

'It escalates,' said Mordrake.

'Yes. But once Davies was convicted, she became totally shut off and wouldn't eat or communicate. It was Angela who snapped her out of her spell. She worked with her tirelessly. I'm not a shrink but…'

Mordrake was already nodding. 'She was saving someone.'

Jeff continued, 'Yeah, maybe as salvation for her father she couldn't save in the fire.'

'Life offers us such chances of redemption,' said Mordrake, his eyes gleaming.

'Davies could potentially get early release through your simulation. She's studying journalism through one of our prison programmes. Takes stunning photographs. She has a great eye, so I've been told,' said Jeff. 'But Pinkney is in for a long time. And, as I said, she won't want to be released even if it were offered. She has a new life here. New meaning.'

'A new family,' said Mordrake.

Jeff nodded. Yes, that felt right. And in many ways, he felt like a father to her. Someone to keep an eye on her.

'Guardian Angel,' said Mordrake waking Jeff from his spell.

'Sorry?'

'I was saying, Angela Pinkney. She really is a Guardian Angel.'

Jeff nodded. 'And they're applying to adopt a baby. If successful it'll be a huge boost to the women. Tasha and Angela are in a relationship and…'

Mordrake interrupted. 'What would happen to the baby if Davies was successful in the programme and did get parole?'

Jeff paused, considering the hypothesis. He hadn't considered any of this, what with the meeting today being the first he'd heard of the simulation.

'Well, I guess in that situation, the baby would go with Davies. More of a life for it on the outside.'

Mordrake smiled. 'Well, let's see what happens. What sex is the baby they wish to adopt?'

Jeff turned one of the files back toward him and lifted pages looking for the notes on the adoption.

'A girl,' he said.

3.

'Why are these files green and not brown?'

The Doctor waved the file at the Governor as if the colour wasn't already clear enough. Jeff maintained his professional calm.

'They will have hidden identities within the prison,' he said.

The Doctor raised his eyebrows.

'Bent coppers,' said Jeff, offering nothing more. *And bent in more ways than one,* he thought, knowing that Paul Ross and Daniel Chad had been more than just partners while working the beat.

'Corrupt policeman, eh?' said Mordrake, flipping through the file. 'Drug dealing!'

'Indeed,' said Jeff, wanting to move on, away from those who gave his profession a bad name. Whether Police or Prison Service, it was One Big Happy Family and bent coppers were quickly rejected.

Mordrake wasn't as keen to move on.

'It says here Paul Ross had served nearly eight years with the force with an exemplary career until Daniel Chad crapped on him?'

Jeff sighed. He hated talking about corrupt officers, especially in The Family.

'Yeah, so long story short: Officer Chad was working under Ross for around two years. In that time, they went from a stellar number of drug arrests to literally zero. It didn't take a Columbo to work out what was going on. Ross would never break, but Chad finally did. They'd been nicking the runners and then selling back the supply to the dealers. They worked their way up, supplying the head-honcho and his team. I think I've got his file here somewhere.' He began to rummage through the many files on his desk. 'A guy called Fletcher. Adam Fletcher.'

Mordrake looked up, eyes wide, almost salivating. A puppy hearing a tin being opened.

Jeff found the file on Fletcher.

'I remember this being in the papers. It was a massive bust. Fletcher was the top of the pyramid. Well, if he wasn't, he wasn't grassing on who was. He's taken the fall. I don't think we can give that bastard any chance of early release.'

Mordrake took the file and read in silence. He went back to the file on Paul Ross, glancing between his and Fletcher's.

'So, Paul Ross was arresting Fletcher's runners, seizing their supply and then selling it back to Fletcher? Didn't that just give Fletcher less runners as they were arrested?'

'No, it's actually quite smart if you think about it. Well, obviously not that smart as they finally caught the bastards. What was happening was Ross and Chad would get a text from one of Fletcher's head-honchos telling them the name and location of the lowlife who was dealing on the street. Basically, setting them up. So, the dealer had already paid Fletcher for the supply, right? Then Fletcher would tell Ross. Ross would arrest the small-time dealer, seize the supply. No minor drug offence gets anywhere near prosecution these days, so in the end Ross realised he could seize the drugs, give the dealer a caution and then Fletcher would buy the supply back at far less than he sold it to the dealer.'

'Only to…'

'Exactly. Sell it on again to the same bloody dealer!'

Mordrake looked back at Fletcher's file, marvelling at the mastermind behind such a ploy. He couldn't wait to see how he'd act in the simulation.

'And it was Ross' partner who eventually gave the game away?' asked Mordrake.

'Indeed. He and Ross had become involved together outside of work.' Mordrake's mouth tightened. Jeff held up his hands. 'Hey, whatever, that's their business. But it was being in a relationship that allowed Ross to keep control over Chad so he kept his mouth shut. His conscience finally got the better of him though and he came forward on his own admission.

Mordrake looked at Chad's file and compared the sentence to Ross'. A much lighter sentence. He wondered how they'd both react once inside The Eden Game. Especially if the AI threw them both back together *and* with Fletcher in the simulation too! Mordrake licked his lips.

Jeff wanted to move on.

But Mordrake wouldn't give up Fletcher's file.

'You say you don't want him to get early release?' asked Mordrake. Jeff sighed. 'There's a lot in that file and it doesn't even touch the surface. They couldn't pin other things on him thanks to his lawyers. Slimy bastards they are too.'

'Such as…?' Mordrake let the words hang waiting for Jeff to provide an ending. Their eyes met and Jeff took the bait.

'Such as rape, murder, arson let alone the countless lives ruined thanks to his cartel. He was getting the supplies from an overseas dealer, a big one from what I've since been told.' Jeff waved a hand. He leaned forward eyes narrowing capturing the Doctor in his stare. 'But you watch that bastard in your game. I tell you now, if he gets so much as a whiff of some kind of parole, he'll play you and your team like a game of chess. He'll win. It's what he does, he's a strategist. He's a survivor. His lawyers are still working round the clock to get him out, hoping to find a loophole.'

Mordrake broke the spell and averted his eyes back to the file. The Governor found he wasn't as keen to move on as he previously had been. He reached forward and lightly knocked the desk, commanding the Doctor's attention once again. 'You can't let him get away with what he's done. You understand me? I don't care what tech or science you think you have to control him; he will see through it and he will manipulate you.' Jeff finally sat back. 'As he has with everyone he's ever come into contact with,' he muttered. 'But not me.' Almost a whisper. 'Not on my watch.'

Mordrake nodded. 'I understand. But I assure you, once he's submerged, he'll have no idea that what he's experiencing isn't reality. He won't be able to manipulate anybody.'

Jeff's hands came together, fingers resting under his chin. 'I've made my point, Doctor.'

Much to Jeff's satisfaction, it was Mordrake who now wished to move on.

'What about this guy?' Jeff handed over a fat brown file. 'He'll make your eyes water.'

Mordrake placed the green files to one side, adding a quick scribble to his pad. It seemed he was keen to consider the two coppers after all.

'And what did this one do?' he asked, taking the file, smiling as opened it.

The Governor hoped that smile would quickly disappear off the Doctor's smug face. He wasn't disappointed.

'Luke Brown. Wealthy, powerful. He enjoyed photographing and making art of his victims.'

'The bathtub killer,' read Mordrake aloud.

'Yeah, he'd kill them, usually prostitutes, by strangulation and then leave them in a bathtub full of cash. After raping them, of course.'

Mordrake's face turned pale. It was the Governor's turn to smile.

Mordrake closed the file, turning his attention to the one cookie left on the plate. Jeff hoped the fat Doctor's appetite was finally gone.

Mordrake sighed, scribbling the name on his ever-expanding list.

'Ah, now here's an interesting one. Kleptomaniac. But with an extra twist.'

Mordrake extended one hand to take the proffered file, while his other absentmindedly reached for the remaining cookie. The Governor watched in mild disgust as the fat Doctor continued on auto-pilot.

'A klepto. Hmmm… why a prison sentence? Did she steal the crown jewels?' he smirked, still chewing the cookie, crumbs joining the others already dotted around the floor.

'No, she blinded someone. Stole their eyesight, I guess you could say.'

The Doctor stopped chewing. It appeared no further scrutiny was needed. Mordrake added the name Paula Asketh to his list.

'Just a few more Jeff and I think we'll be done. I'll have my driver come collect me in, say, an hour?' Mordrake consulted his watch. 'Maybe time for one more cuppa and…' he let the request trail off.

Jeff pressed the intercom, inviting further coffee and cookies. Mordrake smiled.

'Speaking of drivers… how about this inmate. Doug Kinsman. A repeat sex offender. Then he went all-in and began kidnapping too. Used to keep various sex toys in the car.' Jeff was reading from the file, reminding himself of the case. He laughed out loud. 'Ah yes, they finally got him and found a large vibrator in his glove box. Said it was a self-administered drink driving guage!'

Mordrake laughed. 'Imagine being asked to blow into that!'

Jeff smiled.

Within the hour, the final list had been completed.

CHAPTER 6

THE INTRODUCTION - PART TWO
AT THE INSTITUTE - BEFORE

1.

After lunch, the introduction to The Eden Game resumed.

'Like any role-play, there is an objective which we hope you'll undertake as a team. I must remind you all that what we are discussing here today is not to be disclosed, hence the forms you signed yesterday,' said Mordrake.

'Not that we'll remember anyway,' murmured Adam.

'Quite,' replied the doctor. 'So, there will be something generated by the AI – the artificial intelligence - in the simulation which you will collectively have to… shall we say, protect and keep safe.'

'Well? What is this *thing*?' Adam Fletcher seemed to be taking the role as spokesman for the participants. Doctor Hampstead eyed him coolly.

Mordrake laughed.

'Now, now Adam. We can't give the game away. And besides, given the simulation is created as it happens, we're not exactly sure what it may be. The AI will create something, based on your collective consciousness.' Mordrake stopped. Perhaps he'd said too much. He quickly moved on before a discussion on mind-altering, subliminal messaging charges would be aimed at him. He doubted if any of them knew what that was anyway.

'So, it's like subliminal messaging?'

Fletcher. *Criminal mastermind and goddam pain in the ass,* thought Mordrake.

'No, not at all. The simulation will create a world, for you very real when you experience it, but, as I keep saying, you'll only experience it mentally. You cannot be harmed in reality and you can exit at any time.'

'Just by standing up,' said Nancy, seeking clarification that she'd heard everything correctly.

'Indeed,' nodded Mordrake. 'Simple as that.'

'What we ask the AI to do is to create some kind of object. Now, it may be a physical object or it may be something more organic, like a person or animal. We also ask the AI to put in a small…', the Doctor paused, searching for the best way to continue without causing panic, '…problem that gives the game a hint of jeopardy to keep you all moving. Otherwise, you would perhaps just sit down and do nothing!' he laughed, his mirth not shared by anyone else in the room. Even Hampstead.

'Given I've been locked up twenty-three hours a day for the past ten years, I'm happy to do anything but sit on my arse and do nothing,' said Jamie, eliciting laughs from some of the others.

Mordrake continued. 'There'll also be someone in the simulation who will try and stop you achieving the objective. So, in summary, you'll have two hours to work together as you see fit, discover and protect the objective all the while avoiding the threats around you.' He regretted saying it and almost clapped his hand over his mouth like a child caught telling a lie.

'Threats?' said Adam. 'What fucking threats? We have enough of that in here.'

'Here being prison and not my facility,' said Mordrake a harshness to his tone. Fletcher was beginning to grate with him.

The Doctor forced a smile. 'Now, now, it's nothing that will harm you. It's just to keep you on your toes.' He looked around the room, his eyes trying to guage the response to the day's discussion so far.

Unprompted, Hampstead spoke up next to him, much to the surprise of the participants and Mordrake himself. 'So, I assume you fearless people will have no excuse to not participate given it's only a bit of make-believe?'

Well played, thought Mordrake. *Good cop, bad cop.*

Hampstead smiled, locking eyes with Fletcher, her clipboard once again hugged to her chest. She stood indicating the event was over, the discussion done.

By 6pm that evening every participant in the room had agreed to be involved in The Eden Game.

2.

Shortly before 7pm, the participants had been returned to their accommodation within the facility, each with an armed guard. Some with two.

Julia Hampstead walked back into the main room where the introduction session had happened earlier. She found Mordrake slumped in his chair, eyes closed. At first, she froze thinking he'd had a heart attack, but then saw his heavy chest rise and fall.

'I'm not asleep, Julia' he mumbled, eyes still closed.

She didn't respond as she walked across the hard floor, her high heels echoing loudly. She took a seat next to John.

'What's on your mind?' she asked.

Mordrake sighed, opening his eyes and shifting his body back into the chair proper.

'It's the object that they'll be drawn to. The one the AI will create in the game that's concerning me.'

Julia frowned. There was no way of knowing what the simulation would create as the participants collective goal in the game itself.

She let her silence fill the air, knowing Mordrake would continue in his own time.

'Aren't you concerned?' he asked.

Julia thought for a moment and shook her head. 'Why would I be, John?'

Mordrake sighed again, more in fatigue than frustration.

'We know that the AI will actively create something from each participant's subconscious mind, correct?'

Julia nodded.

'And we know that it will base the creation on a similarity between as many of the participants as possible, whether it is part of their crime, their present or past life,' Mordrake looked for her acknowledgement. Julia met his eyes and gave a small nod, seeking more detail.

'And my concern is that the vast majority have killed other people. I've been going through their files, their stories, meticulously.'

'Haven't we *both*, John?' Hampstead chided.

'I know, I know,' he said waving his hand dismissively. 'My point is that many of them have also experienced a traumatic childhood. So, I'm concerned that the object may be too strong a trigger for too many of them.'

It was Hampstead's turn to sigh. 'John, we haven't got time to try and re-work the AI tonight. We submerge them tomorrow!'

'That's what's bothering me!' he said louder than he had intended. He calmed himself. Now was not the time to fall out.

'I'm sorry, Julia. I'm just going through every little detail in my mind and trying to prevent anything bad happening if we can.'

'Well, we've done the risk assessments endlessly and everyone has signed the legal paperwork.' She put her hand on his knee. 'We're protected, John, come what may.'

Mordrake nodded.

'And anyway,' she said, removing her hand, 'most of them are a waste of human flesh as far as I'm concerned.'

Mordrake took a sharp intake of breath in surprise. 'Well, well, Doctor Hampstead. What happened to *do-no-harm*?' She saw he was smiling.

'All I'm saying is, we're giving these people a second chance. Society would prefer many of them rot in prison for the rest of their lives. Not all of them, granted. But some of them. So, don't beat yourself up too much. We've planned as much as we can.'

They sat in silence, each with their own thoughts for company.

After a while, Julia stood and kissed Mordrake softly on top of his head.

'It'll be alright, John. We're doing good work here.'

Mordrake patted her leg.

She left him alone, walking toward the door.

'It's going to be a living object,' she heard him say. 'Maybe a vulnerable human.'

She turned back toward him, wondering if she should reply. She decided to leave him to it. She needed her rest. It was going to be a long day tomorrow.

'Maybe a child,' she heard him mumble as she pulled the door open to leave.

'Even a baby.'

CHAPTER 7
SUBMERGED

1.

It had been his life's work.

Doctor John Edward Mordrake sat at the main control desk with Hampstead seated alongside. All the participants were connected to the system. He looked at one of the camera screens on his desk, showing each participant seated in their cubicle, eyes closed, fully immersed, their own dedicated medical specialist and scientist near-by. Nurses in white dotted the room. Just in case.

The trials with Commander Jared Gibson had gone well. The first few simulations had teething problems, some of which they still hadn't been able to iron out. (Jared reported how some of the CGI characters in the game kept pixelating and disappearing, while others all looked identical. Mordrake had asked his tech team to try and correct this, so wasn't sure if the participants in The Eden Game would see identical people in their world or people flickering in and out of existence. The issue was too small to hold up the programme any longer. Mordrake had been waiting for years to finally trial his therapeutic system with real criminals. Plus, the money was running out and funders wanted results.)

Jared's first few submersions also proved to have few side effects (*apart from that one*, thought Mordrake, still haunted by the memory). Jared did report bouts of confusion while immersed in the simulation, often experiencing Déjà Vu, thinking and feeling he'd done this before, but unable to pin-point it. The Doctor had addressed these concerns early on, informing Jared that he wouldn't recall much of a past life when he was submerged but they couldn't be sure that snippets of his real life wouldn't present themselves within the simulation.

But yes, there was the one side-effect that had threatened everything; the trial simulation when they almost lost Jared's life. His vitals spiked and it took every ounce of skill and timing to drag him out of the game alive. What Jared reported back still haunted Mordrake; he had become *fused* with another character generated by the AI. Mordrake and his team did everything to try and understand how this could have happened, but they had no answer. According to their calculations and experience - the total sum of their collective knowledge - what Jared had reported was *impossible.* There wasn't *any* way that a human consciousness could be fused with another within the game, especially one that was artificially created. Jared reported post-simulation headaches, feeling that something had come back with him from the game. Parts of another. He reported how he could see and experience the artificial consciousness of the character he had fused with. An abomination to Mordrake's mind. A slur on his work and reputation. *On his art.* If what Jared was saying was true, it opened Pandora's Box on ethical questions beyond where Mordrake wanted to delve; was the AI seeking to exist somehow *outside* of the simulation? Was it, therefore, thinking for itself beyond the remit of its programming? Was it trying to *possess* Jared? Mordrake laughed at the idea in the daylight, but spent hours awake during the night when the nightmares of 'what-if?' stalked his mind. The team were warned not to repeat a word of what Jared had told them and were to continue come what may. As for Jared himself, he was only too happy to go back into the trials. It allowed him to kill. Legally. Mordrake was glad the experience hadn't terrified Gibson out of participation.

Or, indeed, himself.

The Eden Game was Mordrake's baby. He'd spawned it, crafted it, *birthed it.* And no delirious veteran was going to taint his masterpiece.

And now it was live. The first trial.

2.

Mordrake looked at the monitors and screens all around him. He could see almost everything. Everything except what the participants were *actually seeing*. To do that, he'd have to immerse himself in the game and he wasn't able to do that *and* monitor the experiment.

He wondered what threat - besides Jared of course, sent in to hinder their objective - they were experiencing. Would it be a natural disaster? An act of terrorism? He had no idea. The AI would generate that. All he did see was what imagery flashed into their subconscious as they participated in the game.

Each player would have around a fortnight of false memory planted which would be accessible to them from the moment the simulation began. People they came into contact with would seem real. Relationships and careers believable. All to observe how they act in a high-pressured environment.

He knew that those who immediately, or eventually, within the game went back to their old ways, their old criminal behaviour, would succumb to the generated threat. For the others, he'd have visions from each scrolling across his screens as their minds translated the data from the virtual world back to the real world.

Although he wasn't a betting man, Mordrake would have bet the house that Hegessay would reoffend, the child abuser showing visions of paedophilic activity being triggered almost immediately. Mordrake knew he wouldn't last long. No way that bastard was getting early release.

Ahmed and Aabid didn't surprise him or his team either. Their ideology so ingrained in them that they were happy to continue their terror plans in the virtual world with no hint of helping others.

As the game unfolded, he began to change his mind about some of the participants.

Lihua Kwok was struggling, almost a shadow of the cruel gang-leader she'd been in the real world. Saffi and Cyrus were appearing to show signs of empathy and selflessness, so he'd be interested to see how things finally turned out for them.

During the two hours, they began to drop one by one, James Whitbourne being one of the first to exit the game.

Mordrake thought Whitbourne may have lasted longer. He recalled his file and the crimes he had committed; Whitbourne was an experienced conman, charming his way into the lives, wills and beds of wealthy women. He'd been living quite the high life until one of his victims was smothered to death by a pillow. That was the straw that broke the camel's back. Whitbourne was given an eighteen-year sentence.

As it got to the final three, Mordrake and Hampstead both agreed they hadn't expected Fletcher to still be involved, he was showing signs of almost complete rehabilitation.

Mordrake recalled the Governor's warning; *He will play you. Don't let him fool you.* He dismissed Jeff's warning, having total faith in his simulation.

When Saffi exited with only minutes to go in the game, they were most surprised. Commander Gibson joined them a few moments later - that was the biggest shock. They had expected him to stop them all reaching their objective. Especially given his vast military experience and trials on other simulations.

But Adam Fletcher? It seemed he was the experiment's most surprising outcome. A criminal mastermind showing signs of almost complete personality reversal in the space of two hours, something a fifteen-year prison sentence looked very unlikely to achieve.

Mordrake allowed himself a little giggle as he thought of the future.

Who else would they rehabilitate over the coming years and simulations? He thought of the prestige, the awards, the money.

There emerged only one problem.

Adam Fletcher never returned from the game to the real world.

PART TWO

CHAPTER 1
NANCY - BEFORE

She didn't like being fat.

By the time she was 16, she'd been shown no interest by boys, had few friends and no ambition. She hated herself.

And then she'd met Jordan.

At first, he'd been as unkind as the others; hurling insults, making fun. But then he'd saw beyond her physical looks and saw a sharp brain. He could use that. He just needed her body to be as fast.

He'd begun helping her with her confidence. He had a thing for Catwoman and kept telling Nancy how she could easily be slim and fit if she had the discipline to follow his routines and habits.

Plus, the smoking helped.

They'd walk the high streets, often stopping by a classy restaurant, Jordan describing how the two of them would celebrate her 21st birthday there; she'd be slim, she'd have cash and they'd be together.

Forever.

Within two years, Nancy had shed almost half her body weight, working out with Jordan, eating hardly anything, drinking coffee and smoking.

By the time she was 21, she was slim.

And for her 21st birthday, he'd gotten her a leather catsuit. It hugged her figure tight. He loved it and she felt good.

And they'd celebrated in that restaurant. Nancy feeling like she was finally on the right path.

A special night.

They talked about possibly getting married, about having kids. About the future.

Nancy told Jordan that night that she doesn't make plans. She told him of her mother's favourite saying, 'when I make plans, God laughs.'

They began with soft core drugs around that time. Just for personal use. Then came the opportunity to sell a little. The extra cash would help Jordan through medical school; all nine years of it.

And then came the chance to take the next step up the ladder. Within weeks, they had runners, some kids as young as eleven. They were supplying everything a junkie could want. Or a banker.

They had the brains and the supply.

And it was all going well, cash flowing in, for the first year. And then their world collapsed.

They got caught, charged and sentenced.

Nancy and Jordan got seven years each. A third of her life. Not the future she and Jordan had planned.

Somewhere, she was sure God was laughing.

CHAPTER 2

CYRUS - BEFORE

He'd do anything for her. Anything.

At first, it was just the two of them. Gradually, her sheer power had attracted others. Cyrus always wanted to keep her just for him. But she was too powerful to be contained. And he was glad others could see it too.

Could *feel* it.

It didn't take long for word to spread to others who were leading nowhere lives. Nowhere people like him. Without home. Without purpose.

Without love.

Saffi could give them everything.

She would call him her Chosen One. They were all Chosen Ones.

Some came and left, others stayed.

Life was simple.

They travelled, the road their home. A comfy camper van housed all they needed. They'd steal whatever they required. Cyrus was the best at stealing electronics. Many they'd keep, others they'd sell. He'd steal laptops, phones, cameras. He loved cameras. Loved simply watching people through the lens. Not taking photos, just watching. Like a god spying on a meaningless world. He enjoyed the feeling of power of watching people without their knowing. All through the lens of a stolen camera.

It felt good to be powerful.

At first, people were afraid of them. The usual words bandied around their group; Cult. Sect. Freaks. He didn't mind. As long as Saffi was with him and he was her Chosen One. He couldn't care less what the others thought.

She began writing, talking and sharing her philosophy. Teaching others of her gift. She taught them how to use telekinesis, hypnotic suggestion and even astral travel, the spirit leaving the body to travel and observe elsewhere. Cyrus never experienced any of these gifts himself but imagined the feeling to be like that of him staring at others through his camera lens. A secret watcher. All seeing.

All powerful.

Cyrus and the other Chosen Ones would hand out her books, pamphlets really. Some were discarded but most worked their magic and spread her gifts to the public.

A few seekers came to find out more.

It was the surgery sessions that ended their tranquillity.

Many sick and dying came to her. Saffi didn't want to turn them away. Cyrus helped as she used her fingers as surgical tools, using nothing but her psychic energies to diagnose their tumours, their cancers, their ailments.

Their blocks.

She'd reach into them, drawing blood, removing the infected parts.

More and more came.

And so did the prosecutions.

At the trial, no-one believed that Saffi had been able to remove the cancers. Cyrus was trialled with her, him being the only other to have participated in the surgeries. The other Chosen Ones had chosen to vanish, returning to their purposeless lives.

Convicted of four murders, his faith in Saffi never wavered.

****

After the trial, the pedestal he had put her on was violently kicked away. She'd lied to him.

He'd been unwell. Suffering. Constant arthritis in the knuckles of his hands, he was unable to even hold a pencil let alone his beloved camera.

His hands and fingers constantly ached in pain.

He begged her to help, to use her magic - her gift - and relieve the pain.

She hadn't even tried.

Not that he saw her.

He knew she was being detained in the same prison. He tried endlessly to talk to her in his mind using their special connection. But whether he had the gift or not, she never replied. She didn't use any of her magic to help him.

It took years, but gradually Cyrus began to see her for the fraud she was.

For the murderer she was.

And there was one murder for which he could never, *would* never, forgive her.

Yet…

He loved her.

Always had.

Always would.

****

She told him out of pure spite.

Cyrus convinced himself there couldn't have been any other reason for her selfish - no, her *satanic* act.

He played the conversation over and over driving himself to the brink of madness.

She'd killed her without even asking him.

Their baby.

His baby.

He hadn't even known she was pregnant with the baby girl. He was the father; Saffi had told him that. Told him he could be an excellent father. And, after laying it all out for him, getting his hopes up of a future where they'd share an eternal bond, a blood-bond, she'd dropped the bombshell and said she'd had an abortion.

She'd taken another life, this one as yet unlived.

And yet Cyrus had stayed with Saffi, continuing to love her, to help her, to worship her. On the occasions he had tried to broach the subject of why she had not wanted the baby, all she would do was say she knew that its life would have been a wasted one.

Its life.

Cyrus had wanted to scream at her; 'It's a she, *she…* my fucking daughter!', the baby being perhaps the only act of goodness he would ever have had to show for his otherwise pathetic life.

But Saffi had shown no emotion, simply shrugging, feigning nonchalance to the entire affair. Saffi: the woman who modelled herself as a mother figure to all and sundry, couldn't be a real mother to her own baby girl.

Yet, he loved her. And hated himself for doing so.

'Cyrus, you have no idea what I've been through! You know nothing about my childhood. I hated carrying it

(It!)

In me. Hated the idea of It being in there, growing, *festering*. If I could go back in time, I'd do it all over again. I'd kill it. I didn't want a baby, never have and never will.'

And with that, Cyrus never talked to Saffi about his unborn baby daughter again.

****

SAFFI – BEFORE

Her mother died from complications after giving birth to her baby sister, Lauren, when Saffi was only seven.

Her father worked during the night, taking care of both her and her little sister in the daytime as best he could around his own sleep. He'd drink heavily and Saffi was wise enough even at her young age to know it was his way of handling his wife's death.

From the moment Lauren was born, Saffi blamed her for killing her mum. Saffi had begun hurting herself, too young to understand and deal with her emotions, her pain, her loss, of being alone.

Especially at night.

When the monsters came out to play.

Her baby sister would cry in the night, waking Saffi from what little sleep she ever managed to get when her dad was at work.

When her father came home, he'd smell of drink and would make a fuss of the baby, tussling Saffi's hair as the only sign of affection on his way to bed.

Saffi would look down at Lauren in her cot, digging her nails deep into the palms of her hand, unknowingly creating a lifelong habit of grounding herself when she was stressed and issues of abandonment threatened to overwhelm her. Saffi wanted to hurt Lauren, not only blaming her for killing her mum but also taking her father's attention and love away from Saffi. She regarded the baby as a curse. Something other, something non-human, not to be loved, a monster planted in her mum's tummy with only one ambition; to ruin Saffi's life.

And she'd never let that happen.

Eventually, she ran away and continued to run all her life, looking everywhere for a new family, chosen ones who would never leave her. She'd become strong, powerful, using magic to counteract any spell that might be placed upon her which would threaten the life of control she would eventually create. It would take time, but she would heal; herself and others.

And she'd make sure no-one, especially a baby girl, would ever, *ever* threaten her life again.

CHAPTER 3

JAMIE – AFTER

'Carter!'

The prison officer held the letter out, not caring which inmate took it. The letter did its dance from hand-to-hand as it was passed back through the group until it reached Jamie.

Jamie turned away from the throng of gathered hopefuls, desperate men hoping to receive some light from the world outside. He held the envelope close. He saw its torn edge where it had been checked before being passed for his perusal. He bought it to his nose and sniffed, hoping to get a hint of her scent.

No such luck.

Jamie walked back to his cell, heart pounding. It was less than three days ago that he'd approached the Governor to ask if he could write to the lady in the simulation trial. The one called Lucy. The one who looked like his sister. Governor Jeff Pullin had agreed on the understanding he'd deliver Carter's letter but that he wouldn't push for a response. Jamie had no option but to agree.

And now, within 72 hours, he held a reply. *Her* reply.

Before the Eden Game, Jamie was depressed; his parole was not for another 22 years. He had nothing to look forward to. Dr. Mordrake had given him a chance; a slither of hope to an earlier release or, at the very least, a transfer to an open prison where life would be easier. Here, he was forever looking over his shoulder.

Jamie couldn't recall much of what had happened in the simulation itself. He'd had fleeting memories and vivid dreams since the experiment. He vaguely remembered an underground station, being with the lady called Lucy, seeing scars on her wrists. He also remembered something about protecting a baby.

But what he did remember, crystal clear, was the day of the introduction to the Doctors at the facility, the circle of participants. And the lady opposite him. The one called Lucy.

His sister.

He knew it wasn't really her. But the likeness was incredible.

Once the simulation had ended and everyone realised the fuck-up it had been, he was sent back to his old cell. With that, his hope had died all over again.

Until he thought to send her a letter.

And now in his hands, as yet unread, dangled once again a tiny thread of hope. A glimpse of a future. Would she want to correspond with him? Could they establish some kind of relationship giving him a purpose to exist, even by letter? Surely the speed of her reply suggested she was as excited as he was?

His hands shook. He placed the envelope down, the letter inside still retaining its secrets.

He realised he was holding his breath. He released it slowly, unsteady. He hadn't felt this nervous going into the simulation.

'Get a grip man. You can't keep running away from things!' he told himself.

With a deep breath, he snatched the envelope up and pulled the letter free. He unfolded it and began to read.

****

Dear Jamie,

Your letter both scared and scarred me. Our stories are incredibly similar and it is somewhat of a disturbing comfort to know there's another who is also going through the daily hell I live with.

We're both murderers.

What good can come from our meeting or continuing to write? I find it troubling that you also have a fixation over me with your words about how I look like your sister.

I don't think it is wise for us to stay in touch.

I hope you find peace as you go through this life living with what you have done. In my dreams I sometimes find peace.

I think the day will come soon when I sleep for good.
L.

****

He read and re-read the note over and over. For that's what it was. It wasn't a letter. It was a *note*. A quick scribble making him feel as if molten lead was being poured over his heart.

He felt cold.

Run, Jamie, run away.

No. I can't keep running.

He read the note again.

In my dreams I sometimes find peace. I think the day will come soon when I sleep for good.

The thread had snapped. All hope gone.

Jamie went to his bunk and pulled the small paper bundle from under the mattress. He carefully unfolded it, the razor glinting in the light.

He held it for a long while, vaguely aware of other inmates passing by his cell door. He crossed the tiny room and pushed the door closed.

Death is a private matter.

He couldn't recall where he'd heard or read that, but it felt right.

Jamie sat on the edge of his bunk, his eyes still glued to the razor and the way the light danced in it. Images reflected from its smooth surface inviting him into their world. Into the world of dreams and reflections.

Into a world of forever sleep.

He carefully rolled up his right sleeve, keeping the razor held gently in his left hand. He thought of Lucy - the simulation one. The Great Rejector. He thought of her scarred wrists

(Your letter both scared and scarred me. Our stories are incredibly similar)

of how he'd hoped she would be his saviour, his light at the end of the tunnel.

He thought of his dreams, the ones from the simulation. Were they real? He didn't know if he'd really lived them or dreamt them. They were blurred like the reflections in the razor. He thought of running in the darkness, holding her hand, holding a baby. He thought of how he'd felt empowered then. Running with purpose. Running to protect those he loved. Running toward the light at the end of the tunnel.

Running.

Always running.

The time had come for one final run. From the inside out.

He put the razor to his wrist and, with one swift, graceful motion, dragged its smooth blade up the middle of his forearm, to the inside elbow. The blood gushed free of its mortal prison.

It ran.

Free.

At last.

POSTSCRIPT

ADAM - FIVE YEARS AFTER SUBMERSION

The doctors treated him as best they could.

Of all the participants in The Eden Game he was their one lab rat in the experiment who had shown signs of potentially being rehabilitated. They'd never know until he gained consciousness.

If he were ever to wake from his coma.

The paperwork protected everyone involved. Each participant had signed the same declaration, same disclaimer. They all signed without duress and with the option of legal counsel. They all knew the risks.

Adam's care was covered by the Government. Undisclosed millions had been spent on the simulation so keeping one man on life-support was a price worth paying if it meant they may one-day have a positive result from the ill-fated project.

His nurses all signed Non-Disclosure Agreements. They'd check his feed-tube, empty his waste. They'd mop his brow, speaking his name, wondering if he was dreaming and what he was dreaming of.

Wondering if he could hear them somewhere in the darkest corners of his mind.

They'd talk in the staff room between shifts, hypothesising dreamscapes, wishing that he would wake so they could get on with their own lives.

Fletcher's sentence was for life without parole. But what if he woke? What if he *was* a different person?

So, they kept him artificially alive - not conscious but not dead. They left him floating on a dream-sea somewhere between life and death.

A prison of sleep.

ADAM

I'm unsure if they know I'm here.

Sometimes, they even seemed to know his name.

He was vaguely aware of other voices that came and went.

For now, he'd just stay here, a floating consciousness in a world devoid of light.

Maybe soon I'll try to find out where the voices are coming from.

Maybe.

He slept.

THE END.

'The first downfall; we forget we made it all up.'
Robert. E. Neale

Coming Soon by Jay Fortune

SPOILER ALERT:
Don't read this until you've finished
reading All Fall Down.

'Jared's Story'

From early trials through to the first submersion with criminals, Commander Jared Gibson was immersed in The Eden Game more than any other participant. Fusing with the AI, *Jared's Story* follows Gibson as he continues his life post-Eden working illegally with Dr. John Mordrake as they continue to refine the technology determined to prove the effectiveness of the Doctor's life's work at rehabilitating prisoners.

With vulnerable people groomed from the fringes of society, throwaways and loners, forced into a crude version of the original state-sponsored simulation, this explosive novel explores how much the human mind and spirit can take with ever increasing exposure to reality-altering technology.

This is the story of what happens when a top-secret Government project goes underground, so secret that not even those involved in funding its conception knows it's continuing...

This is the story of Jared and what came back with him from The Eden Game.

JARED'S STORY
By Jay Fortune

About The Author

Jay Fortune has lived all over England. He currently resides in Blackpool which embodies his love of entertainment and art. A full-time artist and writer, Jay spends his days reading, painting, writing and 'Tourist Dodging', cycling along the promenade whilst avoiding the holiday-makers. He loves books, art, magic, camomile tea* and cake. Jay recently celebrated his second decade of non-TV ownership. All Fall Down is his first novel.

(*Or 'Green Jasmine' if they're out of Camomile)